TIERRA
MILAGRO

TIERRA MILAGRO

A NOVEL

THEODORE LANE MILLER

Cover and Interior Design: Creative Publishing Book Design

ISBN Paperback: 979-8218-97756-6

Printed in the United States of America

In Loving Memory
Victoria Miller

Contents

Prologue

Gospel of John 19:33-34

But when they came to Jesus and saw that he was already dead, they did not break his legs. Instead, a Roman soldier pierced Jesus' side with a long spear, bringing forth a sudden flow of water and blood.

A crimson stream snaked its way down the harsh terrain and puddled close to where Mary knelt in prayer. Even while she was cloaked in the comfort of the Holy Ghost, tears of anguish gathered in the grieving mother's eyes. These salt-tinged tears descended and coalesced, forming translucent orbs at the tip of her nose. Perfectly timed, these blessed spheres of sorrow fell into the pool of cleansing water and sanctifying blood.

No earthly being witnessed the genesis of a miracle.

The Discovery

A precocious Christian girl, who risked dressing as a boy because she'd envied her brother's better treatment, knew that the Messiah had been crucified at this disgusting place called *Golgotha* just a few days earlier. As she approached the putrid trash dump and, much too often, crucifying field, she thought: *I really hate going through this nasty place. But it is the quickest way, and if I don't get home and change before Abba gets there, he's really going to whip my tush.* She mumbled a little prayer and began to jog through the *Place of the Skull.*

Halfway through, she slipped on some loose gravel and fell to her knees. While regaining her footing, something remarkable attracted her attention. Leaning closer, she saw a young flower glowing with the most perfect colors she'd ever seen. Aware of her surroundings, she decided: *This has got to be a special little flower to be growing in the only dark patch of ground around here.*

She found a broken clay pot and a stick to use as a trowel. Taking great care to scoop up the infant lily and some of the dark earth, she whispered, "I'll find a nicer pot to put you in when I get you home." As she placed a handful of the earth into the broken clay pot, a surge of energy raced up her arm and coursed its way through her trembling body. Then a feeling of the purest calm came over her, and this was soon followed by a great sense of joy. It was as if she had been touched by the hand of God.

Forty-Four Years Ago

The sea birds chasing into the last slender strip of blue sky apparently knew. The chickens, clucking and pacing in their pens, seemed to sense it. One of the dogs in the village let go a long, mournful howl. Then it grew eerily quiet. Silence spread across the little Caribbean island like an invisible fog.

A gentle shower began to fall, ordinarily a welcome respite from the smothering heat of late summer. The sun disappeared, and a pale light flickered around the edges of the ominous gray sky. Jagged bolts of lightning fractured the encroaching gray curtain, and these bright splintered spears seemed to provoke aggression in already angry waves.

Huge gusts of wind thundered against the beach. The ungodly roar set free enormous quantities of water that arrived in horizontal sheets. Merciless layers of racing droplets swept up sand, bark, and splinters, piercing everything in their path. Then the larger artillery of wood and metal of all sizes and shapes bombed away, destroying every defenseless target in their wake. Behind these horrors came a windblown nautical attack in the form of twenty-foot waves.

"Hail Mary, full of grace," whispered the little boy. These were the only words of the prayer he could remember, so he repeated them over and over. When the sky suddenly changed from a pleasant pale blue to a threatening gray, the boy felt as if an evil force had invaded his happy world. Before that dreadful moment, he and his adventurous archaeological parents had been gliding over the crystal blue Caribbean in a gleaming white schooner, seemingly without a care in the world. But then Hurricane Lugo appeared.

When the boy's mother stepped out of the cabin and shouted that the radio wasn't working, his father's overly concerned reaction surprised the boy. For the first time in his short life, his brilliant mother didn't seem quite so protective, and his robust father didn't seem quite so invincible.

The little boy's mouth sprang open when the mainsail popped like a cannon shot. The wind slammed into the schooner with an angry surge that sent it pitching and bucking. The gale screamed eerie, singing sounds while it clawed at the canvas, shredding it. And then the mighty force snapped the schooner's mast as if it were merely a twig.

The little boy clung to the rail with a white-knuckle grip while watching his father battle the wind. His hair matted by biting spray, and his clothes pressed tight against his powerful frame, the determined father strained every muscle to turn the stubborn mahogany wheel. The angst on his father's face changed to a look of despair. The search for shelter had come up empty. Saltwater mountains caught up with the wounded sailboat and tossed it about like a rudderless toy. The drowning vessel groaned in protest as swirling saltwater weighed it down.

The father tried to get his wife and son to the lifeboat, but the relentless gale made escape impossible.

His mother screamed hysterically as her only child slipped from her sea-soaked grasp. She shouted out his name, but the word fell silent against the wind.

When a huge wave washed the boy away like a trivial piece of flotsam, he reached out and grabbed the handle of an old wooden chest. Hoping the chest would keep him afloat, he kicked and thrashed, but no amount of effort could prevent him from being sucked into the aquatic beast. He went twisting and turning until he lost all sense of direction. Then, just as he'd exhausted his last ounce of breath, the sea monster spat him out.

He gasped for precious air and flailed with his free arm as a ferocious wind snatched him up. A thunderous roar filled the boy's ears as he flew among stinging raindrops. Consumed by fear, the boy believed he was about to die. But then a reassuring voice blocked out the wind's overwhelming roar. His father's rousing explanation of faith echoed in the boy's mind, and the comforting words encouraged him to whisper a selfless prayer. Praying for his parents somehow erased his fear, and a remarkable sense of calm came over the boy as he clutched the old wooden chest

The Hurricane Hunters

Biloxi Roxy's monotonous drone somehow comforted the pilot, who sat slightly slouched in the vibrating cockpit. The noisy twin engines propelled the dependable old AC-47 through the clearing skies at a resolute 120 knots, several hundred knots less than the speeds the pilot had enjoyed while zooming through the wild blue yonder in a fighter jet.

Two years earlier, Major Cornett had likened accepting this Hurricane Hunter assignment to the way a major league baseball player might feel when being sent down to the minor leagues. However, he soon changed his mind after joining the 53rd Weather Recon Squadron at Keesler Air Force Base in Biloxi, Mississippi. The duty proved to be challenging and rewarding. Flying into the eye of an angry hurricane could still get the adrenaline pumping.

The co-pilot, Lieutenant Albini, gnawed on a humongous wad of bubble gum. He had lowered his mouthpiece to allow room for the gigantic pink bubbles he blew to break the monotony,

This Caribbean hurricane season had been busy—twelve named already with several weeks to go. Lacking two of the usual four-man crew, today's hastily organized mission was planned to search for survivors and make a preliminary damage assessment in the wake of Hurricane Lugo. Sweeping up from the southeast, Lugo had not performed as expected. It had reached Category Five speeds while spinning in a surprisingly small area for the better part of two days, and then made an abrupt turn and fizzled out somewhere near the Yucatan Peninsula.

Biloxi Roxy had reached the outer perimeter of the search grid when the pilot thought he heard something. All too common for former jet pilots, this veteran of the skies suffered from tinnitus, and the ringing in his ears could be hard to distinguish from a faint distress signal.

"According to the flight plan I saw," Albini reminded, "we're running late for the final course change."

"I know," Major Cornett replied. "Bear with me." The pilot adjusted his headset and frowned while listening intently. He needed to convince himself that the beeping sounds were real before mentioning them to the junior officer.

Albini had lowered his mouthpiece and was trying to blow the biggest bubble of the day when he caught sight of an island. Forgetting about the bubble, he shouted, "Whoa!" The exclamation burst the bubble and covered the co-pilot's face with a thin layer of sticky pink gum. "You see that little island?"

Major Cornett shook his head in reaction to the unprofessional behavior, and replied "Yes, I see it and I'm pretty sure I'm picking up a distress signal."

Hurriedly scraping off the gum, Albini said, "Yeah, Pops, I'm hearing it, too. But that island looks like it was blasted with an A-bomb."

The "Pops" insubordinate comment did not go unnoticed, but the pilot's mindset was locked in on the island. "Plot present position and call it in. I'm taking *Roxy* down for a closer look."

Albini's exceptional U.S. Air Force training kicked in. "Yes, Sir. Vectoring coordinates and reporting position to base."

Major Cornett tipped *Roxy*'s wings to the maximum angle the plane could withstand and sliced the bulky AC-47 down at a faster rate than she was designed to achieve. Leveling off at five hundred feet, he aimed the plane straight toward the island. He soon agreed with the co-pilot's assessment—the island did look as if it had been obliterated with an A-bomb.

The few trees still standing had been stripped bare, looking like solitary fence posts. On closer inspection, almost all the vegetation and topsoil had been washed away, leaving naked gray rock and patches of brindle-brown sand.

"I've never seen anything like this," Albini commented.

"I haven't either," Major Cornett replied while flashing back to a bombing run he'd made in Afghanistan. Returning to the moment, he asked, "You get a fix on that distress signal?"

"Roger that, Sir. The signal is faint but steady. Could be from a boat that sank just offshore."

Major Cornett flew the plane in low, thinking there was no chance that anyone could have survived. But as he started to take *Roxy* back up to cruise altitude, something aroused a gut feeling. He turned the plane around and flew in, even lower this time.

"Look!" Albini shouted. "Something's down there."

Major Cornett had already spotted the surprising sight. "You're right, Lieutenant." A distinctive image stood out among the grim expanse of terrain. He slowed *Roxy* and turned her into the tightest circle he could while keeping the bulky aircraft aloft.

Albini found a pair of binoculars and adjusted the focus. "I don't believe what I'm seeing. A small person is lying in what looks like a nest of green leaves and palm fronds. And beyond weird, little flowers are covering some of the body."

"It is a bit mind-boggling," Major Cornett replied

"I think it's a boy," Albini remarked. "He's not moving, but he doesn't look dead."

"This island is not within U.S. jurisdiction," Major Cornett replied, "Call it in and let the brains at the base figure out who is responsible for search and rescue out here."

Albini had received an order he was eager to obey. "Yes, Sir. Calling it in as a maximum priority rescue operation."

The Miracle Boy

Three full days of searching the island had elapsed before a couple of emotionally drained soldiers stumbled upon a young boy who looked to be about five or six years old. Visibly dazed, the boy was found in a crater, most likely created when the wind had ripped a palm tree out by its roots. It appeared as if the boy had been deposited in the safest place possible—the crater had become an unlikely nest that insulated the boy from the hurricane's powerful force. The soldiers seemed overjoyed at finding someone alive after confronting so much death and destruction. But they considered it strange when they saw flowers covering much of the boy's nearly naked body. They both knew that the nearest flower gardens had been on the far side of a large hill, and there was nothing left of them. Devout Catholics, they exchanged nervous glances, looked up toward their heaven, and crossed themselves.

When the third member of the search team walked up to join the other two soldiers, he quickly spotted the old chest the boy was clutching. No doubt hoping it would contain some valuables, the soldier reached down and grabbed it.

Awakened from his trance, the boy held onto the chest with all his might. "No! You can't have it. My mom said it was important."

The soldier ripped the chest from the boy's grasp. He broke off the small lock, and with a sardonic smile, he opened the lid.

"My God! Ashes of the dead!" the soldier shouted in Spanish, Visibly shaken, he handed the chest back to the boy. Then turning to his astonished fellow searchers, he said, "Let's get off of this God forsaken island."

The authorities sent the boy to Our Lady of Carmel Mission on the island of Saint John. Once there, the nuns christened him Francisco Flores, presumably for Saint Francis of Assisi and for the boy's miracle of surviving with the flowers.

Chapter One

Joaquin "Keno" Flores inhaled through flared nostrils as he walked into his mother's delicious-smelling kitchen. He stretched his six-foot-three, two-hundred-forty-pound body and remarked, "Awesome smells, Millie."

"Good morning, Sunshine," his mother, Millicent "Millie" Flores, greeted. "You're up and at 'em early. I thought you'd want to get a little extra sleep on the day of your big game."

Keno shrugged. "I'll catch a nap at the Bear Cave later."

Recalling that Keno was referring to his fraternity's nickname, Millie frowned and said, "Isn't Michigan one of the best football teams in the country?"

"Yeah, they definitely are," Keno replied. "That's why I'm meeting up with our quarterback and some other players to go over plays that might surprise those big bad Wolverines."

Wearing a puzzled expression, Millie asked, "I'm wondering why the University of California would schedule a Thursday night game with such a powerful opponent, especially for your first game of the season."

"Simple. Money and rankings. Cal gets a ton of TV money and Michigan gets to pad their record with what they believe will be an easy win. But they might be in for a big surprise. We're fifteen-point dogs, but the powers that be are rating us by last year's record. They're not taking into account that our quarterback, our middle linebacker, and a few other key players were out with injuries for most of the season. Every one of them was back for spring practice, and we're getting our act together."

"I sure hope so," Millie said as she set his place with an eight-ounce glass of O.J., another one of milk, and a plate with three eggs and six strips of bacon. She brought another plate on which she couldn't resist using her artistic talent. Six large pancakes were decorated with whipped cream and strawberries to create a smiley face.

Keno smiled in appreciation, and said, "Cool," before digging in with gusto.

Millie shook her head. "One might think this is all you're going to get to eat today."

When he'd finished, he stood, hugged his mother, and said, "That was great. Probably hold me till nine or ten."

Millie warned, "Just don't eat too much before the game."

Keno winked and said, "See ya tonight."

"You know you will. It would take a small army to keep your father and me away."

Outside of the brilliantly painted old Victorian, Keno's nasal passages were once again treated to a mix of superb aromas. He slowly inhaled a deep breath laced with the smells of an assortment of beautiful flowers decorating the backyard. When he spotted his father, Francisco "Frank" Flores, loading landscaping tools onto his Ford Ranger pickup, he greeted, "Good morning, Frank. Looks like you're hard at it as usual."

Frank flashed his brilliant smile before responding "Good morning, Joaquin. Ready for your big game tonight?"

"As physically ready as I'm going to get. And I'm meeting up with the quarterback and some other players to go over our game plan and some special plays."

"I suppose you can never be too prepared," Frank remarked. "But sometimes you have to be ready for something unexpected."

"Yeah," Keno replied. "That almost always happens in a football game."

Frank flashed his brilliant smile again. "You Cal Bears are going up against some mean Wolverines tonight, so if you're going to be a bear, be a Grizzly."

"You always come up with some good ones. See ya tonight."

Keno went to the place where he kept his Harley-Davidson out of the weather. The impressive motorcycle was a restored *Knucklehead* his parents had given him for his twenty-first birthday. He donned his helmet, a replica of his Cal football helmet, and fired up his pride and joy. Realizing he was early, he decided to take the scenic tour through Tiburon. He would take the back way to the San Rafael-Richmond Bridge and then on to Berkeley.

On his way through Tiburon, he glanced up toward the hill where the magnificent Simon Bernstein Mansion seemed to hold dominion over the small tourist town. Slowing the Harley, Keno realized why he'd gone that way this morning. He wanted to get as close as he could to his *hot babe*. He looked up at the mansion, and shouted, "Good morning, Tanya, love of my life. Maybe I'll get to be up there with you someday." Then, shaking his head, he mumbled, "Got to get my mind back on football."

Football cleats sent grating sounds careening through the locker room as the team searched for refuge at halftime. Keno Flores and his despondent teammates trudged in and flopped their bruised and battered bodies on benches and assorted pieces of equipment. Only grunts and muttered curses infiltrated the gloom.

There was, however, no place that afforded comfort for wounded egos. Tonight's ESPN telecast was the popular sports channel's first football game of the season, and, unfortunately, the Michigan Wolverines were whipping the Cal Bears 20 to 7. What's worse, the score didn't come close to reflecting the trouncing the home team was suffering out on the field. The score would have been 28-0 but for an amazing touchdown scored by Cal's speedy kick returner and two field goals Michigan had to settle for after a dropped pass in the end zone and a holding penalty that took a touchdown off the scoreboard.

Coach Taylor paraded back and forth in front of his dejected team, one minute venting his disappointment with the overall effort, the next cajoling. The coach was trying to rekindle the fire that blazed before the game began.

A sharp pain penetrating Keno's right shoulder caused a quick intake of breath to whistle through his teeth. He mumbled to a teammate, "To get ready for these Michigan bad boys, we should have scrimmaged with a herd of rhinos."

As a few of his teammates were doing, Keno hung his head and stared into his helmet, which he was holding with both hands. He shook his head, trying to clear the grogginess that lingered from a helmet-to-helmet collision with Michigan's big middle linebacker.

Suddenly, an explosion of erratic dots began to dance in front of Keno's eyes, and a strange aura surrounded his vision. He watched in disbelief as fuzzy images began to take shape and move about inside his helmet. He shook his head again to clear it, but it didn't help. When the surprising images only became more vivid, coming into ever sharper focus and seemingly moving with purpose, he found himself being drawn in and watching a bizarre video. He saw himself catching a pass, powering his body through an enraged mass of humanity, scoring a touchdown, his teammates piling on, and the crowd going wild. A moment later, he was lying in the end zone clutching his ankle and writhing in pain. Then a dense fog descended and erased the implausible helmet video.

"Keno?"

Keno found himself looking into a pair of concerned eyes. It took a moment to realize they belonged to the offensive coordinator.

"You okay, kid?"

"Yeah," Keno replied without being sure that he was. He asked himself: *What the heck just happened? Did that big linebacker ring my bell so hard that it made me hallucinate?*

The offensive coordinator looked long and hard into Keno's eyes. Appearing satisfied that he wasn't dealing with a disoriented player, the coach slashed lines next to X's and O's on a handheld tablet. "Pay attention, Flores." The coach tilted the tablet enough to reveal the play. "They've been cheating up with their safeties to stop our running game and their corners are taking away our passing with bump and run coverage. So, when the time is right, we're going to make those suckers pay with Deke-M Special."

Keno frowned, trying to recall what he was supposed to do in the play the coach called *Deke-M Special*.

As if tuned in to Keno's thoughts, the offensive coordinator explained, "We only ran this play a few times in spring practice, but I designed this play for Michigan's overly aggressive defense." The coach traced Keno's assignment on the tablet while instructing, "You'll go in motion, come to a stop behind Slate for one full count, and then he'll take over your route. If everything is timed perfectly, Slate should take the outside linebacker with him and leave you one-on-one with that slow gorilla in the middle. After a fake screen pass, you streak to the post and the quarterback will get you the ball."

Daryl Slate, the intense fullback, responded with a grin. "I like it. It should definitely fake them out. Especially if you're hidden behind me and the Q.B." He playfully poked Keno with an elbow before adding, "I'll give you a little jab when I go in motion."

Coach Taylor's defensive adjustments included a steady diet of blitzing from unusual defensive formations that confused Michigan's conventional blocking schemes. Also, Michigan's deep-rooted tradition of playing it close to the vest when leading in the second half caused the game to become a slugfest.

The Golden Bears seemed to be gaining confidence with each snap of the ball, and it intensified when their place kicker made a field goal from fifty-three yards. And Cal's middle linebacker, Butch Duggins, was foaming at the mouth as he led the defensive charge— stuffing the run and single-handedly sacking Michigan's quarterback three times for substantial losses. One of Butch's sacks resulted in a safety, making the score 23-12. Then a timely interception by Cal's top cornerback led to a touchdown, bringing the game within reach at 23-18. But the two-point conversion attempt failed.

With momentum swinging in their favor, the aroused Bear defenders collectively sacrificed their bodies to stop the favored Wolverines. But Cal's offense wasn't gaining much ground either, and time was on Michigan's side. Nervous Cal fans behaved as if the scoreboard clock had become a ravenous creature, feasting on time itself. Anxious spectators kept glancing back and forth from the action on the field to the relentless clock

The grunts and thuds of players locked in combat could be heard several rows up in the stands. For many of these players, the first game of the season had become the most important they had ever played. Each team's season was likely hanging in the balance. An upset would bring status and respect for the lowly, humiliation and disappointment for the mighty.

With the score still Wolverines 23, Bears 18, it came down to one final play. It was Cal's ball, fourth-and-ten on Michigan's 31-yard line. When Cal's quarterback signaled the referee for Cal's third and final time-out, only four seconds remained on the scoreboard clock. *04* desperate seconds.

Keno felt an almost tangible sense of anticipation when the quarterback returned from the sideline, kneeled in the huddle, and called the play. "Deke-M Special, on two." The calm and cool young quarterback surprised Keno when he added, "It doesn't get any better than this, boys. Let's block and rock."

Taking his position, Keno noticed that the crowd had gone silent, collectively holding its breath.

Keno went in motion, then stopped behind Slate. After one full count, the fullback tapped Keno's hip and took over his pattern. As hoped, Michigan's outside linebacker took the bait. But the strong safety wasn't cheating up quite as close to the line as expected. And the monster in the middle didn't seem fooled at all, though he was a step slow to react. When Keno ducked and went racing by, the infuriated linebacker vented his frustration with an enraged scream. This alerted both cornerbacks, and the Michigan defenders responded with incredible speed.

The quarterback's pass was delivered on time, but well above the intended target. Keno leaped high, stretched to the limit of his reach, and snagged the spiraling ball out of the air with his fingertips.

One racing cornerback slammed Keno with an explosive shoulder pad, snapping his helmet to one side. Juggling the ball, Keno lashed out with a vindictive straight arm. The other cornerback came flying in, jarring Keno with a crunching body blow. Keno tightened both arms around the ball to secure it, then spun out of the defender's determined grasp. Another defender hurtled into Keno from behind, reshaping his body into an agonizing question mark—the impact fortunately propelled Keno's uncoiling body forward. Finding his balance, he lowered his shoulders and fought for more precious territory. From the corner of his eye, he saw a strong safety racing toward him. A second later, he felt a hard plastic missile slam into his helmet's ear hole. With lights dancing in his head and his knees buckling within inches of the ground, Keno felt octopus-like arms frantically clutching and squeezing. Frenetic fingers clawed and tugged, grasping at cloth, pads, and flesh.

Dragging several tenacious Wolverines, a couple literally breathing down his neck, Keno refused to go down. A massive weight had descended upon him in the form of mauling and cursing animalistic creatures—each determined to halt his advance on their cherished territory. He contracted every muscle, slanted his body, and surged ahead. One more quick step, one final lunge, then Keno strained to reach out as he fell. He looked down to see dirty white turf on his elbow. Feeling a surge of joy, matched only by his amazement, Keno realized he'd made it across the goal line.

Whistles blasted, the crowd erupted, and teammates bellowed triumphantly while piling on. The cacophony of victory swept through Memorial Stadium, roaring up through Strawberry Canyon and echoing into the verdant Berkeley hills. Pandemonium intensified with the emancipation of disbelief.

Feeling claustrophobic by the mountain of bodies pinning him down, Keno shouted to let them know he wanted out from under the tumultuous mass. His jubilant teammates got the message and moved away. But when Keno gathered himself and tried to stand, his right ankle felt as if it had been stabbed with a dull knife. He grabbed Daryl Slate's extended hand and struggled to his feet, but the excruciating pain was more than he could take, and he collapsed back to the turf.

While grabbing his ankle, Keno recalled the bizarre video he'd watched in his helmet at halftime. The accuracy was dizzying. He massaged the ankle while replaying the scene in his mind, then replayed it again. But no matter how authentic it seemed; his mind rejected it. *No, that can't be real. I've been hit in the head way too many times tonight.*

An hour or so later, when Keno appeared from the locker room on crutches, he was surprised to see so many lingering teammates and excited fans still milling about. And even a couple of diligent reporters were waiting for the chance to interview tonight's hero. After responding to a barrage of questions and thanking everyone for their support, Keno was eager to find his parents and Netanya. But that wasn't hard to do. All three came rushing to him when they decided he'd done more than enough to satisfy a hero's obligations.

Frank Flores had watched every football game his son had played, going all the way back to the Pop Warner leagues. Millie Flores hadn't missed a home game since her son's record-breaking high school days at Marin Catholic High School. The parents' faces held the expected looks of concern, which contrasted with beaming eyes that betrayed their pride. They took turns congratulating him and asking about his injury.

Netanya Bernstein gave Keno's parents some private time before making her way to her boyfriend's side. She looked at him with big almond eyes, glossy from shedding happy tears, and kissed him on the cheek. "You were amazing, Joaquin. Lots of people were saying that was the most incredible touchdown they've ever seen. And I heard somebody say you were dragging almost a thousand pounds into the end zone."

Keno liked her using his given name—few did anymore. "I think somebody's exaggerating. And whatever I did during that last play, I did on instinct. I really don't remember much of what happened out there."

"I'll tell you exactly what happened out there, Joaquin. You won the game because you are way too stubborn to lose." She winked to confirm she was kidding, then dropped her glance toward his heavily taped ankle. "How bad is it?"

"Just a sprain."

Millie overheard her son's attempt to minimize the injury and commented, "Don't believe him, Tanya."

Frank smiled and added, "He wouldn't admit how bad it was if the bone was sticking out."

Netanya nodded and said, "Believe me, I know." She rested a hand on one of Keno's shoulders, then added, "We had planned to party after the game, but I guess we'll have to go to Plan B. If it's cool with you guys, I've got a car coming to take him to my place. I promise I'll take good care of him."

Millie shot a glance at Frank before replying, "That's really nice of you, Tanya."

On cue, a stretch limo painted a unique burgundy color came rolling to a stop, just a few feet away. The uniformed driver, looking buff enough to play middle linebacker, hurried out from behind the wheel and opened a door.

Keno leaned on the crutches and held out his hands to divulge his surprise. Fans and teammates applauded, cameras flashed, and the ESPN crew got some interesting bonus footage. Uncomfortable with all the special attention, Keno smiled and waved before plopping down on one of the limo's expensive leather back seats

When Netanya snuggled close, Keno wrapped an arm around her, pulled her close and said, "Life can be totally cool."

Chapter Two

Keno's grimace exposed his clenched white teeth. The slightest pressure to his ankle sent searing pain shooting up his leg. This Saturday morning's assailant was a twisted satin sheet. Like a stylish python, it had seized the foot supporting an Ace bandage.

After carefully working the fancy sheet loose with the toes of his other foot, he yawned, stretched, and fluffed a silky pillow. This was easily the most comfortable bed he'd ever floated on. As Keno's eyes explored the opulent surroundings in Netanya's bedroom, he began to feel out of place. He hadn't given much thought to the posh surroundings when he'd arrived there Thursday night; the excitement of the game was still fresh in his mind and the ankle injury was demanding attention. And then last night presented a considerably more pleasurable distraction. Even so, the more Keno looked around, the more uncomfortable he became, and, like the big TV that seemed to levitate near the opposite wall, a destitute college student didn't fit in.

Netanya had told him the bedroom was decorated in an Arabian Nights motif. She'd also told him the name of the imagery imprinted on the beautiful silk curtains that seemed to descend and flow from every conceivable angle, but the word eluded him. *Din? Gin?* But he did remember the name of the big prehistoric bird—Netanya had called it *Roc*. While observing tapestries with unique Saracen designs, beautiful tile mosaics and a brass lamp that looked like it might even contain a genie, he wondered why a Jewish girl got so carried away with Arab décor.

Keno lost all interest in the luxurious furnishings when last night's amazing event came to mind. The recollection overwhelmed all other thought. The sex—no, the phenomenal lovemaking—had surpassed all expectations. But it had come with a discovery he wasn't prepared to deal with. Not in his wildest dreams would he have imagined that a worldly young woman like Netanya would still be a virgin. *A virgin?*

Keno realized that he hadn't given much thought to the importance of virginity for quite a while. He didn't discuss the subject with his friends—sports and grades controlled their conversations. Most of the girls he'd dated were getting it on in high school, and since the majority of his friends had become active in their mid-teens, sex didn't seem like such a big deal anymore. Also, virginity had come to be equated with abstinence, and, going by some of the things he'd heard, those practicing abstinence were often getting it on in ways that he considered a little weird.

Now, however, Keno found himself thinking that Netanya had given him something incredibly special. It's possible that his Catholic upbringing had surfaced, and it was causing him to reconsider his casual approach to free love. He didn't know whether to feel proud, honored, guilty, or what exactly. In any case he was convinced that last night was especially significant since Netanya could have her pick of just about any guy on the planet.

It occurred to Keno that some heavy responsibility might come with her extraordinary gift. A swarm of significant questions began to race for recognition: *Does this mean serious commitment? Do I really deserve a gorgeous and talented babe like her? And what about her rich old man? What's he going to think about it if, more likely when, he finds out?*

Thinking about Netanya's father added another level to Keno's uncertainty. She'd told him that her father, Simon Bernstein, had amassed a fortune by mining gold and diamonds on far-flung continents, and the clever man had multiplied that extraordinary wealth with shrewd investments in the stock market.

Feeling more than a little insecure, Keno asked himself: *Is a mega-rich man like him going to want a broke, bi-racial dude like me in the family?* The question required very little deliberation. *I seriously doubt it.*

When he sat up to stretch, he noticed Netanya sitting out on the elegant marble balcony. She sat sipping herbal tea from an earthenware cup while enjoying her early morning nature appreciation from the magnificent house perched high above the Marin County town of Tiburon, California. The exclusive real estate offered a panoramic view of Tiburon and the San Francisco Bay. Obviously delighted by this morning's spectacular entrance, her face seemed to glow as she watched the first fiery rays of sunrise set ablaze the majestic towers of the Golden Gate Bridge.

Keno smiled when he noticed that Netanya was lounging in a 49er football jersey, reaching well past her knees. He was glad she was a serious football fan and an early riser; these were two welcome additions to the growing number of things they had in common. When she leaned back and stretched, he suspected that Netanya was naked beneath the crimson jersey—inviting a welcome return to the pleasures they'd enjoyed last night.

As if feeling his focus, Netanya turned and glanced inside. She smiled in acknowledgment, and then ran slender fingers through her boyishly cut hair. Then picking up her cup with both hands, she sauntered inside. "How's my big hottie this morning?"

"Just chillin'." It seemed to take his last ounce of energy to shrug his broad shoulders. "This bed is the best." When she put down the cup and sat beside him, silent seconds seemed to suspend time. *I'm sure she's thinking about last night, but what am I supposed to say?*

Netanya broke the tension by lying down beside him and curling her body to fit against his. She took his hand and guided it around her shoulders. "Hold me."

He gladly obeyed. "You feel good."

"So do you."

When he smelled her neck, Keno took in a deep breath and held onto her wonderful scent for a few pleasurable moments, as a sommelier might do while sampling a fine wine. He'd been exposed to countless aromatic flowers while working with his father in the landscaping business, but he wasn't sure which fragrance best compared to hers. *Maybe one of the roses? Whatever, she's definitely what an angel should smell like.* Of course, he couldn't bring himself to say something that sappy out loud. He condensed all that romantic contemplation into, "You smell good."

"Thanks, I'm glad you think so." She sighed before broaching the awkward subject that lingered. "Was last night as special to you as it was to me?"

"Yeah, it was incredible. But I'm still a little psyched about being your first..." He stumbled to find the right word. "Guy... lover... you know."

"What number was I? Ten...? Twenty...?"

The question surprised him. "What's that about?"

"I could tell you've been around, and then some. You know how to push all the right buttons. And nobody can be that good at it without a whole bunch of experience."

"I'll admit you were the only virgin when we went to bed last night, but why is that so important? You're the only one I've ever been in love with." He stroked her hair, then kissed her inviting neck. "And in case you didn't know, you're pretty good at it yourself."

It was her turn to look surprised. "I am?"

"Yeah, you've got some amazing natural talent. So, what's the big deal with experience?"

She twisted her hips enough to lie on her back, then pursed her lips, clearly mulling over the information she was about to share. "I was raised by my grandmother, Nanna Smatovich, who was born in Russia. She died when I was thirteen. I'm sure you'll think this sounds silly, but she made me promise to save myself for my husband the way she did." She paused before adding, "My friends have always hassled me about being so old-fashioned. Some still call me Tanya-tease. You know, playing the game but never going all the way. And you should know, I've been teasing you all summer. Anyway, I always thought my promise to Nanna was important and I didn't want to break it." She made a guilty face, and said, "But then last night everything was so perfect. The romantic dinner, sitting by the bay, openly sharing our feelings…"

"That's heavy, Tanya. I don't know what to say except I love you very much."

She caressed his cheek with delicate fingertips. "What if I want to go all the way?"

He resisted the urge to joke, *I thought you already did that last night.* But he decided it wouldn't be cool at such a serious moment. "If all the way means total commitment, then I think I'm ready."

Tears began to puddle in her almond eyes. "Me too. I'd like to come close to keeping my promise to Nanna."

"I'm going to give you a ring so everybody will know we're seriously hooked up."

She sat up, turned to face him, and blinked with slow-moving eyelashes—dark lashes that remained bonded together a couple of beats before separating. "And just what kind of ring would that be?"

"I don't know, maybe my frat ring. Or I could buy you one of those friendship rings with your birthstone in it. I've seen some other girls wearing them. Think you'd like that?"

"I can't believe you actually said *hooked up.*"

Her irritated tone surprised him. Then the significance of the Nanna Smatovich revelation sunk in. She'd tossed him an easy softball, and he was too dense to swing at it. "Time out, Tanya. How about an instant replay?"

Her face took on a questioning look. "What…?"

He chose not to explain a football jock's way of asking for a reprieve. "Do you really love me?"

"With all my heart."

Though a permanent relationship with Netanya was something he'd been hoping for with every fiber of his being, the realization that it might be happening right here, right now, was overwhelming. It would be a life-changing non-revocable vow. He paused a moment, considering the possibility that he'd read her wrong. Maybe she would turn him down. He swallowed a large lump of anxiety before asking, "Think we could put up with each other for like... forever?"

She smiled, apparently enjoying the way he'd framed the question. "Longer than forever."

"That's totally romantic."

"Somebody wrote it in a song."

Her reply barely registered. It was time for the big question, and all he had to do was convince himself to ask it. He blew out a deep breath, then took her in his arms. "Netanya Bernstein... will you marry me?"

Her eyes and lips expanded to their elastic limits. Glistening tears rushed down flushed cheeks. A couple of empty seconds intensified the moment, and then her ecstatic reply resonated in his ears. "Yes! Yes! I will marry you, Joaquin Flores." She hurled herself on top of him and peppered his face with rapid-fire kisses. Then she abruptly stopped, raised her head, and asked, "You sure?"

As he was about to reply, a rush of black dots suddenly danced in front of Keno's eyes, and his head began to spin. The left side of Netanya's face seemed to turn cloudy. As he lay watching in disbelief, a tear appeared to slide into the cloud and fall into a gash in her cheek. As more tears descended into the gash, the wound grew deeper, turning uglier, exposing jagged flesh. A steady flow of tears seemed to multiply and soon become a fountain of gushing, crimson blood.

Whoa! What the...? Keno blinked hard as a dense fog surrounded the gruesome wound, engulfed the unsettling image, and then thankfully erased it. While shorter in duration, but certainly more horrific to witness, this vision reminded him of the brief video he'd seen in his football helmet at halftime during Thursday night's game. Keno inhaled a deep breath while thinking, *Am I cracking up, or what?*

Clearly confused, Netanya stared at him with a questioning look. "Is the idea of marrying me that scary?"

Keno returned her stare while working to erase the horrific vision. Thinking fast, he replied, "No, I'm just totally overwhelmed that you're going to marry me. It's almost too incredible to believe."

Sniffing and smiling at the same time, she took his hands and pinned them above his head. "Okay, big boy, you're trapped now. I'm never letting you get away."

When more warm tears began to fall, Keno not only had to avoid thoughts of gushing blood, he had to fight off an emotional meltdown. And not comfortable with tearing up, not even with the woman who'd just agreed to be his wife, he pulled up the 49er jersey and playfully swatted her behind. "You already trying to take control?"

"You're mine now, Joaquin Flores, and I've got you right where I want you."

Needing to lighten the mood, especially the bloody one lingering in the shallow recesses of his mind, he wrapped his arms around her and pulled her under him. Convinced she was helpless, he said, "Forget about control, Babe. The last one on top wins, and I can definitely pin a little pipsqueak like you."

When she couldn't wriggle free, Netanya said, "Oh, yeah?" then reached up and nipped his earlobe.

"Owwww!" He covered his ear with a palm and rolled off the bed, thankfully landing on a plush carpet. "Hey, fight fair, little Miss Tyson."

Netanya slid down beside him and kissed his smarting ear. "I'm sorry, Joaquin. I didn't mean to bite so hard." Quivering stomach muscles betrayed her apology. "But it was so tasty."

While holding his breath to change the color of his face, Keno could feel blood veins stand out while frown lines creased his forehead.

With a visibly reddened face he bared his teeth, werewolf-like. "That does it, you little witch. Now I'm gonna waste you."

Netanya's face took on a terrified look as she pleaded, "Oh, please don't hurt me, you big brute." She jumped to her feet and scampered around the bed, then stopped giggling long enough to compliment, "That's not bad. You really could play a villain."

When he sustained the frightening face, she cocked her head and asked, "You are just acting?" When he still didn't respond, she came back around the bed and asked, "Right?"

His face relaxed into an easy smile. "Maybe I do have a little thespian potential."

"I keep telling you how talented you are, and I'm not the only one who thinks so. Some very respected theater people have said you've got what it takes. And to be honest, I was a little jealous when you got a better review than I did on opening night."

A quick flashback to that memorable night reminded Keno of how thrilling acting could be. "That's cool to hear."

Returning tenderness to the equation, she ran the tips of her fingers over big purple bruises on his body, already yellowing around the edges. "I bet you're still pretty sore."

"Yeah, all over my body."

"Can I get my big handsome hero something?"

"Don't be calling me *hero*. I'm not cool with that."

"No problem, Joaquin. Can I get you something? Maybe a cup of tea?"

The thought of tea this early in the morning was not remotely appealing—one thing they did not have in common.

"No thanks. I'll wait till I get home." When she placed her hands in his and stared with a questioning expression, he asked, "What's up with the look?"

"If you can't play football anymore this season, will you seriously consider becoming an actor?"

Her words "can't play football" jolted him. When Netanya had taken him to Berkeley for therapy yesterday, the team trainer informed him that the X-rays were negative, eliminating the possibility of broken bones. However, he had suffered a severe high ankle sprain, which meant there was severe tendon and ligament damage that would be slow to heal. The trainer's best guess was that he'd be out at least six weeks, but the team doctor would need the results of an MRI before he could provide a more accurate prognosis. Keno was scheduled for that important test early Monday morning.

Netanya frowned and asked, "Well?"

He stared back while considering the answer to probably the second most important decision he'd had to make in his twenty-one years—the first being the proposal. Avoiding a direct answer, he replied, "I'm working on it."

With an exaggerated pout, she said, "I guess I'll have to take working on it as a good thing."

As Keno looked into those big, brown eyes that seemed to devour information, he realized he would do just about anything for her. "But you're not making it easy."

She wrapped her arms around his waist and pressed her face against his chest. "You won't be sorry if you go for it."

"I just want to do the right thing." He put his arms around her and squeezed, careful not to hurt her. "But since we're going to be married, the acting plan does make more sense."

Netanya frowned, then said, "We'll have to wait a while before we can tell anybody about that part."

"That part?"

"If the media finds out, they'll make a big deal out of it. You know, billionaire's daughter engaged to jock, yada, yada, and we can't let that happen before we tell Daddy."

"But I want to go out on the balcony and yell it loud enough for everybody in the whole Bay Area to hear. Have the *Chronicle* use it for tomorrow's headline."

Netanya smiled, and said, "Sorry, Joaquin, but we can't let anybody know about it yet."

"It's weird to be engaged to a beautiful rich babe and not be able to tell anybody about it."

"I'm glad you think I'm beautiful, and I wish it didn't have to be like this, but unfortunately, it does. Promise not to tell."

"Yeah, but I don't have to like it." Feeling a bit subdued, he joked, "If you don't wear an engagement ring, maybe I'll get you a couple of rings for your ears, or maybe one for your belly button. Then I'd know you're committed."

"Or you could just brand my butt."

He grinned and said, "Or how about a strategically placed tattoo?"

She ran her fingers over the big blue and gold Cal Bear logo tattooed on his shoulder. "As long as it's not a silly, smiling bear."

"But no matter what happens," Keno said, "I'm going to be with you every minute I can."

"We can be together a lot if you go to UCLA with me."

Keno blew out a deep breath. "That part is totally confusing, and I'm not capable of committing to anything right now. I'm still too amped about our decision to get married."

"I'm sure you're concerned about what your parents will think. But from everything you've told me about your dad, and what I personally know of Millie, I think they'll be cool with it."

Keno limped over to find his Levi's and Nikes still lying on the floor where he'd slipped them off last night. Putting on his running shoes painfully reminded him of the high ankle sprain. He grimaced when he rotated his foot to check it out; the shooting pain almost bringing tears. "My parents wouldn't try to stop me, but you can bet your sweet little tush they'll be disappointed."

"Tush?" She smiled. "Is my Jewish rubbing off?"

"I have no idea where that one came from."

Netanya smiled and changed the subject. "I'd much rather be with you today, but I promised two of my friends that I'd go to the

City with them to do a little shopping, and then we have tickets for *Les Misérables*. What have you got going on?"

"My day won't be all that exciting. I have to go to Berkeley to get my ankle treated. But if the swelling has gone down enough, I won't have to go back again until Monday. And when I'm through over there, I'm getting my bike serviced."

A frown exposed Netanya's concern. "You sure it's okay to be riding your bike with that ankle?"

"No problem," Keno fibbed. He didn't want to admit that Coach Taylor and the team trainer had expressly warned him not to ride his Harley.

Netanya didn't seem convinced. "I don't think it's a good idea. I don't want you getting hurt more than you already are."

While limping toward the door to leave, he stopped and asked, "We still on for Stinson Beach tomorrow?"

"You bet. And we can do some serious planning while we're there. I'll pick you up bright and early. Eight, okay?"

"You're picking me up?"

"Yeah, I want to check out Daddy's birthday present." She blew a kiss and waved with curled fingers. "Later, my betrothed."

He winked and said, "Later, my unbalanced babe."

While he'd enjoyed her playfulness, Keno left feeling a little inadequate. He was concerned with how the fifty-dollar bracelet he'd given Netanya for her twenty-first birthday measured up to the thousands her father had spent on the new Ferrari. It was his first serious taste of insecurity, and he didn't like it. *Is this going to be a way of life from now on?*

But that train of thought didn't get much shelf life. As he put on his biker's helmet, it occurred to Keno that the vision he'd seen at halftime during the game had come true. Everything he'd seen taking place in his helmet had really happened, down to the smallest detail. He couldn't avoid asking himself: *What could cause that bloody gash I saw on Tanya's face? That's got to be some kind of nightmare, or maybe I should call it a daymare. But whatever it was, or is, things are getting incredibly absurd. There is no* way *I can see into the future... Is there?* A cold chill engulfed him. *These mind trips are getting way too weird.*

Chapter Three

Frank Flores liked his chances in the early morning fog. He didn't have to worry about his scent in the damp, salty air, generously laced with tangy sea smells. He made his way down the bank until he reached a spiny clump of buffalo grass standing guard above the well-hidden den. He paused to listen, put down his gear, then dropped to one knee for a closer look. He could see that the mother raccoon had made her home relatively safe by digging it close to the bay. Any closer, it would have been swamped at high tide.

Frank knew the wary raccoon would be alert for the slightest hint of danger, so he tapped on his snare's aluminum handle with a small rock to make an unusual noise. When she peeked out, he waited for just the right moment, then lowered the plastic loop over her head. Like a fisherman setting a hook, he jerked on the pole to tighten the noose. This method of capture inflicted more discomfort on the surprised raccoon than he liked, but Frank didn't dare expose his hands to her razor-sharp claws. He placed the furious raccoon in an animal carrier and removed the plastic noose. He then reached into the den, scooped up the cute little month-old kits, and placed all three in the cage with their teeth-baring mother.

Frank let go a sigh of relief as he secured the cage latch. He was delighted that he'd managed to rescue the little raccoon family just one day before the rip-rap crew would move in the heavy equipment. He knew it wouldn't take them long to bulldoze the bank and cover it with life-crushing boulders.

After Frank had climbed up the bank, and he was ready to put the animal carrier in his Ford Ranger pickup, a black Mercedes came to a gravel-crunching stop only a few feet away. When Frank peered through the sedan's tinted windshield and saw that it was Nicky Ghilardi, he wondered why the young CEO had decided to stop at this remote spot so early in the morning. He'd learned just yesterday afternoon that Big Nick had suffered a serious stroke that had induced a coma, and this regretful turn of events had allowed Nicholas Ghilardi Jr. to assume control of Ghilardi Development Corporation. But going by the wisecracks he'd heard from some of the other construction guys, Frank doubted that Nicky was there to help rescue endangered wildlife.

Nicky kicked the door open with the toe of his cowboy boot, then slid out of the big luxury car. The pear-shaped young man tipped his cowboy hat back with a thumb before placing pampered hands on neglected hips. Nicky scowled at Frank, made a point of glancing down at the cage, then asked with a pretentious western drawl, "What the hell ya doin' on my property, Flores?"

Frank took a moment to study the surly young man dressed in gaudy cowboy clothes embellished with rhinestone buttons and embroidered pockets. Amused by the outfit, Frank guessed that the wannabe buckaroo hadn't made it to the bunkhouse last night.

While catching a potent whiff of recycled alcohol, Frank explained, "I'm moving a little family of raccoons to a canyon about two miles west of here. There's a nice little creek over there, and they'll be able to find plenty to eat."

"I couldn't care if them varmints starve to death." Nicky blinked his bloodshot eyes, allowing his abused brain time to think. "You just take care of' your landscapin' an' don't be worryin' about them overgrown rats."

Slow to anger, Frank had always tried to avoid the slightest conflict, but Nicky was interfering with a personal matter. "Saving animals' lives is never a waste of my time."

"It is when I say it is, 'cause I'm the head honcho now." Nicky glared for emphasis. "I don't want ya doin' no more o' that Sierra Club crap on my property."

Sinewy muscles rippled beneath Frank's tanned face. "Big Nick promised the county he would protect the environment. He told his superintendent, Jack Murphy, to let some of us rescue endangered animals as long as it doesn't interfere with our work."

Nicky's acne-scarred face became pigment blotched. "Didn't ya hear me, Flores? Big Nick ain't runnin' the show at Sea Lion Cove no more. Jack Murphy is my super now, an' I say to hell with you tree huggers an' your environment crap. Besides, those stupid coons just keep sneakin' back an' causin' trouble."

Nicky spun on elevated heels, leaned into the Mercedes, and reached under the front seat. The make-believe cowboy wore an evil grin as he retrieved a pearl-handled revolver. "Put that cage down an' get outta the way, Flores. I'm gonna put them scavengers outta their misery." He sneered as he cocked the big pistol's hammer, then squinted one eye to aim.

"Come on, Nicky, just put down the gun and..."

Nicky squeezed the trigger before Frank could finish his plea. The .45 caliber bullet nearly ripped the cage out of Frank's hand, and the unexpected explosion, booming like a cannon shot in the peaceful bayside morning, reverberated in his ears. The startled landscaper stared with surprise, not wanting to believe anybody could be so cruel. When a sharp squeal of pain registered, Frank looked into the animal carrier and saw that one of the kits had been mortally wounded. He grew sick to his stomach when he saw that the little guy's hindquarters had been blown away, and even sicker when the distraught mother began to lick the wound.

When Nicky said, "Put that cage down so I can finish 'em all off," a startling change came over the mild-mannered landscaper. A fierce, heat-laced energy accelerated through every fiber of Frank's being.

An awareness of danger appeared on Nicky's pockmarked face, and the tenderfoot retreated, brandishing the pistol.

Frank locked his incredible gaze on Nicky's drug-dilated eyes and stared into them with an intense, laser-like focus. His nostrils flared as he shielded the bullet-torn cage with his body and strode toward the obnoxious young CEO.

Nicky stumbled back while threatening with an unconvincing voice, "Don't mess with me, Flores, or I'll have ta blast ya."

Frank snaked out a powerful hand and clamped hold of Nicky's wrist with a vise-like grip, then squeezed until the pistol dropped harmlessly to the sandy ground. He pushed Nicky back with a flick of his strong, callused hand, then retrieved the pistol. Frank cast an incensed glare at the terrified young man before striding over to the bank. He blew out a long, slow breath and threw the gun out about forty yards, where it made a foamy splash in the gray-green waters of the San Francisco Bay.

This was an aberrant experience for Frank; it was behavior contrary to his nature. It seemed as if all the imprisoned anger of a lifetime had exploded in a few furious seconds. And even when this fury was directed at such heartless cruelty—too despicable for any sensible person to accept—Frank took no pleasure in it. He fought for self-control, doing his best to shake off that alien emotion.

Nicky sounded shaken and confused when he gathered enough courage to bluster, "You shouldn't disrespect me like that, Flores. You crossed the line, an' you don't know who you're messin' with. I got all the juice aroun' here, an' I'm gonna cancel your landscapin' contract. I want ya to get all o' your stuff an' get off my property. Ya hear me? I want you gone this mornin'."

Frank breathed deeply and slowly until he felt the internal fire begin to ebb. Though he managed to regain his self-control, he didn't bother to conceal his contempt. "I have a contract that would be hard to break. You'd better check with your superintendent, Jack Murphy, before you do something stupid that will cost your company a lot of money, not to mention what all the environmentalists in Marin County will do if they find out you killed that poor little kit. And what are you going to tell Jack? You are going to cancel my contract because I wanted to save some raccoons?"

"You threw my best gun in the bay," Nicky protested. "It was my favorite pistol. A Forty-five Special that cost me more'n two grand." When Frank didn't react, Nicky's voice gained some confidence. "It was worth more than all the stinkin' coons in the county. An' I ain't lettin' ya get away with it. I'm callin' the law an' have you arrested."

Frank glanced out at the bay's murky waters, then shook his head. "Even if it were legal for you to be carrying that pistol in your car, which I doubt, the law would still have to find it. I know you have a lot of pull because of your family name, but even that won't convince them to dive in that cold algae soup." Frank glared while adding, "I'm going to move these raccoons, and then I'm going to come back and plant flowers at the model home Jack Murphy wants me to finish. If you have a problem with that, talk to him."

Nicky got into his Mercedes and powered down the window. "You'd better have them model homes finished before the Grand Openin.' If ya don't, you will be in breach o' contract, an' then I'll legally fire your wetback ass."

The broad-shouldered landscaper warned through gritted teeth, "Get out of my sight while you still can."

Chapter Four

Keno rode his Harley more carefully than usual while cruising along the narrow asphalt street that snaked its way through Mill Valley's oldest residential district. He had to avoid putting unnecessary weight on his freshly taped ankle. He shifted down a gear and revved the engine for extra compression before turning onto the concrete driveway leading up to the carport.

The ivy-covered carport was somebody's afterthought. It was attached to the house several decades after the old redwood Victorian was built. Keno didn't see Millie's Volvo or Frank's Ford Ranger parked in their usual places, all but guaranteeing that neither was at home. He parked his Harley in its special nook, chained and locked it, then skipped and hopped up the steep wooden steps and headed for the kitchen. He grabbed a banana, an oatmeal muffin, and a quart of milk as he passed through, then hopped and skipped upstairs to his bedroom.

He flopped down on the bed and stretched out his big body to take a rare timeout. Another whirlwind summer had zoomed by, and it was time to make an attitude adjustment. It was supposed to be his senior year at Cal, except now he might be heading in a different direction.

Keno took a moment to reflect on his hectic summer before embarking on that serious train of thought. Colorful memories began to flash across his mind like the Travel Channel on fast-forward. He recalled sparkling sunrises and golden-hued Pacific sunsets while surfing at Stinson Beach and Half Moon Bay. He smiled when he recalled gettin' down and dirty while putting in long, hard days with Frank in his Milagrozo Landscaping business. Keno's shoulders involuntarily twitched when he recalled the sweat-soaked days of bangin' bodies, getting ready for his final season with the California Golden Bears. He could almost smell the football field's rich green grass just after it had been mown. This stream of consciousness reminded him that the high ankle sprain might have ended his football career. He considered the possibility that fate had intervened.

The next reverie caused him to get up and look out his bedroom window. He stared at the brilliant array of flowers and verdant garden that Frank had so masterfully assembled but observing that spectacular flora barely registered. His thoughts had traveled back to early June when Millie had talked him into trying out for a play she was directing. As a longtime member of the Marin County Repertory Theatre, his mother had acted, directed, designed sets, sold tickets, and even done a little janitorial work while putting plays together each summer. She'd been after her son to try his hand at acting for years, but he'd always avoided it by rattling off a long list of prior commitments. This year, however, he found himself defenseless against Millie and her indomitable collaborator—vehicular circumstance. Her old Volvo was in the shop with a broken valve, which meant he had to take her to the casting call, and since he was there...

Millie seemed thrilled, though not all that surprised, when Keno landed the lead role of Stanley Kowalski in *A Streetcar Named Desire*. The part featured a strong, handsome guy who's smarter than he looks, and it proved easy to cast Keno in the part. Thinking he'd just go along for the ride, Keno got caught up in this exhilarating world of emotionally charged imagination. He found himself acting opposite Netanya Bernstein, cast in the part of Stella Kowalski, and their chemistry seemed to unleash a potent explosion of talent. Netanya, a dedicated young actor with a few plays under her belt, seemed to feed off Keno's enthusiasm, and he enjoyed hearing her say that he'd elevated her performance.

Many associated with the play said Keno exhibited natural talent, but he wasn't so sure about the *natural* part. He was extremely attracted to Netanya and was trying with every fiber of his being to impress her. While he'd enjoyed the company of several girls, and had even gone steady on one disappointing occasion, he'd never gone out of his way to impress any of them.

Keno had used the excuse of rehearsing scenes one-on-one to be close to Netanya, then came grabbing a quick bite to eat, getting closer with a couple of casual strolls, and eventually a drive that ended on Mount Tamalpais. Their first kiss was forever imprinted on his brain, and those that followed unleashed a torrent of emotion. It took little more than a month from that first tender meeting of willing lips for him to declare his unconditional love. Free-spirited Joaquin Flores, the popular jock who'd been sailing through life with a light hand on the tiller, had felt the current take a dramatic turn.

Keno didn't hear Millie's light knock or her soft greeting when she opened his bedroom door. But the squeaking hinge, the one that hadn't gotten the WD-40 he'd kept forgetting, warned that someone had entered the room.

His mother placed an affectionate hand on his shoulder and questioned, "You okay, Sunshine?"

"Yeah, I was just tripping. You know, thinking about things that went down this summer."

Millie's pliant mouth curved into a smile. "A lot of things *go down* during your summers."

He thought about his mother's involvement with the theater, her devotion to oil painting, her volunteer work at the hospital, and her never-quite-finished remodeling project. "Yeah, like somebody else I know."

"Is everything okay with you and Tanya?"

He wanted to tell his mother how wonderful things really were, but he'd promised not to tell anyone about the proposal, and he assumed that included his parents. "Yeah, everything is cool."

Millie had a way of questioning with elevated eyebrows. "Then what's on your mind? I can tell something's bugging you."

Keno decided that he might as well unload at least one heavy thought. "Being with Tanya has made me seriously think about the big picture. Like what I'm actually going to do with my life. Coach Taylor thinks I still have a shot at being a decent draft choice; especially if my ankle heals and I can play in a couple games before the end of the season. And I've thought about being a landscape architect before I could spell *Milagrozo*."

"So, what's the problem? I was under the impression that you planned to play pro football and then expand the landscaping business when that career was over." When Keno was slow to respond, Millie added, "And I'm sure that's what Frank thinks, too."

Keno grimaced while confronting his mother's stare, wishing he could tell her about the sworn-to-secret proposal. "Okay, here's the deal. I might be going in a totally new direction. Tanya is leaving for UCLA in a couple weeks, and I'm thinking about transferring down there, too."

Millie retreated a step, as though distancing herself from her son's revelation. "You've got to be kidding. You'd be giving up your full scholarship and a chance to be drafted in the pros, to say nothing of getting your bachelor's degree." She took a deep breath and frowned, clearly searching for logic not yet provided. "Is the ankle injury responsible for this sudden change of plans?"

Keno shrugged his big shoulders. "That's probably a major part, but it's not the only reason. Bottom line, I really love Tanya, and I don't want to be four hundred miles away from her." He challenged his mother's lingering stare with a determined look of his own. "She doesn't want to be that far from me either."

"I don't believe this." Millie shook her long blonde hair, as if to shed unwelcome information. "Then why doesn't Tanya change schools? She'd have a lot less to lose."

"Because I would be switching my major, and UCLA has the top Performing Arts curriculum in the country. Tanya can afford to go anywhere in the world, and she thinks it's the best."

Millie nodded knowingly. "Ah hah. Me thinks you were bitten by the acting bug."

"Yeah, I guess I'm hung up on acting, too."

"Are you sure it's not just a passing infatuation?"

"I hope not. You know how much I like football, and I totally enjoy landscaping, but when the curtain goes up, acting gives me a bigger blast than when I score a touchdown or see a scruffy piece of ground turn into something beautiful." He bit his bottom lip while recapturing the thrill of being on stage. "My adrenaline pumps and my stomach feels like it's full of psyched butterflies. It's like..."

"It's called passion, Keno, which is hard for me to discourage. But you have to realize that you acquired those intoxicating feelings in a comfortable environment at the same time as you were falling in love with Tanya. Audiences and critics won't always be so kind, and you will be pitting yourself against hundreds of other handsome young men like yourself. And it isn't always the most talented or most deserving who make it. So much depends on chance and connections. I hate to say it, but the chances of making it as an actor are probably about the same as winning the Lotto."

Keno shrugged, wordlessly pleading for his mother's support. "I know the odds are against me becoming a star, but I'm seriously thinking about giving it an honest shot."

Millie's sigh held a sound of resignation. "Your honest shot is like most people's sworn commitment. And to think, I was the one who encouraged you to try your hand at acting." As she turned to leave, another shake of Millie's blonde hair seemed to add an exclamation point to her exasperation. While grasping the antique glass doorknob, she turned and said, "I wish you wouldn't make a final decision until after you've really thought things through. And when you do, consider your father's feelings. He has a lot of himself invested in your future."

Keno had thought about his father's unselfish investment, and there would be a lot of guilt-baggage attached if Frank disapproved. Happy-go-lucky Frank had never missed one of his football games, and he'd spent countless hours sharing his landscaping expertise. Concern for Frank's feelings instigated a defensive reply. "I remember you telling me about going against your father's wishes when you fell in love with Frank."

Millie glared and warned, "Don't even go there. It's ridiculous to compare the two situations." The neglected hinge let go a high-pitched screech as she emphatically closed the door.

Keno began to think about the chain of events that had brought about his current dilemma, but chains of events can often be connected as far back as a person wants to add another link, and today there seemed to be an abundant supply of connectors. His remarks about Millie going against her father's wishes brought to mind some of the family history that she'd narrated for his benefit.

Millicent Elizabeth Hutchinson was the only child of Herbert J. "Hutch" Hutchinson and Mary Belle Carter Hutchinson. They'd lived on a big Spanish-style spread just fifteen miles from downtown Houston, Texas. Hutch, a bull of a man, was a part-time rancher, a wheeling-dealing livestock broker, and an occasional partner in wildcat oil drilling schemes. Mary Belle was a University of Houston homecoming queen who, after years of neglect, had become lonely and disillusioned. Suffering from depression, Mary Belle began to spend a great deal of her time in a terry-cloth bathrobe sipping chilled Stolichnaya vodka. Millie had described her relationship with her mother as sister-like, while her relationship with her father had been dutiful, but quietly resentful. Mary Belle had let Millie do as she pleased, while Hutch had projected himself as the macho authority figure who enjoyed rewarding his *good little gal* when she did something special. Hutch was fit to be tied when Millie chose to "go off to that damned University of Miamah, full o' wetbacks, spearchuckers, kikes, and pinko liberals," instead of attending his beloved University of Houston. Millie was determined to pursue her artistic dreams someplace that didn't include a preponderance of ten-gallon hats, cowboy boots, and pickup trucks with gun racks.

Mary Belle later told Millie that Hutch had gone ballistic when he'd learned that his blonde, fair-skinned daughter had ventured down to Puerto Rico on Spring break and succumbed to disgraceful conduct with one of the island's low-life inhabitants. His red neck had turned a deeper shade of crimson when an inebriated Mary Belle, no doubt enjoying his discomfort, confided that Millie's new beau had a dark complexion, was Catholic, and was of questionable ancestry.

Millie had also told Keno that his father had survived a hurricane when he was a boy, and he'd come to be known as *Chico Milagro de las flores*, Miracle boy of the flowers. Millie had speculated that Frank had not been a native of the island where they'd found him. She'd seemed convinced that Frank's chiseled features and olive complexion confirmed a European lineage and that his family had been vacationing in the Caribbean when all but Frank had perished in the storm. Millie truly believed that her husband had been "touched by the hand of God."

The extraordinary night with Netanya and the associated emotional struggles began to take their toll. Keno closed his eyes and welcomed sleep when it benevolently carried him away to Dreamland with visons of his father's story

The little boy didn't have a care in the world as the gleaming white schooner glided over the crystal blue Caribbean. With his feet dangling over the side of the boat and the cool waves tickling the bottoms of his feet, the boy couldn't have been happier. The boy's cheerful mood vanished when his mother announced that the radio had stopped working, and she didn't seem quite so protective while arguing for dropping sail and riding out the storm. And his father didn't seem quite so invincible while insisting that they try to make it to the island. When the sky changed from a pale blue to a threatening gray, the boy began to pray. "Hail Mary, full of grace..."

The wind slammed into the schooner with an angry surge that sent the boat pitching and bucking, causing the boy's stomach to churn in time with the menacing sea. He grasped the rail with both hands, but it was too slippery, and he couldn't hang on. The boy latched onto a cedar box floating by just an enormous wave crashed over the deck and washed him away. Still clutching the box, he went down kicking and thrashing in the aquatic darkness.

Keno suddenly sat up, wide awake, with no drowsy transition from his deep sleep. His heart continued to race as he watched fading storm images dance among the ceiling's shadows. The dream had seemed so vivid, so real, as if he'd somehow entered the little boy's head and shared every intense emotion. Confused, Keno lay wondering how something so bizarre had worked its way into his subconscious. He eventually decided that Millie had provided the connection. She'd told him quite a bit about his father's traumatic experience, though her vague depictions wouldn't even begin to justify the detailed reality he'd just witnessed.

While recalling the style of clothes the woman in the dream was wearing, it occurred to Keno that she could have been Frank's mother, which would make her his grandmother. Considering that particular relationship caused him to ask with a hoarse whisper, "Shouldn't that be my father's dream?" It would, he decided, take a sharp shrink to explain his involvement in a nightmarish event that happened decades before he was born.

The sound of Frank's pickup caught Keno's attention. The ten-year-old Ford Ranger was probably attracting a lot of the neighbors' attention as well. Frank had run over a big rock that made a hole in the muffler about a week ago, but he wasn't one to sweat the small stuff. Keno had overheard him telling Millie, "I'll get it fixed *mañana.*"

Keno lay there a few moments, realizing that he'd made the decision. It was the second most important of his twenty-one years; the first, of course, being the proposal. He got up and forced himself to confront the moment he'd been dreading since he'd considered transferring to UCLA. He knew Frank wouldn't try to stop him, but he was afraid his good-natured father would be disappointed. This was a price Keno was reluctant to pay.

Frank was not a creature of habit, but when the weather was nice he often sat out on the patio and relaxed with a beer after a hard day's work. Keno checked to make sure his father was out there, then grabbed a Corona from the fridge and limped out to join him.

Frank frowned while glancing at the beer. "I thought you were in training."

Keno sensed something was wrong and guessed it might have something to do with the big landscaping job at Sea Lion Cove Estates. His father certainly wasn't his usual jovial self. "A beer just sounded good." He took a swallow before adding, "Besides, I might need a little courage."

Frank took a swallow of his Corona, then tilted his head a little to stare at his son. "I don't like the sound of that. Why would you be needing courage?"

He couldn't recall his father ever sounding so gruff, let alone seeing him wear such a prolonged scowl. Keno took another long swallow of his beer to delay his response. "I'm considering some new plans that we should talk about."

Frank ran a callused hand through his wavy hair. "What kind of new plans?" His face took on a curious look. "You thinking of getting married?"

Caught off guard by the question, Keno desperately wanted to tell his father about the proposal. But he'd given his word. "I doubt that's going to happen for a while. Netanya's lasered in on an acting career."

"I'm guessing *lasered in* means focused in your lingo."

"Yeah, you're on to me."

"Quit beating around the bush. What's on your mind?"

Frank's brusqueness surprised Keno again, but he did appreciate his father getting right to the point. "Okay, here's the deal. I might be transferring to UCLA to study acting."

"That's a new plan, alright." Frank's face took a studious look. "Does this have anything to do with your ankle injury?"

"Maybe, but that's not the only reason."

"I'm glad you're being honest about it. I know a little thing like an ankle injury wouldn't make you quit the team. I remember when you played the whole second half of a game with a separated shoulder, and then last season you played three games with a broken thumb." Frank frowned before asking, "You worried that I'm not going to like your change of plans?"

Keno nodded. "You know me pretty well."

"I'm glad you're worried about what I think. But you know what?" Frank turned up his palms. "God will help you decide what to do with your life. Life is short, and a man should spend it doing what he enjoys. Most people aren't lucky enough to do that."

Feeling as if he had gotten his father's blessings, Keno wanted to hug him more than at any time he could remember. He couldn't fight back the moisture forming on his eyes, so he looked down at his Nikes and blinked away immature tears. "I think it's totally cool that you're only concerned about my happiness."

Frank waved away his son's gratitude. "You talked to your mother about this?"

"Yeah, she thinks I'd be a fool."

"She's probably right. Not too many people make it in the acting business."

"The same goes for football. Even if the ankle heals perfectly, I could blow out a knee at any time."

"Don't you still enjoy playing? It sure looked like you did last Thursday night."

Keno felt the reality of it sink in. He would definitely miss being a Cal Bear. "Yeah, giving up football is going to be tough. I've been playing on teams since I was about nine years old."

"I think you were eight." Frank's expression turned solemn. "Cal gave you a good scholarship, my boy. You owe it to the coach and the team to tell them if you're not going to play anymore."

"True. I'll tell them Monday morning."

Frank folded his hands and studied his knuckles. "Have you thought about finishing out the season before transferring?"

As usual, Frank had offered a logical alternative, making Keno feel even more distressed that he couldn't tell his father about the proposal. "That's a good idea, but Tanya and I don't want to be apart that long."

Frank managed a little chuckle. "When you're twenty-one, months can drag by and seem like years. But when you get to be my age, time zooms by so fast you don't know which month it is if you don't check the calendar."

"I guess time really is relative."

The Corona and discussing Keno's plans had clearly improved Frank's mood. He leaned back in a more relaxed position, and said, "Your situation reminds me of the old guy who owned three goats. His favorite one was pretty and sweet, another one was little and cute, and the third one was big and mean. Times were tough, and winter was coming on, so the old man had to sell one of the goats to buy warm clothes, butcher one for meat, and keep one to supply his milk and cheese. His favorite goat gave the least amount of milk, but he couldn't bring himself to sell her, let alone butcher her. Then he couldn't butcher the little cute one, so he sold her to somebody for a pet, even though she brought the least amount of money. The old man finally butchered the big mean one, even knowing its meat was going to be so tough he could barely chew it."

Keno smiled and said, "Let's see if I got this straight. The old dude kept the goat that gave the least amount of milk, sold the goat that got him the least amount of money, and ate the goat that had the toughest meat." When Frank smiled and nodded, Keno asked, "And the moral is?"

"Don't trust your heart to make important decisions."

Keno leaned back and laughed, appreciating the way his father had approached the touchy situation. "You sure come up with some cool off-the-wall stuff."

Millie suddenly appeared with another Corona for Frank.

Frank didn't even try to hide his surprise. "Thanks, honey." When she held her smile and didn't make an effort to leave, it became obvious that the beer was a ploy to join them. "Why don't you sit down and shoot the breeze with us?"

She nodded and sat down next to her husband. "I haven't heard that one for a while. What kind of breeze is in season?"

"Goats," Keno said with a straight face. "Frank's teaching me a lot of stuff about them."

"Goats?" Millie frowned. "What about goats?"

Frank shook his head and flashed his brilliant smile. "No, honey, we were talking about Keno's new plans."

Keno decided to bring his mother up to speed. "Frank suggested that I stay at Cal to finish the season before switching to UCLA. It's a good idea, except I don't even know if I'll get to play anymore this year. The trainer is guessing I'll be out at least six weeks, which would only leave me two or three games at the end of the season, and that's if I'm lucky. And more than anything else, I don't want to be away from Tanya for that long."

Millie scowled at her son's rationale. "Good grief, Keno, she'd only be a few hundred miles away. You could be together for holidays, and if it gets so bad you can't stand it, one of you can always jump on a plane for the weekend. Surely, you can handle that kind of arrangement for one short school year." When Keno didn't immediately respond, she asked, "Who's going to pay your way at UCLA? We certainly can't afford it." She shook her head for emphasis. "You probably don't have a clue about how expensive college is without a scholarship."

Keno felt a little sheepish while admitting, "Tanya's going to loan me the money."

Frank grunted, then took another swallow of beer. "I'd think twice about that idea. What if you give up everything, and then you two can't get along? You could find yourself left out in the cold. You'd be surprised at how many young people get together thinking that nothing could ever come between them, and then they part ways over something stupid." Frank paused to pat the top of Millie's hand before adding, "It's not always easy to get along with a headstrong woman. Especially a spoiled, stubborn woman."

Millie swatted his shoulder. "Thanks a lot, dear."

Frank flashed his brilliant smile. "You know I wasn't talking about you, my love."

"Yeah, right." Millie playfully swatted Frank again before turning to Keno. "Seriously, though, your father has raised a valid point. As impossible as it may sound to you now, you could be exposing yourself to a tenuous situation."

Once again, Frank's logic had made a lot of sense, except of course, for the sworn-to-secret proposal. "If I can't trust Tanya, I can't trust anybody."

Frank nodded in agreement. "I can't argue with that, my boy. Trusting the one you love is one of the most important things in life." He turned to Millie and patted her hand again. "I remember a time when I trusted you with my whole future."

"Yes, and we were in it together, sweetheart. I put mine in your hands, as well." Millie's face took on a distant look. "Have you ever told Keno about the unlikely way we met?"

"No, I've never told anybody about it. But who's going to believe a beautiful angel came to me from right out of the blue?"

"That's really sweet, Frank." Millie's eyes shone as she turned to Keno, eager to tell her version. "Our first meeting wasn't exactly what anyone would call romantic." A chuckle escaped before Millie went on, "Actually, it was very nearly a fatal encounter. That year

I went down to Puerto Rico for spring break with Conchita Perez, one of my sorority sisters. She had a cousin living there, and we stayed with her family. Anyway, we decided to take a tour of San Juan the day before we were supposed to return to Miami, and we rented mopeds for our day of adventure. Conchita and I decided to ride up to one of the exclusive districts to check out the rich people's houses and views, so off we went. We were having a ball until we reached the top of one of the highest streets, but then the throttle on my moped stuck wide open. Before I knew it, I was speeding over the hill and zooming down the other side. When I missed a sharp turn, the moped slammed into a bank and sent me flying. I must have hit my head pretty hard because I'm pretty sure I lost consciousness."

Frank's mind raced back, recalling the clairvoyant feeling he'd felt that remarkable day. He could still hear the compelling voice he'd heard a minute or so before he would see Millie come hurtling through the air. He'd rushed to move the heavy steel wheelbarrow away from the precise spot where she would land, and he'd known where to stand to help break her fall. All because of succumbing to a mystical feeling and believing in the warning voice he'd heard. Though later, he suspected that unusual sounds and other outside influences had made it possible for him to reach such a remarkable deduction, which culminated in a spectacular rescue. He'd never shared that extraordinary event with anyone, not with his loving life partner, and not even a priest. And he certainly couldn't bring himself to talk about it after all this time.

Millie's face took on a curious look. "Are you still with us?"

"Yeah, I was just... drifting back."

"Tell Keno what happened after I landed."

"All I can say is luck was riding with your mother that day. I couldn't believe it when I saw a blonde head sliding face-first into one of my flowerbeds. Thank God, it was covered with a lot of my Milagrozo mulch."

Millie nodded and said, "I remember looking up into a concerned man's Cocker spaniel eyes, and the next thing I knew, I was floating up in a pair of powerful arms. And this handsome guy named Francisco rushed me to the nearest hospital, and then he was thoughtful enough to come by later to check on me." Millie reached for Frank's hand and gave it an affectionate squeeze. "This led to a moonlight stroll on the beautiful white sands of Luquillo Beach, and the rest—Millie paused to let go a sigh—was romantic history."

Keno had heard parts of the story before, but he enjoyed hearing his parents telling it together. He glanced at his mother and asked, "Didn't you almost decide to stay in Puerto Rico?"

Keno's question opened the gates to another rush of memory. Millie paused and looked off into the distance, recapturing details dimmed by time. "Yes, Francisco and I fell so hard that neither of us gave any thought to real-world consequences. I decided not to go back to the University of Miami that spring, thinking that finding the love of my life was certainly more important. My father, however, strongly disagreed. He bombarded me with phone calls and telegrams, which I didn't respond to fast enough to suit him."

Millie's face lost its cheerful look. "Your grandfather, the hard-headed rascal, chartered a private plane and headed for Puerto Rico to bring me home. Unfortunately, the plane flew into a tropical storm no one had forecast. The pilot told my mother that Hutch was so worried about going down in the Bermuda Triangle that he had a heart attack. He died before the poor pilot could get him to a hospital."

While noticing that his mother had used her father's first name, which she'd criticized him for doing since he'd turned twenty-one, Keno had become entranced. "My grandfather died in a plane?"

Millie's voice softened, "Yes, a massive coronary."

With a somber voice, Frank added, "It was a couple of days before we learned that Hutch had died, but when we did your mother felt responsible. Though nobody with any sense would think it was her fault, she felt like she had to go home and help your grandmother take care of things."

Visibly moved, Millie chimed in, "The thought of leaving my new love behind was at least as disturbing as my father's death. I contacted Immigration and learned that if I were to marry Francisco Flores, he could go to Texas with me."

Frank grinned and said, "I thought it was a great idea."

Millie winked at Frank, then shook her head while recalling the next dire memory. "A big can of worms was waiting for us in Houston. A mortgage company was foreclosing on the ranch, and the IRS had placed liens on just about everything Hutch owned. Mary Belle sipped a lot of vodka without bothering to hide it and spent a lot of time in the company of a handsome rascal named Hank, one of Hutch's shady business partners." Millie paused to recapture an intimate moment before adding, "One day when she was sober, my mother took me aside and said, 'The Lord works in mysterious ways. He took away your mean-spirited daddy and gave you a good man with a gentle soul.'"

Frank shrugged. "I'm glad Mary Belle thought so, but then she didn't know me very well."

"My mother might have been an alcoholic, but she was very bright." Millie stared at Frank, as if to emphasize her point. "Anyway, we eventually got around to giving Hutch a memorial service that attracted a lot of Texans." She shrugged before adding, "Curiosity draws crowds."

Frank added, "We heard people whisper and knew that Millie's future with me, Francisco Flores, would be limited in Houston, especially since some of the locals blamed us for Hutch's heart attack. But Mary Belle seemed to be in good hands..."

"At least busy hands," Millie interjected.

Frank finished his thought. "So we didn't see any reason to stay in Texas."

In a resentful tone, Millie said, "I explained some of the prejudicial drawbacks that your father wasn't completely aware of at the time.

I thought it would be a good idea to Anglicize his name, so he met me halfway and agreed to change his name. The soon-to-be Frank Flores and I sat down with a map to plot our future. Frank's only concerns were that we wouldn't go anywhere that was too cold or too crowded, while I only cared that the local populace wasn't too bigoted. That narrowed our options more than you might think. I put a few names in a paper bag and let him pick one. By the luck of the draw, he chose Northern California."

"I doubt that luck had anything to do with it," Frank said. "My prayers were answered when we were allowed to live in this wonderful place called Marin County."

"You guys should write a romance novel," Keno joked. But when he saw his parents staring at each other affectionately, he felt awkwardly out of place. Not sure they cared, he stood and announced, "I'm going to go watch the 49ers' pre-season game with the Raiders."

After Keno had limped out of earshot, Millie said, "Are you okay, Frank? You seemed a little distant when we were tripping down Memory Lane. Especially when we were talking about Hutch dying in the plane."

Frank stared at his wife, knowing she could always tell when he'd escaped their singular bond. "I have something to confess." He shrugged, and said, "It was my fault that Hutch died."

"Your fault?" Millie frowned. "How could you possibly think it was your fault?"

"I don't know if *fault* is the right word, but I'm pretty sure I caused it."

Millie questioned, "Are you kidding me?"

"No, I'm serious as a..." Frank paused, deciding that the old heart attack metaphor wouldn't be in good taste. "Anyway, I prayed really hard that you and I would always be together, and I think my prayers turned out to be lethal."

"Now you are being silly."

"You'll have to admit, God did answer my prayers."

"You're getting a little far out, sweetheart."

"Maybe so, but you can't argue with results."

"I guess not. But since we're putting the past under a microscope, I'd like to ask you about something that's been bothering me for a long time. Are you sorry I asked you to change your name? Looking back, it seems narrow-minded of me."

"I've never really thought about it, but the name I changed wasn't given to me when I was born anyway. Besides, I think I was meant to be a Frank. I feel like a Frank." He smiled and winked at his wife. "That's just who I am."

Mille leaned toward her husband and caressed his cheek with her fingertips. "No, my love, you're more than just an ordinary Frank. You were blessed, singled out by God, and I was lucky enough to find you."

"If I was singled out, God was nice enough to give me a beautiful blonde angel."

She sighed dreamily and whispered, "You really are special."

Their awakened attraction drew them together, and their lips met as eagerly as they had on that long-ago moonlit night on Luquillo Beach.

Chapter Five

A frantic voice announced that the radio receiver had quit working; there wouldn't be any more news about the weather. A flock of hastily departing seabirds seemed to know what was coming. A flop-eared hound let go a long, mournful howl. Then an eerie silence spread across the small Caribbean Island.

The wind picked up its pace and bolts of lightning fractured the encroaching gray curtain. Enormous explosions thundered against the beach, setting free tons of water that arrived in horizontal sheets. Wind-propelled rain swept up particles of sand, bark, and splinters piercing everything they touched. Then flying trees, sheet metal, and lumber destroyed everything in their path.

Frank woke with his body feeling hot and clammy, as if he'd been exposed to the steaming humidity that saturated the island that day. Fighting for clarity, he found himself becoming even more confused. For a man accustomed to spectacular dreams, he knew this one was different. It was as if he'd been on the island when Hurricane Lugo had arrived. He had somehow become an eyewitness to a catastrophic event that happened more than forty years ago. He couldn't begin to comprehend the logic of a tragedy trapped in a time warp. Though hurricane dreams had haunted him for years, they seemed to be visiting with increasing regularity. But before tonight's, the dreams had mostly been of him as a little boy on a sailboat with his mother and father, reliving the horror that Hurricane Lugo had wrought. It always amazed him how vividly those dreams had endured.

Millie turned toward her husband and draped a limp arm across his waist. Sleep made her voice sound husky. "A hurricane dream again, honey?"

Frank glanced down at his drowsy wife, whose pale complexion appeared luminescent in the dim light. He stroked her tousled blonde hair, and asked, "You could tell?"

"Yeah, but tonight's was a little different. You usually wave your hands and arms around like a little kid learning to swim." Unsure whether to pursue this disagreeable topic, she snuggled closer and said, "It must have been horrible."

A rush of memories invaded Frank's thoughts, unguarded by layers of time. Now, more than ever, he was convinced that no one could appreciate the storm's terror and devastation unless they'd actually experienced it. Hurricane Lugo had decimated the island's flora, annihilated all the people, and left little evidence of man-made things. When Frank realized that Millie was staring at him, expecting more, he said, "It seemed like everything on the island was erased from the face of the earth." Frank chose not to mention his parents' lost schooner, which had coupled the wrong place with the wrong time.

"You don't have to talk about it, sweetheart."

"No, it's okay." These vivid recollections, like old black-and-white movies, were hard to stop watching once they got going. "Sometimes I'm not sure if I really remember seeing certain things or if somebody just told me about them. But I clearly remember when the soldiers found me in a big hole, probably where the wind had ripped out a tree. I was told that I was only five or six years old at the time." Frank shrugged and said, "I guess my guardian angel dropped me in the safest place she could find."

Millie seemed surprised that her husband was elaborating on the event. "I think more than luck was involved."

"No doubt about it," Frank replied. "But the soldiers seemed happy about finding me alive, probably because no one else..." He paused to let that ugly thought pass, then recaptured another vivid memory. "I was almost naked, but flowers were covering some of me. I'm sure that surprised them because there weren't any plants left standing, let alone flowers. And I remember how those soldiers looked up to heaven and crossed themselves."

"It's easy to understand why they reacted that way," Millie replied. "Anyone would have found your situation remarkable, to put it mildly. And when you think about it, that could be why you became so involved in landscaping,"

"You're getting pretty deep, Doctor Millie." Frank smiled before adding, "Anyway, they sent me to a Catholic mission where the Mother Superior named me Francisco Flores. But some of the nuns called me *Chico Milagro de las flores.* But I didn't care which name they used, as long as they called me when it was time to eat."

Millie smiled at the old joke. "I'm kind of partial to *Chico Milagro.* It rolls off your tongue."

Frank was focused on the past as if he were watching an old video containing outtakes of his childhood. "I don't remember speaking any language for quite a while, and then I started speaking the nun's brand of Spanish. But nobody knew which language I spoke before they found me. They said that trauma had erased my memory after I washed up on the beach with no name, no family, not even a nationality."

"I'm sure the nuns insisted that it was God's will."

"Yeah, I heard that a lot." Frank paused a moment to reflect on a long-held secret. "I had my arms wrapped around a special box when the soldiers found me." He decided not to recount how a soldier had grabbed the cedar box and opened it, and how the terrified soldier had quickly closed it and crossed himself after handing it back. "And I think the nuns let me keep the old cedar box because I really protested when they tried to take it from me. More than one of them said it was my security blanket."

"That was nice of them." Millie said while pressing her cheek against her husband's muscular chest.

Surprised that his curious wife didn't ask about the cedar box's contents, Frank replied, "Yes, it was."

"After losing your parents so tragically, your childhood must have been difficult."

"I didn't let it bother me too much, probably because I was so young. But one good thing did come from spending those years with the nuns. They found out that I was good at growing things."

"I'm sure that didn't tax their imaginations."

Modesty prevented Frank from telling his wife that by the time he'd reached his late teens, he'd transformed the mission's grounds into a botanical masterpiece. And how one day, a visiting Papal Nuncio—one of the diplomatic ambassadors assigned by the Pope to inspect Catholic dioceses—had come to the mission and saw the improvements he'd made.

"This man they called a Papal Nuncio, a big old fat guy, said he knew talent when he saw it. He called me 'The Boy with the Amazing Green Thumb.'" Frank chuckled before adding, "He used his influence to get me moved to San Juan, where I could 'better serve the Church.' I must have done a good job because some of Puerto Rico's richest Catholics were making big donations for the services of Chico Milagro de las Flores." Frank flashed his brilliant smile. "Hope I'm not sounding too conceited."

"No, my dear. If I know you, you're minimizing things."

Frank glanced at the clock, which glowed 6:11 a.m. "I've got a rush job, so I'd better get up and get going." He kissed his wife's forehead and slipped out of bed.

Millie murmured, "You really are something," then burrowed herself deeper under the covers.

When Frank paused to look down at Millie, morning's first light played across her profile, accentuating her beauty. He had to resist a powerful urge to climb back in bed.

Keno walked into the kitchen just in time to see Frank heading for the back door, carrying his lunch pail and a Stanley thermos. "You're working on Sunday?"

"Yes, they're having the grand opening at Sea Lion Cove next Saturday. That only gives me 'til Friday to finish that phase of model homes."

Keno was familiar with the large housing development in northern Marin County. He'd helped do a lot of preliminary groundwork there. He also knew that Frank didn't enjoy repetitive landscaping, even if it was for expensive housing. It had the feel of production line work, and that was diametrically opposed to Frank's nature. But it was a lucrative contract, and the Flores family could use the money.

Keno hoped that Frank's two full-time employees—a sixty-year-old man and his mentally challenged son—would be working today. "Are Hector and Luiz going to be helping today?"

"No, they get very religious when I have Sunday work."

Keno smiled, knowing his father wouldn't avoid mass himself unless something important required it. "What about getting a couple of day-labor guys who hang out at Home Depot?"

"No, the ones there on Sunday are usually hung over, or I have to spend too much time teaching them what to do."

It would have required some serious torture to persuade Keno to break his date with Netanya, but he felt obligated to offer without being asked "Want me to help?"

"I don't think you should be working on that ankle."

Keno shrugged. "It's a lot better. And as long as I don't put too much weight on it, it should be okay."

"You already made plans for the day?"

"Yeah, Tanya and I were going over to Stinson Beach this morning, but if you need me..."

"Hector and Luiz will be there tomorrow, and we'll be able to finish the work by Friday. Summer's just about over, so go ahead and have a little fun. You're only young once."

Keno wanted to tell his father how much he loved him but settled for something cool. "You rock."

Frank flashed his brilliant smile. "I love you too, son."

A moment after Frank had closed the kitchen door, a burst of black dots exploded in front of Keno's eyes. An aura consumed his vision, then changed to a bright glow that surrounded a small cloud on the door. A snapshot of Frank's smiling face formed within the ethereal haze. As the image expanded, Frank raised one arm, as if signaling for Keno to follow him. A split-second later, the image was assaulted with an explosion of shattered glass that sliced open wounds on Frank's tanned face. As with the bloody image he'd seen on Netanya's face, a foggy curtain soon descended on this disturbing vision.

Keno stood staring at the door while thinking: *Whoa! I think I think I really am cracking up. But what could be causing all this weirdness? Things I saw in my helmet did actually happen, but nothing bad has happened to Tanya, so maybe nothing bad will happen to my dad. It better not...*

Netanya braked her Ferrari to a sliding stop in front of the old Victorian, then tormented the peaceful Mill Valley morning with a few beeps of the annoying Italian horn.

Keno would rather have taken his Harley but realized it wouldn't be safe with his injured ankle. Besides, riding in Netanya's hot wheels might be a blast. He paused for a moment to admire the expensive convertible. He held up his thumbs and fingers, framing a make-believe photograph. "That's you, girl." On closer inspection, the car's ultra-glossy paint seemed to project the third dimension of depth. He felt as if he were looking into a vat of wine that continued to change colors. "Cool paint job."

"*Bernstein Burgundy*. Daddy has all our cars painted this color." She shrugged and said, "It was my mom's favorite."

Keno wasn't about to touch that one. "Want me to drive?"

Netanya made a point of glancing at his ankle, then wrinkled her freckled nose. "No, I want to break this baby in."

Keno barely had time to buckle his seatbelt before she accelerated so hard that several unexpected G-forces slammed him into the bucket seat. He glanced back at the cloud of gravel and dust, then raised his voice enough to be heard above the engine's piercing whine, "What's the rush?"

She grinned, burned more rubber with a split-second shift, and said, "Is this baby cool, or what?"

As a tight end, Keno had caught passes over the middle, knowing that at least one burly linebacker was going to knock the snot out of him. As a surfer, he'd been crunched by the awesome power of twenty-foot waves. And he'd even bungee-jumped from a three-hundred-foot bridge to satisfy a bet. But the ride through the twisting, curving coast road to Stinson Beach exposed him to more fright than all his thrill-seeking life put together.

He couldn't have been happier to release his white-knuckled grip and climb out of the high-performance sports car when it came sliding to a stop. While wanting to shout, *You are totally wacko,* he forced a smile and said, "That was incredible."

Netanya tilted her head back and laughed with delight. "You really showed me something, Joaquin. Not many guys would have hung in there without freaking."

Keno forced a smile and said, "Who knows, flying off a cliff in a heavier-than-air vehicle without wings might be a blast."

As Netanya began to gather her things, she said, "Besides everything else I like about you, you are an incredibly good sport."

Ignoring the complement, he replied, "Well, at least you got us here early enough to find a good spot."

Her cell phone jingled, and when she checked the caller's I.D., the number prompted a smile. She swiped open the cell and said, "Daddy, I am so glad you called. Where are you?"

Keno removed his gym bag from the car and waited while Netanya finished her conversation, which from her end were mostly abbreviated sounds of agreement. When she closed the cell, she stared at him with a pained expression. "I'm really, really sorry, Joaquin, but I have to go home."

He stared in open-mouthed disbelief. "Are you serious?"

She moved close and wrapped her arms around his waist. "I know it's disappointing, but Daddy needs my help."

Keno thought about how he'd sacrificed his father's needs to be with her and how he was going to tell her about his monumental decision to go with her to UCLA. She had ruined his surprise. "I don't believe this. My dad could have really used my help this morning, but I stiffed him to be with you. Remember the part where we were going to do some serious planning while we relaxed on the beach? A little thing like our entire future is still out there, hanging in the fog."

She reached up and kissed his unshaven chin. "Don't be so dramatic, Joaquin. We'll have plenty of time to work things out."

"Then how about I go to your place with you? It's about time I met your father anyway."

"Today wouldn't be good. Daddy doesn't like having other people around when we are doing business stuff."

"Is that the only reason you don't want me around? Are you worried that Daddy Bernstein isn't going to approve of me?"

"Now you're being silly."

"I'm not so sure about that. It doesn't seem like you're all that excited about us meeting."

"I'm sorry if it looks that way, but it really wouldn't be a good idea for you to show up when he's got important business stuff on his mind."

Keno released a little animosity by tossing his gym bag into the car. "Okay, but I'd appreciate it if you'd slow down enough for us to talk about some important things on the way back."

As Netanya strode toward the driver's side of the car, the ocean and sand dunes became a background for her profile. Keno felt a vague twinge of déjà vu, as if he'd seen a similar image somewhere before.

Keno did a poor job of hiding his disappointment doing the return trip, and conversation was mostly one-sided. When they reached the Flores' Victorian, Keno climbed out of the passenger's seat and retrieved his gym bag. He had plenty he wanted to say about her leaving him hanging, but he just stared at Netanya with a blank expression.

She asked, "Call me later?"

"Maybe, maybe not."

"You're so cute." She revved the engine and gave him an amused wink as she waved goodbye with curled fingers.

He waved half-heartedly, seeing nothing amusing about her spraying him with dusty gravel while zooming away.

Turning his attention toward the Victorian, Keno noticed that the Volvo wasn't in the carport; this meant he'd been given a reprieve from explaining things to Millie. The word *reprieve* suddenly inspired the idea of making things right with Frank—he'd go help with the rush job. He knew his father would appreciate it, and a side benefit would be working off some of the frustration Netanya had caused. After devouring a peanut butter sandwich, Keno climbed on his Harley and cruised north on Highway 101 toward the Sea Lion Cove Estates.

The exclusive housing development was being built on a fill-enhanced peninsula that curved out into the northwest quadrant of the San Francisco Bay. The model homes were located on the southeast side of the peninsula, where they offered the better views. Much like any new housing development, there were houses in various stages of completion; even a few empty lots lay waiting with flagged grade markers and freshly dug utility trenches. Only the main thoroughfare was finished with sidewalks, curbs, and street signs. The finished street ran parallel to a rock-lined bank, constantly being splashed with choppy waves skipping off the bay. Keno wasn't at all surprised to see that the street had been named Ghilardi Drive.

He barely twisted the Harley's throttle as he rode down the deserted street toward the model homes. When he glanced out at the bay, he saw a few sailboats gliding along in the distance. About fifty yards out, two fishermen bobbed up and down in a small boat with its outboard motor tilted up out of the water. He couldn't make out the fishermen's faces hidden under hooded sweatshirts, but he could see that the boat's navy blue and white paint was chipped and peeling. When Keno glanced at his rearview mirror, he noticed a small black object reflecting a bright metallic light.

Nicky Ghilardi couldn't see much of anything. Coming down from an all-night cocaine binge, he nursed on a can of Coors while speeding his big black Mercedes at nearly eighty miles per hour. Even wearing chromium-coated sunglasses and swerving the car from lane to lane in search of a better angle, he'd nearly blinded his light-sensitive eyes by driving into the sun's dazzling glare. To make matters worse, Nicky had slept less than six hours during the past seventy-two. He'd been celebrating almost non-stop since his mother, Yvette, had handed him the reins to the Ghilardi Development Corporation.

Julie Lemmon was providing another distraction by massaging Nicky's crotch. Julie, ten years older than the fledgling CEO, was sparing none of her impressive mental and physical attributes to land the exclusive sales rights for the Sea Lion Cove Estates. Indeed, she was making the supreme sacrifice to satisfy her compelling need to succeed, for Nicky was a femininely soft, twenty-five-year-old brat. With her eyes closed to diminish the revulsion, Julie began to unzip Nicky's Levi's.

When Keno glanced back a couple of seconds later, the reflection revealed that the black object was a car whose image had tripled in size, which meant that it was approaching very fast. When he turned his attention back toward the model homes, he saw Frank driving his Ford pickup out from a side street that intersected with Ghilardi Drive.

When Frank spotted his son riding toward him on the Harley, his brilliant smile illuminated his tanned face. He raised one hand and waved, then motioned for Keno to follow him. Still smiling, Frank shifted the pickup into first gear, let out the clutch, and stepped on the gas. The engine sputtered, and the pickup coughed and jerked its way onto Ghilardi Drive, where it stalled.

Keno glanced at his mirror again and saw the grill of a Mercedes so close that the famous encircled propeller logo was speeding toward him like the nosecone of a heat-seeking missile. He performed adrenaline-enhanced calculations, and they added up to disaster. He jerked the Harley's handlebars hard and fell into a pavement-scraping slide, just a split-second before the big car veered sharply to avoid running him over.

Nicky Ghilardi yanked the steering wheel hard to the left to avoid hitting the Harley-Davidson, which had unexpectedly taken shape in the blinding glare. Only then did he see the Ford Ranger. Panicked, he struggled to swing the powerful sedan back to the right to miss the stalled pickup. As he fought for control, his cowboy boot slipped off the brake pedal, hit the gas, and then he instinctively pounded the brake pedal again.

When the speeding Mercedes abruptly veered to avoid one tragedy, it created another. The big car slammed into Frank's pickup, striking it broadside at an acute angle. It looked as if the heavy German sedan had played kick the can with the Ford Ranger, which immediately went airborne, violently twisting and turning until it came to a sudden, crunching stop.

Suffering confusing momentum changes, Julie's head flew toward the extravagant silver belt buckle that only partially succeeded in supporting Nicky's potbelly. Then airbags exploded from almost every angle. The steering wheel's airbag slammed into the back of Julie's head, smashing her face into the belt buckle. Blood immediately gushed from her broken nose and lacerated upper lip.

The blow to the stomach sent a disgusting spray of vomit spewing from Nicky's mouth, quickly followed by a girlish scream. Julie had reflexively tightened her grip before removing her hand from inside his pants.

Keno lay on the pavement watching the horrific scene, seemingly in slow motion, unfold in front of him. While shouting, "Noooo! This can't be happening!" he squeezed his eyelids together, hoping this would somehow erase the dreadful reality. Then a nauseous feeling swept over him as he fought to recover from the shocking spectacle. The brutal collision had sent the Ford Ranger rolling and bouncing across a manicured lawn and partially through a model home's picture window. When Keno struggled to his feet, bolts of pain shot through a broken ankle and ruptured tendons in his knee. Blocking out the nerve-searing pain with sheer determination, he limped, hopped, and crawled toward a scene he didn't want to see.

When he reached the rear of the crumpled pickup, dread constricted his ability to breathe and short-circuited his ability to think. Swollen veins pulsed against the lining of his motorcycle helmet. Tears felt like liquid fire burning around the edges of his eyes, and he was forced to focus and look for his father. From somewhere out of his past, a prayer emerged, and he whispered it aloud as he searched, hoping against hope. "Hail Mary, full of grace..."

Frank had been thrown clear of the mangled mass of metal and shattered glass. His bloodied body lay sprawled at the front of the model home—ironically, on a bed of beautiful flowers.

Shock benevolently shielded some of Keno's heartbreak. The magnitude of the tragedy had somehow made the situation seem surreal. He took off his motorcycle helmet and flopped on the ground beside his father's mangled body. In a dazed state, he assumed his father was dead. Even a powerful man like Frank couldn't survive those kinds of injuries.

His first rational thought was to get his cell phone from his back pocket and call for help. But frustration mounted when he discovered that it had been smashed—the cell had undoubtedly received the full force of the impact when he'd hit the pavement. But Keno didn't know what to do next. When he looked up and down the street he didn't see anyone. He glanced out at the bay with hopes of catching the attention of the two fishermen, but the outboard motor was churning up a lot of foaming wake while powering the boat away.

The Mercedes, which had skidded to a stop about fifty yards down the street, seemed to present the best chance of getting help. While it was impossible to tell if anyone in it had survived the high-speed crash, the big car didn't appear to have sustained much damage. Keno could only see a smashed front fender, a blown tire, and a buckled hood. Nevertheless, the longer he watched the car without seeing signs of life, the more he was convinced that its occupants had suffered some serious injuries.

Then the faintest of groans surprised Keno. For a couple of bewildered seconds, the feeble sounds startled him. Thinking he was probably imagining things, he scooted closer to Frank and stared at his father's battered face. Now grasping at a slender thread of hope, he watched for any kind of movement: the slightest breath; a twitch in the eyelids; a contortion of the shredded lips.

When a second groan, more of a rattling sound, came from deep within Frank's throat, Keno stared in disbelief. Frank batted his eyelids open to narrow, blood-glazed slits, then worked at moving his ravaged lips. Somehow, he managed to speak barely audible, raspy words. "Listen, don't... much time."

The urge to go for help assaulted Keno's stunned thought processes. A moment's deliberation convinced him that his only chance to save his father lay in contacting someone in the Mercedes. *There should,* he thought, *be a cell phone in an expensive car like that.* But paralyzing pain shot through him when he tried to get up.

Challenging the limits of human will, Frank managed to reach out and grab hold of Keno's wrist. The weak, raspy voice immobilized his son. "Wait... jus' stay... jus' listen..."

Keno collapsed in a state of shock while staring at the bloody hand that gripped him. His urge to go for help pleaded with him, but an even stronger force compelled him to stay and listen. Tears rushed down his cheeks as he gently peeled his father's fingers from his wrist, then held the injured hand in both of his. "Okay, Dad, I'm listening."

Frank's inconsistent words, some broken, some chopped, some stumbled over, formed with extraordinary effort. "I never told anybody... not your mother... not a priest... but sometimes... saw things... Sometimes... knew things... before they happened."

This phenomenal input struck Keno speechless. Astonished seconds passed before he could bring himself to muster, "You were, like... clairvoyant?"

Frank managed a nod. "Yes... knew things... like secret proposal... you an' Tanya."

Keno felt physically jolted by that one. A disbelieving "Wow" escaped, and a fleeting recollection of his own recent visions flashed across his mind.

Frank made a gurgling, shushing sound, then continued, "My life spared... me and Millie could have you. Now I see... it's His plan. You... chosen... do good things... For Tierra Milagro. Believed I had... more time... teach you... everything. Like miracle earth... needs little saltwater to make more. Evil stopped me... now try... stop you..."

Frank spat some blackish-red blood, then cleared his throat with a guttural cough. While continuing to come in a barely audible whisper, his words grew in intensity. "Must help the world... feed itself. Promise... won't sacrifice... destiny." His strength clearly fading, Frank made a valiant effort to elevate his raspy voice. "Don't be... avenger of blood."

Keno couldn't stand it a second longer. The situation had surpassed critical. He had to get help. Somehow. Now! But when he started to move, Frank's body visibly contracted. "Hang on, Dad, I'm going for help."

Frank managed to shake his head an inch or so. "Too late... promise... give the world... Tierra Milagro... Miracle Earth..."

Keno struggled to remember the words. Without the slightest idea of what the promise meant, let alone the reason for it, he wanted to placate his persistent father. "Okay, Dad, I promise I won't be an avenger of blood, and I promise I'll give the world Tierra Milagro and anything else you want me to do. I hope you're okay with that, cause now I'm going for help."

As he moved Frank's hand, intending to place it on his father's chest with the other one already resting there, Keno felt a sudden, powerful surge of energy. This surprising force coursed through Frank's calloused hand and streamed into his own. Petrified with disbelief, Keno felt this unrelenting force course up his arms and race through him until it seemed to reach every last cell. This incredible energy engulfed him, embraced him, consumed him. Countless electrical tentacles held him in their grasp, and even more startling, they provided an amazing mystical comfort.

The energy gradually ebbed, then simply vanished. But it had left its mark. It had left something uniquely spiritual at the core of Keno's essence.

Frank's eyelids had closed, and he lay quiet and still. Keno realized that he looked exactly as he had when he first found him, which meant that he looked quite dead. It occurred to Keno to feel for a pulse. He placed two fingers on the inside of Frank's wrist but didn't feel a heartbeat. Then he pressed two middle fingers next to Frank's Adam's apple. Still nothing. He pressed harder, this time hoping beyond hope. No beat. Nothing. Frank was gone.

Julie's mind finally cleared enough to realize that vomit covered much of her face and hair, blood oozed from her nose and mouth, and a slowly deflating airbag pressed against the back of her aching head. When she looked up at Nicky, obviously frozen in place with fear, she could see he was pinned in by her head and a confusing assortment of airbags. Feeling sticky vomit slide on her face made her angry, and she couldn't resist one final squeeze before removing her hand from inside his pants. Nicky's squeal offered a measure of satisfaction as she struggled to get free, then wriggled and slid her way onto the back seat.

While wiping some of the vomit from her face, she spied Nicky's expensive jacket lying beside her. As she cleaned herself with the black suede, she muttered, "I always wondered how far you'd go for the big bucks, Julie girl, and now I know. You're nothing but a high-priced prostitute."

Her grumbling alerted Nicky that she'd made it to the back seat. He pleaded, "Help me, Julie. I'm trapped, an' I wanna get outta here."

She wanted to spout a hateful wisecrack about his being a wimp, but she was too busy spitting blood.

It surprised Keno to see a woman climb out of the Mercedes' rear door. She held one hand to her mouth while stomping her high heels up and down as if she needed to go to the bathroom. She glanced up toward the sky and then an exaggerated shrug revealed her reluctance to open the driver's door. When she did, an airbag fell out and dangled like a balloon.

A pear-shaped man wearing gaudy cowboy clothes kicked aside the airbag with a fancy boot and slid out of the driver's seat. The sight of the man who'd senselessly killed Frank sent revulsion racing through Keno. He felt his stomach contract into a knot and his face flush with anger-heated blood. More like Millie in that regard, Keno had a quick temper, which he'd usually been able to let go as quickly as it came. Though this was different, much different. He'd just been intimately introduced to hate, the bitter side of passion. As he glared, Keno felt his ferocious loathing build, intensified by each second of watching the revolting murderer.

"Hey!" he yelled. "I could use some help over here."

Julie glanced in Keno's direction when she heard him shout, then turned to face Nicky. "That guy needs help. We'd better go over there and see what we can do."

"You take care of it, Lemmon. I gotta call Maloney."

Julie knew that Maloney was the Ghilardi family's lawyer. Nicky had mentioned his name several times during their negotiations, which had gone on as often as she could keep him focused on them during the seemingly endless night. She glared at the obnoxious man she was learning to despise, then climbed back in the car and found her purse.

Julie muttered through swollen lips, "What a jerk," as she marched toward Keno.

When he saw the woman approaching, Keno spread his shirt over Frank's mutilated face and upper body. He didn't want anyone to see his father looking like that. As he grabbed hold of the pickup's crumpled fender and pulled himself to his feet, the pain shooting through his knee and ankle convinced him that his new injuries were serious. He abandoned his idea of moving toward the woman and settled for steadying himself on one leg while leaning against the wrecked Ford Ranger.

"Hello, I'm Julie Lemmon." An obvious effort to force a smile failed, and her severely swollen upper lip caused her last name to sound like *Lemmum*.

Keno couldn't resist staring at her hair. It was easy to understand how her nose and mouth had been injured in the crash, but he couldn't imagine why some of her long red hair looked frizzled and other parts were matted and glistening in the sunlight. He finally managed, "I'm Keno Flores." Then he glanced down at Frank but couldn't let his gaze linger. "That's my father, Frank. He's dead. I wish you'd gotten here sooner; we might have saved him."

Julie glanced down at Frank's emaciated body, lying on smashed and flattened flowers that were drenched with a large pool of congealing blood. She thought: *No chance of that, big boy. You can't guilt me with that one.* Awkward seconds passed before she responded, "I'm really sorry. Is there anything I can...?"

"Yeah, I need to make a couple of calls. You have a cell?"

Julie seemed relieved that she could do something. "Oh, sure," she said as she retrieved a cell phone from her purse.

Keno dialed his home number, but as usual on Sunday morning his mother wasn't there. And Millie didn't have a cell phone because she didn't want to become a slave to a phone like so many other people she knew. Keno couldn't think of a message that wouldn't upset her, so he decided not to leave one on the answering machine. Knowing his mother, she was at church or helping out at the hospital, but he wasn't sure about that and couldn't remember either of the numbers anyway. He tried Netanya's cell, but she had turned hers off. He assumed that she didn't want to be bothered while helping her father with *business stuff.*

Julie seemed aware of his mounting frustration and offered, "Why don't you let me call for an ambulance?"

"I'd appreciate that." Another thought came to mind while Keno was handing back the cell. "I think it would also be a good idea to call the police."

"Of course," Julie replied. "But his area isn't incorporated, which I'm guessing means that it's under the County Sheriff's jurisdiction. I'll call them, and they should be able to handle everything." She quickly made the call.

The elevated heels of Nicky's cowboy boots made a clomping sound as he ambled up. Then focusing on Julie's cell, he asked, who the hell ya talkin' to, Lemmon?"

Julie snapped a look. She didn't appreciate Nicky interrogating her as if she were a hired hand.

Keno felt anger scorch his face as he looked down at his father's killer. The arrogant man's proximity made him feel as if a potent toxin had permeated his skin, creating a volatile compound that caused his blood to boil. "She called the County Sheriff's office like I asked her to."

Nicky had figured out who was involved in the accident when he saw the wrecked Ford Ranger. He'd felt a perverse sense of justification for eliminating the crazy wetback who had scared him spitless yesterday. Even now, a quick glance at the bloodied corpse sent a chill racing through him. Nicky turned away from the source of his fear and allowed his twisted mind to revel in the moment. He had to fight back a smile while thinking: *That stupid spick had it coming. That was some great payback for disrespecting me and throwing away my favorite pistol. Yeah, he messed with the wrong dude.*

Keno continued to glare at the monster who had just committed blatant vehicular manslaughter and, adding insult to injury, wasn't showing the slightest hint of remorse. "When the sheriff gets here, I'll make sure he throws your ugly butt in jail."

The obnoxious CEO scowled in response to Keno's threatening glare. "I'm Nicky Ghilardi, an' you're standin' on my property, Biker Boy. If you don't shut your big yap, I'll have you arrested for trespassin'."

Keno digested the pretentious cowboy drawl for a moment, then lost control. He lunged forward and punched Nicky in his soft paunch. But the impulsive effort caused his injured knee to buckle, and he went down in an awkward pile of pain.

Though the punch did carry enough force to knock him on his butt, it quickly became clear to Nicky that he had the advantage. He scrambled to his feet and delivered several hard kicks to Keno's ribs with the pointed toe of his cowboy boot. "I ain't nobody to mess with, Biker Boy. I got a nine-millimeter in my car, an' I won't think twice about blowin' your big ass away."

Obviously feeling proud of himself, Nicky turned to Julie and made a commanding motion with a quick jerk of his head. "Let's go over there where Biker Boy can't hear us an' have us a little powwow."

Julie reluctantly followed Nicky to a place on the sidewalk about twenty yards away. "I don't know why I'm even talking to a jerk like you. You treated that poor guy like dirt just after killing his father. You really should apologize."

"I ain't apologizing to nobody, 'specially not to a spick biker. Besides, it was an unavoidable accident, so zip your hamburger lip an' pay attention." Nicky hooked his thumbs in his cowhide belt, trying to look convincing. "I had a little talk with Maloney, and we came up with what to tell the law when they get here. An' I wanna make damn sure you tell 'em the same thing as I do." He paused to make sure Julie was paying attention. "Now, here's the deal. I was drivin' along about forty miles an hour when this idiot on the Harley rides up from outta nowhere an' starts doin' wheelies right in front o' me. Then he dumps his bike, so I put the pedal to the metal to get aroun' him. That's when this other wetback in the pickup, doin' at least thirty, comes drivin' outta the side street an' pulls right out in front o' me. I tried, but there was no way to miss that stupid greaser. It was some weird crap that happened real fast, but there was nothin' I could do about it."

Nicky fixed his beady eyes on Julie and stared a few extra seconds for emphasis. "An' that's exactly what you're gonna tell the sheriff an' anybody else who asks."

"You expect me to lie for you?" Julie couldn't resist a derisive chuckle. "Are you forgetting the fact, a very significant fact, that you just killed a man because you were high on coke, drunk out of your mind, and driving like a maniac?"

Nicky shook his head like a bobblehead doll. "Are you forgettin' about several hundred thousand bucks? That's how much you'll be making if I'm nice an' give you the sales contract."

For all his faults, Nicky wasn't stupid where money was concerned—a surprising lesson Julie had learned during the long night of negotiations she'd suffered through. He'd made her feel inadequate when it came to crunching numbers, even rattling them off effortlessly when he was wasted. However, the math regarding the sales contract was easy enough for her to process. Her percentage of the gross sales of the Sea Lion Cove Estates would net her privately owned Lemmon Brokerage Company a minimum of $700,000 in less than two years. While thinking, *I really am a high-priced prostitute,* she challenged his arrogant look with an icy stare. "And you'll give me a signed contract if I agree to confirm your fictitious version of events?"

Not only was he good with numbers, Nicky was quick to sense when he was cornered. "That's how it's goin' down."

"Alright, we've got a deal. Lying about how a poor innocent guy got snuffed can't possibly be as revolting as having sex with a disgusting creature like you."

Just as Nicky warned, "Don't press your luck, bitch," screaming sirens approached.

The ambulance was first on the scene, but the paramedic in charge took one look at Frank and said they couldn't touch him until after the county coroner had examined the body. A green and white county sheriff's squad car came roaring up with its lights flashing. A minute later, a county coroner's plain white sedan pulled up behind the squad car. About as opposite as two county officials can get—the deputy sheriff physically fit and the deputy coroner quite obese—climbed out of their respective vehicles and began to discuss procedure.

Then an older Lincoln Town Car came screeching to a halt just a few feet from where Nicky and Julie were standing. An exasperated John Paul Maloney powered down his window and advised Nicky, "Don't say a word. Not a single word to anybody until we get our story straight."

The deputy sheriff asked Keno a few basic questions to establish identities. But Keno found it strange that the deputy wasn't interested in hearing his account of the accident.

The deputy coroner made a cursory examination. When he finished, the paramedics placed Frank's body in a body bag specifically designed for corpses and slid it into the ambulance. Keno declined when asked if he wanted to ride along with his father's body, thinking it was more important to stay behind and make sure the facts pertaining to the accident were documented.

Keno tried to stop the deputy sheriff to relate those important facts, but the man just ignored him. He quickly concluded that the deputy didn't respect bikers, especially a young biker who was shirtless, needed a shave and a haircut, and sported a large blue and gold bear tattoo on one shoulder. Frustrated by being snubbed, Keno held onto the pickup with one hand, then reached out and grabbed the deputy coroner's arm when he passed by.

The pale man smiled weakly, then sympathized, "I'm very sorry about your father."

Keno's grip on the flabby arm grew tighter. "Don't you want to take my statement?"

"I really don't need your statement. I'm only required to make a preliminary report on the cause of death."

Keno spoke through clenched teeth. "Then make sure you report the real cause of death. That ugly punk over there hit my father's pickup with his Mercedes while doing about eighty."

The deputy coroner stepped back, futilely trying to free the arm that was growing numb from diminished blood flow. When he couldn't pull free, he assumed his practiced heartfelt look and said, "At least your father didn't suffer. I can assure you that his death was instantaneous."

Intended to console that remark only made Keno angrier. "You don't know what the hell you're talking about. My father suffered a helluva lot!"

"No," the flabby man protested, "that's quite impossible. A large section of the victim's cranium suffered severe damage, and his neck was broken." He made a knowing face before adding, "Those traumas were quite apparent to my trained eye."

"I don't care what your *trained eye* thinks it saw. You're wrong."

Clearly miffed at having his professionalism questioned, the deputy coroner replied, "If you insist on hearing the sordid details, I will share them." While Keno glared skeptically, the death expert explained, "Though there was more than one fracture, one sizeable section of the victim's skull was, for lack of a better word, crushed. Within an area of approximately twenty square centimeters, large fragments of the skull were splintered and embedded in the cerebral cortex. Also, the C-3 and C-4 vertebrae in the neck were misaligned by more than two centimeters, which strongly indicates that the spinal cord was severed." Pleased with himself, the flabby man asked, "Is that convincing enough?"

"That's total bull," Keno protested. "My father talked to me while he was dying."

The deputy coroner shook his head and spoke consolingly, "I understand that you're experiencing a lot of grief, and your loss makes it difficult to accept the facts. I've seen many of these kinds of reactions by bereaved loved ones throughout the years. And while I'm convinced there were multiple causes of death, it would be inappropriate for me to speculate as to exactly how the deceased incurred his injuries. I will have to wait for the deputy sheriff's accident report, which I will include with the final autopsy findings."

Keno pushed the bulky arm away. "You don't have to speculate about what really happened. It wasn't just an accident; it was murder by stupidity."

Visibly concerned for his safety, the fat man apologized again and hurriedly waddled to the sanctuary of his car.

Still fuming about the deputy coroner's remarks, Keno noticed that the deputy sheriff was conversing with Nicky, Julie, and an older man with a pronounced slouch. He had no idea who the old guy was, and though she'd been nice to him, he didn't know what to think about Julie Lemmon and her frizzled hair. Still, he had no doubt that Nicky Ghilardi would be lying about how the accident had happened.

While his newly injured ankle had swelled and had become somewhat numb, the slightest weight shift sent intense pain shooting through Keno's knee. This prevented him from negotiating the twenty yards to reach the deputy sheriff. Even so, he knew how important it was to let the officer know the truth before Nicky had contaminated it beyond repair.

Keno shouted, "Hey, deputy," to get his attention, but the straight-backed officer merely held up a hand to silence him and then turned back to continue listening to Nicky. His pain increasing by the minute, and his frustration growing by the second, Keno banged his fist hard against the pickup's crumpled rear fender. "Hey! You! Deputy! That guy killed my father. He's not going to tell the truth about what really happened here."

The deputy wheeled and gave Keno a stern look. Then it was his turn to shout. "Do not interfere with my investigation."

"I'm not interfering. I just want you to hear the truth. Don't listen to that murderer."

The deputy waved a threatening finger. "If you keep interfering, I will be forced to physically restrain you."

Emotionally devastated, helpless, frustrated, and growing angrier by the second, Keno shouted from the bottom of his lungs, "Restrain me? You must be an idiot. That punk killed my father, and you'd better listen to what I have to say about it!"

The deputy's lips compressed into thin lines. He slammed his notebook shut, blew out a breath, and charged toward Keno. "You'd better cool it, young man. I understand that you're upset because your father was killed in this accident, but that doesn't give you a free pass to interfere with an officer of the law."

Keno was in no mood for lectures. "No, you'd better cool it and listen, officer. You need to arrest that ugly punk. He was going at least eighty miles an hour when he slammed into Frank and killed him. Any dummy could see that's what happened."

Red blotches exploded on the deputy's cheeks. "I'm cutting you more slack than I normally would because of your loss, but I'm only going to ask you one more time to keep your mouth shut while I complete my investigation. If you don't, I will arrest you and take you to jail."

"What more is there to investigate, officer? Are you blind? Look at this pickup. Look at where the skid marks started. Look at where the Mercedes ended up. Remember what my father looked like? It's totally obvious what happened here."

The deputy stared at Keno, clearly examining his pupils. "Are you high on speed or some other drug?"

"Why? You think I fit the biker profile?"

"Yes, as a matter of fact, I do. A loaded biker's profile." The deputy snatched the handcuffs from the back of his belt and spun Keno around, but he only managed to cuff one wrist.

The deputy was not a small man, but Keno easily pushed him away with the back of his cuffed hand. Unfortunately, the free handcuff swung around and struck the surprised deputy on the bridge of his nose.

Without grasping the seriousness of what he'd done, Keno ranted, "You really are an idiot. Barney Fife could see that you're arresting the wrong guy."

A surprising amount of blood flowed from the small cut, and the sight of it alarmed the deputy when he touched the wound with a fingertip. Staring at the blood with a look of disbelief, the deputy stepped back and drew his gun.

"Clasp your hands together on your head and get face down on the ground." When Keno only frowned and glared, the deputy shouted, "Do it! Now! Get down on the ground!"

The trails of blood trickling down both sides of the deputy's nose finally registered in Keno's incensed mind. As the gravity of it sunk in, he realized that arguing was hopeless. He clasped his hands on his head, blew out a prolonged breath, twisted sideways to make the fall as painless as possible, and then slumped to the ground. The deputy handcuffed him to a chain he had placed around his assailant's waist and even with Keno's help, struggled to get his big prisoner on the squad car's back seat.

While catching his breath, the deputy said, "I'm going to let you cool your heels while I complete my investigation." Then he returned to where Nicky was standing for what Keno considered an unnecessarily long conversation.

As he waited, Keno had a difficult time grasping the reality of his situation. He began to feel as if his world had been turned upside down, and everything in it had spilled into a pit of insanity.

An air of confrontation hovered in the squad car as the deputy and his prisoner rode away from the Sea Lion Cove Estates, though their elevated testosterone levels festered in silence. Riding along quietly gave Keno time to consider his situation, and he realized it was futile to resist. He recalled seeing the deputy's nametag and thought this might be a good time to put his acting skills to the test. Keno swallowed hard, then spoke with a hoarse voice, "I didn't mean to hurt you, Deputy Wertz. I know you were only trying to do your job. I'm sorry I blew my cool."

Appearing surprised by the contrition, the deputy studied Keno's depressed face in the mirror. "You should have gone in the ambulance and left the investigating to me."

Keno decided to press the sympathy angle. "I wish I would have now because I am really hurting. My ankle feels like it's broken, and I'm pretty sure a ligament in my knee is ruptured."

Deputy Wertz leaned over far enough to see his own wound in the mirror. "My nose should be looked at by a doctor. And since it's Sunday, I'm going to be a good Christian and take you to the hospital to get you checked out, too. But that won't change anything as far as arresting you is concerned. I'm still charging you with trespassing, reckless driving, obstruction of justice, resisting arrest, striking an officer of the law during the performance of his duties, and anything else I can think of."

"I guess you have to do what you have to do, but you still need to hear how that ugly punk killed my father. Don't I have the right to tell you what really happened?"

"That ugly punk just happens to be Nicky Ghilardi, whose corporation just happens to own the property you were illegally riding your Harley on. He said you didn't have permission to be there, which means you were trespassing, which means you've abandoned your legal rights."

"That's not true. My father has... had... a contract for the landscaping at the Sea Lion Cove Estates, and I've worked there part-time during the summer. But that's beside the point. The only thing that matters is that the punk killed my father by driving like a maniac. You can't kill somebody while driving like a crazy man, even if you do it on your own property. And not only that, he looked like he was drunk or high on something."

"You'll have the opportunity to tell your side of the story in court, but I don't want to hear any more about it right now. So shut up and appreciate the fact that I'm taking you to the hospital."

It occurred to Keno that Deputy Wertz wasn't being fair in the way he was handling things. He hadn't even bothered to give Nicky Ghilardi a sobriety test, which on its own would suggest preferential treatment.

The deputy solicited the help of two male nurses and a wheelchair to transport Keno into the Emergency Room. While they were waiting to see a doctor, Keno pleaded with the deputy to let him use the payphone in the hall.

Wertz shrugged and said, "Yeah, okay, but make it quick. I want you finished by the time I get my nose patched up."

Before he left, the deputy took the precaution of handcuffing one of Keno's wrists to the wheelchair.

Keno was glad to hear the warm, familiar voice when Millie answered, but an avalanche of emotion swept over him as he searched for the right words. It was a futile search. There just weren't any. "Hi, Mom..."

His hesitation and then addressing her as *Mom* alerted Millie to the fact that something terrible had happened. Her voice elevated an octave while asking, "What is it, Keno?" When he was slow to respond, alarm grew in her voice. "What's going on? Where are you?"

"I'm at Marin General, but..."

"Oh, my God! Are you hurt? Did you wreck your bike?"

Keno blew out a prolonged breath. "Yeah, to both of those, but that's not what's important..."

'Not important? What could be more important than you getting hurt?"

"Well, Mom... it's Frank."

The unmistakable sounds of heavy breathing came through the receiver before she finally asked, "How bad is it?"

Tears scorched Keno's eyes. "As bad as it gets."

Her woeful wail assaulted his ears and pierced his heart. She eventually managed, "How did it hap...?" but didn't finish the agonizing question. "Oh, God, nooooo!"

Keno chose to keep it simple. "A speeding car hit Frank's truck." He waited a few seconds for her to respond, but the wailing screams and heart-wrenching sobs only intensified. Pressed for time, he felt compelled to blurt out the rest of the dreadful scenario. "I don't know how much longer I'll be at the hospital. I blew my cool and got in trouble. I hate to tell you this, knowing what you're going through, but I've been arrested. I guess they'll be taking me to the county jail."

Millie blurted, "God no, Sunshine. I really need you..."

Keno managed, "We'll get through it together, Mom." He knew she'd lost all control, so he finished with: "Call Tanya as soon you can and tell her I'm on my way to jail. Oh, yeah, tell her to bring me a shirt and the crutches in my room."

Millie's woeful wails were still coming through the receiver when he replaced it on the chrome-plated hook.

Keno spotted Deputy Wertz coming down the hallway, sporting a small bandage on the bridge of his swollen nose, but then the resolute man of the law stopped to flirt with a cute nurse. Hoping this distraction would give him enough time, he dropped the correct change into the payphone and quickly punched in Netanya's cell number, but his hopes, like a heavy anchor in a shallow pond, quickly struck bottom. A recorded message droned: "We're sorry, the party you called is not answering..."

The Emergency Room doctor's preliminary diagnosis was a torn anterior cruciate ligament, a chipped or broken talus, and multiple soft tissue injuries. Temporary casts were applied to Keno's knee and ankle and dressings were applied to the more serious cuts and scrapes. He was given a prescription for Hydrocodone, a narcotic pain medication, but wasn't allowed to have it filled. Deputy Wertz decided that it wouldn't be legal to transport narcotics into the county jail.

Keno had seen the magnificent structure that housed the Marin County Civic Center dozens of times and knew it was one of Frank Lloyd Wright's more famous works, but he'd never really studied the elaborate building in detail. And he certainly didn't know that the Marin County Sheriff's Department had a jail there.

As the squad car traversed the perimeter of the tree-dotted parking lot, Keno got a good look. The striking building's two long and narrow wings seemed to be resting on a huge Roman aqueduct. On closer inspection, it looked as if a mosque-like dome, decorated with a surprising amount of ornamental detail, stood command over the converging wings, each made up of a complex series of aqueducts. Three rows of arches, the second of them inverted, diminished in size as they ascended to the upper floors. Much wider and flatter arches at the bottom of the building allowed vehicles to pass under it and through to the other side. A lengthy row of perfectly round windows, like eyes in the sky, peered out beneath the slender eaves of the sky-blue roof.

Deputy Wertz drove under a wide arch spanning a two-lane asphalt road and parked in front of the Marin County Jail, which was located at the extreme west end of the unique edifice. Then as he'd done at Marin General Hospital, Wertz went inside and recruited a jailer to transport his prisoner in a wheelchair.

Keno felt as if he were entering a bunker when he was pushed down a windowless underground tunnel to an elevator, which carried the deputy and the prisoner up to the write-up room on the first floor.

After completing the necessary paperwork, Deputy Wertz took the jailer aside and exaggerated the extent and intent of Keno's assault with the loose handcuff. He touched a finger to the bandage on his nose and said, "A little payback might be in order." He winked and added, "Know what I mean?"

Keno was fingerprinted, photographed, tested for drugs and alcohol, and then his personal belongings were confiscated. The ensuing strip search was not only as humiliating as he expected, but it inflicted some unnecessary pain when the misguided jailor pretended not to notice the injuries. This blatant lack of consideration aroused Keno's anger, simmering close to the surface. And this only served to exaggerate his helplessness, a feeling with which he wasn't familiar.

The stern jailer pointed to the wheelchair and commanded, "Stay right there." Then he crossed the room and had a conversation with a uniformed woman sitting at a computer.

She handed her scowling cohort a piece of paper, which he carefully studied as he ambled back toward Keno. With an emotionless voice, he said, "Your bail is set at one hundred thousand dollars, Flores. You get one phone call."

"One hundred thousand? How did you come up with that?"

The jailer glanced at the printout. "It's done automatically. We feed in the info, and the computer spits it out. You're lookin' at five charges, two of 'em felonies." His face compressed with a look of disgust. "If you ask me, the bail should be a helluva lot higher for striking an officer of the law."

Keno's mind raced. *Has Netanya turned her cell phone on by now? If she hasn't, I'm totally screwed. I don't know anybody else who could come up with that kind of bail.* He looked at the jailer and asked, "What if I can't get a hold of the person I need to talk to? Can I try again later?"

The hard-boiled jailer wisecracked, "What part of *one phone call* don't you understand?"

Keno decided it would only be a waste of time to call Millie. Even if she were emotionally stable by now, which seemed very unlikely, she couldn't raise that kind of bail. Besides, she already knew where he was, and she'd already be doing everything in her power to get him out. He blew out a hopeful breath and punched Netanya's cell number one more time. His heart sank again when he heard the recorded monotone: "We're sorry, the party you called is not answering..." He shrugged and slammed down the receiver. The helpless feeling engulfed him again—more powerfully this time.

The hint of a smile flashed across the jailer's surly face as he pushed the wheelchair toward a door leading to the solitary confinement cells. It appeared as if he found perverse pleasure in knowing that Keno couldn't make bail.

Keno found himself in an empty steel cage furnished with one narrow steel bench and one stainless steel commode. As he struggled to find a comfortable position on the steel bench, it occurred to him that it couldn't be much past noon. The booking sergeant informed him that he'd be arraigned at 1:30 p.m. tomorrow. If he couldn't make bail or get a lawyer, he wouldn't be allowed any visitors. He had no idea of just how insufferably long twenty-four jail hours could seem. But he was about to find out.

While confined in the steel cell, dozens of competing thoughts assaulted Keno's haggard mind. Tangled, jumbled, and scrambled waves of thought swarmed in a free-for-all, each convinced of its supreme importance. This rampant confusion soon overwhelmed him, and his mind took a time out. Emptiness consumed him, and he stared into a void without seeing, feeling, or thinking. With no conception of time, he appreciated the silence of his own composition.

As afternoon turned into night, pain goaded him back to reality. When he noticed that it was dark outside, Keno felt as if he were living in a different dimension of time. He'd seen weeks go by faster. Pain proved to be his ally for a while; it kept his thoughts focused on things other than the agonizing loss of his father. So far, he'd been able to use every trick his mind could devise to evade that recollection. However, he couldn't continue to ignore Frank's last words.

He asked himself: *Were all those things Frank said real, or did the accident freak me out and cause me to imagine them?* His thoughts triggered a recollection of his own recent encounters with visions. *Is it possible that I have the same ability to see things that Frank did? Did we have some kind of genetic connection, or would that be more of a spiritual thing?* Keno shook his head, hoping these perplexing questions would just go away—they were simply too hard to deal with.

Revisiting the helmet vision, however, had allowed some self-pity to creep in. He realized that his football career was over, and he didn't have a choice in the matter. His new injuries had removed that possibility from the equation, and his plans to become an actor, which were probably delusional anyway, would be delayed for who knows how long.

His growing hate toward Nicky Ghilardi took a long turn controlling his thoughts, and he conjured up gruesome ways to punish that punk. Plans for revenge ranged from legal means to medieval torture devices. When he allowed his imagination to get carried away, he saw himself happily choking the life out of Nicky.

Then he recalled feeling the *something* that had coursed through him when Frank was dying, and he remembered that the something was attached to a promise. He'd promised Frank that he wouldn't be an avenger of blood. He asked himself: *Does that mean I promised not to kill Nicky? From the sound of them, those words probably came from the Bible. I'll have to check it out.*

Then blame, guilt, and what-ifs took turns messing with his mind. If only he'd gone to help Frank. But things would've still been okay if Tanya hadn't cut their day short. So, really, he decided it wasn't reaching too far to say the catastrophe was partly her fault. If she hadn't been speeding like an idiot, he wouldn't have been at the Sea Lion Cove Estates at exactly the wrong time. Then Keno suffered a punishing wave of guilt for thinking such terrible things about the love of his life. He realized that Netanya held the one bright spot he could dwell on. He soon found himself revisiting those magical hours when they'd first consummated their love, and then he replayed the proposal several times. The glow of love washed over him, soothed him, and let him imagine being with Netanya again.

But the pleasant feelings dimmed when his promise to Netanya regarding the secret proposal led to the conversation on the patio with his parents, which ultimately led to his last healthy conversation with his father. When he recalled Frank's words as he was leaving for work, "I love you too, son," grief conquered all emotion. His heartache grew until it was all-consuming. It imprisoned his tormented mind as surely as the steel box incarcerated his aching body.

Chapter Six

At 7:10 a.m., a surprisingly jolly jailer arrived with an unappealing breakfast. Keno put aside the cold, limp toast, forced down two bites of gooey oatmeal that rivaled the adhesive qualities of Elmer's glue, then settled for two gulps of watery orange juice from a small plastic container. He spent the next twenty minutes stretching and working out steel-induced kinks. The restricted workout was followed by more seemingly endless waiting.

At 8:30 a.m., the genial jailer returned. He unlocked the door and dramatically waved one hand toward a bargain-basement variety wheelchair. "Climb on, Rambo. I'm taking you up to the luxury suites."

Keno didn't have a clue as to what the jailer meant by *luxury suites,* but he liked the ring of it. Escaping the steel cube had to be a change for the better. "So, where are you taking me?"

"Up to the regular cells," the jailer replied matter-of-factly. "They gotta disinfect these down here." He began to whistle a merry tune as he pushed Keno toward the elevator.

When Keno turned to look up at the jailer, he saw the antithesis of the surly man he'd encountered yesterday. This guy seemed reasonable, so he decided to test him. "I couldn't get through to anybody when I made my one phone call yesterday. Any chance I could try again?"

The jailer stopped the wheelchair, looked down at Keno, then asked, "Gary didn't let you call nobody?"

Keno assumed that *Gary* was the hateful jailer. "No, my mother was out of it because my dad was killed in a bizarre accident. Then my girlfriend's cell was turned off. Gary wouldn't let me make another call after that."

The good-natured jailer pushed Keno back to the write-up room. He moved his passenger close to a desk, and then announced loud enough for all in the room to hear, "This prisoner didn't get to make his phone call." He raised his voice, and added, "That wasn't right, so I'm lettin' him make it now." With his chest puffed out, he pointed to the phone. "Make it snappy, Rambo."

Keno was at a loss for words when Netanya's pleasant voice came bubbling through the receiver. Knowing that she couldn't have possibly recognized the caller's number on her call screen, he was a little surprised to hear the cheeriness in her voice. "Good morning, stranger. What can I do for you?"

A conflicting mix of agony and relief swelled within Keno, applying emotional pressure to the fragile dam that he'd created during the interminable night. He only managed a loud sigh.

Apparently thinking it was a crank call, Netanya said, "If this is not a weirdo, you have three seconds to identify yourself. Three... two..."

Keno managed to reply, "Hey, Tanya," just in time.

"Joaquin? What's up?"

"Nothing good."

She paused, then asked, "Are you bummed?"

His situation caused him to sound harsher than he had intended. "Don't say another word. Just be quiet and listen."

"Are you pissed? Have I done..."

"I said be quiet and listen. This is really important."

Her reply sounded submissive. "Okay... I'm listening."

"My father was killed by a speeding idiot yesterday. I blew my cool, and now I'm in the Marin County Jail."

Her sharp intake of breath was audible. "Oh, baby..."

"Sorry I can't go into the disgusting details, but I don't have time right now. See what you can do for my mom, and then see what you can do about getting me bailed out. And I could really use a shirt and my crutches."

"You got it, Joaquin. I'll take care of everything."

"Love ya, girl. Gotta go."

"I love you, too. You hang in there." Her voice cracked as she commiserated, "Oh, baby..."

After returning to the jail cell, Keno recalled a conversation he'd had with himself. He looked up at the jailer and asked, "Think you could find me a Bible?"

The jailer reacted with surprise in his voice. "You? A Bible?"

"Yeah, who could need a Bible more than a sinner like me?"

"You want the one King James wrote?"

Keno smiled. "Yeah, that one would be good."

The jailer nodded, and said, "I'll see what I can do."

The jailer returned a few minutes later with a Bible, which looked as if it had just been taken out of the wrapper. "Here you go, Rambo, I don't know who wrote it but it's the only one I could find."

"Thanks, I'm sure it will be okay."

The jailer smiled and said, "You sure don't look like no Bible thumper I ever saw."

"I guess you never can tell."

While leaving the cell, the jailer murmured, "Now there's solid proof that you can't judge a book by its cover."

Keno searched the index until he found *an avenger of blood*. He flipped through the pages until they opened to *The Book of Joshua 20:1 The Lord also spoke unto Joshua, saying, (2) Speak to the children of Israel, saying, "Appoint out for your cities of refuge, whereof I spoke unto by the hand of Moses: (3) That the slayer that killeth any person unawares and unwittingly may flee thither. And they shall be your refuge from the Avenger of Blood (4) And when he that doth flee into one of those cities shall stand at the entering of the gate to the city and shall declare his cause in the ears of the elders of that city, they shall take him into the city unto them, and give him a place, that he may dwell among them. (5) And if the Avenger of Blood pursues after him, then they shall not deliver the slayer up unto his hand, because he smote his neighbor unwittingly and hated him not before time.*

Keno thought it over, then decided that he'd been right last night. Even if it applied in some metaphorical sense, he'd promised Frank that he wouldn't kill Nicky Ghilardi. And now he knew why—the idiot hadn't murdered Frank on purpose. He chuckled to himself, thinking: *That promise wasn't necessary. No matter how much I hate the ugly punk for what he did, I could never really be an Avenger of Blood. But then again, this had seemed very important to Frank. And if it weren't, why would he bring it up when he was dying? It had literally taken his last ounce of breath to warn me about it.*

At 1:05 p.m., the jolly jailer opened the door of the two-man cell and tossed a new dress shirt at Keno. "Put this on, Rambo. Your lawyer wants to see you."

Keno wondered who his lawyer was as he slipped on the perfectly fitting long-sleeved shirt. Then he enjoyed a sense of relief when the jailer carted him away in the cheap wheelchair. Even though it had been like a suite at the Hilton compared to the small steel cell, the two-man cell imposed its share of claustrophobic confinement.

The merry man whistled a catchy Irish tune as he pushed Keno down a long hallway leading away from the bunker housing the jail. The hallway led them to a sterile room furnished with two plastic chairs and one metal table with a Formica top.

A minute later, a tall man came bursting into the room with long, bold strides. The dapper defense attorney—a strikingly handsome man of mixed race—had a swarthy bronze complexion that contrasted nicely with his silver-gray hair. He held out his hand to satisfy his obligation to niceties and spoke with an all-business tone. "Hello, Joaquin, I'm Nathaniel Clay."

Keno realized that the lawyer already knew his name, so he shook the perfectly manicured hand without a pointless reply.

Clay placed his briefcase on the table and took out a copy of the arrest report, the criminal complaint, and a legal pad. As he reached inside his Armani coat for a pen, he sized up Keno with an intense look, then spoke with impressive diction. "I've been retained by Simon Bernstein to represent you. I could have had you bailed out a couple of hours ago, but the bonding company would have charged ten thousand dollars for their trouble. Since I expected to get bail reduced, I didn't think it was worth the time and effort. Also, every chance I get to argue your case in front of the presiding judge will benefit you in the long run."

Keno nodded, thinking: *If confidence counts, I've got it made.* "Okay, Mr. Clay, I'll have to agree that my freedom wasn't worth five grand an hour."

"I'm glad you see it that way."

Keno recalled seeing a news reporter on Channel Eight discussing Nathaniel Clay's involvement in a recent high-profile murder case in San Francisco. He guessed that it would cost a great deal of money to acquire the services of such a prominent defense attorney on such short notice. He felt honored that Netanya, undoubtedly with her father's help, had obtained the best that money could rent. He then considered the downside of needing such an expensive lawyer. It could mean he was in serious trouble. "I'm glad you're here to defend me, but do I really need somebody like you?"

"I'll take that as a compliment, Joaquin, but I suppose we'll soon find out whether you need somebody like me." Clay locked his eyes onto Keno's as if wordlessly asking for the truth, the whole truth, and nothing but the truth. "Tell me what happened at the Sea Lion Cove Estates yesterday. I want every detail."

Keno felt like raising his hand and swearing, *So help me God,* before relating his version of yesterday's dreadful events. He related everything he could remember but left out the jarring conversation with his father. He was still struggling with that extraordinary conversation and considered it a personal matter.

The lawyer jotted down comprehensive notes, occasionally insisting that his client elaborate on a particular point. When Keno finished telling his version of events, Clay stared at the criminal complaint while tapping his fingers on the desk. Then he surprised Keno with: "This sucks."

Keno couldn't resist a smile. "I agree. But I have a question about the accident report. How can anybody explain all the damage to my father's pickup, and how it ended up halfway in that model home without acknowledging that the Mercedes was going way too fast?"

"They're saying that the pickup was moving at approximately thirty miles per hour and that the Mercedes had accelerated to about fifty to avoid hitting you and your Harley. When both speeds are added together, they conveniently arrive at an eighty mile-per-hour collision."

"That's total bull. Frank's pickup wasn't even moving when that punk hit him. Besides, their convenient deduction would only be true if they'd hit head-on."

"That's certainly something we'll be investigating, Joaquin, but we won't be going into those kinds of details today. The judge will only be looking at the arrest report and the criminal complaint. You will plead not guilty, and I will attempt to get your bail reduced. Mr. Bernstein has agreed to pay whatever it takes to get you released and I've already contacted a bonding company. The entire process should be wrapped up rather quickly."

"I really appreciate what everybody's doing for me."

Clay appeared to ignore Keno's gratitude as he returned his things to his briefcase. While picking up the arrest report, he paused and asked, "Did the arresting officer Mirandize you?"

Keno knew the word; he'd heard it used in detectives shows. "I don't think so." He searched his memory and grew convinced that he hadn't been offered Miranda protection. "No, I'm positive he didn't read me my rights. He probably forgot to because he was so pissed about getting hit in the nose."

"Unfortunately, it appears to be your word against his. The arrest report has *Yes* and *No* boxes behind a column of questions designed to help the arresting officer satisfy procedure. Question nine asks: *Satisfied Miranda?* Deputy Wertz checked, yes."

"He's lying."

Clay placed the report in his briefcase, then shut the expensive leather case with a little extra force. "It appears that Deputy Weitz's behavior leaves something to be desired. Did he appear to be experienced?"

"Yeah, I'd say he's in his late thirties or early forties."

"Then either he's inept, or he's gone out of his way to tip the scales against you." Clay stood and gripped the briefcase handle, ready to leave. "I suspect the latter."

Keno nodded his agreement, then asked "Got time for a couple of questions?"

Clay glanced at his Rolex. "Sure, we have a few minutes."

"Do you know how my mother is doing?"

"I'm sorry, but no one's told me anything about her."

"What about my Harley? Do you know anything about it?"

"Yes, they've impounded your motorcycle. Anything else?"

"I was wondering where they took my father's body, but I guess I'll find that out after they let me go."

Keno rode the wheelchair to an anteroom next to the courtroom. He waited with four other prisoners, three of whom were wearing Day-Glo coveralls issued by Marin County. He soon learned that prisoners with their own lawyers get to appear in court before those at the mercy of public defenders. As expected, Clay had arranged for his client to be the first defendant called.

When a bailiff wheeled him into the circular courtroom, Keno was struck with the impression that he'd been transported into a spaceship; the ceiling lights looked as if they belonged to something extraterrestrial. He took a moment to admire the richly paneled walls and the ultra-modern furnishings, which included a pair of stylish Scandinavian tables that looked to be about eight feet long—one for the defense and one for the prosecution. But the judge's bench was plain and unimpressive in appearance, especially when compared to those imposing bastions of justice Keno had seen on TV.

Keno spotted Netanya sitting in the front row of royal blue movie theatre-like seats. She sat behind a partition with her legs crossed and her full crimson lips spread in a cheerful smile, but he knew what a convincing actor she could be.

A more inclusive scan told him that Millie hadn't made it to court, and her absence added to his already elevated concern. He spotted a scowling, older man seated near the back—he looked familiar, but Keno couldn't put a name to the face. All in all, he found it to be a comfortable setting. But when Judge Gerhardt Krueger stomped in with a visible growl stamped on his stern face, Keno was reminded of his reason for being there.

His Honor was a big-boned man whose noticeable concessions to time were heavily magnified glasses and at least three generations of bags drooping beneath his probing eyes. He glared out over the top of his bifocals, casting a warning to those who had dared to enter his domain. When he spotted Nathaniel Clay, the judge locked his stern gaze on him for several inquisitive seconds. Jason Bridger, the Marin County District Attorney, attracted the same attention.

"Well, well. What brings such distinguished counsel to my court today?" The judge's pliable features stretched into a surprisingly broad grin when he wisecracked, "Has somebody rich and famous been murdered?"

Clay and Bridger wore practiced smiles while chorusing, "Good morning, Your Honor."

The clerk called out in a staccato voice, "State of California versus Joaquin Flores," and then shouted out the case number loud enough for the people out in the hall to hear.

The judge mumbled, "Joaquin Flores... that name rings a bell." He shuffled through a stack of papers until he found the one he was looking for. "Okay, gentlemen, what's up? Isn't this just a simple arraignment?"

The judge's informal manner surprised Keno.

Jason Bridger had decided to handle the Flores case just two hours earlier—that was when his secretary informed him that Nathaniel Clay would be counsel for the defense. With lofty political ambitions, the DA was aware of the media attention this case would receive simply because of Clay's involvement.

"If it pleases the court, Your Honor, I will speak for the State." Jason stole a quick glance at the report, which he hadn't read, then boldly proceeded. "The charges are plainly spelled out in the criminal complaint. Due to the seriousness of the offenses, the State requests that bail be increased to two hundred thousand dollars." He forced a humorless smile and said, "Thank you, Your Honor," then found his chair.

Clay stood and smoothed the bottom of his Armani suit coat. "If it pleases the court, I will be representing Mr. Flores. My client will be entering a plea of not guilty, but might I beg a moment of the court's precious time before he does so?"

The judge's pliable face compressed. "I don't entertain argument at arraignment."

"I understand, Your Honor, but the State is requesting an exorbitant bail. The amount is not only excessive, but the charges are without merit."

The judge leaned back in his chair. "Your reputation precedes you, Mr. Clay, but this is my court, and we do things my way around here." He paused a moment before adding, "I'll give you two minutes." Then the judge winced when he realized that he'd just contradicted himself.

"Joaquin Flores is a student at the University of California at Berkeley, where he has made the Dean's List each of the past two semesters. He is also the starting tight end for the California Golden Bears football team, and last year, he received the prestigious honor of being named Academic All-Conference."

The judge, himself a Cal alum who had once been an adequate left guard for the Golden Bears, said louder than he'd intended to, "Oh, yes, that's where I know the name."

Clay's smile seemed genuine this time. "Joaquin has been employed during this past summer by Milagrozo Landscaping, a small company owned by his father, Mr. Frank Flores. Yesterday morning, a Sunday, my client was on his way to help his father finish a rush job at the Sea Lion Cove Estates. Shortly after arriving at the job site, Joaquin was nearly run over by an irresponsible speeder who barely avoided hitting him. And unfortunately, this out-of-control speeder then recklessly proceeded to crash into and kill Mr. Frank Flores. The offender was none other than Nicholas Ghilardi, Jr., whose family owns the development company responsible for building the Sea Lion Cove Estates. Mr. Ghilardi may have been mentally impaired by drugs and or alcohol at the time of the accident, but we can't be sure because he wasn't tested. Not only is that malfeasance of duty conspicuous, but my client insists that the arresting officer failed to Mirandize him. This obviously raises the question of whether Deputy Albert Wertz conducted his investigation with bias."

The judge scowled as he rearranged a couple of papers. "I don't see anything about driving under the influence. But Question Nine is checked *Yes*, and the arrest report is signed. Are you accusing Deputy Wertz of something as serious as filing a false report?"

Clay seemed to stand taller. "I suppose I am, Your Honor, but that matter will be addressed at a later time."

The judge scowled harder at the arrest report. "It says here that the defendant struck the deputy in the nose with a handcuff. Is the deputy lying about that as well?"

"That isn't quite the way it happened, Your Honor, and I'd like to elaborate on that for just a moment."

Watching with admiration, Keno realized that Clay's two minutes had long since ticked by, but the clever lawyer hadn't bothered to wait for the judge's consent to continue.

Clay cleared his throat and went on. "Deputy Wertz blatantly refused to listen to my client's version of how the accident had occurred. Considering that my client had just witnessed the needless death of his father, growing angry was a natural reaction. Even so, Joaquin merely meant to push Deputy Wertz away to avoid being unjustly handcuffed. Unfortunately, and inadvertently, the loose end of the handcuff swung around and struck the deputy on his nose, inflicting a very minor wound. However, the most important thing to consider is intent. And though he may have had just cause to do so, my client had no intention of harming the deputy in any manner whatsoever."

His Honor absentmindedly rubbed the bridge of his nose. "I've heard enough. In fact, a lot more than enough." He leveled his stern gaze at Keno. "Do you understand the charges against you, Mr. Flores?"

Caught up in reliving yesterday's events, Keno took a moment to realize that the judge was addressing him. "Oh... yeah. I mean, yes. Yes, I do, Your Honor."

"Have you ever been arrested before?"

"No, Sir. Never."

"How do you plead?"

"Not guilty."

The judge leaned back as if searching for the appropriate number somewhere in the extraterrestrial ceiling. "Bail is set in the amount of five thousand dollars. The clerk will provide all concerned with the next hearing dates, et cetera."

After being wheeled down another long, narrow hallway, which led to another arch that curved over another asphalt street traveling beneath the building, Keno traded the wheelchair for the pair of aluminum crutches Netanya had brought. He hobbled outside and looked up at the sky. He couldn't remember seeing a prettier blue. He took a deep breath, and the Marin County air tasted sweeter than ever. When Netanya wrapped her arms around his waist, he hugged her until she begged for mercy.

Clay appeared to be annoyed when he caught up with the young couple. "This is the most ill-conceived, inefficient civic center I have ever had the displeasure of hiking. Perhaps Frank Lloyd Wright thought we lawyers would need the exercise." He smiled to let them know he wasn't serious. "That being said, things went rather well. It's always a good sign when the judge sets such reasonable bail."

Keno was about to respond when a couple of enthusiastic reporters appeared and stuck microphones in his face, and then signaled for their cameras to start shooting. Surprised, he didn't fully grasp the content of their rapid-fire questions. Though small in number, they had become a swarming pack of word-wolves, salivating for something sensational.

Clay forcefully moved in front of Keno. "Sorry, people, but my client will not be responding to your questions today. As you might appreciate, he's quite distressed over the passing of his beloved father." Clay tilted his head to one side, clearly playing on their sympathy. "Give him a break."

The reporters grumbled as they reluctantly disbursed, but they were kind enough to give the grieving son a break.

Netanya went to get the car while Keno and Clay discussed the next court appearance and some of the things Keno should expect in the days ahead. The lawyer also touched on the necessity of Keno cooperating with a private investigator who would be contacting him.

Keno couldn't contain his surprise when Netanya drove up in a new Cadillac.

She smiled and said, "It's one of Daddy's."

"I could've guessed. You don't see many cars painted Bernstein Burgundy."

"After what you've been through," she said while helping him collapse onto the leather seat, "I thought the Caddy would be more comfortable than my Hot Wheels."

When Netanya got behind the steering wheel, he pulled her to him and let his feelings flow through his lips to hers. "You are one thoughtful babe. And be sure to tell your daddy how much I appreciate his help. Maybe one of these days I'll get to meet the mysterious Simon Bernstein and thank him in person."

"I'm sure it will be happening pretty soon. This situation has definitely elevated his curiosity."

"At least he knows I exist." A sharp pain reminded Keno of his injuries. "How about taking me to the nearest pharmacy so I can get my prescription filled? I could use a bunch of painkillers."

"I'll bet you could." She compressed her lips and shook her head. "It really pisses me off when I think how that deputy sheriff arrested you and took you to jail right after your dad..." They exchanged frowns, and she dropped the subject.

As Netanya drove the Cadillac toward a nearby CVS pharmacy, Keno remembered to ask about his mother. "What's up with Millie? Have you had a chance to talk to her?"

Netanya grimaced. "I'm not sure how to answer that one."

"Why not?"

"I tried calling her right after I talked to you, but she didn't answer. That bothered me, so I went over to your place this morning. I knocked and knocked, but she wouldn't come to the door." Netanya squinched her nose before continuing. "This will probably sound silly, but you have to understand how worried I was." She shrugged and explained, "I looked around until I found a window that wasn't locked, then let myself in. I was a little scared, feeling like a clumsy cat burglar. Anyway, I found Millie in the living room, sprawled on the couch. I could tell right away that she'd been crying her eyes out. Poor woman, I felt so sorry for her." Netanya frowned while searching for the right words. "The next part is really hard to talk about..."

"What could be so hard?"

Netanya sighed and said, "She was wasted."

"Wasted? Like in drunk?"

"Yeah, zombie drunk."

"That's wild. I can only remember once in my entire life when Millie took more than two drinks, and that was champagne for her twenty-fifth wedding anniversary."

"She definitely had more than two this morning."

Keno bit his bottom lip, then speculated, "She must have started drinking right after I called her yesterday."

"She'd been at it awhile, that's for sure. I tried to get her to drink some coffee and have something to eat, but she wasn't going for it. Though I did finally get her to drink some orange juice. I stayed with her until she dozed off on the couch again, and then I covered her with a blanket before I left."

"I hope she doesn't get heavy into the booze like my grandmother did."

"Your grandmother had a drinking problem?"

"Yeah, Millie's mother had a serious problem. She died of cirrhosis of the liver when I was fifteen."

"Have you tried calling Millie again?"

"Yeah, I tried a little while ago, but she didn't answer."

Netanya grimaced again. "I guess I shouldn't have left her alone, but I had to go meet with Mr. Clay..."

"Don't go getting on a guilt trip. You did good, Tanya, and I totally appreciate everything." He leaned over and kissed her again. "Things would really be messed up without you."

The pharmacist wouldn't fill the narcotic prescription for Netanya, so Keno had to climb on the crutches and struggle his way into the drugstore to get it himself. He needed relief in a hurry, so he asked Netanya to buy a bottle of Perrier to wash down the Hydrocodone pills. The instructions read: *Take one every four hours for pain.* Keno decided he needed immediate relief and took two. With very little on his stomach and having a virginal system regarding drugs, the narcotic assaulted his mind like a tornado in a phone booth.

Netanya had her hands full, helping Keno negotiate the steps rising up to the old Victorian. He had trouble climbing the stairs with his debilitating injuries, though considerably less painful ones.

Looking somewhat stupefied, Millie sat sipping from a glass of super-chilled Stolichnaya. When Keno came stumbling through the front door, the glass slipped from her shaky grasp and exploded on the hardwood floor. Speechless, she ignored the broken glass and staggered toward her son.

Keno fought for clarity in his whirling mind, and when Millie finally did come into focus, the sight was devastating. An all-consuming grief and the unexpected bout with alcohol had taken a heavy toll on his beautiful mother. The back of her hair was matted, her pale skin sagged, and puffiness surrounded her red-rimmed eyes. She had aged at least a decade since they'd talked on the patio two interminable days ago.

Netanya helped steady Keno as he wrapped one arm around his mother's shoulders and pulled her close. When Millie looked up at her son, a faint glimmer of joy broke through the entrenched gloom. "I'm so glad to see you, Sunshine. I don't think I could have survived another minute."

Warm tears mingled on their cheeks as they hugged for several important seconds. "It's a bitch, Mom, but we'll get through it together."

Meant to comfort, his words seemed to have the opposite effect. Millie's body began to tremble, and she moaned, "I don't know, Sunshine. I don't know..."

Netanya helped Keno take a seat on the couch and then helped Millie sit down beside him. The intoxicated mother and the drugged son held on to one another without speaking—no words of comfort were good enough.

Netanya offered, "Is there anything I can do? Can I get you guys something?"

Keno sat back and struggled to think. It came as something of a surprise when he realized he felt hungry. A bit of guilt crept into his hazy mind, but it didn't prevent him from asking, "Is there anything to eat around here? I'm starved."

Millie frowned, and said, "I'm not sure. I haven't given much thought to food lately."

Netanya seemed glad to have something to do. "I'll go check out the kitchen. I'm not much of a cook, but maybe I can slap together a couple sandwiches."

After Netanya had left the room, Keno forced himself to address a painful subject. "What are we going to do about Frank?"

Millie took a deep breath and raised her chin to regain a little composure. "Well, we'll give him a good Catholic funeral, that's what we're going to do." Her thoughts seemed to drift off course as she went on, "I joined the Catholic Church for him, you know. Even though I didn't agree with their positions on abortion and birth control, I joined anyway." She looked off into the distance while explaining, "It meant so much to Frank."

"I know, Mom, but we need to contact the county morgue and see what's going on." He shrugged and forced himself to confront another reality. "We'll have to make arrangements with a funeral home and..."

"I know," Millie said, cutting him off. She folded her fingers to form a steeple, then rested her chin on it. "I'm not sure I'm ready for that, Sunshine. Frank was half of me, you know." She leaned her head on Keno's shoulder and began to sob. "My better half."

Fighting back tears, Keno managed, "Okay, as soon as I grab a sandwich, I'll have Netanya drive me over to the morgue."

Keno had only gulped down half of his turkey sandwich before he heard someone pounding his fist on the front door. Then an authoritative voice shouted, "Hey, in there! Answer the door!" The pounding started again, harder. And it was followed by, "This is an officer of the law. Answer this door!"

All three exchanged looks of disbelief.

Keno recognized the voice, and anger fought its way into his murky mind. "I wonder what the hell he wants?"

Voicing her alarm, Millie asked, "Oh, my God, who is it?"

Keno glared. "It's Deputy Wertz, the one who arrested me."

Netanya looked bewildered. "What do you think he wants, Joaquin?"

Keno shrugged. "I have no idea."

Netanya grimaced. "Want me to answer the door?"

When Deputy Wertz shouted, "You'd better open this door before I break it down," a remarkable change came over Millie.

Perhaps it was as basic as a mother's instinct to protect her young when she took in a deep breath and said with resolve, "No, let me get it."

Millie jumped to her feet and stomped to the door. She hooked the safety latch, opened the door as far as the chain permitted, and then peered out through the narrow opening.

Deputy Drable, standing a few feet away, avoided any chance of eye contact.

Millie glared as she hissed, "You had better have a damned good reason for pounding on my door, Deputy."

"I'd say I have a damned good reason. I have an arrest warrant for Joaquin Flores."

"On what charge?"

"Possession of a controlled substance with intent to sell." Wertz's face took on a smug look. "Is that a good enough reason?"

Millie wanted to bore holes through him with her aching eyes. "That's bizarre. Even if you did have a legitimate reason for being on my property, it doesn't give you the right to destroy it."

"Send Joaquin Flores out or I will exercise my lawful right to do just that."

"You go right ahead, Deputy, but if you're stupid enough to destroy my property, I'll have your picture plastered all over the front pages of *The Independent Journal a*nd the *San Francisco Chronicle.* I have some very influential friends who will not take kindly to an abusive law enforcement officer breaking into the home of a grieving widow." She turned and shouted over her shoulder, "Tanya, be a dear and bring my camera. It's sitting on my bedroom dresser."

Her threat caused Deputy Wertz to rethink his strategy. "Okay, we'll be waiting for Joaquin out front. But if he doesn't come out in three minutes, we'll be coming in."

"Don't you dare threaten me, you pitiful excuse for a deputy. He'll come out when he's damn good and ready."

Deputy Wertz adjusted his aviator sunglasses. "He's got five minutes, but that's it."

Millie blew out an exasperated breath, then slammed the door in the deputy's face.

Returning to Keno's side, Millie asked, "Did you hear what that officer said about possession of a controlled substance?"

"Somebody's setting me up, Mom." The excitement had helped clear Keno's mind, and the deduction came easy. "It's Nicky Ghilardi." Mentioning the name sent a blast of revulsion shooting across his mind. "That punk has got to be behind it."

Netanya sat down beside Keno, clearly finding comfort in the big arm he wrapped around her. "I'll call Mr. Clay right away."

"That would be a good idea. Now I need you to help my Mom." He looked up at Millie, whose face brought to mind one of her Texan expressions, *Mad as an old wet hen.* "Are you going to be able to take care of finding a mortuary and everything, Mom?"

"Don't worry about a thing, Sunshine. Frank's not going anywhere, and we'll manage just fine."

Keno finished eating the sandwich before surrendering. Then he remembered the pain pills. He took two, then stuffed the plastic bottle down as far as he could in the knee cast.

Netanya bit her lip as she helped Keno struggle to his feet. "Oh, baby..."

He kissed her, and said, "I guess I gotta go." He grimaced, and added, "I'm learning more than I ever wanted to know about how Jean Valjean probably felt."

Deputy Wertz's crude behavior and Keno's subsequent arrest had somehow tapped a vein of Millie's inner strength. She comforted Netanya for a little while before hitting the shower. She knew it was time to make herself presentable and take charge.

Their roles reversed; while Millie showered, Netanya sat sobbing on the couch.

The two most important women in Keno's life had met more than a year ago when Millie directed *Charlie Brown* and Netanya starred as Lucy. And they'd grown quite fond of each other that summer. This year's play brought them even closer, not even counting Keno's addition to the equation.

When Millie emerged from her bedroom, looking more like her attractive self, Netanya remarked, "You look great, Millie."

Millie gave Netanya a much-needed hug. "You okay?"

Netanya rubbed her eyes with the backs of her knuckles. "Yeah, I'm good."

Millie hugged her again and suggested in motherly fashion, "Why don't you go freshen up, and then we'll see what we can do about taking care of things."

"Okay, I'll call Mr. Clay to see about getting Joaquin bailed out, and then we'll go to the..."

Millie patted her shoulder. "It's okay to say morgue, my dear. I have to face reality."

While Netanya was still in the bathroom, the doorbell rang. Millie's metaphorical feathers ruffled as she marched toward the door, thinking it might be somebody from the sheriff's department. This time, she flung the door wide open, but much to her surprise, she found herself staring at Hector Garcia's woeful face.

He took off his straw cowboy hat and nervously fingered it with both hands. "I'm sorry to bother you at such a sad time, Mrs. Flores, but I want to tell you how sorry me and Luiz are."

"Well, thank you, Hector. It was thoughtful of you to stop by." When she noticed that Hector's face maintained a look of concern, she asked, "Is there something else?"

"Yes, Mrs. Flores. I was wondering what you wanted to do about the landscaping business. There are many jobs that need to be done. What do you want Luiz and me to do?"

Millie had never been involved in Frank's business at any level. To her way of thinking, maintaining the joy of marriage was largely dependent upon each partner doing his or her own thing. "What do you think we should do, Hector?"

"There is the big job at the Sea Lion Cove, but I don't want to go over there yet."

"That's understandable."

"But there are the regular customers and some other small jobs that me and Luiz can handle."

"That would be great, Hector."

"What about Keno? I heard he was hurt and put in jail."

"Yes, and I'm afraid he was arrested again."

"Again?" Hector looked pained. "That's too bad. He's a good young man who don't belong in no jail."

"Yes, he is, but there are some people who aren't so good."

Hector twirled the straw hat again. "Would you let me know when you have the...?"

"Yes, I'll make sure you know when we have the Wake and the Funeral Mass."

When Hector behaved as if he didn't want to leave, Millie asked, "Is there something else?"

The hat twirled faster. "Luiz and I would be very much honored to..."

Millie frowned. "What is it, Hector?"

"We would like to be pallbearers if you want us to."

The mental image dealt a blow to Millie's newfound resolve. "It's kind of you to offer, Hector. And yes, I think Frank would be honored to have you and Luiz take part. And so would I."

"Thank you very much, Mrs. Flores."

"No, I should be thanking you, Hector."

As she returned to the living room, Millie glanced at the phone and saw that the message light was blinking furiously. The machine could handle one hour of messages, and it was now completely full. It occurred to her that a lot of people were feeling much like Hector.

Marin County is relatively small compared to most of the other counties in California, but it's one of the wealthiest in the United States. As is often the case where wealth resides, prominent movers and shakers maintain generations of tradition by meeting in time-honored watering holes. They especially enjoy meeting during Happy Hour to schmooze, crow, or wangle a deal. Jason Bridger, the Marin County District Attorney, often joined an ambitious crowd at The Wharf on Canal Street, where they entertained themselves with a game of Liar's dice—often jokingly referred to as Lawyer's dice.

J.P. Maloney patiently waited in a booth by himself, closely watching Jason Bridger's every move. When the time was right, he had the cocktail server deliver a Heineken, the DA's beer of choice. And he made sure that Jason knew who sent it.

Jason turned and gave an appreciative nod. J.P. returned a barely noticeable wave and the hint of a yellow, timeworn smile. The DA knew who the big fish were in his little pond, and, as far as he was concerned, J.P. qualified as a Great White. Jason Bridger also understood the subtle message.

Jason lagged behind after most of his group had left. As casually as possible, he made it appear as if he'd run into the very person he'd been wanting to meet all day. He sat down and smiled across the table at the hunched, gray-haired attorney. He greeted, "Nice to see you again, Mr. Maloney." Then Jason forced another lie. "You're looking well."

"Never mind the small talk. I see they arrested that Flores boy again."

"Yes, they did." Jason's wheels spun until they found the connection, and it was named Nicky Ghilardi. "I filed a charge of possession with intent to sell. We have a law that prevents making bail twice in the same calendar day, so Joaquin Flores will be spending at least one more night in jail."

"Speaking of bail, I happened to see the pitiful amount that lily-livered Judge Krueger set this afternoon. What are the chances of getting a different judge for tomorrow's arraignment? It galls me to see a criminal like Flores walking the streets."

Jason made a face and shook his head. "It's late summer, vacation time for the high and mighty. There aren't any other judges available, even if we had just cause to get him recused."

"I'm curious to know how a broke college brat got a hotshot lawyer like Nathaniel Clay?"

"I understand it was Simon Bernstein money."

The news hit J.P. like a heavyweight's body blow. "Dammit! It figures that a rich Jew is behind it. Those kikes will rob you blind with one hand while spreading liberal crap with the other."

Jason's forced smile was mirthless—he detested racists. "My sources tell me that Bernstein's daughter was behind it."

J.P. tightened his fists and muttered, "Jesus H," through clenched teeth. He coughed to regain control, then said, "I wouldn't dream of telling you how to do your job, but in my humble opinion you need to keep the cases separate. You know how easy it is to start dropping charges once they get lumped together, especially in front of a liberal-minded judge."

Jason searched for J.P.'s logic and found it without much effort. If Joaquin Flores were convicted of any of the first five charges, this would establish a prior, and then a conviction on the new drug charge would automatically receive a doubled sentence. "That's something I'll keep in mind."

J.P. reached over and patted the back of Jason's hand as if they were old pals, then slid a fat manila envelope across the table. "The Flores case aside, Jason, the main reason I wanted to talk to you today is that I know you're going to be running for Congress next year." He nodded toward the envelope. "I want you to know that my associates and I are behind you one hundred percent. This campaign contribution is only the first of many if things go the way we'd like them to."

A mental picture flashed in Jason Bridger's mind, and he didn't enjoy the image of J.P. Maloney standing behind him. He fingered the envelope for a moment, then deposited it in his coat's breast pocket. "Your support is greatly appreciated."

When J.P. stood to leave, he shook Jason's hand and winked. "Stick it to that young Flores."

As he watched the clever old rascal slink away, Jason wondered if he'd just accepted a down payment on his soul.

Chapter Seven

Even in the more comfortable cell, the night had seemed like another protracted stint in purgatory. The cleverly stashed pain pills had helped minimize Keno's physical suffering but had done nothing for the mental anguish. While his body had been immobilized, his mind raced a cerebral marathon, resting only during a couple of hours of fitful sleep. He had revisited his father's death scene so many times that the vivid memories had seemed to come alive.

After getting past the gruesome recollections, he dwelled on the way Frank had shocked him by divulging that he was clairvoyant. Keno wondered if this revelation was somehow related to his own recent visions. But even while realizing that two of those premonitions had already come true, he refused to dwell on the ugly gash he'd seen on Netanya's face. And Frank's last prophecy was intimidating: *Evil and anger will try to stop you. Promise you won't sacrifice destiny.* And the promise extracted by his dying father commanded its full share of attention: *I promise I won't be an avenger of blood, and I'll tell the world about Tierra Milagro. Miracle earth?* Attempting to rationalize that event, he thought, *Maybe Frank's words had just been the rantings of a dying man with a crushed skull, or maybe shock had caused me to have some bizarre hallucinations. After all, that fat Deputy Coroner seemed convinced that Frank had died instantly.*

However, nothing could explain the powerful force that surged through his body and left him feeling something deep inside at the exact moment that Frank died. It was beyond his mental capacity to explain this mystical energy and its connection to Frank's prescience.

Keno also had spent much of the long night dwelling on his unjust incarceration, and the man responsible for it. While aware that nurturing this kind of malicious anger could undermine the promise to his father, it was impossible to ignore his loathing for Nicky Ghilardi.

The jolly jailer swung the cell door open and made a sweeping gesture toward the same flimsy wheelchair he'd used yesterday. "Drop your butt in the chariot, Rambo. Your lawyer's waiting."

Keno appreciated the cheerful man's attempt at humor, but a smile eluded him. "Okay, let's go."

"I don't know how your big shot lawyer pulled it off," the jailer said respectfully, "but you're getting a morning arraignment. They never have 'em in this court 'til the afternoon."

"I guess that's why Clay gets paid the big bucks."

Rewarding the hackneyed remark with more smile than it deserved, the pleasant jailer whistled a spirited Irish tune as he pushed his prisoner down the same long hallway they'd traveled yesterday, then backed the wheelchair into the same sterile room.

This replay ended when Keno saw that Clay was already there. The lawyer and his exhausted client exchanged brief pleasantries, neither offering a handshake this time.

Nathaniel Clay would have been the first to admit that his sensitivities had become callused through the years—so much exposure to so many kinds of criminals—but a pang of sympathy worked its way through when he looked across the table at the young man with a four-day growth of beard. This poor guy, still a kid to Clay's way of thinking, had watched his father die a horrific death; had suffered several painful injuries; and been twice unjustly incarcerated in only two days. Keno's eyes, truly a window to the soul, had hardened in that short amount of time.

Clay picked up a paper revealing the new criminal complaint and directed Keno's attention to an item highlighted in yellow. "Do you know anything about the cocaine they found in one of your Harley's saddlebags?"

Convinced it was another piece of the frame-up puzzle, Keno felt his jaw muscles constrict. "I have no idea why the coke was there, but I'm pretty sure Nicky Ghilardi does. That punk is going to extremes to set me up and I don't know why. I only punched him once in his pot gut and he more than got even by kicking me in the ribs with his fancy cowboy boots."

Clay nodded, and said, "I believe his purpose is to discredit you as a witness. I'm sure he thinks the new drug charge will undermine your testimony."

"That punk didn't look smart enough to figure out something that clever."

"While I'm reluctant to judge intellect by appearance, I'm assuming that Nicky Ghilardi has obtained some good legal advice, and probably further assistance from the omnipresent Deputy Wertz. It's beyond coincidence that the same deputy at the scene of Sunday's accident was responsible for obtaining the warrant to search your saddlebags, and then conveniently discover a large quantity of cocaine in order to arrest you the second time."

"Yeah," Keno replied. "That deputy had to know the coke was there. If not, why would he need a warrant?"

Clay shrugged. "I suspect Nicky Ghilardi planted the cocaine before your Harley was impounded on Sunday, and Wertz was then smart enough to have an inculpable deputy with him while conducting the search the following day."

Keno nodded while assembling pieces of the frame-up puzzle. "Yeah, he conveniently had Deputy Drable with him when he arrested me at my house yesterday. Plus, Wertz made sure he did everything by the book this time."

Clay held up a piece of paper that provided positive information. "Speaking of pluses, your blood tests came back clean for drugs and alcohol."

"That's a relief. I was a little worried about that last test."

Concern lined Clay's tanned face. "Why is that?"

"I'd taken a few painkillers."

"Had I known, I would have told you not to worry. The tests currently being administered by the local law enforcement agencies are rarely sophisticated enough to detect low levels of pharmaceutical narcotics." As he gathered his things, Clay's usually serene face became a mask of determination. "Judge Krueger needs to know about this frame-up, and he'll be getting his first clue on the matter this morning."

Keno was pleased to see Millie sitting in the first row of the courtroom comporting herself with stoic resolve. Netanya sat next to her, obviously concerned but thoughtful enough to flash her pretty smile. As he scanned the gallery, he noticed two of Millie's closest friends, Gladys and Faye, sitting behind her. Then in the back row, Keno spotted the elderly man he'd seen at the first arraignment.

Judge Gerhardt Krueger maintained his normal routine at the beginning of each session, which included casting his commanding glare out over the top of his bifocals. He elevated his bushy eyebrows as he locked his stern focus on Clay and then gave Jason Bridger the same treatment, the penetrating stares lasting a little longer than they had on the previous day. His Honor muttered, "If I didn't know it was late summer, I'd think it was Ground Hog Day. We seem to be repeating the same procedure with the same cast of characters like they did in that silly movie." His eyes lingered on the complaint for a few seconds before questioning the DA. "Tell me, Mr. Bridger, why wasn't this matter included with the complaint you filed yesterday?"

"Good morning, Your Honor. This is a new and far more serious felony offense that did not come to my attention until well after yesterday's proceedings were concluded."

"How long was *well after*?"

The DA didn't seem prepared for that one. "Let's see… probably four or five hours."

His Honor studied the complaint for several deliberate seconds. "Okay, tell the court what you've got, Mr. Bridger."

"Thank you, Your Honor. The defendant has been charged with possession of fifteen grams of cocaine, which is a tad more than half an ounce. This, as I'm sure Your Honor knows, surpasses the legal standard for intent to sell. Considering the other serious charges, the state is asking the court to increase bail to two hundred and fifty thousand dollars."

His Honor tugged a fleshy earlobe while digesting the DA's input. "Since we haven't had a preliminary hearing yet, it should be easy enough to add this charge to those pending against the defendant. I don't see why it shouldn't be a continuation of Sunday's events."

"*Sunday* is the keyword, Your Honor. The deputy sheriffs assigned to this case could not obtain a search warrant until they came on duty yesterday, which was Monday. A legal search of the impounded vehicle, one Harley-Davidson motorcycle, revealed that fifteen grams of cocaine were concealed in the bottom of a saddlebag attached to the rear fender. It took some time to get this illegal drug analyzed, which explains why I didn't find out about it until well after yesterday's proceedings were concluded. Since no charges were filed for the defendant being under the influence at the time of the accident, this offense has nothing whatsoever to do with the unfortunate events that occurred on Sunday."

The judge scowled for a pensive moment before commenting, "They wouldn't have had any reason to get a search warrant if it weren't for Sunday's unfortunate events."

"Your Honor," Jason Bridger argued, "there is precedent for the state's position. In the State of California versus Hulbert, a shoplifter's belongings were searched for stolen merchandise, and a murder weapon was discovered. The Ninth Circuit Court of Appeals ruled that possession of the murder weapon was an unrelated offense and it was subsequently treated as such."

"That was a Fourth Amendment question about search and seizure," the judge snapped. "That question hasn't been raised."

"We must assume that it will be, Your Honor. We clearly have independent offenses, and they must be treated accordingly."

"It's a stretch to compare shoplifting and murder to events involving a vehicular accident and drug possession." The judge turned his attention to Clay. "Along the lines of drug possession, I see that your client's drug and alcohol tests came back clean." He compressed his rubbery features before adding," That always carries a lot of weight with me. What have you got to say about all this, Mr. Clay?"

"Good morning, Your Honor. I'm not challenging the legality of the search, at least not at this time. I'm primarily concerned with the planting of evidence."

"Planting of evidence?"

"Yes, Your Honor. I contend there is a conspiracy afoot to damage my client's impeccable reputation. If allowed to stand, this drug charge will undermine his credibility as a witness to the tragic vehicular event that resulted in the killing of his father. As you may recall..."

The judge interrupted. "Hold on, Mr. Clay, you know better. Save the extraneous oratory for the preliminary hearing."

Of course, Clay knew better. He was employing his customary practice of introducing biased remarks for the court, the media, potential jurors, and the public. "I apologize for my extraneous oratory, but Your Honor should consider the glaring possibility that these are trumped-up charges. I opine that they were cleverly designed to negate my client's future testimony, which will directly conflict with Deputy Wertz's arrest report concerning Sunday's fatal incident."

"You're orating again, Mr. Clay."

"I apologize again, Your Honor, but the court must consider this opinion in order to place the charges in proper perspective. On that basis, the defense asks that the court include this latest complaint with the pitifully weak ones filed by the state yesterday and continue existing bail. I further contend that it would be a shameful waste of the court's valuable time to do otherwise."

The judge tapped the ends of his fingers together. "How do you plead to this new charge, Mr. Flores?"

Keno was ready this time. "Absolutely not guilty."

"Have you ever used drugs or alcohol?"

"I drink a little beer when I'm not in training for football, and I took a couple of hits of weed about two years ago. Other than that, I've never used any drugs that weren't prescribed."

"Sounds like an honest answer." Judge Krueger leaned back and once again appeared to search the extraterrestrial ceiling for decisions and numbers. "Mr. Clay made a valid argument when he said it will save the court a lot of time and money if we put all the charges into one pot, and I'm inclined to agree." He tugged on a fleshy earlobe, then ordered, "Mr. Bridger, include this complaint with the charges you filed yesterday. Then we can deal with them at the same preliminary hearing." He paused a moment to study Keno. "From the looks of those casts, Mr. Flores, I doubt you're much of a flight risk. However, as Mr. Bridger has pointed out, these are some serious charges, trumped-up or not, and I'm compelled to increase bail to fifty thousand dollars."

When Keno had crutched his way outside, he found himself confronted by several reporters, and this time they were determined not to go away empty-handed.

Clay displayed his consistent attention to detail by handing Keno a three-by-five card with a prepared statement. "Read this, Joaquin, then I'll take over."

Keno cleared his throat and read: "As some of you may know, my mother and I have suffered a terrible loss. Our grief has been compounded by the ridiculous and unfounded criminal charges filed against me. I'm confident that I will be exonerated of these trumped-up charges in the not-too-distant future. We will appreciate your continued support. Thank you very much."

Clay stepped forward and handled a steady stream of questions with practiced skill and poise. The reporters left much happier this time.

While this was going on, Netanya went to get the Bernstein Burgundy Cadillac. As soon as Keno had plopped his big body on the passenger's seat, she drove under one of the building's unique arches and down the hill to a park located behind the civic center.

Keno noticed a carved wooden sign that read: *Marin Center Park*. Large flocks of ducks and geese were scattered on and around a cobblestone-lined lake that inundated several acres of unspoiled property—extremely valuable property for which greedy developers might trade a very close family member. A variety of trees and at least a dozen park benches dotted the lush, sprawling lawns. Burnt orange lamps, looking like coolie hats perched on slender poles, lined curving gravel paths.

Keno wondered how such a pleasant place existed without his knowing about it. "I had no idea there was a park back here."

Netanya remarked, "I didn't either. Millie clued me in."

"It's weird how you can drive right by a cool place for years without knowing it's there."

"Yeah, we get wrapped up in our own little trips and don't pay enough attention to some of the beautiful things around us." Netanya, parked beneath a large willow tree near the edge of the lake, leaned over and released some of her suppressed feelings with a lingering kiss. "So, how ya doin,' Joaquin?"

"A lot better now that I'm not locked in a cage."

She playfully massaged his four-day beard, and said, "It kinda grows on you."

He grinned while rubbing the itching stubble. "It's definitely longer than it's been in a while." With a curious look, he asked, "So, what's up? Why we did you bring me back here?"

"We're hooking up with Millie to coordinate Plan A."

"Plan A?"

"Yeah, we've got your day all planned. After you talk to Millie, I'm taking you to get an MRI, and then we're going to the City to deliver you and the results to Doctor Sanford."

"The orthopedic doctor who takes care of the 49ers?"

"That's the guy."

Keno frowned. "Did Daddy Bernstein arrange it?"

Netanya squinched her nose and admitted, "He has a way of managing things." Then she tapped her cell phone and said, "And we'd better get you a new one of these guys. We need to stay connected."

Before Keno could respond, Millie pulled up alongside them in the chugging Volvo and lowered her window.

As Keno powered down the Cadillac's window, he noticed that Gladys and Faye were in his mother's car. "You doin' okay?"

Millie got out of the Volvo and leaned into the Cadillac to plant a kiss on one whiskered cheek while patting the other. "I'm doing okay, Sunshine. How are you holding up?"

"I couldn't ask for much better. I've got the best defense lawyer in the West, and now I'm going to see the best bone doctor on the planet."

"After all you've been through, you deserve the best." Millie turned and smiled at her friends in the Volvo. "And with Faye and Gladys, I've got the best, too."

Keno gave the delightfully embarrassed ladies a little wave to show his gratitude. "That's cool, Mom."

"With some much-appreciated help"—Millie wiggled her fingers at Netanya— "I managed to make arrangements with a mortuary. Now I have to finalize things with the church and plan for the wake."

Keno thought having a lot to do was definitely in Millie's best interest, even if it meant dealing with unpleasant tasks. "I'll be there to help as soon as I get patched up. I feel bad that we haven't had much time to talk, but Netanya says I've got an appointment for an MRI, so I guess we'd better get going."

Millie couldn't quite pull off the smile she was trying for. "Bye, Sunshine. See you soon."

Netanya started the Cadillac but hesitated a moment before driving off. "Do you think I'm too controlling?"

"About what?"

"You know, asking Daddy to get a lawyer and a doctor without first discussing those things with you."

"Hey, you and your daddy take care of me anyway you want." He leaned over and kissed her cheek. "I hope you know how much I appreciate everything. And I'm going to thank Daddy Bernstein in person as soon as we can make it happen."

"He's looking forward to meeting you, too, and that should make you feel special. He's never been interested in meeting any of my boyfriends." She made an exasperated face before adding, "Not one."

Keno liked the sound of being special to Simon Bernstein. "Maybe you didn't have good taste with boyfriends until you got lucky with me."

"Don't be getting full of yourself because of one meeting with Daddy. He doesn't think any guy is good enough for me."

Keno couldn't have agreed more with Daddy Bernstein.

When J.P. Maloney steered his Lincoln onto Lucas Valley Road, he revisited a thought he'd dwelled on numerous times. It was a disgrace for the road to be named for some Johnny-come-lately movie mogul rather than for the family who had founded and nurtured this valley. After all, the Ghilardi family, going all the way back to the 1870s, once owned five sections, or thirty-two hundred acres of this prime land. Even that secretive sci-fi movie compound was built on property once owned by a Ghilardi.

J.P. slowed the Lincoln, found a wide spot just off the two-lane asphalt road, and parked. He lit up a Cuban cigar before powering down his window to gaze across a plush meadow and up the tree-dotted hill. He let his gaze stop on the extravagant new Ghilardi house, which seemed to be standing watch over the ranch's remaining 640 acres. Describing it as a California ranch, the architect had created an 8,000-square-foot, U-shaped masterpiece, which J.P. felt was out of place. The old two-story family house and the hay barn, now listing and bleached with time, had seemed big to J.P. when he'd first laid eyes on them all those years ago. But he realized that you can't stop time and change, even when it isn't for the better.

J.P. reminisced about the good old days with Big Nick. The suave gentleman with the dark wavy hair and ready smile could charm the pants off anybody, especially the ladies. He dwelled on the day he convinced Big Nick to get out of the dairy business and get into real estate—a brilliant move that made them both a barn full of money. J.P. allowed himself a rare smile, thinking about how his brains and negotiating skills and Big Nick's iron will had been an unbeatable combination. Not only had they made the right move, but they'd made it at the right time. They'd gotten in on the ground floor just before real estate in Marin County had gone through the roof.

J.P. realized he had made one colossal mistake back then, and now that critical error had come back to haunt him. Although he and Big Nick were close to the same age, never once in his wildest dreams had he imagined himself outlasting that seemingly indestructible man. J.P. hadn't given five minutes' thought to watching his diet and staying in shape, let alone worrying about consuming vats of alcohol and smoking countless boxes of cigars. While he'd been quite pleased with himself for finagling thirty-three percent of Ghilardi Development Corporation's privately held stock, with a current value exceeding twenty million dollars, he'd dropped the ball when it came to naming the executor in case of Big Nick's death or incapacitation. It had seemed like an insignificant bone to throw Yvette thirty years ago. And now she made her idiot son CEO...

J.P. angrily snuffed out his cigar and threw it out the window. Now he had to deal with that egotistical brat. Hell, Nicky wasn't even a Ghilardi. A cruel twist of fate had left Big Nick sterile, and the poor bastard didn't know whether to blame the mumps or gonorrhea. The old lawyer bit his bottom lip so hard it brought tears. Yvette, with that piss-weak French blood, had insisted on in vitro fertilization with sperm provided by some genius she'd picked out of a book. He likened it to a Holstein cow getting artificially inseminated. That supposed genius must have been one mean, butt-ugly retard. Just look at what she birthed.

J.P. jerked the gearshift into drive, steered the Lincoln across the county road, and opened the expansive gate with a remote clipped to the Lincoln's sun visor. He waited impatiently as the twin wrought-iron gate halves automatically parted. Once on Ghilardi's smoother asphalt road, he sped the Lincoln up the hill to the parking area in front of the magnificent house. J.P. paused a moment to glance down at the heavy equipment parked in the field where the dairy cows used to graze, then smiled for the second time in one morning. Those D-9 Cats and giant earthmovers had made the corporation a ton of money. Now those were some real cash cows.

Deputy Wertz was surprised to see J.P. still sitting in his car. While climbing out of his squad car, he wondered why the crusty old lawyer hadn't gone inside. When he tapped the Lincoln's front door with the backs of his knuckles, he provoked the expected scowl. "How's it going, J.P.?"

J.P. struggled to get out of his car, then glared up at the deputy. "I'd be doing a helluva lot better if I didn't have to deal with a miserable brat named"—he grimaced and spat— "Nicky."

The vitriol was more than Wertz expected, even coming from the cantankerous old lawyer. The deputy removed his aviator sunglasses and shrugged. "I don't like the pampered jerk any more than you do, but he is the top dog now."

"Stop insulting dogs." J.P. couldn't explain that Ghilardi Development Corporation was his brainchild, his baby, and he wasn't about to let that young egomaniac ruin all those years of building and nurturing. He glared at Wertz and said, "If the truth gets out and Nicky is convicted of vehicular manslaughter, not to mention obstruction of justice and conspiracy, the insurance company will wash their hands of our entire operation. The corporation will be liable for millions, and we could lose the entire investment in the Sea Lion Cove Estates.

Wertz shrugged and said, "I'm doing everything I can."

J.P. glared again, growing even more concerned when considering the potential for disaster. "The fact that Nicky is in control doesn't make his idiotic behavior any easier to swallow." He snorted before adding, "I guess we better go on in and see what we can do about keeping the ugly brat out of trouble."

Nicky's office—Big Nick's office until he'd had a stroke— occupied the eastern leg of the house's "U" shape, mirroring the leg with the five-car garage at the west end. The richly paneled interior had plush, brown shag carpet, which seemed to sink a couple of inches when walked on. The press of a button raised roll-up metal shutters, exposing wall-to-wall windows that provided a spectacular panoramic view of the verdant valley. Two small mahogany desks, noticeably vacant, were placed several feet from a brilliantly polished oak desk that seemed oversized, even in the expansive office.

His face furrowed with a manufactured scowl; Nicky sat slumped in a big leather chair with his arms folded. His chrome-tipped cowboy boots rested on papers scattered on the desk. He tilted his cowboy hat back with a thumb and made a show of studying his Rolex. "Where the hell you guys been? I got better things to do than waitin' aroun' here for you suckers all mornin'."

J.P. looked at the empty desks and decided not to ask about Amy, the all-purpose secretary, or Diane, the middle-aged bookkeeper/comptroller—both pleasant and efficient women who had been with Big Nick for almost two decades. He gritted his worn teeth, thinking that the obnoxious brat was lucky he showed up at all, never mind the ten minutes late. He cracked his knobby knuckles to release a little tension, then responded with restrained sarcasm, "I wouldn't want to keep you from your busy schedule, Nicky, so let's get down to business. Jason Bridger didn't win the ruling we were hoping for this morning. Judge Krueger showed his lily-livered liberal side again by combining the two complaints and setting an unreasonable bail."

Nicky's face darkened. "Dammit! Any lamebrain oughta be able to nail somebody with half an ounce o' coke. That much dope should've got bail set so high that Biker Boy couldn't make it." Nicky glared. "Doesn't sound like you impressed our friendly DA too much, J.P." He drummed his fingers on the desk before adding, "Or maybe Jason Bridger ain't the sharpest knife in the drawer."

"Probably not," J.P. replied "The DA wasn't very impressive in court this morning, and it's probably going to get worse. Before this is over, Nathaniel Clay is going to chew him up and spit him out like a piece of stale gum."

"Nathaniel Clay?" Wertz's mustache twitched, and his ruddy face paled. "How in the hell can a landscaper's son afford a high-powered lawyer like him? That Flores kid looked like some down-and-out Hells Angel who couldn't afford the colors."

J.P. spat, "Simon Bernstein money," as if they were dirty words. "It seems that Joaquin Flores is an upstanding citizen who has never done anything worse than get a parking ticket. Not only is he an honor student and star football player at Cal, the lucky s.o.b. is more than likely banging Bernstein's beautiful daughter."

"This is not good," Wertz responded with visible apprehension. "If I would've had that info Sunday morning, there's no way I would be involved in this phony frame-up."

"But you are involved," Nicky snapped. "An' I'm thinkin' we're gonna have to help that lame-brained Bridger nail Biker Boy. He's gonna need somethin' more convincin' to work with."

J.P. raised his bushy eyebrows, obviously wondering what malicious thoughts the brat was brewing up this time. "Are you considering more trumped-up charges?"

"Not trump 'em up, make 'em happen. Get Biker Boy so pissed, he'll do somethin' crazy."

J.P. formed a mental picture of Joaquin Flores being really angry. "I'm not sure that's such a good idea, Nicky."

"Yeah," Wertz agreed. "That big dude could be hazardous to your health."

Nicky opened a drawer and brought out a Glock 9mm. "I already kicked the hell outta him once. An' if he messes with me, I'll blow his big ass away."

J.P. had to fight back a chuckle while visualizing Nicky fighting Joaquin Flores. "I say we stick to more civilized plans."

"You pull that gun on him," Wertz warned, "you'll probably have to use it."

Nicky's beady eyes narrowed. "Don't think I won't."

J.P. massaged his temples, wondering what he'd done to deserve being involved with such a pathological nutcase. "Violence is not going to get us anywhere."

"Don't sweat it, J.P.," Nicky said while performing an exaggerated bobblehead doll imitation. "I got it all figured out. Biker Boy an' his ol' man caused that freakin' accident, an' that freakin' accident caused me a whole lotta property damage. It also cost me a lotta freakin' money by delayin' the grand openin' of the Sea Lion Cove Estates, which was supposed to be happenin' this Saturday, an' which now it ain't."

J.P. deliberated a moment before remarking, "If you're thinking about suing, I don't see how that could personally affect Joaquin Flores. Even if you can show cause, which I can't see happening, Milagrozo Landscaping's insurance company would be liable." J.P. paused to shake his head. "And I'm advising against having their insurance investigators come digging through our convoluted can of worms."

Nicky let go a malicious giggle, sounding something like a child's squeal. "That's where you got it wrong, old man. I already checked it out, an' Frank Flores didn't have the million-dollar liability insurance policy he was supposed to have accordin' to our contract." Nicky giggled again. "An' it gets better. Flores had a pissy little one hundred-thousand-dollar liability policy, but the premium on it is already a month late. So, I'm thinkin' that one's probably worthless."

J.P. massaged his temples again, with more intensity this time. "And your brilliant plan is?"

"Sue the poor grievin' widow for every penny she's got." Nicky grinned while smacking a fist into his palm. "An' if that doesn't get Biker Boy totally pissed, nothin' will."

Realizing this plan was beneath even his prostituted morals, Wertz said, "You and J.P. don't need my input on anything concerning lawsuits, Nicky G. I need to check in with my dispatcher, so I'd appreciate it if we could go over the details of our agreement."

Nicky glared at the deputy. "Just what freakin' agreement are you talkin' about?"

Surprised by the question, Wertz replied, "You know damn good and well what agreement. The one where you sell me the model home below market value, and then I sell it back to you next year for a nice profit. That's what we agreed to, and finalizing the details is the only reason I'm here."

Nicky slammed the oak desk with the flat of his hand, leaned back, and giggled again. "I'm just messin' with ya, Wertz. We got the contract all worked out. I'm gonna sell you a model home for seven hundred thou, an' that's with no down an' no closin'. Hell, you don't even have to make a payment. Then next year I buy it back for eight hundred thou. You walk away with a clean one hundred grand, all for doin' me a couple o' little favors.

"Sounds good," Wertz replied. "Where's the contract?"

"We're goin' all the way to make the deal look legit. I'll meet you at Lemmon's office tomorrow to sign the papers. She'll notarize everything." When he realized that Wertz didn't recognize the name, he reminded, "You know, Julie Lemmon, the real estate broad who was in the car with me when I crashed into the wetback's pickup." He grinned when he thought about how cleverly he'd handled that situation. "She's the babe I talked into backin' up my story. Anyway, she just opened her sales office at the Cove, an' she'll do exactly what I tell her to do."

Somewhat relieved, Wertz said, "Okay, I'll be there at exactly two p.m. tomorrow." As he was about to go, he remembered another detail that needed to be addressed. "By the way, what did you do with your wrecked Mercedes?" He didn't like to think about Nicky's nasty vomit that he'd seen on the airbag, but it was necessary to tie up loose ends. "Remember when I told you that it contained damaging evidence?"

Nicky nodded and said, "I had the tow truck driver put it here in the old barn so I could have my spicks clean it out before I got it fixed. But I got Big Nick's car now, which is exactly like that one, so I might just junk it to make sure nobody finds any o' that *damagin' evidence*."

This tenuous input caused alarms to go off in Wertz's professional mind. He knew that anyone involved with a crime, no matter how minimally, could become a dangerous witness. "You sure you can trust that tow truck driver to keep his mouth shut?"

"That ain't a problem. He's just a dimwitted cokehead. I gave him five hundred bucks for zip-your-lip money, then set him up with a big-time coke dealer."

Wertz felt as if he'd been professionally castrated. He'd sold his right to enforce the law, and now he had to ignore one crime after another. "Just make sure you pay attention to the details, Nicky G." Wertz gave J.P. a pat on the shoulder, said, "Hang in there, partner," and marched toward the door. He couldn't leave soon enough.

J.P., who'd been thinking things over, ran his gnarled fingers through his wispy gray hair. "You sure you want to sue the poor widow, Nicky?

"Damn right I do. That's a good way to get to Biker Boy."

For the briefest of moments, J.P. considered throwing in the towel, but then considered how the corporation, his baby, would do without his stewardship. He knew it wouldn't survive for long. "I'll file the papers this afternoon, and I'll see that she gets served within a day or two."

"Speakin' o' papers," Nicky said with a calculating tone, "do I have to worry about any legal crap if I fire Jack Murphy?"

J.P. couldn't believe his ears. "Are you serious? Why in God's name would you want to fire Jack Murphy? He's the backbone of our field operations. With Big Nick out of commission, we'd be completely screwed without Jack to keep the ball rolling."

"Well, Murphy ain't rollin' the ball fast enough to suit me. Besides, I don't have to explain anything to you. Can I just pay him off, or what?"

J.P. began to visualize his life's work going down a giant drain. Beautiful houses and prime properties twisting and twirling in a great whirlpool—all caused by Nicky's ego. A sharp angina pain pierced J.P.'s chest as he imagined tossing Nicky's lifeless body into the swirling void.

Nicky stared at the cranky old lawyer, then said, "Don't go blankin' on me, J.P. Can I fire Murphy without it costin' us an arm an' leg, or what?"

J.P. responded with a dire warning, "It wouldn't cost us in the short term. Jack Murphy only has a handshake deal with Big Nick, but I'm strongly advising against letting him go. He's one of the best supers in the construction business, and it's going to cost us more than a few limbs if you terminate him. Our bare butts will be exposed."

"You just stick to your legal crap. I'll be making all the personnel decisions aroun' here."

Having endured more than enough of Nicky's warped logic for one day, J.P. was eager to leave. But just as he was about to struggle to his feet, he spotted Yvette entering the office.

The pretty woman wore a white silk dress, so light that it seemed to float, and transparent enough to entice J.P.'s old watery eyes to explore her shapely curves. Looking like a Greek goddess with a fixed happy face, she carried a silver serving tray that required the support of both slender arms. Yvette carefully placed the tray on the huge desk, then leaned over and kissed Nicky full on the mouth. She looked up, smiled at J.P., then greeted with a cheery voice, "Hello, Mr. Maloney. Can I offer you a homemade croissant and a cup of my freshly brewed coffee?"

Flabbergasted by the incestuous kiss, J.P. stared with an unhinged jaw, wondering how such a beauty could have conceived a monster like Nicky. She had to be over fifty, but she didn't look a day over thirty—a gorgeous thirty at that. No wonder Big Nick had violated all those generations of family tradition by marrying a woman who wasn't Italian. "Don't mind if I do. If memory serves, you make the best croissants I've ever tasted."

"Why, thank you, Mr. Maloney. It's kind of you to say so." She served Nicky first, placing two of the flakey pastries on a cloth napkin and pouring rich-smelling coffee into a cup made of expensive China. As she served J.P., she confided, "You'll be pleased to know that Mr. Ghilardi regained consciousness for a few minutes last night."

J.P. had never liked the way she addressed him formally. In fact, he'd come to resent it, and now she was giving Big Nick the same treatment. He also noticed that she'd offered this fantastic news without the slightest hint of emotion. He forced a thin smile and replied, "Does this suggest a more encouraging prognosis?"

Yvette shrugged her sun-challenged shoulders and made a face of resignation. "The doctors always want to instill some hope, but I've come to expect the worst. After all, Mr. Ghilardi isn't getting any younger." She moved behind Nicky's chair and began to massage his hairy neck with her dainty hands. "As always, life must go on. The heir has assumed the throne."

The lemon croissant was delicious, but the remark caused J.P. to choke on it. He swallowed hard, coughed to clear his throat, then said, "I'd sure like to see him."

She curved her heart-shaped lips into a pretentious-looking smile and said, "I seriously doubt that Mr. Ghilardi will be entertaining visitors any time soon, but you will be among the first to be invited, when and if that time ever comes, Mr. Maloney."

J.P. bristled at being regarded as a visitor. This final insult, added to Nicky's blatant disrespect, was more than he could stomach for one day. It was time to go. As he shuffled toward the door, he grumbled, "You do that, *Mrs. Ghilardi*. You be sure to invite me, if and when that time ever comes."

When the crusty old lawyer slammed the door with unnecessary force, Nicky snapped, "I'd like to waste that grouchy ol' goat. He's gettin' to be a real pain in the you-know-what."

Yvette's smile became genuine as she stroked her son's slicked-back hair. "Time is your ally, lambkins. His age will dispatch him soon enough, just as it has extricated Mr. Ghilardi from his position. In the meantime, remember that Mr. Maloney is still quite efficient at dealing with certain unpleasant tasks."

"Yeah, I guess the ol' fart is still good for somethin'." Nicky turned and looked up at his mother with a questioning frown. "So, what's the deal with Big Nick? Do I have to worry about him gettin' well an' takin' over again?"

"Don't you worry your brilliant head about that, my pet. Mr. Ghilardi will never again regain control." Yvette smiled while affectionately massaging her pride-and-joy's rounded shoulders. "Not as long as I am executor of the estate."

Chapter Eight

Millie had prepared the hide-a-bed in the living room, which seemed like a sensible solution. The steep stairs leading up to Keno's bedroom presented a challenge. Keno appreciated Millie's thoughtfulness, though a mat on the floor would have been just fine with him after the two brutal nights in jail. He had entertained thoughts of spending the night with Netanya, but Simon Bernstein was home, and he wasn't sure how the enigmatic mam might feel about his daughter sharing her bed.

Keno stretched and yawned, then observed the new cast on his knee. While raising his leg to expose the smaller cast on his ankle, he reminded himself of how fortunate he was to have been treated by Doctor Sanford, the renowned orthopedist. Although the Emergency Room doctor at Marin General had correctly diagnosed two of his injuries—a tear in the anterior cruciate ligament, or ACL, and a small chip of an anklebone called talus—the MRI had been worth the extra precaution. It revealed two additional tears in his knee—one in the tibial collateral ligament and another in the medial meniscus cartilage. Keno knew that sports orthopedists commonly referred to having all three injuries at the same time as the *unhappy triad*. The ankle injury would heal in about six weeks, but the knee was going to need months of rehab. He'd been provided crutches to support his upper body, and the ankle cast had a rubber support attached beneath the heel, providing cushion as well as traction. Doctor Sanford advised him not to put any more weight on the foot than necessary, but the ingenious support would provide him with some limited mobility.

Keno soon detected delicious aromas escaping from the kitchen. Inhaling through delighted nostrils, he recognized that Millie was cooking French toast and Canadian bacon, his all-time favorite breakfast. When an image of the jail's gooey oatmeal sprang to mind, the comparison encouraged him to bang a fist into the sofa and shout, "Yeah!"

Peeking around the corner, Millie said, "Good morning, Sunshine. What's with the shouting?"

"Your cooking smells too good to be real."

Millie allowed herself a full smile for the first time since getting the news about Frank; having her son home dispelled some of the gloom overwhelming her life. "I thought you'd enjoy a good breakfast."

Yesterday's jail breakfast popped into Keno's mind. "You can't even begin to imagine," he said as he hopped up on one foot and found his crutches. "I'm going to run, well not run exactly, to the bathroom, and then I'm going to break my record of twelve pieces of French toast."

The telephone's abrasive ring froze him in place. When Millie just ignored it, he asked, "Aren't you going to answer that"?

"No, I'm going to let the machine get it. I've been a slave to that telephone lately. At least fifty people have called, and there's no telling how many didn't get through."

Keno's shrug was limited by his hold on the crutches. "Isn't it a good thing to know that so many people care?"

"Yes, of course, but a lot of them ask about the wake and the Funeral Mass." Millie let go a sigh of resignation. "I hate to admit that I haven't finished making all the arrangements."

"I can see how that would make you uncomfortable." Keno thoughtfully shifted the conversation. "I can't wait to dig into that breakfast, but first I gotta use the john."

When his breakfast was served, Keno left most of the talking to Millie. He'd been taught not to talk with his mouth full, which left him with a distinct disadvantage. After two glasses of orange juice, eight slices of Canadian bacon, and ten pieces of French toast, he abandoned the quest to break his record. He pushed his chair back, sighed, and rubbed his belly. "That's it. I give up." He blew out a big breath and said, "I think that rotten jail food shrunk my stomach."

"No offense," Millie said as she gathered his dishes, "but it didn't shrink that much. You consumed enough for three or four normal people."

She finished tidying up, then poured herself a cup of coffee and sat down across from him. She stared at her son curiously before asking, "Why is that awful man trying to frame you with those terrible crimes?"

The reference to Nicky Ghilardi ignited the predictable burst of anger. "Mr. Clay thinks the ugly punk wants to discredit me as a witness. If the truth gets out about what really happened, Nicky and the Ghilardi Development Company can be in serious trouble, criminally and financially. That punk could be charged with vehicular manslaughter, not to mention all the other laws he's broken. And if he's convicted, you can sue him and his company for some major bucks."

Millie obviously didn't like that idea. "The last thing I need is to get involved in a lawsuit."

"You don't have to worry about suing them right now, but the criminal part is totally important. Think about it. If Nicky gets convicted, I'm off the hook. And I'm sure he's got to be hiding something that could affect that happy outcome."

"Oh?" Millie's eyebrows arched. "And that is?"

"I can't say for sure, but I'd bet some serious cash that he was drinking or high on drugs at the time of the accident." Keno paused to entertain a connecting thought. "I think Nicky already had the cocaine in his car. It would've been hard to find a dealer to buy that much coke on Sunday morning, then still have enough time to hide it in my saddlebags before my bike was impounded." Keno's conjecture had become fact in his mind. "Yeah, the punk already had the coke and planted it after Deputy Wertz took me away."

"That seems so excessive." Millie paused and frowned, clearly trying to make sense of it all. "If you didn't have a wealthy friend like Netanya, you would still be in jail without getting the proper medical attention. And without Mr. Clay, you would have been swallowed up by the criminal system without the truth ever coming out."

"You'd better believe I know it." Keno wasn't ready to discuss any of the mystical events that occurred at the accident scene, but he was willing to share one private thought. "Maybe I'm a convenience Christian. I spent some serious time praying last night. I'm really thankful that I have you and Tanya to care about me and that I'm connected with so many good people."

"Convenience Christian?" Millie asked with a puzzled expression. "Oh, I get it. That's like what my father's generation would have called a Foxhole Christian." Millie patted the back of her son's hand before adding, "And yes, it is good to know that you're loved, Sunshine."

Needing to escape this emotional minefield, Keno changed the subject. "But the bottom line is money. If you're rich enough you can get a good lawyer and a fair trial, but if you're poor you can get totally screwed by the system."

Millie held her coffee cup with both hands and stared into the brown liquid. "Sometimes God's works are not only mysterious, they can be inexplicable. Think about it. Frank miraculously survives a hurricane when he was a boy, then is senselessly killed by a drunken idiot. It doesn't make any sense."

"No, it doesn't. And speaking of things that don't make any sense, I had a weird dream the other day. It was about a little kid on a sailboat in the middle of a terrifying storm. I don't know why, but I kept thinking it was Frank." He vaguely noticed his mother's slacked jaw while recapturing the horrific dream. "It was like I was really there. I could feel the awesome power of the wind and hear scary noises just before the boy got washed overboard and felt helpless in some really big waves."

Her face a colorless mask, Millie said, "I've heard almost identical descriptions coming from Frank. It's as if you dreamed his dream."

For a moment, Keno thought his brain was going to freeze. "It was my dream, but I'm pretty convinced it was about Frank when he was a little boy."

Millie frowned and asked, "How is that possible?"

Keno tried to make light of it. "Who knows? My subconscious was probably working overtime, having a little fun with some of the stuff Frank told me about the hurricane." He couldn't begin to explain his recent visions nor the paranormal experience that took place when Frank lay dying. So how could he even begin to understand the strangest dream of his life? Then thinking, *Okay, it's time to get away from this weirdness*, he forced a smile and said, "Let's get back to trashing the system. How unfair it is, and how you need lots of money to survive in it."

Millie bit her bottom lip, clearly fighting back tears.

"You okay, Millie? Did I say something...?"

"I'm sorry, Sunshine, but money is not a good subject for us to discuss right now."

Keno knew his progressive-minded mother wouldn't pass up an opportunity to attack the republic's inequitable capitalistic system unless something important prevented it. "What's up?"

"This is hard to admit, but"—Millie interrupted herself with an exasperated breath— "we're broke. After I wrote checks for the funeral home and a few other things, the bank manager called to inform me that I was almost two thousand dollars overdrawn. He's a nice man who really liked Frank and was kind enough to cover the account. And then I got more bad news when I called to get the balances on the credit cards." She paused to shake her head. "They're almost maxed out. I don't know what I'm going to do. I can't bring myself to ask anyone to loan me money. For one thing, none of my friends would ever let me repay it." She blew out another big breath before adding, "But I still have to make those checks good, and pay some past due bills, and..."

Keno didn't want to broach the subject but felt compelled to interrupt. "What about life insurance?"

The question was clearly a blow to Millie's fragile psyche. Her hands tightened into clenched fists as she told him, "There isn't any. Not a cent. Your father and I discussed it several times, but we always decided that neither of us wanted to be rewarded for the other one dying."

Keno knew he could get money from Netanya if he asked. But asking was the problem. He had the same distaste for charity that Millie did, and he needed to find another solution. Though Frank was too softhearted to be a good businessman, Keno knew his father always had more customers than he needed, and he'd always worked more than his share of long hours just to keep up. "I'll bet a lot of people owe money to Milagrozo Landscaping." The more he thought about it, the more convinced he became. "Yeah, I'll bet there are a lot of receivables out there."

Millie shrugged. "I'm feeling very ignorant at the moment. I was so wrapped up in what I was doing that I never got involved with the business end of things. Frank always took care of our financial matters. I have no idea about receivables, or anything else associated with Milagrozo Landscaping.

"Maybe we should go down to the Yard and check out his books."

"That's a wonderful idea," Millie said with a glimmer of hope. "At least we can see where we stand."

As they were preparing to leave, the phone rang. Netanya had told Keno she was taking her father into the City for a doctor's appointment. Since this wouldn't prevent her from calling, he hopped over to answer the demanding instrument.

Keno listened to the caller introduce himself, then held out the receiver toward Millie. "It's for you." When Millie's exaggerated pantomime revealed that she didn't want to talk to anyone, he extended the receiver to the limit of his reach. "I think you might want to talk to Father Garrity."

Millie's eyebrows remained arched as she listened. Her side of the conversation mostly consisted of muted sounds of concurrence and appreciation. She ended the call by expressing her gratitude. "I can't thank you enough, Father." After replacing the receiver, her look of disbelief lingered. "That was Father Garrity calling from the Church of Saint Raphael. That's the big church next to the old mission on Fourth Street, which is actually the Mission San Rafael Arcangel..."

"I know, Mom," Keno interrupted. "I've been by there lots of times. So what did he want?"

He said they would be honored to provide the Funeral Mass at Saint Raphael's. Father Sartori informed him that our Mill Valley parish is too small to handle the expected turnout. He also said that San Rafael Joe's has offered the use of their restaurant for a celebration of life reception." She folded her hands, as if in prayer, and rested her chin on them. "This is all so wonderful. The church seats hundreds, the restaurant is right down the street, and there is public parking close by..." She shook her head with a look of disbelief. "It's all so perfect."

"If the Mill Valley parish is too small, is San Rafael Joe's going to be big enough to handle that kind of crowd?"

"Father Garrity thinks so." Almost giddy, Millie began to ramble. "Some people will be coming and going at different times. Some will pop in for a minute, and then some won't have time to eat after the service..." She grimaced, and said, "Oh, I almost forgot to tell you, Father Garrity said the Funeral Mass will be held at two o'clock on Friday. I'm guessing that the restaurant will be available during its slow period. I need to call them when we get back. You know, decide what we're going to do about the menu..." Millie seemed to forget that she was having a conversation as she stared into the distance.

"That's great, Mom. That solves two major problems."

A curious frown crossed Millies face. "I wonder how Father Sartori knows how many people are going to attend the Funeral Mass."

Keno did his crutch-limited shoulder shrug. "Priests always know about that kind of stuff. It's part of their job."

Millie sighed and said, "This is all so thoughtful of them."

"Yeah, I bet Father Garrity doesn't get involved very often."

"Probably not," Millie agreed. "But then there are many in the Church who think Frank was special. And I'm probably not the only one who thinks he was touched by the hand of God.

It had taken about a half hour but Netanya had insisted that Keno practice driving the Bernstein Burgundy Cadillac She wanted to makes sure he was comfortable applying the brake with his left foot and getting the feel of the accelerator with the toes protruding from the cast on his right foot. When Netanya was satisfied, she'd insisted that he use the luxury car for as long as he needed it. Daddy Bernstein had a fleet of cars, and he certainly wouldn't miss this one.

While explaining that she couldn't cope with the slightest negative, let alone another auto accident, Millie argued longer than she normally would have before accepting that Keno had made up his stubborn mind to drive. He was determined to prove he wasn't helpless.

It was just over three miles to the isolated property where Milagrozo Landscaping occupied five acres. Known as *the Yard* by those involved in the business, the property had once been part of a large rock quarry that was abandoned shortly after Highway 101 had been expanded to four lanes in the 1950s. Looking as if it might have been imported from Mars, the reddish, rocky terrain surrounding the Yard largely consisted of silica, garnet, and granite minerals that seemed unsuitable for growing almost any kind of vegetation. However, several rows of beautiful flowers bordering the cyclone fence dispelled. that notion. This colorful border gave the impression that the Yard was surrounded by a gigantic rainbow.

Perhaps even more impressive, much of the ground within the cyclone fence was covered with beautiful green grass, bringing to mind a huge emerald carpet.

The hot house sat on the southeast corner of the property. Clearly the newest and largest structure, it was an impressive rectangular building painted a gleaming white. The only contrasting color was provided by a large number of gray solar cell panels on the roof.

In the northwest corner of the Yard, an obsolete nineteen-foot aluminum house trailer sat perched on the most elevated piece of the property. Much too old to be called a mobile home, the house trailer had long served as Frank's office.

A good-sized tool shed, made of galvanized sheet metal, stood about fifteen yards south of the house trailer/office. Another sheet metal building, known as the *Gonzo shed,* sat midway between the hothouse and the tool shed. This building got its name by housing the new Gonzo chipping machine, Frank's pride and joy. This amazing machine could crunch a six-inch log into quarter-inch chips in a matter of seconds or be adjusted with enough precision to pulverize leaves into powder.

Strategically positioned along the interior of the cyclone fence, large bins contained cuttings from a wide variety of tree branches, bushes, and vines. A few smaller bins contained a vast assortment of leaves in various stages of decay. At least a dozen large mounds, most approaching fifty feet in diameter, occupied much of the remaining yard. Each mound had been painstakingly covered with a thin, glossy plastic known as Visqueen.

Keno had been to the Yard many times, but he'd never lingered any longer than he had to. He didn't appreciate the ever-present smell of decay—a musty odor that permeated everything within its domain. Keno had helped make his father's renowned Milagrozo mulch several times, but his duties at the Yard were usually limited to loading tools and mulch, which he would haul to various jobsites.

When he brought the Cadillac to a stop, Keno was surprised to see the front gate standing open. He glanced at Millie and remarked, "Hector must be here." He tilted his head toward the hot house. "You want to take a look inside?"

Millie looked off into the distance, almost as if she hadn't heard the question. "What's in there?"

"I'm not sure. Frank never told me to go in there. But I'm guessing Frank would've been growing tropical flowers. You know, things like orchids and other types that need heat and humidity."

"Let's not bother with it today," Millie said matter-of-factly. "Hopefully, there will be a nice breeze blowing the next time we come. Even though this yard is quite remarkable with the beautiful flowers and all the green grass, there's an overwhelming odor that's hard to... ignore. I suppose that's why Frank never asked me to come down here."

"Yeah, probably was," Keno agreed.

"Thank God it's so secluded." She blew out a breath before adding, "It's hard to believe that such a deserted place exists only about twenty miles from San Francisco."

Keno spotted a green Ford pickup parked beside the Gonzo shed, and remarked, "Hector must be making mulch."

Millie glanced around at the large mounds. "Is that productive? It looks like there's enough of that stuff to last for months, if not years."

"Frank had a standing rule that the mulch used during one week had to be replaced by the end of the next week. That way he had a perpetual supply that was always aged just right."

"I know his mulch had to be perfect," Mille said. "You would think he was making fine wines."

"Yeah, he had different recipes for almost every kind of plant or flower. He added special kinds of grape vines, branches from different fruit trees, and he even mixed certain kinds of leaves together. Screwing up his mulch was the only thing I ever saw him get pissed about."

Millie's face had taken on a wistful look. "He didn't take most things too seriously, but he could be quite fussy at times."

Keno pulled the Cadillac up close to the Gonzo shed and honked. Within seconds, Hector looked out to see who was interrupting his work. The squat man, pushing sixty but still going strong, removed his dust mask and brushed himself off as he approached the Cadillac. He tipped the brim of his straw hat toward Millie, and greeted, "Mrs. Flores." Deep lines creased his leathered face as he smiled at one of his favorite people on the planet. He turned to Keno and said, "Hola, muchacho."

Keno reached out and playfully slapped Hector's shoulder. "*Qué paso*, old man?" Making it clear that he'd noticed Keno's casts, Hector closed his hands into fists and assumed a boxers stance. "Old man, huh? Step out here and I will give you the beating of your life."

Keno enjoyed a good laugh for the first time in days. "I surrender. You are one *muy mal hombre*."

"And don't forget it, muchacho." Hector smiled before adding, "Me and Luiz are making mulch this morning."

Keno replied, "Me and my mom are going to check out some business stuff in Frank's office."

"That's a good idea. You are the new jefe now, and I know you can run this business the way..." Hector let that thought escape. "Maybe later we can talk about the jobs we need to do."

Keno nodded, realizing that he and Millie would soon have to make some significant decisions regarding the future of Milagrozo Landscaping. "Yeah, we need to do that."

Millie leaned forward to get Hector's attention. "We're going to have the Funeral Mass at the Church of Saint Raphael this Friday afternoon at two o'clock. As you probably know, it's the church near the old mission."

Hector's weathered face revealed that he was impressed. "I never been there, but I heard it's a very nice church."

"We're having the wake service at the Redwood Mortuary at seven o'clock tomorrow night. If you and Luiz can attend, we can go over the pallbearer duties when it's over."

Hector respectfully touched the brim of his hat. "Me and Luiz will be there. You can count on us."

Keno gave a little wave, said, "Later, Hector," and steered the Cadillac toward the house trailer/office.

When they were out of hearing range, Millie grimaced and remarked, "Remind me that I still need to get four more pallbearers. When Hector mentioned Luiz, I remembered that I hadn't discussed the funeral arrangements with them. And worse, I haven't given a moment's thought to choosing the other four."

"That shouldn't be a problem. Frank had plenty of friends."

"Yes, but picking four without offending anyone..."

When Millie fumbled with Frank's large key ring, wondering how she could possibly find the right key to the house trailer/office, Keno told her that she didn't have to bother. He explained that Frank had always hidden spare keys to each gate and building. The right key was always hidden on the right-hand side of each driveway or path, under the third rock.

Millie got out of the Cadillac, turned over the third rock, and sure enough, a brass key was lying there in plain sight.

When they entered Frank's office, the look on Millie's face told Keno that her impressions were similar to his own. Furnished with one small metal desk, a metal chair with worn padded arms, and two upright metal file cabinets, the tidiness and order of things was impressive. A stained cedar board on one wall held spare keys arranged in alphabetical order, and each key had a little paper tag attached to reveal its purpose. A small stove, a half-size refrigerator, and a large HEPA filter appeared to be Frank's only concessions to comfort. A large redwood crucifix near the door, a picture of the Virgin Mary on the wall, and a worn Bible resting on one corner of the desk confirmed Frank's dedication to his faith. One wall was plastered with pictures of Millie and Keno. It was obvious that pictures had been added to the collection over several years—essentially, a chronological family history.

Millie and Keno stood there in silence for a few moments, absorbing the essence of the man they loved.

Millie finally went to the desk and lifted the front cover of a large Rolodex. She ran a fingernail over the tightly bunched cards, each revealing a neatly printed name, address, and phone number. She swallowed, cleared her throat, and said, "He wasn't this neat at home, except for his personal hygiene of course. He went to extremes in that regard."

Keno forced a chuckle, and said, "Things that we'd think was important usually didn't seem like it to him, but then some things that we'd think were trivial couldn't be done good enough to suit him."

Millie allowed herself a little smile as she thought about her husband's idiosyncrasies, penchants, and passions. But the reverie soon left her with an empty feeling—a huge void that could never be refilled.

As the somber pair investigated, they became even more impressed with Frank's attention to detail. They saw that each card on the Rolodex not only included a client's personal information, but each one also had a small map of a particular client's property with neatly printed numbers and letters.

Millie studied the backs of the cards, then shook her head. "What do you make of these?"

"I think he had a code for the plants and flowers that he planted for every customer."

An even more compelling example of Frank's attention to detail surfaced when Millie examined the top drawer of a metal file cabinet. A binder contained row upon row of abbreviated initials for the names of flowers, herbs, grasses, vines, shrubs, and even certain kinds of weeds. Still other binders were filled with meticulous landscaping plans. Each of Frank's customers was provided before and after drawings.

"I think he did it to eliminate second-guessing after a specific plan had been formulated," Keno commented.

"I didn't realize he put so much effort into his work," Millie replied. "I knew he was very good at landscaping, but this rises above and beyond what anyone would expect."

In the bottom drawer of the second file cabinet, Millie found the ledgers they were looking for. "Ah hah! Financial records." She flipped through pages until she found one of the current accounts with money owed Milagrozo Landscaping. "Oh my God, Sunshine, this confirms that Frank wasn't good at collecting money."

"That should be a good thing."

Obviously excited, Millie held the ledger so that Keno could see it as she turned the pages. "Look at all these."

"Yeah, a whole bunch of customers owe the company money." Some quick calculations led Keno to conclude, "I'm guessing it's five or six grand."

"That is a good thing," Millie said with an unmistakable sense of relief. "But what do we do about collecting it?"

"I guess we need to start calling people."

Millie made a face. "I hate doing that."

"Frank obviously did, too. But we don't have a choice."

"Okay, let's just get what we need and take it home. We can make our phone calls from there. Even with the HEPA filter running, there's still a nauseating odor in here."

Just as Keno said, "Yeah, it will definitely be a lot more comfortable to do it at home," he noticed the edge of a legal document protruding from the ledger Millie had just closed. "What's that paper sticking out?"

Millie extracted the document and spread it open. "I'll be... it's a contract with the Ghilardi Development Corporation." As she studied it, her gaze came to rest on the agreed upon dollar amount. "Oh, my goodness. Each phase of the contract is worth twenty thousand dollars, payable within thirty days of completion."

"That's outstanding," Keno said. "I know the first phase of the contract was for ten houses, and I'm almost positive that Frank completed eight of those. As he was leaving Sunday morning, he told me that he only had two more model homes to finish by next Friday. That means he was at least eighty percent complete with the first phase, which means Ghilardi Development Corporation owes Milagrozo Landscaping sixteen grand."

Millie said, "That sounds like a lot for landscaping work."

He nodded and replied, "There's a lot that goes into it. You have to prepare the ground, put in sprinkler systems, then lawns, plants, and flowers. It's a lot of hard work."

Millie's eyes had brightened with excitement, but then a little doubt sneaked in. "You think we'll have a problem collecting the money? I assume we'll be dealing with Nicky Ghilardi."

Hearing the name sent the expected flash of anger coursing through Keno's mind. He had to take in a deep breath and let it out slowly—like a pop-off valve releasing steam from an overheated tank. "You are going to get that money. The state has strict contracting laws that guarantee payment in these kinds of situations, but if we can't do it legally…"

"Let's not get carried away, Sunshine. You've had more than enough trouble with the law." Millie elevated her chin and said with resolve, "Let's get the Rolodex, ledgers, and whatever else we need, and then go home and see what we can do about collecting. I'm sure most of the customers will be more than happy to pay up."

When Keno struggled to balance a few ledgers on one arm, he lost his balance and the bulky load tumbled to the floor.

Millie patted his shoulder and said, "Just sit down and relax. I'll carry everything out to the car." She grimaced before adding, "I've had as much of this place as I can stand—emotionally and aromatically."

While Millie carried out the first load, Keno plopped down on the metal chair to wait. No sooner had she gone outside than he noticed a small desk drawer they'd neglected to inspect. When he opened it, he discovered a small, timeworn book. Closer inspection revealed that it was an old journal written in Spanish. The quality of the penmanship was remarkable.

The first entry had been written several decades earlier Though Keno's Spanish was more than a little rusty, he was able to translate *Pensamiento en Prevado de Francisco Flores* to Private Thoughts of Francisco Flores. Keno wasn't sure what to do with the old journal, but he suspected that this astonishing discovery might be too difficult for his mother to deal with at the moment. Also, who knew what kind of information it might contain? Recalling his father's dying words, he realized that Frank's old secrets might be hard for his mother to accept.

Keno decided to translate the journal at his first private opportunity. If the contents didn't prove to be too shocking, he would share them with Millie at the appropriate time. No matter what, though, it would be best to wait until after her heartache had healed a little. Hoping Frank would approve of an act that his mother might consider deceitful, he slid the little book into the waist of his Levi's.

Millie and Keno took turns calling customers who owed Milagrozo Landscaping money. To make their work easier, they'd prepared a short statement which they usually didn't get to finish before the customer eagerly agreed to send the entire balance due. Some customers added a little extra to the check they put in the mail, and a few even went as far as to hand-deliver a check to the mailbox in front of the old Victorian.

They'd been at the collecting for more than an hour when the front doorbell rang. It was during Keno's turn on the phone, so Millie went to answer the door. She grumbled to herself as she charged across the living room, "It better not be that damned Deputy Wertz again, or I swear..." Prepared for the worst, she flung the door open to find herself glaring at a sportily dressed man, whose youthful good looks belied the fact that he'd recently turned forty.

"Hi, I'm Buzz Aldridge, and I'm assuming that you're Mrs. Flores. Did I catch you at a bad time?"

Millie couldn't help wondering if this man called himself "Buzz," because of his flat-top haircut or because his last name sounded a lot like Aldrin, the astronaut who'd gone to the moon. "Yes, I'm Mrs. Flores, and I am busy. What can I do for you?"

"May I come in and explain the reason I'm here?"

"I suppose that depends on your reason."

Buzz flashed a disarming smile. "I've been hired to investigate matters pertaining to Joaquin's case and to do everything I can to clear him."

Millie's relief replaced her scowl with the beginnings of a smile. It felt good to have someone on her son's side—especially someone so polite and charming. "Please come in, Mr. Aldridge."

"Call me Buzz."

"Then call me Millie," she said as she closed the door and led him to the dining room where Keno was on the phone.

Millie waited until Keno had finished the call to introduce the investigator. "Joaquin, this is Mr. Aldridge." She made a face and quickly added, "Who goes by Buzz."

Unsure of the man's intentions, Keno greeted, "Hey, Buzz, what's up?"

Buzz extended his hand, which Keno couldn't avoid shaking. "Nice to meet you, Joaquin. I'm a private investigator. Mr. Clay has instructed me to work on your case and do everything I can to exonerate you."

Keno was just as pleased as Millie to learn that a professional was working on his case. "Cool. Exactly what will you be doing?"

"To begin with, I'm going to visit the scene of the accident. If you're up to it, I'd like you to go there with me. I'm hoping you can walk me through it. Tell me how it all happened from your point of view."

Keno made a point of staring down at his casts. "I'll probably have to hop you through it."

Buzz smiled. "That will work. Are you free to go now?"

When Keno glanced questioningly at Millie, she responded, "I think you should go with Buzz. It's important for him to get your input as soon as possible. Besides, we've already done better than I expected with the phone calls. I'll make a few more, and then I'll be going to Faye's house. She and Gladys are going to help me finalize plans for the wake.

Keno slipped his hands onto the crutches and winked at Millie. "Don't be stressing, Mom."

Keno was pleasantly surprised when he plopped his big body on the passenger seat of a red BMW convertible. The car, which Buzz referred to as his *Beamer*, was considerably roomier than it appeared from the outside.

Traffic was light on Highway 101, so it only took about twenty minutes to reach the not-yet-gated entrance to the Sea Lion Cove Estates.

Almost too realistically, Keno relived the nightmarish sequence of events as he and Buzz cruised down Ghilardi Drive. The street was busy with various kinds of vehicles, many of which belonged to subcontractors associated with the construction project. When they reached the intersection where Frank had been killed, Keno's recollection of the accident came rushing back in vivid detail. His solemn descriptions, sometimes painful, sometimes bitter, gave a surprisingly accurate depiction of that tragic event. By the time he'd finished describing how Deputy Wertz had hauled him away in the squad car, Keno's fists had tightened into balls, and he could feel beads of sweat on his forehead. When he revisited the paranormal scene that included Frank's cryptic message—a private communication he couldn't possibly share with Buzz—an inner voice seemed to be saying: *That's enough for now.*

Sensing Keno's distress, Buzz pulled the Beamer over to the side of the road. He closed his cell and said, "If this is too difficult..."

Keno said, "I'm good." Then he stared out at the choppy waves skipping over the San Francisco Bay and dwelled on the noises the saltwater made while slapping against the rocks on the bank. Somehow, the soothing sounds told him that the tide was in. From these comforting distractions came a nautical recollection that seeped through the fog shielding his grief. He recalled seeing a small boat out on the bay that Sunday morning. He frowned as he brought the picture into focus. "Oh, yeah, there were two fishermen out there."

Responding quickly, Buzz aimed the cell phone recorder toward Keno, and asked, "You saw two fishermen on the bay prior to the accident?"

"Yeah, they were in an old boat. It was navy blue and white, and some of the paint was peeling."

"Do you think they could have witnessed the accident?"

Keno shrugged, and said, "I have no idea. I remember seeing them just before a Mercedes appeared in my mirror, and then I saw them leaving when I was with my father." He paused to let the picture form in his mind. "Yeah, their outboard motor was churning up a lot of foam."

"How far out do you think they were at the time of the accident?"

"I'd say about forty or fifty yards when I first saw them, and then about a hundred when they were leaving."

"I'll need to talk to these fishermen. And if they fish near here often, I'll reel them in."

Keno appreciated Buzz's effort to amuse him, but it didn't quite earn a smile. "I don't know what else I can tell you. I covered about everything I could think of."

Buzz closed his cell, and then steered the Beamer back onto Ghilardi Drive. He had only intended to drive down to the end of the project, but as they neared the model homes, he saw colorful banners announcing the opening of a new sales office. A bold sign in a model home's front yard read:

SEA LION COVE ESTATES
SALES OFFERED BY
LEMMON BROKERAGE COMPANY

Noticing three vehicles parked in front of the model home caused Buzz to slow the Beamer. He saw a metallic-gray Jaguar, a black

Mercedes, and a green and white Marin County Sheriff's car with the distinctive gold and black insignia. When he realized that Keno was staring out at the bay, deep in thought, Buzz gently nudged him with an elbow. "Check this out."

Keno's eyes snapped open when he noticed that the black Mercedes was identical to the one that had crashed into Frank's pickup, and they narrowed into angry slits when he saw that the squad car was identical to the one driven by Deputy Wertz.

Buzz opened his cell, hit the recording app, and asked Keno, "Do you suppose Lemmon Brokerage is owned by Julie Lemmon, the woman you described as helpful and having frizzled red hair?"

"Yeah, I do. And now I'm wondering if Miss Lemmon is in on the frame-up."

Buzz nodded and spoke into the cell phone recorder with a professional-sounding monotone: "I think we can safely assume that, as I speak, Julie Lemmon, Deputy Wertz, and Nicholas Ghilardi, Jr., a.k.a. Nicky, are meeting inside the sales office located at the Sea Lion Cove Estates. And there is good reason to believe they are discussing the conspiracy to cover up Nicky's culpability in the accident that resulted in the death of Frank Flores." Buzz closed his cell, then glanced at Keno and apologized. "Sorry if I seem callused, but it's important that I record my observations."

"No problem," Keno replied. "So we know they're meeting in there. What good is that? There's no way we can find out what they're talking about."

Buzz winked, and said, "I've suddenly become very interested in buying a new house at the Sea Lion Cove Estates."

"That would definitely get you inside."

"You understand that I'll have to take you home and come back alone."

Keno didn't mind; he was drained. "No sweat. Do what ya gotta do to nail those bastards."

Julie Lemmon was busily preparing the required paperwork for Deputy Wertz's bargain-basement purchase—a luxurious home he would never visit, let alone occupy. Julie hadn't staffed her new office yet, so she was attending to all the particulars herself. She hadn't expected to be open for business so soon, but Nicky had given her no choice.

"You need to make me some money, Lemmon. I want ya to get your butt busy and sell a bunch o' these high-dollar cracker boxes."

Julie had used ice and make-up to overcome the swelling, but tinted glasses hid the discoloration in the corners of her eyes, near the bridge of her swollen nose. Her upper lip was still a bit puffy, but it had assumed the sensual look that wealthy and famous women pay extraordinary sums of money to achieve. As her fingers danced over the keyboard of her new computer, she overheard Nicky discussing another of his evil plans—the contemptible one that involved suing Mrs. Flores.

Nicky sat sprawled in one of the expensive leather chairs, which had been strategically placed to make clients feel comfortable while being coerced. He'd crossed his cowboy boots on top of an elegant coffee table, inconsiderately bending and crinkling expensive sales brochures. "I want ya to be on your toes, Wertz. If I got it figured right, Biker Boy is gonna blow his cool when he finds out I'm suin' his poor widowed mama." Looking something like a silent-screen movie villain, Nicky chuckled and rubbed his hands together. "I hope to hell Biker Boy comes after me. I'd like nothin' better than to blow his big butt away."

Deputy Wertz smiled to himself while muttering, "Better be careful what you wish for, cowboy." Not even slightly suspicious of its passengers, he stood at the window watching Buzz's Beamer become an ever-smaller red dot in the distance. The deputy was doing his best to ignore Nicky's obnoxious dialogue but felt obligated to go along. He was, after all, going to be making more money on the house deal than he'd managed to save during his eighteen years of serving the criminal justice system. He turned and said, "Don't worry. I'll be ready, Nicky G."

"Damn right you will." Nicky let go another malicious chuckle. "For what you're makin' on this deal, you oughta be livin' with me until we get Biker Boy put away."

Julie quipped, "I'd pay to see that."

Clearly annoyed, Nicky jumped to his feet and demanded, "What's the hold-up, Lemmon? I ain't got all day."

"Oh," Julie replied with a teasing voice, "are you running late to score some coke, or is it to buy a hooker?"

Nicky glared, and warned, "Watch your mouth, Lemmon."

Julie finished printing out the final legal document, then placed all the papers on her desk. "Okay, go ahead and sign these. I'll notarize them later."

Nicky picked up a pen and glared at her. "If you ever breathe one word of this transaction to anybody, an' I mean anybody, your little butt will be crab food at the bottom of the bay. Ya got me, Lemmon?"

Julie fought back a smile, knowing that each and every one of these documents would become public knowledge as soon as they were recorded in the Office of the County Clerk. "You know your secrets are always safe with me, Nicky. I would never do anything to put you at risk. I've got way too much to lose."

An affluent-looking middle-aged couple entered the sales office just as Nicky and Deputy Wertz were leaving.

Julie gave her well-polished spiel to the interested couple as she showed them the architect's impressive renderings of the finished Sea Lion Cove Estates, and then guided them through two model homes. Julie was good at what she did. In less than an hour the couple had tentatively agreed to "Go for the gusto." The husband cheerfully wrote an earnest money check for five thousand dollars, although the deal was contingent upon their selling the house they owned in Madison, Wisconsin.

Julie was standing in front of the sales office, waving goodbye to her happy new clients when Buzz pulled up in the Beamer. He flashed his disarming smile while climbing out of the sports car, then extended his hand while introducing himself.

"Hi there. I'm Buzz Aldridge." Before she could respond, he asked, "Who would I see about buying a house?"

Other than the hand she was subconsciously shaking, Julie stood transfixed. She thought: *Is this my lucky day, or what?* A couple of empty seconds ticked by before she managed, "That would be me." Then she remembered to smile and introduce herself. "Hi, I'm Julie Lemmon."

After they went inside, Buzz frowned and said, "I saw a sheriff's car leaving as I turned onto Ghilardi Drive. Was there a criminal problem?"

Julie had begun to worry about her appearance, so the question didn't immediately get her full attention. "Oh, no, he was just..." She caught herself and cleared her throat. "Mr. Ghilardi asked a deputy to offer some suggestions regarding security. Things pertaining to vandalism, that sort of thing."

Buzz thought: *That recovery wasn't too bad, but a bright babe like you could do better.* After taking a seat in the captain's chair next to her desk, he decided to play a little mind game. "Is there a lot of vandalism going on in this area? If there is, I wouldn't even consider buying here."

Miffed with herself, she said, "No, this is actually one of the safest crime areas in the state. Mr. Ghilardi is just a worrywart who doesn't leave anything to chance. Besides, within a couple of weeks we'll have the perimeter fence enclosed and the security gate in service. You can rest assured that the Sea Lion Cove Estates will be safe and secure."

That was a nice recovery, Buzz thought. He grinned and said, "I feel safer already."

Julie smiled and asked, "So what kind of house are you interested in, Mr. Aldridge?"

"Call me Buzz."

"Thanks, I prefer informality myself. Please call me Julie."

Buzz figured it was time to toss out the first fictitious bait. "I'm looking for something with four bedrooms and at least two full baths.

I was divorced last year, and I have two young children. My boy is six, my daughter is eight. I want to make them feel comfortable when they spend time with me." Buzz was a bachelor who lived in a swank apartment on Russian Hill in San Francisco, but he often relied on deception to achieve his goals. Sometimes he even enjoyed the game. "I'm presently living in a cramped third floor apartment in the City, definitely no place for children. I'd like to have a place big enough so that my kids can each have their own room. Something big enough for their grandparents to stay with them on holidays. Maybe even get them a dog."

With a slightly glazed look, she said, "That's very thoughtful. So, what do you do for a living, Buzz?"

Much of Buzz's success had come from providing convincing misinformation. He handed Julie a gold-embossed business card that read: C.J. "Buzz" Aldridge, Senior Investments Advisor. This time the name was real, but the occupation was fictitious. "As the card says...."

While studying the card, she said, "I can imagine being a financial advisor is interesting work. Especially in this unpredictable economy."

"It has its ups and downs."

Julie was already attracted to this charming man. She thought: *God, what a dreamy guy. Why can't I find somebody like him instead of the egomaniacs and losers I always end up with?* She unconsciously elevated her breasts a couple of notches and smoothed her pin-striped suit coat with her moistening palms before beginning her practiced spiel.

"We have six different floor plans, Buzz, twelve if you consider that they can all be reversed. And we can do an amazing amount of customizing to fit specific needs, especially if you buy before the foundation is in place."

Buzz nodded with great interest.

Julie retrieved a matte-finished book that displayed the floor plan of each available house and an architect's rendition of what the finished product would look like. Her throat suddenly felt dry, and she began to fret about her lipstick, and then her appearance in general. "I'm sorry, but I need to run to the little girl's room. Why don't you look through these while I'm gone? See if there's anything that appeals to you."

He smiled, confident that his charm was working its usual magic. "Take your time, Julie. I really would like to study these floor plans."

She liked the way he said her name. On further thought, she liked a lot of things about him. "Okay, I'll be right back." She resisted the urge to add, *You sexy rascal.*

When Julie had disappeared into the bathroom, Buzz pounced on the opportunity to examine the papers on her desk. It took a minute to analyze the purchase made by Albert W. Wertz, who had to be Deputy Wertz. It took another minute to figure out how the buy-back payoff worked. "Clever," he whispered with a certain amount of respect.

With rearranged hair, a new layer of lipstick, and touched up make-up, Julie's walk had a little added pizzazz as she came strolling back. "See anything you like, Buzz?"

He smiled his captivating smile while tempted to say, *Yeah, your nice bod,* but resisted. "All the models are impressive, but I'd be hard pressed to choose one without knowing more about them."

"Then let me take you on the guided tour. That will give you a better feel for what I have to offer."

He smiled, resisting another obvious double entendre. "I'm sure you're right. I'll have a better idea after a walk-through."

When Julie started to lead him toward the model homes at the far end of the peninsula, Buzz objected. "I don't think I'd like anything out there. The weather could be a problem if you get too far out in the bay."

He was directing her to the model home that had taken the hit last Sunday. He let her walk him through the model home next to it, then casually strolled over and stood in front of the scarred lawn and the damaged model home—mostly repaired by busy carpenters and glaziers. He turned and asked with feigned alarm, "What the heck happened here?"

"There was an unfortunate accident." Julie paused while considering how much to explain. "One of our subcontractors drove his truck out in front of a car."

"How serious was it?"

Julie grimaced and said, "The poor guy was killed."

Buzz frowned, then nodded knowingly, "Oh, yeah, I remember reading something about that. Didn't it happen last Sunday?"

"Yes, last Sunday morning."

"Now that I think about it, wasn't a Mr. Ghilardi involved?"

Julie made a pained face before confiding, "I'd only met the poor guy a couple of times and he seemed really nice. If you don't mind, I'd rather not talk about it."

Buzz thought: *We'll see about that.* Then replied, "I understand."

Julie asked, "So what do you think? Would you like to look at another model?"

He said, "Sure," while scheming on an excuse to meet her later for a cocktail. Julie was about to make it easy for him.

"This may seem a bit forward, Buzz, but you're looking for a house and I just happen to be in the market for a financial adviser. Maybe we can work something out that will benefit us both."

Buzz saw the opening and pounced. He glanced at his watch, as busy people are wont to do, and made an apologetic face. "That sounds intriguing, Julie, but I just remembered that I have an afternoon appointment that I can't avoid." While appearing to search for a solution, he said, "My schedule is really crazy for the rest of this week, but I'd sure like to discuss these things further." He let his blue eyes linger on her enthused green ones, and said, "I don't believe either of us is the type to procrastinate. Would you think I was being too forward if I were to ask you to join me later for a cocktail?"

I'd meet you later to have your child, you sexy man, she thought. But she didn't want to seem too eager. "I've got a lot going on myself today, though I can probably wind things up by seven or so. What do you have in mind?"

"How about a restaurant in Sausalito? That's about halfway between here and my place in San Francisco."

"That's really convenient since I live in Sausalito. And on the plus side, if I drink too much, I can always stagger home. How about Scoma's? You know where it is?"

"I'll find it. See you there at seven-thirty?"

"Okay, Buzz. See you then."

As Buzz drove away, he called and placed an order for Telecom Service & Testing, or TS&T, to service the Lemmon Brokerage Company's sales office at Sea Lion Cove Estates.

Wearing gray coveralls and white hard hats, members of his team would soon arrive in a specially equipped van with magnetic red, white and blue TS&T signs attached. They would tap into the appropriate phone lines and install a small black box that would intercept calls. It would feed the desired information to a computer located in the basement of a delivery service company on Howard Street in San Francisco. The powerful computer had a state-of-the-art search program. A person's voice articulating any one of a list of keywords—a specific person's name such as Nicky, or an illegal drug such as cocaine—would automatically trigger sophisticated equipment to trace the caller's number, record the conversation, and activate a signal. The flashing signal would then alert a TS&T employee, known to the team as a com-op.

Events had finally caught up with Keno, and he was sound asleep on the couch when Netanya called. Fortunately, he'd had the foresight to place his new cell phone on the coffee table before taking a Hydrocodone pain pill and lying down. But it still took a few seconds of fumbling to find the annoying instrument. "Hello."

"Joaquin?"

"Yeah?"

"You, okay?"

He finally realized who was calling. "Hey, girl. What's up?"

"I wanted to ask you to have dinner with me and Daddy tonight, but from the way you're sounding it might not be such a good idea."

Keno took a moment. "Dinner with Daddy?"

"You made the big time. He really wants to meet you, and he's never invited any of my guy friends to dinner."

"I'm glad he wasn't interested in dining with any of your other *guy friends*, but I'm thinking Daddy wants to check out his investment. I've already cost him a bundle."

Netanya's melodious laugh resonated through the receiver. "You're hilarious, Joaquin. But he's not concerned about the money. He knows I'm really hot for you, so he's more curious than anything else."

"You're really hot for me?"

"Scorching, sizzling, blazing..."

"That's probably a good thing since we're committed to taking the big plunge."

"Plunge sounds dangerous."

"At least a little risky."

"So, what about it? Want to come to dinner?"

Keno stretched while thinking how good the sofa felt. "I don't know, babe. I'm pretty zonked. But I definitely don't want Daddy Bernstein to think I don't want to meet him."

"Don't sweat it. We'll go to Plan B."

Keno smiled. Netanya always had a Plan B. "And that is?"

"We'll do brunch tomorrow morning."

"That sounds way better."

"Okay, Joaquin, you're on for tomorrow morning at ten."

He liked her decisiveness. "I'll be there. Love ya, girl."

"Back atcha."

When Keno returned his head to the pillow, hoping to extend his escape to Dreamland, a nagging thought persisted. It was as if a metaphysical alarm clock was telling him he had to wake up. He'd forgotten to deal with something, and whatever it was, it wasn't going to let go. As his clearing mind scanned possibilities, his anxiety peaked when his search landed on this morning's visit to the Yard. Then it didn't take long to realize that the source of his concern was the little journal he'd found in Frank's desk drawer.

Millie had gone to Faye's house to finalize plans for the funeral, so this was as good a time as any to begin the translation. Keno found an old Spanish-to-English dictionary on the bottom shelf of his mother's bookcase. It was wedged in between *William Shakespeare: The Complete Works*, and *Partridge's Concise Dictionary of Slang and Unconventional English*.

Keno retrieved the journal from his backpack, and then made himself comfortable on the couch. While flipping through the journal's brittle pages, he noticed that there were only about twenty-five of them, each drafted with the same impressive penmanship. He felt a little guilty for violating his father's privacy, even if they were at least thirty-year-old secrets. But curiosity soon dispatched those pangs of shame.

It surprised him to discover how well he could understand Spanish, given that his history with the language was limited to two classes in high school and what he'd absorbed while working with Hector and Luiz. The journal's first page presented an introduction to Francisco Flores at age sixteen in San Juan, Puerto Rico. Approaching manhood, Francisco had wanted to record his thoughts and feelings before the transition was complete. He would explore his blossoming sexual desires, plans for his life's work, and spiritual considerations. Keno decided that his father had been surprisingly well-educated for a young man of his time and place. This conclusion was reinforced when Francisco suggested that recording these insights might make his life easier to deal with if he could reflect on them someday—*Tiempo suficiente para reflexión.*

The second page included thoughts similar to those of disadvantaged Catholic teenagers of the day—long before kids could spend countless hours watching TV and become immersed in electronic marvels.

Keno skimmed over a page in which young Francisco wrote about his studies. His next entry described a shiny new red Chevrolet that a wealthy merchant had recently purchased. This triggered an apologetic comment about coveting. Francico next complimented some nice people who had hired him to do their landscaping, and, it so happened, they had a beautiful daughter named Felicia. The girl's name was written twelve times before he asked God to forgive him for lustful thoughts.

Keno skipped over a couple of pages that contained adolescent musings before something unusual captured his attention. Francisco had begun the page discussing the highlight of his day, which was a flirtatious conversation with Felicia.

However, the mood of his words suddenly changed. On his way to his landscaping job, Francisco had come upon a cruel man whipping a young boy. The frail boy was lying on the ground, shielding his face with his arms while screaming in pain. The brutal man was shouting that the boy had stolen food and deserved a good beating. When Francisco begged him to stop, the cruel man lashed out with the whip, striking Francisco while warning him not to interfere. This was Francisco's first introduction to anger, and he couldn't believe how quickly the fury consumed him. Big for his age, and unusually strong from the physical demands of landscaping, Francisco attacked the cruel man. Even worse, he went out of his mind with rage and, though he wasn't sure, he might have used his hoe to knock the man unconscious. And though he felt his anger was justified, like the righteous anger he had read about in the Bible, Francisco harbored terrible guilt for losing control. He begged God to forgive him, and, knowing the harsh punishment this sin deserved, Francisco prayed that he would have the courage to confess this deplorable behavior to Father Rodriquez.

The next installment dealt with Francisco's growing infatuation with Felicia, and how he dreaded going to confession. Father Rodriquez strongly disapproved of lust. This sin drew more of the priest's ire than any fit of anger.

Concerned that Millie might be returning soon, Keno skimmed over the next few pages, most of which were much harder to translate. Especially difficult were the parts that included Francisco's detailed conclusions of working with worms, maggots, termites, bugs, and other tiny insects in *la tierra* (the earth). Francisco had meticulously recorded data pertaining to these diminutive creature's diets and their resulting excrements which enriched the soil. Francisco had underlined a sentence that translated to: *Soil growth dramatically improved with a tiny amount of salt...* Yellowed stains, perhaps old water damage, covered the rest of this page and made most of the text illegible.

Keno dwelled on the word, *Soil,* or *Tierra,* for a moment. *Why was it capitalized?* He recalled the extreme importance his father had placed on the name, Tierra Milagro, when he was dying. *Miracle Soil? Could this be related to the promise?*

He skipped to the journal's last page, which thankfully had escaped the worst of the discoloration.

Very little translation became necessary as the stunning revelation ripped through Keno's mind. The shocking, frightening, implausible words seized all thought. When he finally blinked his way back to a semblance of control, Keno reread the page.

I have never revealed my dreams and visions to any living person, not even to Father Rodriquez. People would think I was crazy if I told them about the dreams and visions that almost always come true. They let me know about certain things ahead of time, sometimes only minutes before they happen, and sometimes days. Last night a dream came again, only with more power and light than any before. The shimmering light spoke to me in a voice as clear as day. It told me that my life had been spared when I was a little boy, and I was granted more years of mortal life for a Divine purpose. I was chosen to share a miracle with a special son. And someday my son will share this miracle with poor people all around the world. I am overwhelmed, but I will try my best to deserve this honor God has bestowed upon me. If someone is reading this, I am probably dead. I hope and pray that I deserve to be in Heaven. I hope and pray my son will do the miraculous work God expects of him.

Go with God

His faithful servant,

Francisco Flores

Feeling numb, almost anesthetized, Keno lied back and stared at the ceiling. What he'd just read was beyond his comprehension. Beyond anyone's comprehension. But he couldn't deny that Frank had whispered similar words to him as he lay dying. Remarkably similar words.

Keno returned the journal to its hiding place in his backpack while thinking, *How am I supposed to do miraculous work? Just how am I supposed to do something all that special? I've got about twelve bucks to my name, and I'm lucky to take care of myself, let alone anybody else. And why would I be chosen? I'm not even a good Catholic; I quit going to church when I graduated high school. And I know absolutely nothing about miracles. What's up with that? Besides, doing something like that would take total commitment. And even if I could, I'm not so sure I'd want to sacrifice my life that way.*

A chill ran down Keno's spine. *What if all the weird stuff I've been seeing lately is related to this...? What if God is trying to tell me something?* Goose bumps covered much of Keno's body when he realized that he could be contacted at any moment, or through his dreams on any given night.

Millie interrupted his anxiety by greeting, "Hi, Sunshine," when she came through the front door carrying a bag of groceries. When she got close, Millie seemed surprised by his appearance. "Are you alright?"

"Yeah, I'm good."

She obviously didn't believe him. "I'll fix you a nice big bowl of minestrone soup and some hot garlic bread. I just bought some fresh sourdough."

Keno felt a huge sense of relief. His mother had returned his thoughts to earthly concepts. "Sounds good."

Chapter Nine

B uzz sat sipping his usual Johnnie Walker Black Label on the rocks when Julie entered Scoma's at 7:40 p.m. Suddenly forgotten, his cocktail glass hung suspended. Watching her curvaceous hips move and sway beneath a slinky, black cocktail dress, triggered a thought: *Wow, the old powers of observation must have been out to lunch when I met her today. I didn't realize she was that gorgeous.*

Twin mother of pearl combs restrained the sides of Julie's auburn locks. Cascading over a black lace wrap, the colors contrasted nicely with her tanned shoulders. Her emerald eyes, highlighted with the perfect amounts of eye shadow and mascara, busily searched the room. Those exploring eyes expanded when they located her date.

Assuming she was adhering to the *ten minutes late to be cool rule,* Buzz stood to greet her. When she offered her hand to shake, he held the tips of her fingers and brushed them with a kiss. He smiled and complimented louder than he'd intended, "You look absolutely stunning."

When this courtesy was followed by his moving a chair to seat her, Julie was clearly impressed. "Thanks, Buzz, you look nice yourself."

Hoping to distract attention from his exuberant compliment, he joked, "It's always good to begin a date with a little mutual admiration."

She smiled and offered the obligatory apology. "Sorry for running late, but things were even more hectic than usual today. I had to rush home to change."

Buzz couldn't get over how ravishing Julie looked now compared to the businessperson he'd met that afternoon. She'd been wearing a tailored khaki suit that obscured her curvaceous body, her hair had been up in a French twist, and her dazzling eyes had been hidden behind horn-rimmed glasses. He was certainly no expert on how much time women spend on date preparations, but he guessed she'd spent at least an hour getting ready. This pleased him; it suggested that she was interested in more than just business. He said, "Let me get you a cocktail," and held up a finger to attract a server's attention.

Julie ordered a glass of chardonnay, a drink she was not thrilled with, and at the last second changed her mind. "Oh, the hell with it. I could use a boost. Make that a Margarita, Jose Cuervo Gold."

Buzz smiled while toasting, "Here's to attractive company."

With an appreciative nod, Julie raised her glass. "Here's to a handsome man buying a new house and helping an inept businesswoman attain financial independence."

"I seriously doubt the inept part," he said while tipping his glass. "And here's to making a new friend in the process."

"I'll drink to that." After a healthy sip of her Margarita, she said, "And speaking of liking, I'm very fond of Jose Cuervo, but that devious rascal doesn't feel the same way about me. He's been abusive more times than I'd care to admit."

Buzz glared at his glass of scotch. "I know exactly what you mean. Old Johnnie Walker has turned on me more than once. In fact, he's been downright sadistic at times."

Julie smiled and replied, "I should warn you that if I drink too much, I may not comport myself in a ladylike manner."

Buzz's team discovered that Julie once had a serious drinking problem, much of it linked to an unhappy marriage, but she'd been keeping it in check for the past few years. Hoisting his glass again he replied, "Here's to unladylike manners."

"Seriously, Buzz, if I embarrass you, just pour me in a cab. I live close by." After another sip, her face took on a serious expression. "But let's get back to business. I really do need some sound financial advice, and nothing is going to prevent me from selling you a house."

Owning a respectable portfolio that occasionally needed his attention, Buzz knew the basics of investing. So by sprinkling in terms such as mid-cap stocks and price-to-earnings ratios he was able to convince her that he knew much more about the subject than he actually did. And Buzz satisfied his purpose for the date by artfully interjecting questions related to Nicky Ghilardi and events surrounding Frank Flores' death. He soon realized that Julie was razor-sharp, but he doubted that she suspected his ulterior motive, and with each sip of tequila she provided more valuable information.

Each feeling a pleasant alcoholic glow as the evening wore on, their conversation grew more comfortable by the minute. Then they enjoyed a tasty crab dinner, which they drowned with a bottle of fine champagne.

Buzz found himself enjoying her company so much that it became hard to focus on his objective. He reminded himself: *Forget about how good she looks, and how witty she is, and...* He mentally slapped himself. *Pay attention, dimwit. Dig deeper, learn everything she knows about Nicky Ghilardi and Deputy Wertz.*

Over her unconvincing protests, he escorted her to a quaint little nightclub that offered good brandy and slow dancing. Neither had danced that way in years, but their bodies meshed as if engineered to fit together. Lost in the moment, time seemed to evaporate with each soulful tune. Buzz couldn't believe it when he looked at his watch and saw that it was 1:45 a.m.

Buzz had been around. He knew that countless nightclubs in countless cities on Pacific Standard Time would soon be turning on their lights. Bright lights that would lay waste to romantic spells and annihilate enchanted moods that had taken considerable amounts of time and alcohol to achieve. Assuming this Sausalito nightclub would be guilty of this heartless act, and not wanting Julie to be finding her way back to reality, he whisked her off the dance floor. He only slowed long enough for Julie to gather her things before rushing her out the door.

Julie stood with surprised eyes blinking rapidly, though it wasn't a reaction to any bright lights. The combination of alcohol and moving so quickly had made her dizzy. "Where's the fire?"

He started to say he wanted to walk with her under the stars, but a dense fog had rolled in while they were enjoying themselves inside. He adjusted quickly. "I'm sorry, I just had a sudden urge to walk with you in the fog. Do you remember Casablanca, where Bogie and Ingrid were parting company?"

Julie encircled her breasts with goose-bump covered arms before replying, "Yeah, that scene was really romantic, but I think they were dressed for the occasion. If I remember right, they were wearing raincoats and big hats."

Buzz grimaced as he slipped off his sports coat and draped it over her shoulders. "I'm sorry, Julie. I didn't think about the fog making it so cold." Attempting to lighten the moment, he added, "As Mark Twain once said, 'the coldest winter I ever spent was one summer in San Francisco.'"

"I'll bet he was standing close to the bay when he came up with that one." She kissed him on one cheek while gently patting the other. "It's sweet that you're so romantic, Buzz, but right now I just want to get warm. I only live a few blocks up the hill from here, so why don't you take me home?"

Buzz was afraid he'd deflated the romance balloon, but after they got to her place Julie regained her warmth rather quickly. In fact, around 4:00 a.m. he staggered out to her patio, needing to catch a few breaths of that fog-chilled air.

Later that morning, it took Buzz a bleary moment to realize he was alone in Julie's bed, which had a space-age mattress that seemed to fit around every inch of his body. He couldn't resist the urge to press his fist into the mattress, then watch it regain its shape when he pulled his hand out. He tried to remember if this extraordinary bed had affected last night's marathon bout of lovemaking. Though not sure whether it had contributed, he could testify that it hadn't hindered Julie's performance in perhaps the most enjoyable sexual experience of his life. He closed his eyes, hoping to recapture a moment of that incredible ecstasy.

But dedication to his work cut short that futile notion. He looked at his watch, which read: *7:52 am,* then remembered that Julie was already up and about. He hated to abandon the space-age comfort but forced himself to slide out of bed and find his shorts, which happened to be lying next to his shoes. His head spun as he got to his feet, an abrupt reminder of too much alcohol and too little sleep.

He peeked into the master bath, but Julie wasn't there. He tiptoed down the hall and found her in a well-stocked gym. Wearing a gray T-shirt and tight Spandex, Julie had worked up a glistening sweat by climbing a Stairmaster and pulling on ropes attached to a series of pulleys and weights. She acknowledged his presence with elevated eyebrows but kept going until a display screen congratulated her for completing the challenging program.

Still breathing hard, she grabbed a big fuzzy towel and wiped away most of the light-refracting sweat. "Good morning, Buzz. How are you feeling?"

"Definitely not good enough to exercise the way you did."

Her eyes traveled over his six-pack abs and rippling arm muscles. "You certainly look like you work out."

"Thanks, I try to stay fit, but I'm not dedicated enough to torture myself more than I already have by getting toasted and depriving myself of a night's sleep."

"It's not that hard when you're as dedicated to greed and hedonism as I am." With a matter-of-fact shrug, she added, "I think some of the old rules will always apply. Especially the one that goes: *If ya wanna play, ya gotta pay.*"

She took a quick shower and dressed in a crisp khaki pants suit. With her hair up in a tight French twist and her horn-rimmed glasses concealing her beautiful eyes, she'd reverted to the businessperson he'd met yesterday. While sipping her great smelling coffee, she said, "You're welcome to stay as long as you like, Buzz, but I've gotta run. I'm meeting my new secretary and a new salesman at the Sea Lion Cove Estates in—she glanced at her watch— "exactly twenty-three minutes."

Still in his shorts, Buzz took a sip of the rich coffee, then said, "This is a terrific blend, Julie. You say you buy your beans in Mill Valley?"

"Yes, I get them at a little coffee shop in the town square. I shouldn't brag, but this is my own concoction."

Buzz said, "You have excellent taste." Then he made a curious face, as if he'd just remembered something. "Didn't I read that the landscaper killed at the Sea Lion Cove Estates was a resident of Mill Valley?"

"Yes, that's right. Mr. Flores did live in Mill Valley." She glanced at her watch and made an apologetic face. "I hate to leave such fantastic company, but I really gotta go." She put down her cup, then leaned over and kissed him. "I want you to know that last night was very special." She squeezed his shoulder for emphasis. "Really special. You have my number, and I expect you to call me. We still have important business matters to discuss."

"Yeah, it was a special night, and I will call you."

As soon as she'd gone, Buzz forced himself to make use of Julie's personal gym, punishing himself with a grueling workout that eliminated some of the hangover's effects. While showering, he realized that he had to keep the investigation separate from the romantic notions creeping in. It wasn't the first time he'd used his charm and looks to ferret information from a woman, but it was the first time he was concerned about letting his personal feelings get in the way. Even so, he had gleaned some valuable information pertaining to the Flores accident. He corrected himself—from now on it's *the Flores incident.*

After dressing and pouring himself another cup of the terrific coffee, Buzz regained the discipline that had served him so well. With his thoughts focused on pertinent information, he sat at the kitchen table with a notebook and the cell phone's recorder.

Facts

1. Julie was born Juliet Alice Higginbotham in Bakersfield, California to hardworking but uneducated parents who lived in a mobile home and drank lots of beer. She was determined to rise above this kind of behavior.

2. She married an alcoholic real estate broker in San Rafael, California who physically abused her. But Arnold Lemmon committed suicide (he actually jumped off the Golden Gate Bridge!) when she filed for divorce eight years ago. Thankfully, no children.

3. She retained the last name of Lemmon because of the established brokerage company name, and she had always hated her maiden name. Also, real estate was her only means of attaining significant wealth.

4. She was riding in the Mercedes with Nicky Ghilardi the morning of the "incident".

5. A tow truck came to the scene and hauled away Nicky's damaged Mercedes soon after the incident. (How long after?)

Suspicions

1. Julie made a deal with Nicky to keep quiet in exchange for a huge sales contract.

2. Julie knows Nicky was drinking and loaded on drugs.

3. Julie knows Nicky was speeding.

4. Julie knows Nicky made an "unusual" real estate transaction with Deputy Wertz.

Observations

Julie is driven, intelligent, beautiful, witty, a good dancer, fun to be with, and great in bed. (She was wildly convincing when she "admitted" she hadn't been with a man for two years) Basically a good person but has her price, like most of us.

Buzz studied his notes to see if there was anything he wanted to add, then spent the next twenty minutes searching Julie's residence. In the bottom drawer of her dressing table, he discovered a jewelry pouch that didn't contain any jewelry. Disappointment flooded his mind when he saw that the pouch contained a small mirror, a single-edged razor blade, a short straw, and a plastic baggy that held about a quarter of an ounce of cocaine. He licked a fingertip, touched it to the white powder, and tasted the substance—the cocaine was of a higher quality than most local dealers could, or would, sell.

He returned to the kitchen table and added some more notes.

Questions???

1. Is Julie hooked on coke?
2. What about Nicky's cocaine habit?
3. Name(s) of drug dealer(s)?
4. Name of tow truck driver?

Buzz found his cell and called TS&T. He instructed the duty com-op to have the team service Julie's home number. Unprecedented for him on a personal level, spying on her caused an unpleasant twinge of guilt. But he had a job to do, and the job always comes first.

Keno arrived at the Bernstein mansion at precisely 10:00 a.m. This morning's brunch date reminded him of the time when he was sixteen and escorted the most popular girl in his class to the Junior Prom. Much like this morning, he hadn't been the least bit intimidated by the girl; the challenging part was meeting the parents. Noticing that the palms of his hands were sweaty, he wiped them on his Levi's, which Millie had altered to make room for his casts. When he reached to press the doorbell, Netanya opened the door an instant before his finger made contact.

"How's my big hottie?"

Relieved to see that she was wearing faded jeans and a loose-fitting sweater, he replied, "I'm good." Then he leaned forward and whispered, "Was I supposed to bring something?"

She leaned over and kissed him on the cheek. "Just your big sexy bod." When he just stood there, leaning on his crutches, she spoke with a hint of amusement. "Come on in. Daddy's waiting and he won't bite very hard."

As he followed Netanya down a museum-like hallway, his mounting apprehension reminded him of the first time he'd gone through the tunnel and out onto the Rose Bowl's manicured football field to play UCLA. But on that occasion, he'd been able to relieve his anxiety by yelling, head-butting a few helmets, and pounding his fists on teammates' shoulder pads. Now he was limited to squeezing the handles of his crutches.

Netanya stopped at the door of an expansive library and waved him into the impressive room.

Keno had conjured up several preconceived notions of what Simon Bernstein might look like, but none were remotely close. Keno felt as if he were staring at a living, breathing caricature. Simon had narrow features, acutely accentuated by a long, boney jaw. A red French beret, jauntily tilted to one side, somehow complimented his blue and white yachting attire. A black velvet patch, fitting nicely around one side of his prominent nose, covered the void where his right eye used to be. With one shoulder tilted at a steep angle, Simon leaned on a glossy oaken cane with a gloved right hand.

As he got closer, Keno noticed that Netanya's father was quite a bit older than he'd assumed he would be, but that discovery did nothing to diminish the extraordinary energy the man projected. More than a little awed, Keno imagined that Simon Bernstein radiated his own force field.

Simon smiled with compressed lips, then greeted with a British-accented voice, "Good morning, Joaquin. I am delighted that you could join us on such a fine morning."

Keno swallowed and replied, "It's my pleasure, Sir. I've been looking forward to meeting you and telling you how much I appreciate everything you've done for me." Keno moved closer and held out his right hand to shake, but he was caught off guard when Simon shook it with a surprisingly strong left hand.

Reacting to Keno's curious frown, Simon lifted the polished cane with his left hand and tapped the back of his gloved right hand. "Plastic, you see." He then tapped the ankle area of his right leg and said, "More plastic." Simon elevated Keno's shock to another level by lifting the beret and tilting his head to reveal an unsightly pattern of burn scars. The discolored skin started at the top of Simon's head and continued down the side of his face until they disappeared beneath a silk ascot. "Lots and lots of plastic surgery."

Startled by the revelation, Keno wanted to ask how the injuries had happened, but he decided Simon would tell him if and when he wanted to.

Netanya grimaced and said, "Don't let him get to you, Joaquin. Daddy enjoys shocking people."

Keno caught them both off guard, even surprising himself a little, when he tapped his ankle cast with a crutch. "Looks like we have something in common, Mr. Bernstein."

Simon's smile revealed his perfectly capped teeth. "Touché, Joaquin. Though I really don't enjoy shocking people. I simply prefer to dispense with awkwardness as quickly as possible."

Keno nodded and said, "I can appreciate that."

Netanya's radiant smile told Keno that she approved of the way he'd handled her daddy's introduction. "Come on you guys, let's go get some brunch."

An extraordinary table, polished as bright as Simon's cane, was made of green teak, so dark that it appeared black at first glance. The round table held a basket of fresh pastries, two large crystal bowls holding assorted fruits and melons, and three glass pitchers filled with different kinds of juices.

Surprised to discover that he could order from a menu lying beside his place setting, Keno felt as if he were dining at a fancy restaurant, not a private residence. When he'd decided on the Dungeness crab omelet, a muscular butler almost magically appeared to fill his coffee cup and take his order.

Simon and Netanya each opted for the shitake mushroom quiche.

Keno felt more than a little uncomfortable in the luxurious surroundings, but he didn't let it affect his appetite. He devoured pastries, consumed melon slices, gulped juices, and nodded a lot while listening to Simon elaborate on his family history.

Simon told how he and his Jewish parents had lived in Vienna, Austria when he was a child, but his father, a banker, had been smart enough to move to Zurich, Switzerland, shortly before the Nazis took control. At this point, Simon took a couple of minutes to expound on the merits of always having the proper information in time to make the correct decision, emphasizing that one can never have too much information. He paused to chuckle before adding, "Except possibly knowing too much about the sexual history of one's spouse or lover."

Simon went on to discuss how ironic it was that the Nazis had robbed the Jews, then hid a large share of their loot in Swiss banks, mostly owned by Jews, and then, of course, Jews sued the Swiss banks, mostly owned by Jews, for reparation. Simon smiled and summed it up, "Strange world we live in."

Simon's narrative was interrupted when the main course arrived. After some unenthusiastic picking at the gourmet meal prepared by his personal chef, the eccentric billionaire leaned back in his chair and talked about his early travels to Africa. He'd made a fortune on the Ivory Coast by acquiring mineral rights to properties containing diamonds and gold—properties that required guarding with his own mercenaries. He then talked about his excursions to South America, particularly Venezuela and Columbia, where the emeralds were lying there for the taking. During these interesting anecdotes, Simon's lone eye revealed his emotions like a mood ring, becoming bright green during light-hearted banter, then becoming a darker green when an issue grew serious.

When Simon first began to talk about his travels to Israel, the fond memories made the eye seem to twinkle. He described an especially happy time when working on one of the early farm settlements, called a kibbutz. He stopped his yarn-spinning long enough to enjoy a couple sips of coffee, then proceeded to tell how he'd met Sasha, Netanya's mother, at a kibbutz in the 1980s. Simon's eye turned a shade darker when he related how he'd admired Netanya's grandmother, Nanna Smatovich, a former White Russian who'd been born to a long line of nobility. While nearly starving and freezing to death, she had carried Sasha on her back for nearly seven hundred miles to escape Stalin's wrath.

Listening with rapt attention, Keno couldn't contain himself. "That's wild. I should've known Tanya was a princess."

"Have you ever heard of an aristocratic Russian Jew?" Netanya shook her head and grinned. "I don't think so. Daddy left out the part where my grandmother married a Jew who was eventually sent to a gulag in Siberia, where I'm sure he didn't last very long."

Simon took another sip of coffee before continuing. "Sasha was a young widow when we first met. Her first husband was a soldier in Israel's army, and he died near Lebanon fighting Hezbollah." After a pause to let that thought dissipate, the eye began to twinkle again. "God, she was beautiful. I wasn't all that handsome, but I had attained considerable wealth by then, so I suppose we each had a lot to offer the other."

Netanya made a face. "You make it sound like a business deal, Abba."

"I'm sorry if I've given that impression, *Motek*." As he let his mind drift back, a film of moisture gathered on Simon's eye. "We fell madly in love. And we were going to do wonderful things for Israel, but then..."

Netanya patted her father's good hand. "You don't have to go there."

"It's alright, my dear, I've learned to accept man's inhumanities to man. Especially the cruelty perpetuated between Arab and Jew, whose hostilities go back thousands of years to Abraham's dysfunctional family." Then directing his attention to Keno, who'd become spellbound, Simon continued. "Sasha was nearly nine months pregnant when we drove in to see her gynecologist that day. Just a routine check-up." He paused to clear his throat. "We'd just reached the sidewalk, and then, just like that, a bomb exploded." While edgily tapping his plastic hand with a fork, his eye grew almost as dark as the teakwood table. "I don't remember anything but the first terrifying seconds of that scorching blast. They told me later that Sasha was killed instantly, and they didn't think I was going to make it. Fortunately, the doctor was able to save my baby girl." He turned to smile at his daughter before adding, "This tragedy happened in the beautiful seaside city of Netanya, so I named my motek after the place where I lost one love and gained another."

Netanya found a napkin to wipe her eyes. She bit her bottom lip and said," On that cheery note, I'm going to the john."

While watching his daughter walk away, Simon made a curious face, then turned to Keno. "Did you know that the flush toilet was invented by an Englishman named John Crapper?"

Keno was impressed by the way Simon had shifted gears, relieving the almost tangible emotion that lingered. "No, I didn't. But if I were him, I think I would've changed my name."

Simon's eye brightened a little as he chuckled. "Very good, Joaquin. It just wouldn't be the same to say I'm going to go use the Bill."

Keno smiled and quipped, "The *Donald* might be more appropriate."

Though not necessarily agreeing with the politics of the barb, Simon chuckled again. "A good sense of humor is an admirable quality in a man."

When Netanya returned, Simon informed her, "I've invited Joaquin down to the Data Dungeon."

The news clearly surprised Netanya, and she stood speechless for several seconds. "Okay... I need to answer a couple of e-mails and text messages anyway." She kissed Keno on the cheek and said, "Come on up to my room when you're finished."

Keno's curiosity was maxing out, but he did his best to hide it with a wisecrack. "Yes, *dear*. Whatever you say, *dear*."

Netanya responded with an exaggerated wink. "Cool, Joaquin. You're catching on."

Simon directed Keno to an elevator that carried them down to the mansion's basement, which had been carved out of the granite hill. Still spry for his age, especially after having suffered such devastating injuries, Simon led the way down a sterile hallway, then stopped in front of a large stainless-steel door. Entry required his typing a complex series of numbers on a keypad and then placing his eye over a small hole that projected a dim beam of light. As Keno watched the bulky metal door move, he imagined that it would take an extremely powerful explosive to blast it open.

Keno stood awestruck in the big windowless room, viewing row upon row of sophisticated electronic equipment and space-age gadgetry. He could only manage, "Whoa!"

So this is where Tanya and Daddy Bernstein do business stuff, he thought as he observed several elevated plasma screens. Each was soundlessly, but ceaselessly disseminating vast amounts of data.

Simon pointed his cane, guiding his incredulous guest's attention toward the viewing area. The plush leather chairs reminded Keno of those in first class in an airplane, except that these chairs were surrounded with turntables bearing all sorts of electronic instruments, whose purposes baffled him. When they'd each sunk into one of the comfortable chairs, Keno noticed how quiet it was. Even though people's mouths were moving on some screens, and colorful charts and graphs were popping up and down on others, he couldn't hear a sound.

After Simon picked up one of the remote controls and pressed a couple of buttons, one of the plasma monitors smoothly moved toward them. When it reached a predetermined point, it quadrupled in size. Simon pressed another button and a serious-sounding man expounded on the weather's long-term effect on this year's wheat crop in Ukraine. Simon listened for several seconds, pressed more buttons, and, as that monitor receded, another moved in to take its place. At the press of still another button, a monotonal voice elaborated on the recent meeting of OPEC, which would significantly affect the price of oil. On still another screen, an obese man with a wild shock of blond hair explained the importance of a corporate merger in Frankfurt, Germany.

Simon continued to manipulate monitors, most of which had nonstop price streamers at the bottoms of their screens, imparting information from stock markets all around the world. Then he surprised Keno by saying, "Give it a go."

Keno had been watching closely, so it didn't take him long to figure out how to move one of the monitors close and make it expand. This enlargement procedure impressed him so much that he couldn't resist an urge to repeat it. Seconds later, a middle-aged woman related statistics regarding the latest rounds of layoffs in the textile industry. Her voice cracked while reporting that thousands of jobs from her home state had been transported to China—she'd allowed a personal opinion to sneak into her report.

When Keno returned the controls, Simon muted all the monitors. "What do you think of my Data Dungeon?"

"It's incredible. And I think it's a good name. You've *captured* data on just about every major business event that's happening around the world. But how could you possibly use so much input?"

"My people have developed software that is specially designed to filter and condense vast amounts of information, providing me with an overall précis."

Feeling a little inferior, Keno grimaced. "Précis?"

"I suppose many Americans would refer to it as a summation. Anyway, I have dozens of experts studying condensed printouts and providing opinions and advice. I've attained much of my success by gathering more information than anyone else, faster than anyone else. For example, I was the first that I'm aware of to use RFID."

Keno was now convinced he was dimwitted. "RFID?"

"Radio frequency identification. Simply put, it's wireless technology achieved by marrying cell phones and bar codes. It is better known as just-in-time supply. Knowing the needs of anyone in the world, anywhere in the world, provides me with a tremendous advantage."

Keno had questions, lots of questions, but simply nodded and said, "That's incredible."

The barest hint of a smile exposed Simon's pride. "Then it merely becomes a matter of application. For example, my data warned me well ahead of time that a recession was coming near the end of President George W. Bush's term. Or 'a slow patch,' as Alan Greenspan referred to it at the time. I made millions by putting that knowledge to work."

"You can make money when the stock market tanks?"

"Yes, it's primarily selling short, but it requires collecting the proper data far enough in advance. It is usually easier to profit in a bull market than a bear market, but I can make money either way. I personally enjoy investing in futures because I have a tremendous advantage in that area. For example, I know what people will be eating for dinner in Hong Kong next year, how much and what kinds of foods they'll need to import, and where they'll go to acquire it."

"Why are you telling me all this, Mr. Bernstein?'

Simon had obviously expected the question. "Netanya told me that she has very strong feelings for you, Joaquin. In fact, she told me that she is very much in love with you. And I believe she is serious, because prior to this, she has never shared information about any of her romantic relationships. And much like her father, if she wants something, she is apt to get it."

"Yeah," Keno agreed, "she definitely has a way of getting what she wants."

"This, of course, leads to the purpose of bringing you to my Data Dungeon. Netanya has her heart set on becoming an actor, and, although she has been helpful at times, she has no interest in the business world. And I don't mind telling you how disappointing this is to me. It leaves me with no one I can trust to take over my businesses when my old, decimated body decides it doesn't want to continue on. Of course, my dilemma is one of my own making. I've always compartmentalized my business affairs, and I've remained reluctant to relinquish authority. No one associated with my business knows how the entire operation works." Simon's single eyebrow elevated for emphasis. "I just couldn't bring myself to trust anyone completely. Having done more than a little head-hunting in my day, I've always assumed that any of my people could be bought as well. And I am appalled at the idea of entrusting my life's work to self-serving bean counters and heartless lawyers who would deplete my hard-earned resources through ineptitude or greed. No, I prefer to hand-select my successor before I go, especially when I consider the possibility of choosing a man who might also provide me with some wonderful grandchildren."

Keno leaned back in the comfortable chair. He was trying, without much success, to digest the astonishing turn the conversation had taken. *Is he sharing all this for the reason I'm thinking he is?*

Simon fixed his eye on Keno. "I'm hoping that one or more of my daughter's offspring will inherit my proclivity for business."

Keno forced himself to ask, "Are you suggesting that I might be the guy you would... hand-select?"

Simon nodded to confirm Keno's assumption. "Yes, I believe you are the guy."

Keno had a hard time swallowing the lump in his throat. "How do you know you can trust me?"

Simon's eye brightened. "I know almost everything there is to know about you, Joaquin. I know when and where you were born, that you weighed nine pounds and five ounces at birth, and that your blood type is O negative. I know the schools you've attended, your grades, your dedication to football, and your penchant for landscaping." He chuckled before adding, "And much more than I cared to know about the girls you've dated. I even know quite a lot about your parents..." Simon suddenly stopped talking, made a grim face, and shook his head contritely. "Please forgive me, Joaquin. I'm so very sorry for the loss of your father, and I apologize for not offering my condolences earlier."

"No problem, Mr. Bernstein. We've all had a lot on our minds lately."

"Thank you. I appreciate your indulgence. But even as embarrassed as I am feeling, I think it's important that I finish what I started to say."

Keno nodded and agreed. "I understand."

"The thing I most enjoyed learning about you is your burning desire to succeed at whatever it is you set out to do. That quality, combined with your innate honesty, is exactly what I'm looking for." Simon paused and stared with the piercing eye. "Are you interested?"

"To tell you the truth, Mr. Bernstein, I'm overwhelmed just thinking about it. And I don't think I'm remotely qualified to handle something as big as"—Keno spread his arms— "all this."

"Let's construct a hypothetical, Joaquin. Suppose you don't marry Netanya and then I die within a couple of years. What's going to happen to my estate?"

Keno shook his head and shrugged. "I don't know. I guess it would be up to Tanya and the lawyers to figure out."

"Exactly. Netanya doesn't want to get involved, so she would turn my business over to the vultures. As we both know, she is"—he paused to make a one-handed quote mark—"lasered in on becoming an actor. I've tried using every trick in my extensive arsenal to persuade her otherwise, but she simply refuses to grasp the potential of what can be done with all this wealth and power."

"Why do you think I'd be any more interested in it than she is? As I'm guessing you already know, I've pretty well decided to become an actor myself."

Simon massaged his chin with a finger and thumb, clearly searching for the proper approach. "I'm sure you've heard the expression, 'Give a man a fish, you'll feed him for a day. Teach a man to fish, and you'll feed him for a lifetime.'"

"Yes, I have heard it."

Simon's eye brightened. "What if you could teach men how to build big boats to fish in? Or even better, what if you could teach men to farm fish in concrete ponds and sell the fish for enough profit to improve the quality of their families' lives while protecting the environment?"

Keno clearly liked hearing that question. "That would be awesome, Mr. Bernstein."

"Sasha and I talked about doing things like that. But, of course, she was..." Simon bit his lip and looked away.

"Those are some incredible ideas, Mr. Bernstein. I really do like the idea of feeding poor people and providing medicinal supplies for impoverished places like Africa and the Middle East."

Simon shook his head. "No, Joaquin, that's not at all what I had in mind. I don't believe it's wise to expend your resources in third-world countries with little chance of a return on your investment. Believe me, I've done plenty of that. Even a billion dollars would merely provide the starving masses with enough food to survive for a few months. Simply put, donating food only serves to give those poor people enough energy to breed and have more offspring, most of whom would continue to suffer their parents' plight, thereby perpetuating the treadmill to deprivation. No, resources must be used to educate as many of the world's poor children as possible. Education instills self-worth, which leads to a desire for a better quality of life, which inevitably leads to birth control, which leads to a man's desire to attain a better quality of life for his children, and his children's children." Simon paused, then elevated his voice for emphasis. "Education is the only valid long-term solution. And at the heart of it, people must learn to tolerate each other's religions."

Keno was impressed at the amount of thought Simon had invested in the big scheme of things. "Then the whole purpose of your getting so rich was to help educate poor people?"

Simon leaned back and laughed so hard it brought a tear to his eye. "No, nothing quite so glorious. Getting so rich, as you put it, began with a selfish obsession to show up my father. He told me I would never amount to anything because I didn't want to live the constricted life of a banker. And it was Sasha who first exposed me to altruistic endeavors. Also, when you get near the end of the road, such as I am, you start thinking of ways to justify your existence." He chuckled again. "I just hope it's not too late to influence my maker."

It was Keno's turn to chuckle. "What about a charitable foundation to memorialize you?"

"Please, I'm a very private person."

Keno suddenly noticed that all his muscles were tense. He blew out a breath, stretched, and leaned back in the chair. "This has been an incredibly heavy conversation, Mr. Bernstein." He shook his head for emphasis. "It's so humongous, I can't begin to get my mind around it."

"I'm aware that I've thrust a great deal on you in a short amount of time, Joaquin, but I am in a bit of a hurry. I'm a pragmatic man, and I know my time on the planet is limited. Simply put, too much damage to my miserable excuse for a body. So let's take a moment to examine the facts: First, you are an exceptionally honest young man; second, you are well above average in intelligence; third, you think in optimistic terms; fourth, you are compulsively driven to succeed; and fifth; certainly foremost in my mind, my daughter loves you. All this leads me to believe that you are more than qualified to one day assume control of my business. Lastly, and somewhat abstractedly I suppose, I am also convinced that you will provide outstanding genes for my grandchildren."

Keno's head swirled. "I'm really honored that you think all that good stuff about me, and I would be lying to say I wouldn't be interested in controlling all that money, but there are a couple things bothering me. First, I have virtually no business experience. And second, I'm not so sure I'd want to be burdened with that much responsibility for the rest of my life."

Simon pursed his lips, then responded, "I have another list as well. First, the business end can be learned if you're willing to apply the effort; second, it's your nature to excel; and third, I won't permit you to marry my daughter unless you are willing to assume the responsibility that goes with it."

Stung by the impact of Simon's words, Keno realized he'd just been given an ultimatum—an inflexible ultimatum. "I do love your daughter, Mr. Bernstein, but..."

"But what? Don't you want to marry her?"

Keno wanted to ask Simon if Netanya had told him about his earlier proposal, but decided he couldn't ask without violating his promise. "Yes, I definitely want to."

"Considering all that we've discussed, and if you knew she would accept, are you prepared to propose to Netanya?"

Keno was convinced that Netanya hadn't exposed their secret. "Yes, I would."

"Do you love my daughter enough to become a Jew?"

Keno felt as if Simon had just thrown him a sneaky curve ball, maybe even an unhittable screwball. He sat there blinking and thinking before responding, "I don't know how to answer that one, Mr. Bernstein. I suppose I could pretend to convert, but being a Catholic is ingrained in me. And I f it really comes down to it, I think I would try to convert Tanya. But if I couldn't do that, maybe we could work out some kind of compromise for the kids, or whatever."

Simon nodded, and said, "That's the honest answer I expected from you, Joaquin. Just so you will know where I stand, I believe religion is a personal matter that can be resolved by two people in love. At the moment, my immediate concern is whether you're interested in accepting my offer."

"Your offer?" Keno unconsciously held his breath while trying to accept the offer concept. He decided that Simon Bernstein couldn't escape his business mentality. "Let's see if I got this straight. You're offering me future control of a business worth billions of dollars and your beautiful daughter's hand in marriage, or I hit the... sidewalk. Duhhh, that's a tough one. I don't even have anything to drive." He smiled and shook his head. "You really drive a hard bargain, Mr. Bernstein. You're not on any hallucinatory drugs, are you?"

Simon smiled at Keno's attempt to lighten the moment. "Seriously, do we have a deal?"

"The ball's in Tanya's court. If she's good with it, we have a deal."

"Excellent, Joaquin. Let's have brunch again tomorrow. Meanwhile, why don't you go spend some time with Netanya? I need to stay here and catch up on a few pressing business matters."

With so much input assaulting his mind, Keno took his time making his way to Netanya's bedroom.

She came trotting to the door after he rapped on it with the backs of his knuckles. With her big eyes advertising her curiosity, she said, "That took a while. What did you and Daddy spend so much time talking about?"

Keno tossed aside his crutches and collapsed on her bed. "Wow! That was one of the heaviest experiences of my life." He thought about it a second, and added, "Not as heavy as my father getting killed, or the first time we made love, or proposing to you, but... Know what I mean?"

Netanya shrugged and shook her head. "No, you lost me. But I do know that Daddy can be extremely heavy at times. What's going on?"

"Your father showed me a lot about collecting business information, and that was incredible. Then we talked about doing different kinds of charity work, and then..." He made a face before confiding, "And then we talked about our future."

"Our future?" Her disbelieving eyes expanded to their limits. "Yours and mine?"

"Yours, mine, his..."

"Daddy talked to you about our collective futures?"

"In surprising detail."

"I don't believe you. Daddy never talks about personal stuff with anybody. And I mean, anybody." When Keno responded with a matter-of-fact shrug, she frowned and added, "But he was talkative at brunch this morning, and he's never talked to anyone so much. Not even me."

Keno grabbed her around the waist and pulled her down beside him. "Daddy Bernstein approves of our secret."

Netanya's jaw became unhinged. "Are you serious?"

Keno nodded smugly. "Totally."

"Are you telling me that Daddy would approve of us making a serious commitment?"

"For starters."

"As serious as getting engaged?"

Keno hoisted her on top of him and kissed her. He blew out a big breath, and asked, "Want to get married?"

She frowned and asked with obvious skepticism, "Daddy gave us the okay?"

"Netanya Bernstein, if you are willing, we can get married anytime you want to."

She sighed dreamily, then smothered his face with kisses. When she came up for air, she said, "Mrs. Joaquin Flores. Or Mrs. Netanya Flores. I kinda like the sound of that. Or what about Netanya Bernstein-Flores? Nah, that's a bit much. Don't you think?"

Keno deftly avoided that line of questioning. "Remember what your father said this morning about losing your mother but gaining you?"

She nodded, and replied, "Yeah..."

"Well that triggered a heavy thought. I won't have my dad to love anymore, but now I'll always have you."

She found his lips with hers and shared the depth of those feelings.

Keno knew they'd each suffered the pain of losing a parent, but now they'd been granted an opportunity to help heal their wounds. They could chase away some of their pain with a different kind of love—a love that could last.

Chapter Ten

After faxing his employer the relevant information he'd acquired thus far, Buzz went to the Marin County impound yard and learned that the mangled Ford Ranger pickup registered to Frank Flores and the Harley-Davidson motorcycle registered to Joaquin Flores were there, as expected. Unfortunately, Nicky Ghilardi's black Mercedes sedan was not. Buzz felt a jolt of concern when he considered the possibility that important evidence in the Mercedes might have been destroyed.

Buzz learned that when a vehicular accident in Marin County includes a fatality, it has long been standard procedure for the responsible law enforcement officer to include specific information in his/ her report. That information must include: *the name(s) of any, and/ or all, towing company(ies) employed to remove any, and/or all, relevant vehicle(s) from the scene.*

The name of the towing company on the Ghilardi/Flores accident report proved to be illegible. *Gee,* Buzz thought facetiously, *think it was scribbled that way on purpose?* Buzz spent the rest of the morning tracking down towing companies. It wasn't that there were so many towing companies in the county, it was that most of their employees weren't inclined to cooperate; they simply didn't want to bother checking their logs and records. With subtle threats and dogged persistence, Buzz learned that only three of the companies had operated tow trucks on the Sunday in question. The duty com-op at TS&T quickly eliminated two of those, leaving only North County Towing, located in the nearby city of Novato.

The owner's name was Travis Cobb, known to many as "Cobb the Slob," or "Cobb the Blob." Travis was the sole proprietor and the only driver of North County Towing, which made sense because the company owned just one truck. Travis's father, Harvey Cobb, who served in the Army during the Iraq War known as Desert Storm, had handed him the business three years ago. The red-blooded patriot had suddenly decided to buy a big Winnebago so that he and Travis's mother could travel and see some of the good old US of A before it was too late. After all, he'd once put his life on the line to defend it. Travis last heard from his parents last spring, when they'd set out for Homer, Alaska. The company, with name changes about once each decade, had a history of doing well financially. It had succeeded because it was located on two acres of prime property, purchased by Travis's grandfather just before Highway 101 was constructed in the 1950s.

The business currently operated out of a sturdy concrete block building, approaching ten years old. Some forty feet behind it stood a somewhat neglected three-bedroom house built in the 1960s The business had started out as a filling station and auto parts store but had gradually transformed through the years to become North County Towing, which still stocked tires, batteries, sparkplugs, hoses, and miscellaneous auto accessories.

Buzz's first unpleasant exposure to Travis reminded him of a cartoon he'd seen on the bathroom wall of a neighborhood bar in San Francisco. In the cartoon, three fat guys were sitting on barstools, each wearing their jeans down so low that most of their big ugly butts were exposed. At the bottom of the page was a warning: Crack Kills!

Travis's grimy T-shirt had ridden up and his oil-stained Levi's had slid down far enough to expose far too much of the unsightly crack.

Oblivious, he sat on a round metal stool, methodically attaching a clamp to the end of a cable.

Buzz inquired, "Travis Cobb?"

In response, the obese man spat a mouthful of tobacco juice in the general direction of a nasty five-gallon bucket, conveniently placed beside his greasy work boot. He turned his head a little, stared at Buzz with dilated, bloodshot eyes, and then asked with an attitude, "Who's askin'?"

Buzz handed him a business card, which Travis didn't bother to read before twirling it onto the metal work bench. The squandered card landed among oily tools and towing apparatus.

"I'm Buzz Aldridge, and I work for State Farm Insurance," Buzz lied. "I'm investigating an accident in which a Mr. Frank Flores was killed. Mr. Flores was our insured, so I'm required to examine all the vehicles involved. The accident report states that North County Towing removed all three vehicles from the scene, and that you were the driver who did the towing. I've located the Ford Ranger pickup, or what is left of it, and the Harley-Davidson motorcycle. But I haven't had any luck finding the Mercedes, which I assume you know is owned by the Ghilardi Development Corporation."

Travis obviously had a lie of his own prepared. "I put the Mercedes on one of Ghilardi's flatbed trucks that Sunday morning. I got no idea what they did with it."

Buzz studied the burly man's vein-lined nose and dilated pupils, and concluded: *This guy's a real doper, probably coke.*

"The Deputy Sheriff's report states that North Count Towing removed the Mercedes from the scene." Buzz could see the man's wheels turning, so he expanded his lie to the liar. "Maybe you're confusing this accident with another you assisted that day. But I spoke to a lady named Julie Lemmon who said that she specifically saw you hook onto the Mercedes and tow it away. She even described your blue and yellow truck."

The mention of an eyewitness clearly upset Travis. "Oh, yeah, that's right. I had to tow it over to where we could load it onto the flatbed with a forklift."

"And where was that?"

Travis pressed his grimy fingers to his temples, as if applying exterior pressure would relieve some of it building in his mind. "It was down there at the turnoff where they keep equipment."

"Which turnoff?"

Travis's face turned a pinkish color. "Didn't you hear me? It's where they keep equipment!"

"Was that on Lucas Valley Road?"

"I couldn't say for sure."

"Don't you keep trip reports?"

"It was Sunday. I went out of my way to be a nice guy."

"Who operated the forklift?"

"I don't know, some other guy that was there."

"They had an operating engineer there on Sunday?"

Travis blew out a breath of exasperation. "Okay, you got me. I drove the freakin' forklift."

Buzz tightened the vice. "Who drove the flatbed truck? Did you drive it, too?"

Travis's coloring darkened to an orangish pink. "No, it was one of Nicky's spicks."

Convinced that Travis's lies were backing him into a corner, Buzz persisted. "Who is Nicky?"

Pulsing veins stood out on Travis's forehead. "I ain't got time to talk about this right now." He stood up and brushed by Buzz, who was practically leaning over his odiferous shoulder. "I gotta go out on a call, so you just get the hell off my place."

"When you mentioned Nicky, were you referring to Nicholas Ghilardi, Jr.?"

Travis's face had swelled, looking like a big pink balloon. "I told you I ain't got time to talk about it right now. I really gotta go."

"You will have to talk about it sooner or later, Mr. Cobb. If I have to subpoena you to answer my questions, I will."

"You do what you gotta do, mister, but get the hell outta here before I throw your prissy ass out on the street."

Buzz smiled, confident that with his mastery of martial arts he could pound the blob into a bloody heap. "I'm curious to know why you are covering for Mr. Ghilardi. Or should I say, Nicky? Think about it, Mr. Cobb. You may want to reconsider your position. If I learn that you're involved in a conspiracy with Nicky, you'll be just as guilty as he is. And without a lot to show for it." Buzz pointed to the business card lying by an old pair of pliers. "Call me if your memory improves."

When he reached the door on his way out, Buzz turned and saw Travis hurrying into the men's room—most likely to get a blast of cocaine courage.

Buzz got in his Beamer and called TS&T to service North County Towing.

Keno could barely restrain himself when he got home. He wanted to tell Millie about his exciting day and all the good news. He wanted to climb up on the Victorian's steep roof and shout it loud enough for everyone in Mill Valley to hear. But Keno knew that he couldn't. How could he share his joy with his mother when she was grieving so much? But thankfully, Netanya had offered a good way to deal with this dilemma. Showing heartfelt concern that pleased Keno, she'd suggested that they wait until at least a week after the funeral to announce their engagement.

Even when suffering, Millie was no fool. She'd noticed the glow on her son's face the minute he hopped in the door. She patted his big shoulder when he sat down on the sofa, and inquired, "I take it you just came from Tanya's house?"

"Yeah, I did." He wanted to blurt it all out, share his inner joy, but it would have to wait. "We got to spend some time together for the first time in days."

"I'm so glad you have Tanya." She forced a smile, and said, "I finally got the arrangements made. It's going to be a nice service and reception. Frank will be going out like a rich man."

"That's great, Mom," Keno replied. He had to resist adding what he was thinking, *If he would have lived a little longer, I really could have made him a rich man.*

"Oh, by the way, your friend Daryl called."

Keno was glad to hear it. He hadn't talked to his best friend for at least a week before Frank's... accident. "Cool, I'll give him a call later." Keno missed spending time with Daryl Slate, the fullback for the Cal Bears, and his fraternity brother and roommate for road games for the past two years. This close friendship stimulated a thought. "You know what, Mom? I'll bet Daryl would like to be a pallbearer. He and Frank got pretty tight when we went away on road games. Frank was always taking us out to eat."

Millie smiled wistfully. "The way to a football player's heart is through his stomach. But, yes, that would be wonderful because we need one more. I don't know if the word got around, or what, but several of Frank's close friends called today. Somehow the subject kept coming up, and three of them offered."

"That was nice of them," Keno said.

Millie suddenly looked very tired. "Completing the arrangements has left me feeling like the wind has gone out of my sails. But we have one more thing to do. The mortuary called to say that Frank is ready for viewing."

Julie had agreed to meet Buzz at Scoma's when he promised "to stick to business, this time." And this time, she didn't rush home to change. She didn't want to get trapped into another long night, even though the prospect was more than a little tempting. She did let her hair down and freshened her make-up before arriving at 7:10 p.m., the obligatory ten minutes late. And this time she couldn't be persuaded to have a margarita, steadfastly settling for the chardonnay.

Julie retrieved a few folders from the gigantic leather bag she usually carried, then tossed them on the table. She took a sip of her wine, made a face, and said, "Okay, mister financial advisor, there's all my info. Tell me what I'm supposed to do with my blossoming fortune."

This time, playing the role didn't come quite as easy for Buzz, and it took a moment to get into character. "I never make decisions by the seat of my pants, Julie. I have to study your assets, your liabilities, your cash flow, your earnings potential, and your present and future tax positions. I'll need to know your short and long-term goals, and how much risk you're willing to assume. All those kinds of things."

Julie grimaced. "I hate that stuff." She opened a folder with SEA LION COVE ESTATES embossed on the cover, then turned it so that Buzz could see the page containing several columns. "I took the liberty of working up some numbers for the house that I think is perfect for you. And I can arrange for some terrific financing." Her face assumed a no nonsense look. "As you well know, interest rates are coming down, and when you consider potential for appreciation, these houses are a bargain at the prices were selling them. With the building moratoriums and all the stringent environmental laws, I doubt there will be anything comparable to this development again. Ghilardi Development had to pull some major strings to get this project approved." Julie grimaced before adding, "I'm sure they did some things I don't want to know about, but they did get it done, and it may be the last affordable housing ever available in Marin County."

Buzz had to admire Julie's persistence. In fact, her arguments had merit. He had seriously begun to consider buying a house at the Sea Lion Cove Estates. He was all but convinced it would be a sound investment. "Tell you what, Julie, let's grab a quick bite here, and then go to your place to finish this conversation." When she just stared at him without responding, he added, "I don't feel like drinking tonight, and besides, we'll be a lot more comfortable there."

"That's what I'm afraid of. I don't trust myself when we're... comfortable."

He smiled, confident that he was about to reel her in. "I promise to leave by ten o'clock."

She leveled her eyes just above the rim of her wine glass and stared devilishly. "Would that be p.m., or a.m.?"

Chapter Eleven

K eno had spent much of the night navigating a turbulent stream of consciousness. His future with Netanya offered thrilling and exciting possibilities; the business opportunities proposed, or imposed, by Simon Bernstein instilled enormous amounts of awe. Meanwhile, the paranormal issues—especially those associated with Frank's senseless death—crowded in more than their fair share of dread and disbelief. And while his dreams hadn't included any paranormal adventures, he had suffered a brief appearance by a devil, not surprisingly named Nicky Ghilardi.

The delicious smells Millie was creating in the kitchen reminded him that he would be having brunch with Netanya and Daddy Bernstein in a couple of hours. Regretfully, he'd have to control his appetite. At least hold it down a little.

Alone in his Russian Hill apartment, Buzz made a mental note to buy a space-age mattress like the one on Julie's bed. He took a moment to dwell on the amazing sex they'd enjoyed on it again last night, but this pleasant reverie was soon brushed aside when he recalled that his devious trap had backfired. Julie had ignored his less-than-subtle hints to enhance their pleasure with a little cocaine, and when he pursued the matter, it only led to a painful admission of his own recreational use. This lie became even harder to sustain when she told him how much she admired his honesty.

Then, with genuine concern, she'd warned, "You're playing with fire, Buzz. You should really think about quitting before things get out of hand." In her own way of baring the truth, she'd confessed that she was terrified of that bewitching drug because of her "excessive compulsive tendencies." Soon thereafter, she demonstrated a bewitching tendency that made him forget all about the cocaine hidden in her dressing table. She'd also added to her rapidly rising plus column by accepting responsibility for his staying past the promised departure time.

Buzz worked out with his weights and did his floor exercises, showered, and then ate his usual bowl of cereal topped off with banana. He next made a call to the duty com-op at TS&T, learning that the telephone taps hadn't captured any useful information as yet. More specifically, neither Julie nor Travis Cobb had called any drug dealers. He emailed a progress report to his employer, and then assimilated the disorganized files that passed for Julie's portfolio. In his way of honoring his promise, he placed the contents in a manila envelope and printed an accountant friend's name and business address on it. His friend, regarded by many as one of San Francisco's top bean counters, owned a prominent accounting firm downtown.

Buzz dropped off the manila envelope before driving across the Golden Gate Bridge to Marin County. He entertained hopes of tracking down the two fishermen who'd been in the dilapidated old boat Keno had described. He knew it was a long shot but decided it couldn't hurt to take a look around while some of his other irons in the fire were heating up.

His first stop was the San Rafael Marina. He didn't see any old boats, but quickly realized that the unmistakable lack of them might be a good thing. None of the dozens of boats he could see were old and dilapidated; there simply wouldn't be many of that sort in the wealthy waters bordering Marin County. Added to the physical reality that other communities were simply too far south of the Sea Lion Cove, this logic eliminated the need for searches at the exclusive docks of Sausalito, Belvedere, and Tiburon. He decided to drive north on Highway 101 with hopes of spotting a clue along the way—possibly uncovering a detail or two that could narrow his search.

After a wild goose chase on the twisting and curving Paradise Drive, Buzz returned to the freeway and continued north. He slowed the Beamer when he noticed a large sign providing directions to the Larkspur Landing Ferry. He turned off at the Lucky Drive Exit and doubled back on the bayside frontage road, passing close to the modernistic ferry facility. From somewhere out of the minutiae-collecting sector of his brain—which at times even he found annoying—he recalled reading somewhere that the Golden Gate Transit Authority had begun offering ferry service at Larkspur Landing during the 1980s.

About half a mile south of the ferry facility, Buzz noticed an isolated cove which had somehow eluded the greedy fingers of progress. A sun-bleached shed sat in front of a weathered pier, both evidently built years before the paved frontage road had come into existence. The old pier stood several feet above a fairly large tide pool. The brackish pool was naturally drained and filled twice each day with a narrow channel that snaked its way through algae-encrusted mudflats. Some twenty feet south of the pier lay the cracked and worn remains of a concrete boat-loading ramp. Overgrown with wild grasses and weeds, the abandoned ramp angled down the sloping bank until it disappeared into the murky green water.

This archaic scene became even more fascinating when two dilapidated old boats came into view. Each was secured with a small rope to the same relatively new two-by-four, which was nailed to two moss-encrusted wood pilings that unconvincingly helped support the old pier. Coincidentally, one of the boats was blue and white, its paint noticeably chipped and peeling.

Buzz parked on a weed-infested patch of pea-gravel, which he guessed was a turnaround when the loading ramp was still in use. A NO TRESPASSING sign—on which the red had faded to washed-out shades of pink, and the white had become a motley yellow—was nailed to a heavy plank door. The door's formidable hinges, long and wide and thick, were caked with flaking layers of orange rust. A seemingly out-of-place shiny carbon-steel padlock, looped through a stout iron hasp, made entry next to impossible without the proper burglar equipment.

Buzz couldn't see an easy way to gain access to the pier, exposed as he was in broad daylight, so he walked down to the water's edge and stood on a large rock that offered a decent view. He could see a short gangway descending from the pier to a small wooden landing that separated the two boats. A closer inspection revealed that only the navy blue and white boat, probably sixteen feet long, had an outboard motor attached to its transom. The motor was tilted up ninety degrees, with the propeller about three feet out of the water.

What are the odds of stumbling onto the right boat so easily? Buzz asked himself. Then he realized that there simply weren't that many old fishing boats in this part of Marin County. The odds weren't so astronomical after all. Probably wouldn't even be considered a long shot.

Buzz looked out at the bay and assumed that experienced fishermen could navigate around San Quentin, under the San Rafael-Richmond Bridge, then over to the Sea Lion Cove without exposing themselves to larger vessels, dangerous tides, or foul weather. They could, he concluded, navigate that far in roughly half an hour—no time at all for dedicated fishermen to reach their favorite spot. Buzz jotted down the name of the boat with the peeling paint. *Phish Phinder*—somebody's idea of humor. Then he located the identification number, which was supposed to be registered with the state. He mumbled, "Good luck with that one."

When a search of the immediate area didn't turn up anyone, Buzz called an acquaintance at the Coast Guard—a sharp guy who might be able to track down the owner of the boat. His friend informed him that he would get the information if humanly possible. Buzz considered asking if it were *computerly possible*, but decided he might be the only one to see the humor in it.

Buzz next placed a call to Timothy Morgan, the youngest member of his team. He instructed him to get to the location ASAP. It was important that Timothy keep an eye on the old fishing boat and I.D. the fishermen, if and when they showed. If questioning these fishermen proved to be too difficult, Timothy should just follow them and find out where they lived. Buzz smiled when he thought about the big man surreptitiously monitoring human targets. For reasons Buzz had yet to figure out, Timothy—six-feet-five and over three hundred pounds of human Teddy Bear—had an uncanny knack of tailing people without being spotted.

While waiting, Buzz opened his notebook and entered relevant information regarding his progress thus far. Certainly, nothing to brag about.

Keno arrived at the Bernstein mansion a few minutes early, but this time he wasn't nearly as anxious about meeting his iron-willed, mega-rich, soon-to-be father-in-law However, he did feel tired from a lack of sleep, and it showed in his eyes when he'd looked in the mirror, even after flushing them with several drops of Visine.

Joy was dancing in Netanya's eyes when she flung the mansion's front door open. She bounced out onto the front porch and planted a big kiss on Keno's mouth, hanging open with surprise. She teased his tongue with hers, then leaned back and let a smile light up her pretty face. "Hey, Joaquin, are you as excited as I am?" Without waiting for his reply, she grabbed him by the hand and almost dragged him inside. "I bet I didn't sleep more than three or four hours last night."

Keno paused to dwell on her "excited" question. Excitement comparable to hers had bounced in and out of his thoughts during his sleep-deprived night, but guilt had taken the edge off his elation.

It just wasn't right to be that happy while still mourning Frank, only dead four days. "I know what you mean. I didn't sleep much either."

When she led him past the library and straight to the impressive teak dining table, Keno was pleased to see that Simon hadn't arrived yet. "We need to talk, Tanya. We got sidetracked yesterday before..."

"Sidetracked?" Netanya asked with an almost equal mix of surprise and disappointment. "That's what you call having some of the greatest sex in the history of the planet?"

He winked to let her know he agreed with the assessment. "Anyway, I need to talk to you about what's going on with us. There are only about a hundred things we need to decide on. Like when are we getting married? Right away, or hold off a while? Are we going to have a big wedding, or do it my way and elope to Vegas? Am I still going to UCLA, or what?" He made a face and shrugged his big shoulders.

"I think you're stressing too much, Joaquin. Why do things have to change so dramatically just because we're going to get married?"

They simultaneously felt Simon's presence, but neither was certain how long he'd been in the room. They jointly chorused, "Good morning," while five moving eyes exchanged contact.

Looking like the kid caught with a hand in the cookie jar, Netanya asked, "Did you hear what we were talking about, Daddy?"

Wearing a red fez decorated with gold Arabic script and a dangling tassel, Simon wasn't about to admit to anything. "Not enough to comprehend any of it without an interpreter. You youngsters speak a different brand of English than I was taught."

Netanya said, "Joaquin and I have something important to tell you." And then she turned to Keno and signaled with a quick tilt of her head—an unmistakable hint to take it from there.

Keno suspected that Simon had heard at least some of their conversation. And since the intimidating man had given him two choices—though just one to Keno's way of thinking—the disclosure came easy. "I asked Tanya to marry me, Mr. Bernstein."

Simon flipped the tassel behind his unscarred ear and held his thin-lipped smile, clearly waiting for more input. A few empty seconds struggled by before he asked, "And how did she respond?"

The question startled Keno at first, but then he smiled and replied, "The way I hoped she would. She accepted."

Simon smiled a rare full smile and patted the back of his daughter's hand. "My hearty congratulations."

Netanya bounced to her feet, kissed her father on the cheek, and then hugged his neck as hard as she dared. "Thank you, Abba. I'm so glad you approve."

"I am very happy for you, Motek." He turned to Keno. "And for you as well, Joaquin."

As if on cue, the muscular English butler arrived to serve coffee and take their orders. This time Simon ordered plain oatmeal with cranberries. Netanya, too excited to think about food, chose to nibble on a muffin and a few odd pieces of fruit. Exhibiting remarkable constraint, Keno ordered six pieces of French toast with a few slices of Canadian bacon.

Simon entertained them with more family history while they ate. When they'd finished, he maneuvered the conversation to a subject he felt compelled to address before vows were exchanged. "Your dissimilar religious beliefs are something I'm sure you have both considered." When the two young people nodded to admit they had, he asked, "How serious is this issue?" Without waiting for a response, he went on. "My guess is that it won't be a problem unless it's one of your own making. While I know this is a personal matter that only the two of you can resolve, I'm going to offer my two-cents worth anyway."

Simon paused to take a sip of coffee. "I didn't give a lot of thought to religion during the course of my lifetime, but then a few months ago, during the early part of June as I recall, I became almost obsessed with learning everything I could about the subject. On a few occasions, I even let it interfere with business matters.

Keno was struck with the timing of it. *Simon's obsession would have started about the same time I met Netanya, which was during early June.*

Netanya stared with open-mouth disbelief. "You actually let religion interfere with business stuff?"

Simon's nod was barely perceptible. "My studies primarily included Judaism, Islamism, and Christianity. All three religions maintain there is one omnipotent God, ostensibly the same deity, and each adhere to many of the same scriptures. In my opinion, Judaism is the trunk of monotheism's tree and Islamism and Christianity are branches, though the branches may have outgrown the trunk."

"That's really reaching for a metaphor," Netanya chided.

"Guilty as charged. But I'll begin with Islamism, which has expanded rapidly during the past few centuries. I've discovered that the Quran contains more biblical scriptures than most people, and I would assume many Muslims, are aware of. It almost verbatim contains the first five books of the Old Testament, commonly known to Jews as the Torah, and to many spiritual leaders, the Pentateuch. Muhammad was born in Mecca, where the locals claim to be descended from Abraham through Ishmael, and it's widely accepted that Abraham built the temple known as Ka'bah for the worship of the One God.

"This is the temple that every Muslim feels compelled to visit at least once during their lifetime. Even though it was ostensibly constructed by Abraham, a Jew, it has become the Islamic world's holiest shrine. Idolaters of the day, known as Quraysh, had taken control of the temple by the time Muhammad came along. He supposedly had a vision saying that it was his destiny to return the temple to God's, or Allah's, people. While in a trance, a voice repeatedly said to Muhammad, *Quran*, which literally means *read*.

Simon shrugged and continued, "This seems more significant when one considers that he wasn't able to read anything at the time. Muhammad's wife, fifteen years older than he, took him to get advice from her cousin, Waraqa bin Nawfal, an old man who knew the scriptures of the Jews and Christians. Later on, when the Quraysh grew angry at Muhammad's teachings, they conspired to kill him. Strange as it may seem, the Christians hid Muhammad for three years, and soon thereafter he traveled to the Jewish city of Yathrib, where he resided with the Jews for seven years."

Simon stretched, and asked, "Are you still with me?" When his engrossed audience simultaneously nodded, he went on. "Glaring differences arose between Jews and Muslims in Yathrib, but I think they were related more to earthly matters than to conflicting religious doctrine. I'm convinced that these old struggles for power and property are at the root of the hatred that continues to this day. I find it curious that the Jews, who taught Muhammad the scriptures, have become the infidel enemy. Nonetheless, those entrenched differences have congealed into a fierce hatred that overwhelms logic."

"The way I see it," Keno interjected, "they've connected those religious differences with political and geographical conflicts that benefit greedy rich leaders wanting money, and religious fanatics wanting power. I don't think many of the current Muslims understand what their ultimate goals are. Do they really think they can kill everybody that isn't a Muslim?"

"Well said," Simon agreed. "I'm glad to hear you've given the subject some serious consideration. But getting back to my dissertation, Christians believe that Jesus Christ is the Son of God, or God incarnate. Islamism teaches that Jesus Christ was merely a wise prophet, and Muhammad was the True Savior sent by Allah. The Jews are still waiting for their Messiah, their King of Kings, to come along. Jewish prophets had promised the coming of a messiah for centuries. Then many of the prophesies described in the scriptures began to be fulfilled around the time Jesus Christ was born. Isaiah said, 'The Savior would be born of a virgin;' Micah said, 'The Messiah would be born in Bethlehem;' Daniel said, 'Messiah the King would make a triumphal entry into the Holy City;' and Zechariah said, 'He would enter the Holy City, lowly and riding on a donkey.'"

Clearly fascinated, Netanya asked, "Did all of those things actually happen?"

"Many millions of Christians are convinced of it."

Netanya frowned and asked, "Why are prophets mostly limited to ancient guys in the Bible? It's funny how millions of people believe everything about visions and prophecies if it were written centuries ago, but now if somebody claims they've had a religious experience, they're called wackos."

Keno felt stunned; it was as if Netanya had somehow learned his secrets. "Yeah, almost anybody would be afraid to admit it if it happened now."

"No, really," Netanya persisted. "Why don't we hear about prophets that aren't at least two thousand years old?"

"I'm sure most Mormons would argue the point," Simon replied. "And while this may not satisfy your question, I'd like to offer what I once heard a wise Rabbi say on the subject. 'God speaks to everyone, but only a few have perfected the art of listening, which must be done with the heart instead of the ears.'"

Feeling a chill snake up his spine, Keno smiled and said, "That's pretty good."

"Most of us would be too afraid to listen," Netanya put in. "It's way too scary to imagine." A frightened look came over her face. "Think about it. A one-on-one with God?"

"I see your point," Simon replied, "but let me finish my train of thought. The name Jesus is Greek for the Hebrew word *Yeshuah*, which means messiah. The Greek, *Kristos*, and the Latin, *Cristus*, basically mean savior. How Jesus and Christ came to be conjoined is beyond me. Though both Peter and Paul referred to Him in letters as Jesus of Nazareth.

"Moving on, John the Baptist was busily traveling about the countryside at that time, convincing a sizeable segment of the populace that the messiah would soon be making His appearance. And, of course, when there is opportunity for fame, glory, power, and wealth, men will jump at it. And many pretenders—each with their own little band of followers; and each performing their promised miracles—came forward during this time.

"These pretenders were considered to be uneducated, fanatical Jews who posed no real threat. Jesus, however, succeeded in angering the Sanhedrin, which was the highest judicial and ecclesiastical council made up of seventy High Priests. Remember, Jesus enraged them when he threw the moneylenders out of the Temple. He further angered the Sanhedrin when He performed healings on the Sabbath, which the Pharisees, the strictest sect of the lot, considered to be blasphemous conduct. And He compounded his transgressions by referring to Himself as *the Son of God.*

"Now a large share of the populace grew disappointed because this so-called King of the Jews wasn't the least bit interested in rebelling against the Romans. To make matters worse, Jesus was resolutely opposed to violence. He preached that if you use evil means to overcome evil, evil wins. The angry masses didn't buy into this dovish philosophy. His preaching peace and love, I believe, was the fundamental reason why the general populace turned against Him in the end."

His face constricted with thought, Keno offered, "Those angry masses were probably stoked by the Sanhedrin."

"That's quite likely," Simon agreed, "but a growing number were convinced that Jesus was the real McCoy. Remember, He met important requirements set down by the scriptures, not to mention miraculous healings. Jesus also treated his followers to the delicious notion that these impoverished peasants would reign in Heaven after the Final Judgment. This would almost certainly send the rich, the powerful, and the elite down to eternal damnation." Simon chuckled and added, "Tempting fodder, indeed."

"If the poor reign in Heaven, Abba," Netanya said with an exaggerated look of concern, "you are in big, big trouble."

Simon smiled his appreciation. "Now I'll touch on something that is perhaps merely legend. The night before Jesus was brought before Pontius Pilate, his wife, Claudia Procula, supposedly dreamed a disturbing premonition. She saw a holy man in her vision, and his brutal death was going to destroy her husband's life. As even the most educated at the time were superstitious, this undoubtedly made a strong impression on Pilate."

Simon paused for another sip of coffee. "I won't bore you with the details, but the Romans had imposed a law that no Jew could kill another Jew without the Procurator's permission. Therefore, when the High Priests had Jesus arrested with hopes of having him executed, they were compelled to bring him before Pontius Pilate. The Prefect tried to persuade Jesus to save his life by denying that He was the Son of God, which Jesus refused to do. Pilate next attempted to toss the ball into the court of Herod Antipas, the King of Galilee, who was more figurehead than king. When that ploy didn't work, Pilate offered the growing mob the life of Barabbas, a convicted murderer, but that strategy didn't work either. Then Pilate was faced with the choice of allowing the angry throng to publicly stone Jesus to death, the accepted punishment for blasphemy, or crucify Him for committing treason against Caesar. The fact that Jesus was crucified with His head elevated and His side pierced with a spear, both of which would certainly hasten death, may indicate that Pilate displayed some out-of-character mercy."

Netanya found herself feeling sympathy for Jesus. "Where are you going with this, Abba?"

Simon smiled and patted the back of her hand. "Sorry to be so longwinded, Motek, but I'm almost finished." He cleared his throat, and continued, "There is little documentation to support their findings, but two important nineteenth century historians arrived at similar conclusions. They each wrote that Pontius Pilate returned to Rome about 37 a.d. and they each concluded that Pilate had become a Christian somewhere along the way. This suggests that his close encounter with Jesus had a profound impact on him. In the end, Pontius Pilate committed suicide, presumably because he was overcome with guilt for having a hand in killing Jesus Christ."

Keno sat thoughtfully, trying to decide whether he was more pleased or disturbed by Simon's version of events. "I'll be the first to admit I'm no student of theology, but I've never read or heard anything about other false messiahs being around at the same time Jesus was, even if they were charlatans."

Simon shrugged his good shoulder. "I'm not attempting to undermine Christianity. I'm merely relating information I've come across during my studies. Whether those devoted to Jesus had an agenda, or if later Christians wanted to suppress that information for obvious reasons..."

"I don't know," Netanya interrupted. "It sounds to me like you're arguing in favor of Christianity. Come on, Pontius Pilate becoming a Christian after a couple of quick meetings with Jesus? That doesn't sound like an Orthodox Jew talking." She stared at her father suspiciously. "You haven't become a Christian without telling me...?"

"No, my dear, but I have entertained the notion that we Jews might have missed a messianic moment."

"A messianic moment?" She cast another questioning look. "Did you just make that up?"

"A simple turn of phrase." Simon rubbed his chin before adding, "And I should remind you that more than a few historians have determined that Jesus did fulfill several biblical prophesies."

Keno enjoyed that confirmation. "There you go. That should convince anybody."

"However," Simon continued, "I have a problem with the Resurrection, which I feel should be Christianity's crowning moment—perhaps mankind's crowning moment. The final pages of the four Gospels each deal with the disposal of Jesus' body in murky ways that arouse my suspicion. For reasons unknown, a man named Joseph of Arimathea went to Pontius Pilate and asked for the body, which he took to a grave site that belonged to him. The Gospel of John mentions that Nicodemus helped him prepare the body according to Jewish custom; Mark says His mother, Mary, and another lady prepared the body; while Luke and Matthew say only Mary Magdalene and another woman, also named Mary, provided traditional ointments and perfumes, and that only these two women witnessed the sealing of the tomb.

"After the third day, a number significant in Judaism, there is fleeting mention of an earthquake and the presence of brightly clothed angels sitting on the rock that was rolled away from the tomb." Simon shook his head pensively. "There is also brief mention of Jesus walking and dining with two men who didn't recognize Him soon after He arose from the dead. And there are short passages of Jesus meeting with the eleven remaining disciples, from which derived the phrase, *Doubting Thomas*. But all in all, it seems rather feeble documentation for the most impressive event mankind has known."

"The Christians might have been too scared to come forward at the time," Netanya offered. "And the Gospels were written decades after Christ's death. Maybe some of the writings about the resurrection were lost, or deliberately destroyed by the Romans, or maybe others with an agenda. Like maybe the Sanhedrin?" She stared blankly, as if it just occurred to her that she might be arguing in favor of Christianity.

Keno leaned back to digest this glut of information, most of which he'd never read or heard before. "Think about how fast Christianity spread in such a short amount of time. It was basically just word of mouth and some letters from Paul. There's even evidence that the Word reached all the way to England by the end of the first century." He turned to Simon and said, "And I think you might be missing the big picture, Mr. Bernstein. We call it the Christian Faith, the key word there being *faith*. If God—who created heaven and earth, caused a catastrophic flood, and then wiped out Sodom and Gomorra in a flash—can't do a simple little thing like resurrecting His Son, one single man, then he isn't the omnipotent God I believe in." Keno collected his thoughts before adding, "And I think Jews and Muslims have missed out on the most important fact of all. Jesus brought absolution into the world. The fact that our sins can be forgiven is huge. I sure wouldn't want to be deprived of confession and denied the promise of Christ saving my soul."

Netanya let go a nervous little laugh. "Yeah, confession might be a good thing, Abba. I wouldn't mind shedding a little of the guilt that Jews have been struggling with, like, forever." After a brief pensive pause, she added, "Come to think of it, I have a girlfriend who became a Christian Jew."

Keno nodded and said, "And when you really think about it, all the Apostles and early converts were Christian Jews."

"Yeah, I guess so," Netanya agreed.

Simon smiled knowingly. "I think that's enough discussion of religion for one day."

It occurred to Keno that Simon seemed to be steering Netanya toward the beliefs of her husband-to-be. He said, "I've got one more question before we drop it." With three curious eyes focused on him, Keno turned to Simon and asked, "What do you know about the avenger of blood?"

Simon thought a moment, then replied, "It comes from the Old Testament. The avenger of blood was the person assigned by the family of a murder victim to take revenge on the killer. However, in the Book of Joshua, a benevolent God commanded that if a person had killed accidentally, and with no malice aforethought, that person should be granted refuge."

Keno frowned while recalling Frank's warning: *Don't be an avenger of blood.* "So the killer gets off the hook if he did it accidentally?"

Simon nodded. "That's what I take it to mean."

Keno mulled things over, then asked, "What if the killer does other bad things to other members of the victim's family? Does he still get to keep his stay-out-of-jail-free card?"

"I wouldn't think the killer could avoid punishment for violating additional laws, but I don't believe *the avenger of blood* should be responsible for imparting justice."

Netanya seemed to be catching on. "How did you come up with that off-the-wall stuff, Joaquin? Does it have something to do with that idiot killing your father?"

Keno blew out a deep breath before avoiding the truth. "I'm not sure, but I think you're right, Simon. It is time to drop all this religious talk."

Simon nodded. "I couldn't agree more, Joaquin. So how would you like to go down to the Data Dungeon and get better acquainted with my business practices?"

Netanya frowned at the idea. "You'd better not keep him too long, Abba; he tends to get carried away if something interests him. And I don't want him obsessing about business stuff when we've got so much important planning to do."

"Of course, Motek, but I hope the three of us can have more of these enlightening conversations soon. Next time it might be fun to attack philosophy, or even politics."

Can I ever be honest about all the weird things I can't explain? This internal question inevitably led to Keno's other thoughts related to Frank's needless death and tomorrow's depressing event. "Tomorrow is out, Mr. Bernstein. We're having the funeral at two o'clock.

"Yes, Netanya told me. We've made plans to attend."

"I appreciate that, Mr. Bernstein."

Simon stared at Keno for a moment. "I think it's time we stopped being so formal. Please call me Simon. And which do you prefer? Joaquin or Keno?"

"I think Joaquin would sound better coming from you, Simon."

Julie's day began on a negative note. Her period had started early, possibly accelerated by the unaccustomed sexual activity. And this made watching the clock even more exasperating. Nicky had promised to bring the twelve-thousand-dollar check for the Wertz deal before ten a.m. Here it was, almost noon, and he hadn't even bothered to return her calls. The closing costs, approximately three thousand dollars, would be coming out of her escrow account if the inconsiderate jerk didn't come through. When the grandfather clock chimed twelve, she couldn't stand it a second longer. She dialed Nicky's private cell number, then nervously tapped a pen against her phone while listening to the grating ring.

"Nicky G. here."

Julie sneered at the egomaniac's new way of relating to himself. "Where the hell are you, Nicky G.?"

Nicky G. obviously didn't appreciate the lack of respect. "What's it to ya, bitch?"

"You were supposed to be here with a check two hours ago."

"I changed my mind. I ain't given you no commission for no phony deal." Nicky chuckled. "You didn't really sell nothin,' did ya?"

Julie's grip on the telephone tightened, wishing it was his scrawny neck. "You told me the deal had to look legitimate. I'm still doing the same amount of work as if it were. And by the way, the deal has fixed closing costs I can't avoid."

"Okay, you snivelin' bitch, I'll pay the three thou. But that's gonna be it."

Julie sat fuming, her mind searching for some way to get back at him. But she knew, at least for the moment, he had her over a barrel. In a chilly monotone, Julie replied, "Okay, Nicky G., if that's the way you want to play it," then she slammed down the receiver. She mumbled, "Someday I'll get you for this, you miserable little egomaniac."

A minute later, the abused phone delivered more bad news. Her banker called to inform Julie that the wife-half of the Wisconsin couple had put a Stop Payment on their five-thousand-dollar earnest money check. The husband had suffered a serious heart attack, and the wife was circling the wagons.

Julie replaced the receiver, just slightly less aggressively this time, and began to massage her temples. Sales at her San Rafael office had been unusually slow during the past couple of months for several reasons: skyrocketing prices eliminating many middle-income buyers; so little new building; and lots of new competition. She'd also had to spend extra cash setting up her new office, not to mention mortgage payments and maintenance for her house and repairs on the money-sucking Jaguar. Like thousands of other Americans, her money market investments had taken a serious beating a few years ago, and she didn't have enough ready cash to catch the market on the rebound. To put it mildly, her financial situation was looking grim. She thought: *Please help me out here, Buzz.*

Chapter Twelve

Travis Cobb had to face the harsh light of day with only enough cocaine to do two lines—maybe three if he really stretched it. He was angry at himself for chasing his high last night with Peggy, his on-again, off-again girlfriend. She always seemed to show up and be nice as pie when he was holding nose candy, even giving him a quickie once in a while. But she would usually disappear when his stash ran out, even though she was supposed to pay him back by answering the office phone, doing a little cleaning, and whatnot. At least he'd gotten smart enough to stash a little coke that she didn't know about. And business had been real good at North County Towing this week, plus Travis had the five hundred Nicky had paid him for the illicit tow job. So buying more cocaine wouldn't be a problem—at least moneywise

He'd already left three messages on Hans Van Exel's answering machine, but the snobby dealer still hadn't returned his calls. This was typical. The stuck-up Dutchman's day rarely started before noon.

And the waiting was even more intense than usual because Travis was stressing over an important decision. After a lengthy mental battle that had given him a splitting headache, he had all but decided to reveal something about Nicky that Hans would definitely want to know. In the first place, Nicky had pissed him off by talking down to him like he was a stupid hired hand. And Travis Cobb, a successful businessman in his own right, didn't like that crap one bit. In the second place, Nicky had put him in an awkward spot with that nosey insurance investigator, causing him to cover his butt with the phony story about the Mercedes. Then the big-mouthed jerk had violated one of Hans Van Exel's cardinal rules, which was divulging the dealer's name to Travis. While Nicky had no way of knowing it, Travis had been buying cocaine from Hans for almost three years—well before Nicky knew the Dutchman existed.

Hans Van Exel was a sophisticated thirty-eight-year-old from Amsterdam who made a ton of money employing America's primary capitalistic tools—supply and demand. He bought cheap denim from Taiwan and traded these popular products to the Russian mafia for automatic weapons, which he promptly traded to a major Colombian cartel for pure, uncut cocaine. Hans survived by trusting absolutely no one and employing half a dozen big, mean bodyguards. He maintained a limited number of customers who bought large quantities, and he often delivered the coke himself to avoid relying on any of the idiots who frequently brought down the big boys by saying or doing something stupid. In addition, each of Han's customers had been thoroughly warned that there would be hell to pay if his identity were ever revealed.

Travis was talking to himself again, a habit he'd developed from working and living alone. "If I tell Hans about Nicky running his big mouth, maybe the Dutchman will give me a break on my next buy. But if Nicky finds out I ratted on him, he'll probably try to get back at me some way. And I know he packs a big gun. But that twerp did diss me like I was slime, and I would be scoring some major points with Van Exel..."

Travis jumped as if he'd been shocked when the phone rang. He snatched the receiver with his meaty paw and answered with hope in his voice, "North County Towing."

The frantic voice of an elderly woman rattling on about how she'd locked her keys in her trusty old Buick let the air out of his hope balloon. Travis said, "Yeah, yeah, alright lady. I'll be over there in few minutes."

Travis slipped on his windbreaker that advertised NORTH COUNTY TOWING in bold letters on the back, and *Travis* stitched inside a red oval above the left front pocket. It was the same food-stained jacket he wore whenever the temperature outside was anywhere below 90 degrees.

On his way out to his tow truck, he stopped, slapped himself on the forehead with the heel of his thick hand, and went back inside to get the keys he'd left lying on his desk. This delay gave him the extra seconds he needed to hear the phone ring. He dove across the paper-littered desk to grab the receiver. "North County Towing."

Van Exel wondered why Travis sounded like he was out of breath but didn't bother to ask. He didn't want to talk to the blubber butt any longer than he had to. "Hello Mr. Cobb, this is Hans with Van Exel Tires. I'm calling to let you know I have some excellent new Michelins in stock."

Travis's voice turned unusually cheery. "Hey, Hans, I'm glad you called. I could really, really use some new tires today."

This business call became even less convincing when Hans asked, "How many tires do you need? I can bring them by your place around six o'clock this evening." Each tire was actually a quarter of an ounce of high-quality cocaine, each little plastic baggie costing five hundred dollars. "I need two tires today, Hans, and I'd appreciate it if you could bring them by a little earlier today. I'd sure like to get the delivery by around three o'clock if you could."

Hans hated it when these junkies tried to rush him. He paused to collect himself, then replied with the politest voice he could fake, "I'll see what I can do for you, Sir."

Unbeknownst to the addict and his dealer, a TS&T computer automatically recorded the call and traced it to a residential number in the affluent town of Belvedere.

Even though it was already a few minutes past noon, Buzz drove out to the Sea Lion Cove Estates with hopes of taking Julie to lunch. He opened the door to the sales office, leaned his head inside, and called out, "Anybody home?" He was a little surprised when Julie didn't immediately respond but went on inside anyway. When he still didn't see her, he called out a little louder, "Julie? Are you here?"

Buzz could tell something was bothering Julie when she came out of the restroom wearing a look of stoic resolve. Her smile seemed forced. "Hi, Buzz. To what do I owe the pleasure?"

"I had to pay a visit to one of my less ambulatory clients in Tiburon, so I thought I would take advantage of the opportunity and steal you away for a quick lunch."

"I'd like nothing better, but I'm still running this office by myself. A new salesman will be here Saturday, and a new secretary is coming next Monday, but that's not helping at the moment."

"Don't you have one of those *Be back in an hour* signs you can stick in the window?"

Julie sighed, and said, "I'm waiting for a three-thousand-dollar check, and, as you've probably noticed in my bank statements, my cash isn't flowing so well at the moment. I desperately need to deposit the check in my escrow account."

Buzz didn't dare touch a discussion regarding bank statements. "I'm in no real hurry. I can wait if you like."

Before she could respond, Nicky Ghilardi, dressed completely in black, came barging through the front door. He slammed it shut with the heel of his cowboy boot, gave Buzz a cursory glance, then stomped over and twirled an envelope toward Julie, as if he were doing her a huge favor. "There ya go, Lemmon. There's the damn closin' money you was buggin' me about.'

When she opened the envelope and carefully studied the check inside, he asked, "What's the matter, don't ya trust me?"

She shook her head slowly from side to side. "Not even a little bit."

Nicky's face flushed, highlighting his acne scars. He turned to Buzz and asked, "Would you mind waitin' outside, pal? Me an' Miss Lemmon has got us a little business to hash out."

Buzz wanted to laugh at Nicky's phony cowboy act, but he shrugged and said, "No problem. I'll be waiting outside, Julie."

As soon as Buzz had closed the door, Nicky pressed his fists on top of Julie's desk and leaned toward her. "It ain't nice to talk to me like that in front o' people." His beady eyes narrowed in the shadow of his black cowboy hat. "An' if you don't start sellin' somethin' real soon like, Miss Smartmouth, you're goin' to be packin' up your stuff an' movin' on outta here, real pronto. Remember, you gotta sell two houses a week to keep up your end o' the sales contract."

Julie was not amused by the cowboy act, and her anger easily surpassed his. "Where are you coming from, Nicky G.? We're not having the open house until Saturday, which is the first official day of our contract."

Nicky chuckled. "I'd like to buy you for what your worth an' sell you for what you think you're worth. You're even too stupid to read the fine print. The contract was effective the minute you signed it."

Julie wasn't about to let him browbeat her, even though she was growing more concerned by the minute. "Okay, have it your way, Nicky G. I'm sure I'll close at least two sales this weekend."

Nicky stood up and rounded the brim of his hat with both hands. "You'd better, Lemmon, 'cause I'm holdin' you to every word o' that contract."

Buzz watched the pear-shaped cowboy stomp out to his Mercedes, slide in, slam the door, and then accelerate away as fast as the powerful car could go.

It was easy to see that Julie was on the verge of tears when he went back inside. He tried not to show it, but he felt his own anger heating up. "I take it that was Nicky Ghilardi?"

Julie nodded as she blinked back tears. "Excuse the expletive, but yes, that was the ugly son of a bitch."

"I take it you two are not on the best of terms."

"You might say that." She opened one of the desk drawers, fished through it for a few seconds, and then raised both arms, shouting, "Voila!" She'd found a sign with a clock printed on its face, and at the bottom large bold letters read, *BE BACK AT:* She set the moveable red hands on the cardboard clock for 3:00 p.m., then with a sultry voice, said, "Take me away, my handsome prince."

Netanya's mood had visibly soured by the time Keno entered her bedroom, more than two hours after he'd left for the Data Dungeon. "Is this a preview of how it's going to be when we get married? Are you going to let Daddy occupy all your time?" She rested her hands on her hips and glared. "He has a way of being really, really controlling."

Looking more than a little spent, Keno's head spun from the vast amount of information it had absorbed in a very short period of time. "Yeah, I did happen to notice, and I think it's a genetic thing that runs in your family." He sat down on the side of her bed and patted a spot next to him.

She scowled to let him know she was still miffed but sat down anyway. He put a big arm around her shoulders, squeezed, and kissed her forehead. "Your dad's business is really fascinating, Tanya, but you will always come first with me."

"It's a good thing I do, or you wouldn't even be here."

Keno frowned, unsure how to react to the ribald double entendre. "I think I'm hooked up with one nasty-minded babe."

She reached up and nipped his ear lobe, inflicting a quick stab of pain. "If I've become depraved, it's all your fault.'

He rubbed where it hurt, and said, "I might as well get an earring. It's already pierced."

She smiled devilishly. "Want me to do the other one?"

He wrestled her down on the bed and kissed her tenderly. The kisses that followed became progressively more passionate. "My mind is fried, but I've still got enough energy left to..."

She wriggled out from under him, then made a curious face. "Did you know that something like eighty percent of all the women on the planet have their period within five days of each other?"

Keno turned on his back and stared at up the dramatic ceiling. "Did you know that ninety percent of beautiful rich babes with big brown eyes and freckles are really full of it, and that you're in the top one percent of those?"

She punched him on the shoulder. "You mess with me, Bub, I'm really going to bite you hard." She bared her teeth and growled. "Someplace where it really hurts."

He pulled her close and kissed her. "I don't know why, or how, but talking about women's statistics reminds me that I haven't been spending enough time with Millie."

Netanya gave him an affectionate squeeze. "Yeah, I'm sure Millie needs you."

Keno said, "Yeah, Millie needs me, Simon needs me, and you need me, and I guess that's a good thing. But at the moment, I'd just like to blank out. All that business stuff with your dad was totally intense. Let's kick back and watch a stupid movie or something, and then I'll go home and take care of Millie."

"Sounds good, Bubba."

"So, I'm Bubba now?" He paused before adding, "You've really got a thing with names. And what's up with Abba and Motek? I noticed that's what you and your dad call each other."

"It's a Hebrew thing for daughter and father. Daddy has called me Motek for as long as I can remember, and I've called him Abba since I was a little girl."

"You want to play games with names, I think I'll shorten Motek and call you, Mo, from now on. Like in, Mo Money."

"Okay, I give. No more silly names." She wriggled her eyebrows, and added, "Unless I come up with a really good one."

Buzz let Julie vent for most of the hour they spent having lunch at La Cantina in Mill Valley. By the time they'd returned to her sales office, she'd regained some confidence. His hinting that he wouldn't let her lose her sales contract had definitely helped, though her venting about Nicky's behavior had added to Buzz's already low opinion of him.

When Buzz called Timothy as he was driving away from the sales office, the big man reported that he hadn't seen one fisherman all day. Buzz told him to wait another hour or so, then return early in the morning—maybe 5:30 a.m. Timothy was anything but an early riser, but he reluctantly agreed.

The next call was considerably more interesting. A TS&T com-op described all three of Travis Cobb's calls to Hans Van Exel's answering machine, and the return call that discussed the "tire delivery". Buzz instructed the com-op to contact him immediately if either Travis or Hans called the other again. He glanced at his watch, then aimed the Beamer toward Novato.

When he hobbled into the old Victorian, Keno found Millie passed out on the couch. A quick inspection of the freezer told him that his mother had been into the super-chilled Stolichnaya again.

Guilt flooded Keno's thoughts as he envisioned his poor mother grieving there all alone. "I'm sorry, Mom. I won't let it happen again." This commitment reminded him that there would be a constant demand on his time from now on. He whispered an amended promise, "I'll really, really try to make sure you're never here alone again."

His caring words seemed to penetrate the heavy fog encompassing Millie's mind. Her eyelids fluttered a little as she felt for his hand, and the hint of a smile tugged at the corners of her mouth. When she sat up, she bit her lip so hard that it drew a little blood. Panic visibly inflicted its torture as she cried out, "Oh, my God!"

"What's the matter, Mom?"

"We're supposed to be at the Redwood Mortuary at seven o'clock for the Wake Service."

Keno had only attended one Wake Service in his life, and that was several years ago when one of his teachers had died unexpectedly. All he remembered about it was the anguish engraved on the mourners' faces and the musky scent of lilies. "I'll tell you what, I'll call Father Sartori and tell him that you're so overcome with grief, you can't make it. He'll understand."

Millie stubbornly shook her head and said, "But Frank won't." She forced herself to stand on shaky legs, and then worked at collecting herself. "I just couldn't live with myself. Besides, I'm ashamed enough already." As she wobbled toward her bedroom, she turned and looked back over her shoulder. "I'm going to shower now. And you be ready by six-thirty. We're not going to embarrass your father by not attending."

Keno thought her "embarrass your father" remark bordered on the absurd. "Okay, Mom, if you can do it, I definitely can."

Buzz parked at the 7-Eleven on the opposite side of the street from North County Towing. He'd positioned himself close enough, and with just the right angle to observe the office and the overhead metal door. He could also see Travis's neglected one-story house in the back.

Only an older model Honda was parked in front of the office, and a quick drive-by revealed that the car belonged to a customer who was inside buying a battery. Buzz thought of calling to have a team member bring him a less conspicuous car but decided against it. He was reasonably sure that Travis hadn't seen his Beamer when he'd paid his earlier visit posing as an insurance investigator. The last he'd seen of him on that day, the fat coke addict was heading for the Men's Room, most likely for a nerve-settling blast.

Buzz went inside the 7-Eleven and got a cup of coffee, then sat in his car with his cell phone glued to his ear in case anyone grew curious about his lingering. Still, Buzz didn't worry too much about that part of his job. He'd learned that honest citizens are generally oblivious to things going on around them. Paranoia is much better acquainted with the corrupt.

Hans called to tell Travis that he would be there by five o'clock. Within seconds, a com-op at TS&T called Buzz to impart that interesting bit of information.

The Dutchman arrived at 4:47 in a silver Corvette that didn't look like it could haul very many tires. Hans slowed to a crawl, and then he gave three quick beeps of his horn. Travis had the metal garage door rolled down and the office locked in little more than a minute. Hans parked the Corvette behind the block building and met Trevor at the front door of his house, and then the odd couple went inside to complete the transaction. In less than five minutes, Hans was cruising away in the Corvette. No tires were off-loaded

Buzz drove up the street, made a U-turn, and parked alongside the North County Towing building where there was no chance his car could be seen from inside Travis's house. He sat there for a minute, allowing enough time for the coke addict to go to work on his new buy. Buzz knew that an important part of an addict's pleasure was preparing for that first good hit—a lot like foreplay. He climbed out of the Beamer, prepared to give Travis an unwelcome surprise.

From out of nowhere, a beat-up Volkswagen came sliding to a stop in front of Travis's house, and a thin peroxide blonde got out. Apparently, she'd been conducting her own stakeout, and had waited for Hans to leave. She stopped to snap the elastic of her panties away from her behind, brushed down her mini-skirt with nervous-looking palms, then went bounding up the steps.

Buzz decided that he'd put his plan on hold. Let the cokeheads indulge a little—all the better to induce paranoia when the time was right.

A couple of minutes later, Buzz looked around to make sure no one was watching before he hurried onto the front porch. He listened for a moment, then leaned over and peeked in the living room window. White powder, obviously cocaine, had been placed on a mirror on the coffee table. Buzz knew something about coke measurements, and it looked as if Travis had spread out about three grams. He could see that Travis and the bleached blonde, each holding a red straw, were leaning back against the sofa with their heads tilted dramatically. Buzz assumed they were each drifting into the drug's fantastic, almost orgasmic, nether world.

Buzz pounded hard on the front door and shouted, "Police! Open up!" The mad scramble taking place inside told Buzz his actions were cruel and unusual, but he needed results, and he needed them quick.

He shouted again, louder. "Open the door or we'll break it down!"

Travis cautiously opened the door a couple of inches to see what in the scary world was going on. That was all Buzz needed. He slammed the edge of the door into the bridge of Travis's nose, then barged into the room. Travis landed hard on his butt, stunned and nearly unconscious.

Obviously freaking out, the young woman, Peggy, wrapped her skinny arms around pencil-thin legs, curling herself into an ungainly ball.

Buzz reached down with one arm and placed Travis in a half-nelson, then jerked the fat man to his feet and flung him onto the couch beside Peggy.

With a telltale ring of white powder glued to his left nostril, Travis looked up at Buzz with terrified eyes. "What the hell?" It suddenly occurred to him that he'd seen this man somewhere before. "Hey, wait a minute... I have seen you before... but you wasn't crazy then." Travis's dimmed mind searched until the pieces came together. "You ain't no real cop. You're that nosy insurance investigator."

Deepening lines on Peggy's pale forehead telegraphed her confusion. "If you ain't no real cop, why'd you come busting in here? And what the hell are you hurting Travis for?"

Buzz narrowed his steel-blue eyes and barked, "I need information, Travis, and I need it ten minutes ago."

Travis glared, as if considering whether to attack this crazy intruder, but then paused to rub his aching shoulder. "What kind of information?"

"I need to know where you towed Nicky Ghilardi's Mercedes."

"That's it?"

Buzz nodded, and replied, "That's it."

Travis's face took on a sudden rush of relief. "If I tell ya, will you get the hell outta here an' not come back?"

"You have my word on that."

Travis shook his head from side to side, almost studiously. "How good is a man's word two minutes after he breaks into your house pretending to be a cop?"

"I guess you'll just have to trust me.'

"And if I do, I ain't gonna get hassled by no more cops?"

"No, you're illegal habits, however disgusting, are not my concern."

"Okay, mister, since I ain't got much choice anyway, we got a deal. But you gotta keep this between us. Rattin' on Nicky could get me shot." When Buzz nodded again, the fat man continued. "I hauled Nicky's wrecked Mercedes out to their place on Lucas Valley Road, an' then put it in the old barn."

Buzz remembered to ask, "What did do with the keys?"

Travis frowned, desperately trying to remember. "I'm not sure, but I usually put keys behind the left front tire of cars after I tow 'em. That's prob'ly where that key fob is."

As Buzz turned and headed for the front door, Peggy unleashed her fury at this revolting man who had ruined her high and freaked her out. "And don't you come back here no more you phony, or else I'll, I'll..." Frustrated, she turned to Travis and began to pummel him with her fists. "How could you let that son of a bitch barge in here like that? Ain't you got no balls?"

Hans didn't often derive pleasure from his work, but he was going to enjoy making this call. Of all his disgusting clients, he disliked

Nicky Ghilardi the most. When Nicky grunted, "Nicky G.," on his cell phone, Hans couldn't resist a derisive little chuckle. "Hello, Mr. Ghilardi, this is Van Exel Concrete Company calling."

Nicky's voice instantly perked up. "Hey, I'm glad you called, pard, I was just about to call you. I'm goin' to need two yards of concrete delivered as soon as possible."

Hans chuckled again. "No can do. I'm out of the concrete business."

Nicky was stunned. "What? What the hell you tellin' me? You're goin' outta business?"

"No, dummkopf, only the concrete business. Somebody has been running their big mouth about my contracts. And when that happens, I close down that particular business."

Nicky forgot to use the pathetic code. "I don't know what you heard, or where ya heard it, but you got it wrong, Hans. I ain't told nobody nothin' about your dealin'."

Nicky's stupidity annoyed Hans more than it usually did. "Don't call me again, Mr. Ghilardi, or your family will be reading about how you suffered a terrible accident."

"Don't threaten me, you Dutch Boy kraut. I got big time connections. I'll take ya down."

"Goodbye, Stoopnagle." Hans chuckled again as he put an end to Nicky's desperate ranting with a click of his cell.

Nicky's mind raced, wondering who had ratted on him. Then he realized that he'd only told one person about Hans, and that one person was Travis Cobb, the fat tub of a tow truck driver. He didn't know how, when, or where, but he'd get that slob for this. However, there was a more immediate concern demanding his attention, and that involved satisfying the relentless Mr. Jones.

He came up empty after checking every one of his secret hiding places. All he had to his name was the one lousy gram he always kept in the Mercedes in case he hooked up with a broad. He wanted to kick himself for stashing so much coke in Biker Boy's saddlebag—especially for all the good it did. Then he had a sudden flash of recall while trying to remember the name of a dealer a hooker had told him about recently. He'd left an eighth of an ounce at Julie Lemmon's place the night before the accident. When he'd gone there to pick her up, he'd taken the coke inside to try to turn her on, but she wasn't going for it. They did have quite a bit to drink, though, and he hadn't wanted to take the chance of getting nailed with that much snow in his car. He'd made her stash the coke for him with the idea of getting her blind drunk and coming back later to nail her.

Nicky punched in Julie's number, which was answered on the second ring. His mentioning her name automatically activated a computer at TS&T. "Hey, Julie, it's Nicky G. What's goin' on?"

The cheerful voice set off every alarm in Julie's suspicious mind. "I'm doing okay, Nicky G. What do you want?"

"I need to come by your house later tonight to talk about some business."

"What do you want to screw me out of this time?"

"Don't be like that. I know I been comin' on a little strong lately, but, hey, business has been kinda slow. Ya know? It can cause a guy to say mean stuff an' act worse than he usually would."

Even more suspicious, Julie asked, "Where are you going with this, Nicky G.? I know you well enough to know that you're not calling me to apologize." She paused a moment, then asked, "What do I have that you want? Or more specifically, need?"

"That ain't right, Julie. You shouldn't diss me like that. I just wanna come by your place tonight and talk a little business."

Julie chuckled with audible disdain. "It just occurred to me, Nicky G., that your business is not only little, it's so trivial that it can be wrapped in a small plastic baggie."

"Yeah, okay, ya busted me, Lemmon. But I still need ta come by an' get it."

Julie saw the opening and pounced. "Sorry, Nicky G., but your stuff is all gone. I got depressed about you taking away my commission for the Wertz deal. In fact, I was so upset that I got carried away and snorted every bit of your coke. And by the way, it was some dynamite stuff."

"You better not have snorted my stash, bitch.'

"Or what, Nicky G.? You'll call a cop?"

"I'm coming by your place tonight at nine o'clock. You better damn well have my stuff ready when I get there."

His tone added fuel to her disgust. "I'll have it ready if you agree to give me my commission on the Wertz deal and agree not to hold me to the starting date on my sales contract."

"Your askin' a lot, ya ungrateful broad."

"Apparently you don't have a lot, or you wouldn't be bugging me."

Nicky surrendered. "Okay, I'll give you half a commission."

"And the sale counts toward my contract."

"Yeah, yeah," Nicky fumed. "I'll see you at nine tonight."

Livid that he'd been outsmarted, Nicky slammed down the phone. After a minute of stewing, he decided to vent some of his anger—he'd get back at the arrogant Dutchman. He dialed Wertz's number, then provided the appreciative deputy with more than enough details and specifics to arrest Hans Van Exel for dealing vast quantities of cocaine.

Wertz liked the idea of doing some real police work for a change. His professionalism had been wanting lately, to put it mildly. It would be good for his career, as well as his ego, to present the glory-seeking sheriff with a significant lead on a major drug trafficker.

Within minutes of Nicky ending his call to Deputy Wertz, Buzz was on his cell—listening to the tape the TS&T com-op was playing for him. He suffered mixed feelings as he listened to every word spoken between Nicky and Julie, and then those between Nicky and Deputy Wertz. Buzz wasn't exactly thrilled to learn that Julie had been with Nicky the night before the incident, but he was pleased to learn that she wasn't a coke addict. On the downside, however, he realized that she would be committing an illegal act by profiting from an exchange of a controlled substance—even though she technically wasn't dealing.

This meant that he couldn't set up Nicky at her place, though it did present him with a different opportunity.

Millie put on a brave face as she and Keno stood by the door, greeting the scores of friends and acquaintances who'd come to honor Frank at the Redwood Mortuary. Pained expressions and teary eyes revealed the sorrow the mourners felt for Keno and the distraught widow. But no one could completely grasp the terrible toll Frank's death had taken on them.

The magnificent casket holding Frank's body had been placed front and center in the large nondenominational prayer room. Millie knew her husband had friends of every persuasion, probably even an atheist or two, and she hadn't wanted anyone to feel left out.

Millie clutched Keno's arm with both hands as they stopped at Frank's casket before taking their seats.

Keno couldn't help thinking how handsome his father looked—someone had done an amazing repair job. He was thankful that this viewing would be the picture carved in his memory, and not the battered face he'd witnessed on the day of the accident. Keno bowed his head and closed his eyes, praying with all his might that their souls would someday soar together in Heaven. But gazing at the lifeless, wax-like body soon sent an agonizing helplessness swelling through him. The reality of his father's loss created a vast emptiness, holding only heartbreak and grief. He felt Millie go limp beside him, and it was all he could do to help her find a seat. They sat down and pressed their heads together, each wanting to share the other's inescapable burden—the permanent loss of irreplaceable love.

When Father Sartori concluded his moving prayer service, he asked if anyone in the large congregation wanted to speak. The response was more than he'd bargained for. Sister Margaret, waiting nearby, steered her electric wheelchair to the podium. "Hello, everyone, thank you for being here tonight to honor such a fine man. I'm sure others will

want to speak, so I will be brief. Eight years ago when I contracted
M.S., I had a beautiful flower garden. I was especially fond of my
yellow roses, but my disease soon prevented me from taking care of
my yard that, no pun intended, was going to pot. I don't know how
Frank learned of my predicament, but he came to my rescue. He
replaced all of my plants with evergreens, and even put in automatic
water feeders. He refused to take a penny for his trouble. He said,
'If you have any extra money, give it to your favorite charity'" She
paused to wipe away a few tears sliding down her sunken cheeks.
"And every Thursday morning, I would find seven yellow roses by my
front door"—she paused to sniff and blink back tears—"but I won't
anymore." Sister Margaret lost her battle with the tears and almost
blindly powered her electric wheelchair away.

A small old lady, pushing ninety but still surprisingly agile, climbed
up to the podium and leaned close to the microphone. She crossed
herself and said, "Hello everybody, my name is Maria Ambrosini. God
be with you tonight." She frowned, as if trying to remember what
she was going to say, then continued "It used to be us Dagos that did
all the work here in Marin County, and then it was the Okies, then
it was the Negroes, and now it's the Mexicans. And the Mexicans
owned all the land in the first place.

"But that's all beside the point. I like to burn firewood in my
fireplace, but my granddaughter told me I was causing pollution,
and I didn't want to cause no pollution. Then that good man, Frank
Flores, fixed it. Starting about five or six years ago, he would bring
me a load of dried oak that don't pollute 'cause it don't smoke much.

"But that's not what I came to tell you. Last year when I was
adding some wood to the fire, I tripped and fell. I hurt my hip real
bad. And when I fell, I knocked some big coals out of the fireplace
with the poker in my hand. The coals started a fire, but I couldn't do
nothing about it 'cause I couldn't move, and the fire just kept getting
bigger. Then lucky for me, Frank showed up just in time. He was like
a guardian angel that came to save me. He carried me outside, then

went back in and put out the fire. Frank saved my life, but he made me promise not to tell anybody. He was a great man. Thank you. God bless you." Mrs. Ambrosini crossed herself before stepping down.

Keno doubted that it was a matter of luck. He suspected that Frank might have foreseen the old lady's predicament before it had even happened.

Next, a thin, pale man almost skipped to the podium. "I should start by saying that I'm not Catholic. I don't even go to church, but I guess I'm a Christian in my own way. No matter, I felt like I had to tell you folks what a wonderful man Frank Flores was. I was his barber for eleven years, and you get to know a man pretty darned good when they come in every other Wednesday like clockwork. Our relationship started off on the wrong foot because I accidentally nicked Frank's mustache the first time I trimmed it. And he never let me touch it again. He was a very particular man that way. But back to the point, Frank talked me into opening at eight o'clock in the morning instead of nine like I always did. He didn't want a haircut to take so much time out of his day. Now I didn't used to do much business on Wednesday morning. But when Frank started coming in, entertaining everybody with his cheerful way, pretty soon it was like a meeting place every Wednesday morning. And not just every other Wednesday either.

"Business got so good that I had to hire another barber. And then that barber introduced me to his pretty sister, who is now my lovely wife and the mother of my beautiful children. When I tried to thank Frank for making my life so good, he told me that if I had any extra money, give some to charity, and I've been doing that ever since." Mr. Hanson tilted his head toward the casket, and said, "Bye, old pal. We're sure going to miss you down at the shop."

A stunning young Black lady turned a few heads as she gracefully strode down the aisle to the podium. "Hello, I'm Lawanda James. God bless each and every one of you as we've assembled to pay tribute to the most wonderful man I've ever had the privilege of knowing."

She stared out at the congregation, gathering the courage to share her exposé. "Six years ago, I was hooked on crack and had alienated every relative and acquaintance I had. Then one morning I woke up on the floor naked in a crack house in Richmond. The sun was beating down on me through the window, like a light shining down from Heaven. Praise the Lord. For some reason, I took it as a sign. I slipped on an old dress and just started walking without any idea of where I was going. And in a little while, Frank picked me up and took me across the bridge to San Raphael. To be honest, I was shocked when he didn't try to hit on me." She made an appreciative face, and said, "I like to think he was my guardian angel. Anyway, Frank dropped me off at the door of Saint Elizabeth's. One of the nuns took me in, cleaned me up, and gave me something to eat. She asked if I knew how to do any work, and I told her that the only real job I ever had was working in my aunt's flower shop when I was seventeen. Of course, I didn't tell her that I had stolen money from my aunt to buy crack and that she'd run me off.

"But getting back to the point, the nun introduced me to Frank Flores without knowing that he was the very man who brought me there in the first place." She shook her head for emphasis. "The world just ain't that small. I know that God led me to him."

She wiped away a few tears and went on. "He set me up with a little flower stand at the mall. He even made it legal by getting permits and whatnot About all I had to start with was one picnic table and one beach umbrella. Then Frank would take me with him every Thursday morning at 3:00 a.m. to the wholesale warehouse in the City to buy flowers for the week, which, of course, he had to front me for the first month or so. I'm happy to say that it only took one year after that to lease my own shop. I can't even begin to tell you how indebted I was to Frank, but the only repayment he would accept was my promise to give some of my profits to a charity called Wayward Girls.

"I have a husband and a daughter now, and we own two flower shops with a busy delivery service called Flowers Express. We're a happy Christian family, and we owe it all to Frank Flores." When she glanced at the casket, she lost her resolve and went hurrying to her husband's comforting arms.

A short, stocky man marched to the podium. He paused to collect himself, then said, "Hi, I'm Gino Matteri. Frank was my best friend, and I only hope to God that he thought of me as one of his best friends, too. I first met him at Pop Warner football practice around twelve years ago. My kid and his kid played on the team, but his kid, Keno there, was a lot better than mine. My poor Tony couldn't help it because he was handicapped with my short legs. Anyway, I hit it off with Frank, and at the time there was me and three other guys who'd go duck hunting up by Bodega Bay every year. I invited Frank to go with us, so he buys himself a brand-new Remington twelve gauge, like he was really serious about hunting. Then every year for the next ten years, the rest of us always bag our limits, but Frank never drops a bird. Not one single bird in all those years.

"So last year I bought a bunch of decoys at a yard sale, and I take 'em with us when we go hunting. This one Saturday morning, me and the other guys had bagged several birds, but there was nothin' else comin' over so we kicked back and had a couple beers. That's when I get the bright idea to teach Frank how to shoot. I pointed to a decoy out about twenty yards and bet him five bucks he can't hit it. Bam! He blows it to bits. I tell him five bucks more on the next decoy out about thirty yards. Same thing. Bam! He blows it to pieces. This went on 'til I'm down fifty bucks. So I see a decoy out there about seventy-five yards that I know I can't hit, and I'm a real good shot, so I tell him double or nothin'. And you know what? He blows it right out of the water. It cost me a hundred bucks to learn that Frank was a crack shot. He just couldn't bring himself to kill nothin.'

"On top of that, Frank made me stop on the way home to give the hundred bucks to some homeless guy we saw walking alongside the road. Then Frank talks me into giving the guy a ride, and before you know it, I'm giving this guy a job. And now he's the best worker

I got." Gino shook his head, and then gave the casket a little wave on his way back to his seat.

A slender Japanese man came to the podium and politely bowed at the congregation. "I, too, am not of the Catholic persuasion, but I think we will all agree that a person must have love in their heart to reach anyone's concept of Heaven. With this in mind, I am sure Frank Flores has gone to his. When I first came to Marin County, I was worried that Frank would not appreciate my business ambitions because I intended to compete with him for many landscaping jobs. But he quickly put my concerns to rest, for I am nothing but a glorified gardener while he was a true landscaping artist. One might compare my work to that of a housepainter and his to that of Rembrandt.

"When I first started, my work was pathetic compared to Frank's, and he took pity on me. One day, out of the blue, he stopped by one of my jobs and offered me a sample of his Milagrozo mulch. In no time at all, my flowers were blossoming beautifully, and even my prized Bonsais loved a special blend of the stuff. Thereafter, he would sell me the Milagrozo mulch at a very reasonable price, though part of the deal was that instead of paying him for it, I was to give the money to my favorite charity." Mr. Mikado pressed his hands together and bowed his head toward Frank's casket, openly honoring his friend. "Sayonara, Franksan."

A tall man nervously hurried to the podium, giving the impression that if he were to slow down he might chicken out. Wearing a brand-new suit with a white shirt, too tight in the neck because of his big Adam's apple, he grabbed the podium with long fingers that revealed faded tattoos on his knuckles. "Hello, I'm Larry Kubiak. I just want to tell you all how Frank changed my life, and that affected a lot of other people who I'm enjoying life with now. I was a low-down common thief before, and now I'm straight. I used to steal just out of habit. Then one day about nine years ago, right after I got out of prison for the third time, I was desperate and went down to the corner by Third Street where all the day workers hang out, hoping somebody would hire them. Frank pulled up and asked me if I was willing to do an honest day's work for an honest day's pay. Well I didn't have a lot of choices.

"We went up by Sebastopol and cut up limbs and gathered leaves from fruit trees, then loaded it all on a big trailer. It was some really hard work, but there was something about working with Frank that made me enjoy it. And that was a brand-new experience for me 'cause I'd never done a hard day's work in my life. But it made me feel real good when we got done that day.

"Then Frank put me to work mowing lawns and trimming things that he didn't have time for. He said he had more business than he could handle, so he got me started doing jobs for myself. Now I have three employees that Frank brought to me, all ex-cons, and we take care of yards all over the county. And I always tell my men what Frank told me: 'Do an honest day's work for an honest day's pay.' And like some of the others that talked here tonight, I give a little something to charity to show my appreciation for Frank changing my life." With that, Larry Kubiak lowered his eyes and hurried back to his seat.

The only other time Hector Garcia had worn a suit was at his wedding, some thirty-five years before, but the stocky man's face took on a determined look as he marched to the podium. He didn't bother to introduce himself. "I know that pride is one of the seven deadly sins, but I must confess that today I am a very proud man. I am proud to say that Frank Flores was my boss and my friend for many years. Me and my son, Luiz, are not the sharpest shovels in the shed, but Frank always treated us good and respected us like men. Even though I am older, I always looked up to Frank like a big brother. And Luiz and I know something that probably nobody else knows. Every Thursday morning when Frank got back from the flower market in the City, either me, him, or Luiz would take flowers around to some special people, and we would put flowers on a few special graves, too. That was all Frank's idea, and he made us promise us not to tell anybody."

Hector paused to rub his eyes with his knuckles and took a deep breath. "A lot of macho men have trouble saying the word *love*. They think saying it will make you look weak, but love is a very strong word." Hector bowed his head, paused a moment, and then said, "I loved Frank Flores with all my heart." He turned toward the casket and said, "*Vaya con Dios*, Jefe."

Daryl Slate, the muscular fullback for the Cal Bears, was fighting back tears with rapidly blinking eyelids. He glanced up once, then focused his attention on the podium. He spoke almost as fast as he blinked. "Hi, I'm Daryl. I play football with Keno Flores. In fact, Keno's my best friend. Cal's got a good team now, which Keno really contributed to, but we didn't win too many games his first year. And after every game we lost, Frank would take a bunch of us out for pizza to cheer us up. And it always worked. Frank used to say something I'd heard lots of times, but it was just an old cliché when anybody else said it. But when Frank said, 'It isn't whether you win or lose, it's how you play the game,' you totally believed it." Daryl lost his battle with tears as he glanced toward the casket. "Frank knew how to play the game."

Sister Ruth affectionately patted Daryl on the shoulder and took his place at the podium. "I, too, am greatly indebted to this wonderful man, but I'd rather read you a poem than speak of my personal story." She adjusted her bifocals, opened a somewhat tattered old book, and said, "I cannot read this poem without thinking it was expressly written for Frank Flores.

"It's titled Drop a Pebble in the Water, by James W. Foley.

"Drop a pebble in the water: just a splash and it is gone: But there's half-a-hundred ripples circling on and on and on, Spreading, spreading from the center, flowing on out to the sea, And there's no way of telling where the end is going to be.

"Drop a pebble in the water: in a minute you forget, But there's little waves a-flowing, and there's ripples circling yet: And those waves a-flowing to a great big wave have grown: You've disturbed a mighty river just by dropping in a stone.

"Drop a word of cheer and kindness: just a flash and it is gone: But there's half-a-hundred ripples circling on and on, Bearing hope and joy and comfort on each splashing dashing wave Till you wouldn't believe the volume of the one kind word you gave

"Drop a word of cheer and kindness: in a minute you forget: But there's gladness still a-swelling, and there's joy a-circling yet, And you've rolled a wave of comfort whose sweet music can be heard Over miles and miles of water just by dropping one kind word."

Sister Ruth clutched the book to her breasts as she turned away.

Chapter Thirteen

Buzz scanned the Ghilardi house with binoculars while slowly cruising down Lucas Valley Road, and he was immediately impressed by the big U-shaped dwelling. A broader scan with the binoculars located the black Mercedes sedan that Nicky had been driving recently. Buzz carefully surveyed the six-foot electric cyclone fence surrounding the property but didn't see a single break in it. Added to that negative, a big Doberman appeared to be roaming free. He glanced at his watch and saw that it was 8:23 p.m., which meant that if Nicky Ghilardi intended to keep his appointment with Julie he would have to be leaving the house within a few minutes.

Buzz parked in a secluded area about twenty-five yards from the main gate, then got out and opened the Beamer's trunk. He retrieved a military-type backpack, which contained meticulously stowed equipment. As he lay in a grassy ditch beside the road waiting for Nicky to leave, he toyed with the idea of calling Hans Van Exel and telling him that Nicky had ratted him out to the Sheriff's Department. This would probably be the quickest way to rid the world of this ugly blot on society, but he realized that Nicky's elimination would make it harder to expose the cover-up and clear Keno of the fabricated charges. Most of the information he'd garnered couldn't be used in a court of law. Besides, it would take some of the fun out of making Nicky squirm.

The black Mercedes came speeding down the asphalt road so fast that Nicky had to slam on the brakes to avoid smashing into the gate. When the two-piece gate opened just far enough, the big car roared through. Buzz alertly jumped to his feet and slipped through the automatically closing gates. This was an unexpected bonus; he didn't have to use the electronic frequency finder he'd brought to open it. His night-vision goggles also proved unnecessary. The full moon was doing an excellent job of lighting up this peaceful, rural setting.

Finding the old barn in the field couldn't have been easier. The slightly listing building reflected an almost phosphorous light as it stood vigil over some very large earth-moving equipment. As Buzz moved from one piece of heavy equipment to another, he thought: *This is almost too easy.* However, the sudden appearance of a ferocious-looking Doberman, boldly standing between him and the barn door, caused a quick retraction of that optimistic notion.

Buzz had seen the dog during his drive-by and had come prepared. He retrieved a wand-like instrument from his backpack and gave it a quick twist. Knowing that he possessed the latest stun-gun technology instilled a certain amount of confidence, but not as much as he would have liked. He extended the wand and cautiously approached the stubborn animal, who was emitting a deep-throated growl and spilling lathered drool from its curled lips.

The big dog suddenly pounced with bared fangs, its menacing teeth flashing a brilliant white in the limited light. Buzz reacted just in time, zapping the powerful canine with 50,000 volts while it was still airborne.

Buzz breathed a sigh of relief when he saw the stunned animal fall to the ground, unconscious and twitching. But his relief was short-lived. As he approached the barn door, about to open it, another big Doberman sprang at him from out of the shadows. It buried its teeth into Buzz's defensive forearm and tried to rip away a mouthful of flesh. The intimidating dog only released its grip when Buzz zapped it with the 50,000 volts. He gritted his teeth and instinctively grabbed the bite wound. He held onto his forearm for a long minute, hoping the intense pain would subside, but it stubbornly persisted. Feeling a little faint, he slid up his sleeve and raised his arm for a closer look. The good news was that the bleeding was sterilizing the wounds. The bad news was that the puncture wounds were going to need medical attention, and soon. He took off his black turtleneck and then his T-shirt, which he tore into strips to create a makeshift bandage.

Realizing time was of the essence, he hurried into the barn, found the key fob behind the left front tire, then opened the driver's side door of the wrecked Mercedes. He took out his penlight, flashed the circular light over the steering wheel, and then played it back and forth across the front seat. Thankfully, the interior hadn't been cleaned.

Buzz only needed a few seconds to decide on the items he would take, but first he needed photographic evidence. He located his digital camera, already loaded with high-speed film, and snapped a series of pictures. He began with the front license plate, took several of the body damage, and finished with interior shots, which included close-ups of the airbags. Next, he used his Swiss Army knife to slice off a piece of the airbag that dangled from the steering wheel. He put this revolting piece of vomit-covered plastic in a large baggy, then placed this crucial piece of evidence in his backpack. As a final precaution, he opened all four doors, super-glued the locks in the down position, and, after closing the doors, super-glued all the keyholes. He hadn't thought about what to do with the key fob, so he just put it in his backpack and took it with him.

Both dogs had regained consciousness by this time. Still stunned and confused, they seemed content to just lie and watch as Buzz hurried into the night.

The phone beside Buzz's bed unleashed its annoying ring at 6:15 a.m. While reaching for the demanding instrument, the pain shooting up his left arm advised him to use the other hand. He finally managed, "This is Buzz."

The shrill voice didn't need to identify itself but did anyway. "Hey, Buzz, it's Timothy."

Buzz tried to shake out the cobwebs as he glanced at his clock radio. "I hope you have a good reason for calling this early, Timothy."

"Well, sure I do. You don't think I'd just...?"

Buzz cut him off when he realized the call was a consequence of his own making. "Okay, I know. What's up?"

Timothy was trying his best to sound professional. "Two Asian types entered the shed at the end of the old pier approximately four minutes ago, no, make that five minutes ago. It took me a minute to find your number."

"Are these fishermen still in the shed?"

"No, they are loading fishing gear on the boat, the one with the outboard motor." Timothy hesitated, then continued in a whispering monotone. "They are now tipping the outboard motor into the water... They are now pulling on a rope and trying to start the motor... Whoa! It started! What should I do? I don't think I can intercept them..." His voice raised an octave while adding, "Now I know I can't intercept them. They're backing the boat away from the pier. What should I do?"

Buzz felt a headache coming on. "Okay, here's what you do, Timothy. You drive over to the west end of the San Rafael-Richmond Bridge and watch to see which way they go. If they head north, drive over to Ghilardi Drive at the Sea Lion Cove Estates. If they're there and stop in the cove to fish, watch them until they're ready to leave. Then call me and I'll meet you back at that old pier where we can intercept them."

"What if they turn south or go east?"

Buzz's cheeks ballooned as he blew out a breath. "In that case, just go back to the old pier and wait for them to return. When they do, try to detain them. But if you can't, just follow them home or wherever they decide to go."

"Should I use force to detain them?"

Buzz frowned at the thought of the big Teddy bear getting physical, but he knew that would never happen. "No, don't use force, Timothy. In fact, don't even bother to detain them. Just observe them and call me."

"Gotcha, Chief."

After the call ended, Buzz stretched his jaws to make room for an irrepressible yawn. He'd slept three hours at most, and the thought of turning over and getting back to sleep was more than a little tempting. But he knew that was out of the question, especially when fragments of last night's events began to swirl in his mind.

It had taken a couple of hours and a few lies to get his puncture wounds bandaged and a tetanus shot administered at Marin General Emergency. He'd told the doctor that a stray dog had attacked him when he'd pulled off the road to check a tire, and then had to elaborate on that lie by insisting that there wasn't any risk of rabies because the dog was wearing a collar with current tags.

After escaping with a lie about returning for outpatient care, Buzz had made a quick trip across the bay to a chemical testing laboratory in Emeryville. Exhausted, but wanting to get the information as fast as he could, he'd roused a grumpy technician who surreptitiously worked for Buzz's employer. It took about an hour for the cantankerous technician to determine that a nasty mix of tomato sauce, hamburger, pasta, beer, and blood was glued to the slice of airbag that Buzz had taken from the Mercedes. Perceptible quantities of cocaine were also found in the revolting mess.

Still holding the phone, Buzz glanced at the clock radio, shrugged, and punched in a private number. "You probably aren't enjoying getting this call so early, old pal, but we've got to move fast on this one.

Clay's voice was surprisingly pleasant considering the time. "Good morning, Buzz. What's so pressing?"

"We've got a Code Red situation in the Flores case. Nicky Ghilardi's wrecked Mercedes wasn't in the county impound yard where it was supposed to be, so I had to track it down. I found it in the old barn at the Ghilardi Ranch, and good news for our side, the steering wheel's airbag was still covered with a disgusting mess of dried vomit. I cut out a section and took it to our friendly lab in Emeryville, where the tech got positives for beer and cocaine. Now the car needs to be moved to a secure location, someplace where that evidence can't be destroyed."

Clay's surprise came through in his voice. "Good work, Buzz. But I'm amazed that this incriminating evidence wasn't already destroyed."

"Yeah, I hear you," Buzz agreed. "Ghilardi must have forgotten about it, or he didn't think we'd find it. Or maybe he's just stupid, which gets my vote."

"I'll petition the court to grant an impound order for testing purposes," Clay informed him. "But I won't mention your discoveries, which I assume are inadmissible. However, it is reasonable to argue that our experts have the right to determine if that Mercedes contains evidence pertaining to the cause of the accident, and that the opportunity to perform the necessary tests is in jeopardy."

Buzz was too tired to explain that his super-glue might make it a little harder to eliminate the evidence. "Can you get it done this morning?"

"I'll be meeting Judge Krueger the moment he arrives at the Marin County Civic Center."

Buzz said, "The ball is in your court, old buddy," and then rolled over and closed his eyes. As he drifted off, he thought: *A good general always relegates, which means having somebody else do the dirty work whenever possible.*

Keno woke to the wonderful aroma of Millie's breakfast cooking. He glanced at his watch lying on the end table and saw that it was already 8:20 a.m. He stretched, sat up, and looked around for his crutches. He went to the bathroom, and then hopped his way back to the kitchen.

"Good morning, Mom."

"Good morning, Sunshine. I'm sorry, but I don't have any Canadian bacon. You're going to have to settle for some good old Jimmy Dean sausage with your French toast."

"I guess I'll just have to tough it out." He sat down at the kitchen table and studied her for a moment. "You're looking good this morning."

Millie grimaced as she turned to face him. "Didn't you leave off 'considering that you made a fool out of yourself by getting blind drunk yesterday'?"

"Don't go there, Mom. We both know how hard this whole thing has been to deal with. Besides, nobody's perfect. We all deal with pain in our own way."

"I was certainly feeling no pain by the time you came home yesterday."

"Let's talk about something more positive."

Millie forced a pretentious smile, and said, "Such as…? We're going to have a wonderful funeral today?"

Keno blew out a breath of exasperation while searching for something positive. "That was an incredible wake last night."

"Yes, it was very moving."

"It was totally cool to hear all those people say so many good things about Frank. I guess you could call him a closet philanthropist, always doing nice stuff for people without wanting anybody to know about it."

Millie's face took on a distant look. Her heartache had evidently migrated to a distant place, somewhere beyond tears. "None of it really surprised me."

Keno wondered if his mother knew anything about Frank's paranormal powers, or even suspected that he had them. "Is there anything else we need to do?"

Millie shook her blonde mane. "I don't think so."

"Is there anything you'd like to do this morning?"

Millie stared off into space for several seconds, as if searching for an elusive answer. "Yeah, there is something I'd like to do. Sometimes when I used to get bummed out, Frank would take me for a drive over to the coast. We would sit there and watch the waves break until I got around to letting him know what was bothering me. He was so patient..." Her face took on a wistful look as her mind's eye traveled back through time. "Then sometimes we'd go wading at the edge of the surf. I just loved the smell of the fresh salt air..."

"That's a great idea, Mom. Let's take a drive over to Stinson Beach."

Millie patted his hand and said, "You're a good guy, Sunshine. Thank God you take after your father."

Nathaniel Clay was already at the Marin County Civic Center when Judge Krueger came trudging down the lengthy hallway. The judge carried a battered briefcase in one hand and had a raincoat draped over the opposite arm. He did a double take when he spotted the renowned criminal defense attorney waiting for him. "Good morning, Mr. Clay." He frowned and asked, "We have something on the docket?"

Clay moved closer to His Honor and walked along beside him. "No, Judge, I'm here because I desperately need a court order to impound the Ghilardi vehicle involved in the Flores accident."

"Really?"

"Yes, the Mercedes isn't at the county impound yard where we expected it to be."

The judge frowned while asking, "Where is the car now?"

"The Ghilardi property on Lucas Valley Road."

Clearly curious, Judge Krueger opened the door to his chambers and said, "Come on in." He hung his raincoat on an antique coat rack, dropped his briefcase by his desk, and flopped into his timeworn chair. He pointed to a captain's chair with a big, bony finger. "Have a seat."

Clay handed the judge the petition and the court order he'd taken the liberty of preparing, then took the proffered seat. "I apologize for interrupting your morning, Judge, but this is a matter of utmost urgency."

Judge Krueger studied the carefully crafted documents and then nodded matter-of-factly. "I don't see a problem with this. All the i's are dotted, and the t's are crossed." The judge's face suddenly took on a pensive look. "But let me ask you something, Mr. Clay. Why wasn't that car impounded on the day of the accident?"

"I made the mistake of assuming that it had been. That's standard procedure when a fatality is involved. But Deputy Wertz's accident report was misleading by omission. Since the accident occurred on private property, the deputy allowed Nicky Ghilardi to move the Mercedes from one piece of his property to a different one. And the deputy allowed this without bothering to include that little detail in his report."

The judge tugged on an earlobe while asking, "Do you think Deputy Wertz has gone out of his way to give preferential treatment to Nicky Ghilardi?"

"No doubt about it."

Judge Krueger signed the court order with a flourish. "Take this over to the sheriff's office. In the meantime, I'll call over there and tell them I want that car impounded."

As Clay reached for the court order, the judge cleared his throat and said, "On the other hand, what with expedited arraignments and rushed court orders, I would say that young Mr. Flores is getting some special treatment of his own. Let's face it, counselor, there's no way that young man could afford to obtain your services, unless perhaps you have a soft spot for football players."

Clay flashed a smile. "I did play a little ball at Oklahoma, but that has nothing to do with it. Joaquin Flores is a very fortunate young man with a prominent patron."

The judge arched his bushy eyebrows. "I heard it was Bernstein money."

"You heard right."

An ex-football player himself, the judge asked, "Oklahoma, huh? Were you fortunate enough to play for Barry Switzer?"

"As a matter of fact, I did." Clay smiled again before adding, "Defense, of course."

"You boys sure had some terrific teams in those days. After Bear Bryant, Switzer was one of the best coaches in the history of college football. And I believe the key to those good men's success was not being afraid to recruit boys of color, back when it wasn't a popular thing to do."

"No doubt about it," Clay agreed. "As well as being two of the all-time great coaches, Bryant and Switzer should be remembered for advancing the cause of minorities. I remember when Switzer came to recruit me at our house in Muskogee, Oklahoma, and somehow, the subject of race came up. My father told him that he was one-third Negro, one-third Cherokee, and one-third horse-trader. It amused Switzer so much that he practically fell on the floor laughing. That sealed the deal with my father, and I became a Sooner."

"One-third horse-trader," Judge Krueger repeated, then let go a chuckle that caused his wide shoulders to bounce up and down. "I'll have to remember that one. Well, it's been nice talking to you, Mr. Clay. Good luck with securing that vehicle."

"Thanks, Your Honor. I really appreciate your help."

Fifteen minutes later, Deputy Wertz tried to call Nicky but he wouldn't answer his cell. After four frustrating attempts he decided to call Yvette.

Yvette almost jumped out of her chair when the house phone rang. Nicky was about the only person who called her on it these days, and she knew he was still in bed.

"Hello... Who's calling?"

"This is Deputy Wertz and I need to talk to Nicky right away. He must have his cell turned off because it doesn't even ring."

"I really hate to disturb him..."

"This could be a matter of life or death," Wertz purposely exaggerated to speed things along. "Tell him to call me on his cell right now."

The exaggeration worked. Yvette replaced the phone and hurried into her son's bedroom to deliver the message. It took a lot of shaking to wake Nicky and convince him that he should talk to the deputy.

Nicky couldn't accept that the deputy had information important enough to require his immediate attention. He angrily through back his bed's expensive quilt, ran one hand through his tousled hair, clicked on his cell phone, and grumbled, "What the hell ya want, Wertz?"

"The sheriff is sending Deputy Drable and a tow truck to your place to impound your wrecked Mercedes," Wertz said with elevated concern in his voice. "They'll be there in less than an hour. I hope you got it cleaned out good."

"Don't sweat it. Right after we put it in the barn, I told my top spick, Javier, to get it cleaned out."

"If I were you, I'd double-check," Wertz advised. "It's too damned important to be taking any chances."

"Yeah, yeah, okay. I'll check it out right now."

Nicky slipped on a pair of Levi's, tugged on his cowboy boots, and put on a wrinkled cowboy shirt. He stopped by his office to get the bullhorn he'd taken to using when summoning his hired hands—all of whom lived in the old house. The workers had a telephone there, but the bullhorn made Nicky feel more in command.

He stepped outside his office, put the loudspeaker close to his mouth, and shouted, "Javier! Get your lazy butt over to the office. You hear me, Javier? Get your wetback ass over here right now!"

Javier had been cleaning rain gutters at the west end of the big house, getting them ready for the seasonal rains. But he threw down the trowel and came running when he heard the amplified voice. He almost tripped while sliding to a stop, took in a quick breath, and then addressed his young boss as he'd recently been instructed to do. "What do you want, Mister G?"

Nicky glared at him. "Did you clean out my wrecked Mercedes like I told ya to do?"

Javier cringed while shaking his head in the negative. "No, Mister G, we couldn't do it."

The unexpected reply stunned Nicky. "What the hell ya mean ya couldn't do it?"

"The dogs, Mister G. The dogs wouldn't let us do it."

"What?" His face growing redder by the second, Nicky raised his voice. "Did ya ask the dogs if ya could, and they told ya that ya couldn't?"

"No, Mister G, they wouldn't let us because their puppies are in the barn."

"Freakin' puppies? I don't believe this crap!"

Nicky shook his head and stormed back into his office. A minute later, the enraged young CEO came stomping out with his freshly loaded Glock 9mm in one hand and the bullhorn in the other. He commanded, "Come with me," as he passed the startled Javier, and then stomped down the hill toward the old barn.

Javier had worked for Big Nick for more than sixteen years, and he knew that the Doberman pinschers had long been his old boss's pride and joy. The dogs on the ranch were the fourth generation of a championship line.

Javier almost trotted to keep up with the angry young man who had become his boss and was making his life miserable. "Please don't shoot the dogs, Mister G. We will get your car cleaned out, and we will do it very, very fast."

Nicky stopped, glared at Javier, and then shouted into the bullhorn. "All spicks, listen up! I want every wetback on the place to meet me down at the old barn in two minutes." He paused, then shouted louder, "No, make that one minute. Get your burrito butts down there right now!" He turned to Javier and snapped, "Let's go get that damned car cleaned out."

Nicky soon spotted the male Doberman standing about ten yards in front of the old barn. While holding the bullhorn at his side, he stopped, aimed the Glock, and snapped off four quick rounds. One of the bullets barely grazed the dog's left hip, but after the run-in with the stun-gun, the big Doberman knew to scamper for the safety of the nearest D-9 Caterpillar.

The female's protective instincts were inherently stronger than her mate's. She stood in front of the barn door and growled a warning, but Nicky didn't break stride as he approached and began blasting away. He kept firing until the valiant dog yelped, went limp, and fell over.

Javier couldn't hide the surge of anger darkening his face. He rushed to the wounded dog, clearly not concerned about anything but comforting her.

Nicky jerked the barn door open and barged inside to inspect the wrecked Mercedes. When he saw that there was still a nasty mess inside the car, he turned and pointed the pistol at Javier, who was kneeling beside the wounded dog. "I should blow away your pea brain, Javier. Get your wetbacks in here and get this car cleaned out. And I mean now!"

Javier defiantly returned Nicky's glare as he cradled the wounded animal in his arms. "This is Big Nick's dog, and I am going to help her if I can." With that, he began to walk away with the female Doberman in his arms, determined to carry her up the hill to the old house.

Nicky shouted, "Stop, or I'll blast ya right in the back." When Javier just kept walking, he growled, "Just keep on goin' then, you stupid spick. An' keep goin' 'til you walk your worthless ass right off my property. You're fired!"

By that time, three Mexican laborers had reached the barn. Nicky realized that these young men had seen the shooting, and they had also seen Javier ignore his commands. Feeling the need to regain control, Nicky waved the pistol and shouted, "Get the hose from that high-pressure washer beside the barn an' clean out the inside of this car. An' don't worry about hurtin' anything inside of it. Just get that freakin' mess cleaned out."

The youngest of the laborers, most likely illegal and desperate for a job, scurried to get the hose. A second laborer shrugged his shoulders with resignation, then went outside to start the high-pressure washer.

The remaining worker reached out to open the car's front door but discovered it was locked. When he asked for the keys to open it, Nicky realized he didn't have them. Then he vaguely recalled Travis Cobb telling him about putting the key fob behind the left front tire. When the key fob wasn't there, Nicky ordered the anxious laborer to get down on his hands and knees and search around all the tires. But, of course, there was no key fob to be found.

While contemplating his next move, Nicky realized that time was growing short. He knew a spare key fob was in his office desk but couldn't remember exactly where. Then he asked himself: *Who the hell can I trust to go rummaging through my desk? I sure as hell don't feel like running all the way up there.*

While considering his options, he stepped closer to the wrecked Mercedes and glanced inside. He saw that a small section had been cut out of the steering wheel's airbag, and then he noticed the reflection of something shiny on the door's keyhole. He felt it with his finger, then shouted, "Freakin' glue! Somebody's been messin' with my car!"

He turned and glared at the workers, one holding the nozzle attached to the end of the high-pressure hose and another waiting for instructions. "The hell with it. Somebody bring me a can o' gas." When the laborers just stood there exchanging confused looks, he shouted, "Can't you spicks understand English? I said somebody get me a can o' freakin' gas!"

The youngest worker scampered outside and soon came trotting back with a five-gallon can.

Nicky tossed the bullhorn out of the barn's door, stuffed the Glock in the waist of his Levi's and grabbed the can. He twisted off the spout, then doused the wrecked Mercedes with the pungent liquid, leaving just enough gas in the can to leave a trail in the thin layer of straw covering the barn's wooden floor. Like a man possessed, he spilled a narrow ribbon of gas all the way to the door

Nicky felt a strange sense of elation while gathering a handful of straw and then taking out his lighter. But just as he was about to light the straw, the eldest of the three laborers cried out, "Alto, Mister G. *Los perritos!*"

Nicky scowled. "What the hell ya talkin' about?"

A different laborer shouted, "Los perritos! The puppies! They are still somewhere in this barn!"

Torching the straw and watching the flame grow in his hand, Nicky snarled, "Ta hell with them perritos," and flipped the blazing straw toward the gas trail. A blue and orange flame snaked its way to a pool of gas puddled beneath the wrecked Mercedes. A ball of fire engulfed the car and sent a blast of searing heat roiling toward the open barn door.

Nicky and the three Mexicans turned and ran as fast as their feet could carry them. Behind the ball of flame came a dense cloud of black smoke billowing out of the barn door.

When the female Doberman had chosen the old barn to birth her litter, she had dug a hole beneath the barn's siding; she instinctively knew that she would need a way to get in and out. Now, like something out of a Disney movie, the male Doberman was at the access hole barking at the puppies—his way of letting them know that they needed to escape. Then, one by one, the chubby little six-week-old pups came scampering out through the hole. Terrified, they ran in circles around the male until he managed to herd them away from the smoke-belching barn.

Holding the pistol in one hand and the bullhorn in the other, Nicky stood watching the barn with disappointment etched on his face. The car's tires and rubber hoses had caught fire, and black smoke continued to belch out of the barn door, but there was very little in the way of flame. He kicked the ground with a boot and grumbled, "Dammit, anyway. I was hopin' for a helluva lot more than..."

Just then, the car's gas tank exploded, shooting flame through every crack in the barn's shingled roof. The ground shook beneath Nicky's boots as the explosion blew massive holes in the barn's roof and sent splintered planks flying off its sides. In a matter of seconds, a roaring blaze engulfed the old barn as if it were a giant stack of kindling. Absorbed with the bright and glimmering shades of yellow and orange, Nicky grinned and said, "Now that's what I'm talkin' about."

When Deputy Drable saw the old Ghilardi barn engulfed in flames, he slammed on the squad car's brakes and was almost rear-ended by the closely following tow truck. The deputy immediately called the dispatcher to report the situation. He instructed her to call the fire department, then put him through to the sheriff.

When Drable asked for further instructions, the sheriff told him to proceed to the Ghilardi property and see if this had anything to do with the wrecked Mercedes. Then he should find out who, or what, had started the fire.

Nicky's devious mind had gone to work, planning a cover-up within seconds of the big blast. He waddled up the hill to the replacement Mercedes parked in front of his office, jumped inside, and sped over to the old house.

Once there, he trudged up the steps and stomped inside. He gritted his teeth and forced a pretentious smile while approaching Javier. In the nicest voice he could muster, he asked, "How's the dog?"

Javier had placed the female Doberman on the kitchen table and was sterilizing her wounds. Without turning around to look at Nicky, he replied, "You hit her three times. I think the most serious wound is the one that hit the top of her head. It made her unconscious." Straining chords in Javier's neck and pronounced veins standing out on his forehead exposed his seething anger, but he stoically continued to prepare the wounds for bandaging.

Being ignored angered Nicky to his core, but he desperately needed Javier's cooperation. He didn't know if any of his other laborers were legal or if any of them even spoke passable English.

"I'll tell ya what, Javier. I'll let ya fix the damned dog if ya do somethin' for me." When Javier turned enough to give him a questioning look, Nicky explained, "I need ya to tell the law that you saw Tomás Martinez set the barn on fire an' then take off runnin'. Tell 'em that Martinez was mad as hell at me for firin' him the other day."

Both men knew that Tomás Martinez was a young illegal who had been fired last Monday afternoon for taking a siesta after lunch—something he'd been doing all his life. Javier paused a moment to give the request some thought, then leveled an unyielding glare at Nicky. "I will lie for you, Mister G., but only if you let me take care of Big Nick's dogs. And that includes the mother, the father, and all the puppies. Also, I will need a pickup truck to take Cleopatra to the vet."

Nicky seethed at Javier's blatant disrespect. Then he realized that the puppies had probably been fried to a crisp anyway. That prospect forced him to suppress a smile; it seemed like reasonable payback for this Mexican's disrespect. "Sure, no problem, Javier. You can take care of all the dogs ya want if ya tell everybody that Martinez started the fire."

Javier hung his head a little, clearly ashamed that he had agreed to lie. "I will do it for you, Mister G. Now leave me alone. I have more bandaging to do before I can take her to the vet."

"Alright, but you just take her there an' come right back. I want ya here when they start askin' questions."

As Nicky sped the Mercedes back to his office, he noticed that the barn's fire had passed its peak; the flames were only flaring up about ten feet now. A longer glance told him that a squad car and a tow truck had arrived at the main gate. And he knew it wasn't Deputy Wertz because Nicky had given him one of his push button gate openers. This observation initiated the first stage of panic.

Nicky's mind raced while driving back his office and then hurrying inside. He immediately called Yvette on the intercom. "Momma, come to the office as quick as you can." While waiting for his mother, he cracked the door open a little to spy on the deputy who'd climbed out of the squad car and was standing by the main gate. His heart picked up its pace—he'd soon have to go down there and open the gate for the deputy.

Yvette came rushing into the office with an anxious look. She'd seen almost everything her son had done but chose not to mention it. She was sure there had to be a reasonable explanation for such extreme behavior. "What is going on, Nicky? I heard the shooting, and then I saw the old barn going up in flames."

"They're gonna think I set that fire, Momma. But it was a spick I fired. He did it outta revenge. They're not gonna believe me, so you havta say that you saw a Mexican pour gas in the barn and set it on fire." Nicky gave his mother a woeful look and pleaded, "Would you tell 'em that, Momma?"

Yvette had questions but didn't really want to know the answers. "Of course, Nicky, I saw the whole thing. I just happened to be looking out the window when I saw a young Mexican man sneaking around the construction equipment. His behavior looked suspicious, so I kept an eye on him. He carried a can of gas into the barn, and a minute later, he came out and made a little straw torch. He threw the flaming straw on a gas trail that he had spilled on purpose, and, of course, that started the fire."

It crossed Nicky's mind that his mother seemed to know almost everything about the things he'd done; she'd described them in amazingly accurate detail. But that didn't seem important at the moment. He winked confidentially, and then climbed in the Mercedes to go down and open the main gate for the deputy.

A screaming fire truck pulled up behind the tow truck within seconds of Nicky opening the main gate. The deputy drove in and parked the squad car beside Nicky's Mercedes. The tow trucker driver took a long look at what was left of the wrecked Mercedes, waved with both hands, and drove away. A fireman drove the fire truck to a safe place about thirty feet from the smoldering barn's remains.

A few minutes later, the DA called J.P. Maloney. "Good morning, J.P., this is Jason Bridger. I hate to tell you, but I've just received some very alarming news.'

J.P. already knew about the alarming news. He had spoken with Deputy Wertz and had just gotten off the phone with Yvette. "Good morning, yourself, Jason. Does this call have anything to do with the idiot I've found myself in bed with?"

"If you're referring to Nicky Ghilardi, then I'm afraid you're right. Apparently, the sheriff sent Deputy Drable to the Ghilardi Ranch to impound the Mercedes involved in the Flores accident. The deputy discovered a blazing barn fire when he arrived at the ranch. And, surprise of all surprises, the targeted Mercedes was destroyed in the fire."

"I already heard, Jason." J.P. decided to throw out a life preserver to see how it would float. "Nicky claimed that a Mexican who ran off the other day burned down the barn. He supposedly did it out of spite."

Jason's chuckle contained no amusement. "And I'm supposed to believe that the Mercedes, containing who knows what kind of evidence, was destroyed in the process? Rather convenient, I'd say."

"Like the old saw, every cloud has a silver..."

"This could be serious," Bridger interrupted. "It's one thing for Nicky to destroy his own property. I could probably arrange for a misdemeanor plea and get him off with probation, community service, and counseling, which I'm sure he could use. But if this proves to be the willful destruction of evidence, he's put himself in an indefensible position that I can't ignore."

More times than he cared to recall, J.P. had considered the disastrous effects of a civil suit. If the truth came out about the Flores accident, Ghilardi Development could be financially crippled, if not mortally wounded. Now it looked as if Nicky had taken drastic steps to destroy damning evidence, which may or may not have been necessary. Nevertheless, it would be a financial disaster if the authorities could prove he did it. The old lawyer chose not to waste any more time with gratuitous small talk. "Let's put our cards on the table, Jason. We need to meet to discuss some very large campaign contributions. Your political ambitions will get a huge boost if you play ball, and I know you need cash for pressing personal obligations."

The receiver remained silent for several seconds. "I have plans for tonight, but I can meet you for lunch tomorrow."

J.P. wanted to tell the DA how much he appreciated his cooperation in the matter but couldn't quite bring himself to spit it out. "See you tomorrow then, Jason."

If not like a new man, at least Buzz felt like a well-rested one. He'd slept until 9:30 a.m., something he couldn't remember doing since college. He completed a rigorous workout, had a leisurely breakfast, and even got to enjoy reading quite a bit of the *Chronicle*. The grating phone warned that his peaceful morning was about to end. The soprano voice, needing no introduction, greeted, "Hey, Buzz, it's Timothy."

"What's up?"

"It just started to rain, so I guess the two Asians were winding it up for the day. They just put the outboard motor back in the water, and now they're trying to get it started."

"Okay, I'll meet you at the old pier. It will take them at least half an hour to get there."

"Oh, and you know what else, Buzz?"

"What else?"

"One of them is a female. She had on a hooded sweatshirt before, so I couldn't tell what sex she was. And a lot of those Asians are kind of little anyway. But when she pushed back the hood, I could tell it was a female."

Surprised, Buzz replied, "That's interesting."

"Oh, and you know what else, Buzz?"

Buzz couldn't restrain a sigh. "What else?"

"Sometimes when I'm surveilling people, I listen to the police scanner. Anyway, a little while ago, people from the sheriff's department were talking about a big fire at the Ghilardi Ranch. And that's quite a coincidence since I'm parked beside a street named Ghilardi Drive."

That information got Buzz's attention. "Thanks for the info, Timothy. Drive carefully and be nice to people."

As he sped the Beamer through the toll booths at the south end of the Golden Gate Bridge, Buzz found his cell and put in Clay's number.

"Yes, Buzz, what can I do for you?"

"Did you get the court order?"

"Of course. Judge Krueger was quite cooperative. In fact, I'm already on my way back to the City."

Buzz realized they would probably pass going in opposite directions when he asked, "I heard there was a big fire at the Ghilardi Ranch. Know anything about it?"

"No, I've been out of touch. I've been escaping with Beethoven's String Quartet Number 13 in B-Flat Major, Opus 130."

Buzz wished he knew more about music. "I'm on my way to intercept some fishermen who might have witnessed the incident on Ghilardi Drive. I'll check out the fire later."

"Good luck with the witnesses. Keep me posted."

"Will do. Drive carefully and be nice to people."

Buzz had to fight off a sudden urge to take the exit to Lucas Valley Road as he whizzed by but realized that potential eyewitnesses might prove to be more crucial than ever. Especially if Nicky had destroyed the incriminating evidence in the wrecked Mercedes.

When Buzz arrived at the old pier, Timothy was there waiting in his Suburban with the heavily tinted windows. The thought of killing time with the overly curious young man was not appealing. So Buzz momentarily escaped Timothy's barrage of questions by calling his friend at the Coast Guard and learning that the old fishing boat was registered to one Charles Chung. Whether this was one of the fishermen in the boat remained to be seen.

Ten long question-and-answer minutes later, the anticipated fishing boat came chugging up to the pier. It had begun to rain a little harder while Buzz launched the plan he'd formulated while waiting. He instructed Timothy to drive to the nearest point of concealment and, if necessary, be prepared to follow the car with the fisherpersons in it.

Buzz waited until the two potential witnesses had carried their catch into the old shed. He waited for several more seconds, then hurried to the plank door. He tried to open it, but it was obviously latched on the inside. He listened for a moment and then knocked on the door loud enough for those inside to hear, but not so loud as to frighten them.

A fisherman opened the door a little and peered out. He frowned, and asked, "Who are you, and what do you want?"

Buzz flipped open a leather I.D. holder that held an impressive badge and an official-looking I.D. with a recent photo. The I.D. read *Special Investigator*, though it didn't specify a particular agency. "Charles Chung?"

The man's expression revealed a mix of surprise and alarm as he stared at the gold-plated badge. "And you are, Mister...?"

"Aldridge."

"Have I broken the law?"

Buzz invited himself into the shed by pushing the door open wide enough to pass by the confused man. He let Charles Chung sweat for a minute, hoping a sense of relief would make him more cooperative. "Not really."

The Chinese woman, who looked to be in her early forties, came over and stood close behind Chung. She stared for a moment, then asked, "What do you want?"

While looking them over, Buzz decided they could easily pass for brother and sister. "I need to ask you two a few questions."

Chung seemed impatient. "We have fish to clean."

Buzz tried to appear friendly. "It's important and won't take much of your time."

"Then ask your questions while we work." With that, Chung hurried over to a large stainless-steel sink, modernly out of place, where four fish were waiting. He grabbed a big knife and began to whack off heads and fins.

The woman, who had taken up a position at his side, began to slit the fish open, clean out the insides, and then wash out the bloody slit with a nozzle attached to a small hose. When she finished with her part, she handed the fish back to Chung. He used a large pair of pliers to peel off the stripers' skin in two equal pieces and then finished the job by whacking off the tail.

It was obvious to Buzz that this efficient team had cleaned fish together many, many times.

Buzz had become so interested that he briefly forgot to ask his questions. But Chung gruffly reminded him to get on with it as he violently ripped off half of a fish's silver and speckled skin. "You have questions, Mr. Aldridge?"

"Were you two fishing in the Sea Lion Cove last Sunday?"

Chung glanced at Buzz, his stoic face not giving anything away. "And if we were?"

"If you were, I want to know if you witnessed a *deadly* accident that occurred that morning." Buzz had purposely added emphasis to "deadly," hoping for a reaction.

Appearing unmoved, Chung ripped off the other half of the fish's skin and then handed the peeled fish to the woman. "I don't recall seeing an accident, Mr. Aldridge."

Buzz turned his attention to the woman who was scraping a red substance off each side of the skinless striped bass, then giving them a final rinse. "What about you, Ma'am? Did you happen to see the fatal accident that occurred last Sunday?"

The woman remained bent over the sink while shaking her head. "I saw nothing."

Buzz had a gut feeling that she was lying; she wasn't quite as inscrutable as Chung. "By the way, what is your name, Ma'am?"

She frantically began to scrub her hands as if trying to scrub away the question.

"Ma'am? Your name, please?"

"My name is Mary."

Buzz fought back a smile—too quick an answer after so much reluctance. "Mary what?"

She wheeled and snapped, "None of your business."

Interesting overreaction, Buzz thought. Then he decided to employ a different approach. "I really don't care what your name is, or the reason why you don't want to reveal it. My only concern is whether either of you witnessed the accident at the Sea Lion Cove Estates last Sunday. If you did and are willing to testify to what you saw, there will be a large reward in it for you."

Chung crossed his arms defiantly and said, "We told you we didn't witness an accident, Mr. Aldrich. Is there anything else?"

An off-the-wall thought popped into Buzz's mind. "Why do you peel the skin off the fish?"

Chung flashed the briefest of smiles. "The red part under the skin of the striped bass is where their digestive waste is stored before it is expelled."

"You're saying it's kind of like their intestines?"

"That is one way to think of it."

This image made Buzz feel a bit queasy. He'd eaten striped bass many times, but he doubted anyone had peeled off the skin and cleaned off that red intestinal crap.

Buzz thanked them for their time, then went outside to his Beamer. Every professional instinct he possessed told him that both fisher-persons had seen the incident but, for reasons of their own, weren't willing to admit it. He called Timothy, parked about a hundred yards down the frontage road, and instructed him to follow the Chinese couple for the rest of the day, wherever that may lead.

Then his curiosity took over, and Buzz aimed the Beamer toward the Ghilardi Ranch—he had to know what happened out there.

On the way to Lucas Valley Road, he took stock of the case against Nicky—which appeared to be growing weaker by the minute. He spent some time dwelling on Julie's involvement in the cover-up and realized that other than Keno, she might be the only eyewitness he could produce. He also realized that there may come a time when he would have to choose between professional duty and this new infatuation. However, *infatuation* seemed too weak a word to describe his accelerating feelings.

Buzz slowed the Beamer as he approached the Ghilardi Ranch, then pulled over and parked at a decent vantage point. It was easy to see that his worst fears had been confirmed. Steamy wisps of smoke still curled up into the misting rain, creating an eerie scene. Most of the barn had burned down to its old concrete foundation. A few blackened, carbon-charred beams and posts provided the only evidence that it had once been a large wooden structure. Smoldering steel skeletons of nearby equipment provided testimony as to how hot the inferno had been. It took a close inspection with his binoculars to find the burnt metal remains of what had once been an expensive luxury car. Now the Mercedes was merely a large piece of junk resting among the muddy, gray ashes; its important evidence gone up in smoke.

Two fire trucks, a Marin County Sheriff's squad car, and Nicky's Mercedes were parked some thirty yards from the barn's remains. The firemen were busily putting away hoses and equipment, while Nicky and a deputy sheriff were down by the main gate. Buzz zoomed in with his binoculars and saw the deputy sitting on his haunches, touching a finger to the ground. The deputy held the extended finger close to his face to examine it and then nodded his head, obviously confirming a suspicion. Buzz immediately realized that the deputy had found some blood—his blood. Questions formed in Buzz's mind: *Why is the deputy looking for blood in the first place? Why hadn't he already arrested Nicky for arson and the willful destruction of evidence?*

A sudden downpour caused the deputy and Nicky to hightail it back to their vehicles, and this provided Buzz with a limited sense of relief. The blood evidence would be washed away, and with it all DNA proof that he'd been on the premises. The rain slowed to a steady peppering as Nicky and the deputy got into their cars. Nicky sped up the hill, and the deputy drove toward the main gate.

Buzz shook his head in disgust. He couldn't imagine why Nicky hadn't been arrested. Puzzled and angry, he drove away before the deputy could spot him.

Just as he was about to turn his car around, Buzz's cell phone jingled. He hit the brakes and swiped open his cell.

The soprano voice greeted, "Buzz? It's Timothy."

"What's up?"

"I followed the two fisherpersons over to Corte Madera and up the hill to a residential area. The male individual was driving a gray Toyota. You want the license number?"

"In a minute. First, tell me what happened."

"Okay, Buzz, they were traveling along at about twenty-five m.p.h., when all of a sudden, the male individual stops and lets the female individual exit the vehicle. She starts walking in one direction, carrying a plastic bag, which I'm guessing has fish in it, and he drives off in the opposite direction. I was going to call you for instructions but didn't have time. What I did was follow the female. Since I got the license number, I figured it would be easier to find the male individual and the gray Toyota later."

"Good thinking, Timothy."

Timothy said, "Thanks," then added, "I stayed back and watched the female walk two blocks to an intersection where she made a right turn. She went down about half a block and inside a really nice house. I wrote down the address. Do you want it?"

"Yes, tell me the address of the residence and the license number of the Toyota," Buzz replied, knowing that his TS&T techs would have the information on Timothy's cell recorded. After Timothy carefully conveyed the information, Buzz said, "Okay, Timothy, drive carefully and be nice to people."

Buzz called the duty com-op at TS&T and instructed him to I.D. the occupants of the female's house and the vehicle's registered owner, then aimed the Beamer toward the City.

The com-op had the information within three minutes. The vehicle was registered to Charles A. Chung, and the house was owned by Mr. Eugene Simmons and his wife, Lulu R. Simmons.

Buzz called Timothy, who was just pulling into a Denny's, and gave him Charles Chung's address. For lack of a better idea, he instructed the big man to enjoy his lunch and then go keep an eye on Chung. Buzz clicked off his cell while Timothy was shaping his next question.

As he drove toward his doctor's office in the City, Buzz called the com-op at TS&T and requested more detailed information on Mr. Eugene Simmons. As he assimilated facts pertaining to the Chinese couple, he took note that they'd gone out of their way to hide the status of their relationship. He decided this could only mean that they were having an affair, even if they did look like siblings. Their fear of exposure was undoubtedly the reason they didn't want to risk admitting they had witnessed the incident.

A couple of minutes later, Buzz learned that Mr. Simmons was a marketing executive for a large firm in the City and an avid golfer with a seven handicap. Buzz's next devious idea caused him to feel uneasy. Blackmailing nice people was always his last resort.

A few minutes later, a com-op called to inform Buzz that they had just finished recording a conversation between Julie and Nicky Ghilardi. Feeling a knot in the pit of his stomach, Buzz instructed the com-op to play it for him.

The recording exposed a sharp edge to Julie's voice. "Dammit, Nicky, you promised a check for six thousand today."

"Hold it a minute, Lemmon. Ya got it wrong, I ain't backin' outta the deal. Didn't I bring ya the three thou like I said I would?"

"That was closing money. It has nothing to do with our latest agreement on the Wertz deal."

"For your information, I just happen to have some very important stuff goin' on at the moment, Lemmon. A spick I fired the other day set fire to my ol' barn this mornin'." Nicky's voice sounded sad. "That ol' barn was really special to my family. It was built by my late grandpa."

Julie said, "That's a shame." Then asked with a softer voice she asked, "Was anyone hurt?"

"Nah, nobody got hurt, but the deputy sheriff found a trail of blood leadin' to my front gate. The spick who set the fire must o' cut himself while he was gettin' away."

"What about property? You lose anything of value?"

"Yeah, my favorite Mercedes, but insurance will cover it."

"Sorry about your loss, Nicky, but I would really appreciate it if you would bring me the check like you promised last night."

"Don't sweat it. I'll get it to you later today or the first thing in the mornin'."

When Buzz finished listening to the recording, he took a moment to analyze Nicky's story. The jerk was blaming some poor Mexican laborer he'd recently fired, and going by Deputy Drable's report, he assumed that people on the ranch were lying to back up Nicky's fabrication. Undoubtedly, his mother was one of them. And a worker named Javier had to be in on the deception, too. This turn of events had put another obstruction in his quest for justice, but in the meantime, he had to go meet with his employer.

Even though a cold squall had cut short their walk on the beach, Keno felt rejuvenated when they returned to the Cadillac. Millie apparently did too because she made it clear she wasn't ready to leave just yet. Searching for the right mood music on the radio, she asked Keno to idle the engine to keep them warm.

Seeing that his mother was blankly staring out at the raging breakers and not interested in conversation, Keno powered the seat back and closed his eyes. Sleep came quickly, and a realistic dream assumed control of his mind.

Strolling along on the beach, a sudden explosion of black dots, and a shimmering aura overwhelmed Keno's ability to see. Shocked and confused, he dropped his surfboard and kneeled down on the sand. A soft, golden glow swiftly surrounded the aura, creating a mystical cloud that seemed close enough to reach out and touch. Then images began to take shape and move about within the cloud. Mesmerized, he watched an implausible mini-movie unfold on a paranormal screen.

Swimming out toward the breakers, a teenage girl slipped through the waves with smooth, accomplished strokes. Suddenly, her head rose up out of the water as if she'd been attacked by something beneath the surface—something that inflicted intense pain. Her wide-eyed expression telegraphed her fear, and her mouth sprang open to unleash a scream that no one seemed to hear. She raised one arm and waved for help, then frantically beat the water with both hands—obviously fighting to the last racing heartbeat before going under.

When the vison faded, a flush of anxiety aroused an inner voice, which decisively instructed Keno to warn the same teenage girl walking toward the ocean. He ran after her and shouted, "Hey, you! Don't go in the water!" Getting no response, he shouted louder, "Wait! Something bad is going to happen to you!"

Two muscular men appeared from out of nowhere and pounced on Keno. When he tried to resist, one of the men punched Keno, knocking the wind out of him. Keno caught his breath and fought back, even landing a couple of punches of his own. But they soon overwhelmed him and pinned him down.

Now up to her knees in small waves, the girl turned to see what was causing all the commotion. When she saw what her bodyguards were doing to some poor guy, she shouted, "Stop that! I can't stand that kind of violence." A sharp pain suddenly struck the girl's abdomen, and she bent forward, as if someone had stabbed her with something sharp. She grimaced and clutched her right side, where her appendix threatened to rupture.

Keno woke with a start and mumbled, "Wow! That was incredibly weird." Then he remembered that most of the things in this dream had actually happened about five years before—his dream was a confusing flashback. Then he asked himself: *But how could I be dreaming about having a vision that told me to warn a girl not to go in the water? That most likely saved her life. But how would I know about her appendix? What's even weirder, the girl in the water looked a lot like Netanya. But remember, it was only a dream, and anything can happen in a dream.*

"Were you talking to me?" Millie asked while returning to her own reality.

Keno shrugged. "I guess I zoned out and was talking to myself."

"Are you alright Sunshine?" Millie asked with a look of concern. "You look like you've just seen a ghost."

Keno shook his head again to clear it. "I dozed off and had a really weird dream."

"You should try living in my head at night," Millie said with a weak attempt to chuckle.

"No thanks, mine's bad enough."

Millie patted his shoulder. "Thanks for bringing me out here today, Sunshine. I really do feel better." She sighed and added "But it's time to go home and face the music."

As they were about to leave Stinson Beach, Keno flashed on the eerie feeling he'd experienced the day Netanya had driven him there in her Ferrari. He recalled that her silhouette had triggered a sense of déjà vu. Keno grimaced while thinking: *Totally weird. But remember, it was only a dream.*

Keno knew that his mother had been to the church several times to celebrate mass with Frank. But like a growing number of places he lived close to but hadn't visited, Keno realized that he hadn't been inside the Church of Saint Raphael or the Mission San Rafael Arcangel. He climbed out of the stretch limo, which had parked on the street behind the matching hearse used to transport Frank's body. Then waited until Netanya had taken Millie's arm before hopping up the long flight of concrete stairs leading up to the church.

Keno felt a sense of awe as he stopped to look up at the magnificent edifice that exemplified elegant Spanish architecture. A large golden cross stood atop a blue, terrazzo tile-capped bell tower, which rose some fifty feet above heavy wooden doors. Just above the massive double doors was a beautiful stain-glass window, surrounded by an intricately clover-like cross carved from colorful wood. A recessed ledge above the window supported an impressive man-size statue of the Archangel, Saint Raphael.

Keno turned to his right and took a moment to study the more modest mission—a stucco and terrazzo building that closely emulated the original, constructed in 1817. However, later additions for the parochial school had made it vastly larger. A few brief flashes of Spanish-American history popped into his mind as he abstractedly tried to imagine what those people's lives might have been like nearly two centuries ago.

When Keno entered the church, the awe he felt while examining the exterior suddenly seemed insignificant compared to the sense of wonder consuming him. He slowly hopped down the aisle and absorbed the entirety of the church's beauty with a deep sense of reference. A magnificent life-sized crucifix, surrounded with marble and gold-plated candelabra, dominated the opulent hard altar at the far end of the church. Some twenty feet in front of that opulence was a stage-like altar covered with plush carpet. This was adorned with another large gold cross and the three largest candles Keno had ever seen. Fittingly, this altar was surrounded by a splendid array of floral arrangements.

He began to notice how much larger the church's interior actually was than it appeared from the outside. Four wide rows of seats looked to be—he often referred to lengths in yards because of his football mentality—at least thirty yards long. When Keno looked up, he saw at least a dozen huge, curved beams, which appeared to be made of solid redwood. Some forty feet at the zenith, they arched over at least a third of the church, hovering above the magnificent altars.

Keno and his mother sat together quietly for several minutes, waiting for the church to fill and the procession to begin. He glanced at Millie, who had closed her red-rimmed eyes. As they'd done at the Wake Service, they held hands and pressed their shoulders together, each gaining strength from the other.

Father Sartori and Father Garrity were outfitted in resplendent white robes, banded with purple and gold. Then came three cherubic altar boys wearing snow-white robes; the tallest of the three boys was carrying a large gold cross and the other two carried big candles. When those in the procession took their place on the carpeted altar, the casket—transported on a gold-plated gurney—was wheeled directly in front.

Father Sartori greeted the congregation and sprinkled the casket with Holy Water, a symbolic remembrance of Frank's baptism and acceptance of his faith. Then a white linen pall was placed over the casket, signifying a baptismal garment and Frank's life in Christ.

The hymns and Responsorial Psalm, led by the Cantor with an angelic voice, the prayers and a touching eulogy by Father Sartori all seemed like a distant ritual to Keno. However, it somehow became more personal when Gino Matteri read a verse from the Book of Wisdom in the Old Testament, and Lawanda James read a verse from the Book of Romans in the New Testament.

Keno and Millie, searching for consolation through faith, ignored Father Sartori's requests for the congregation to stand.

Both priests appeared to be surprised when, just before the Eucharistic Acclamations, Millie let it be known that she wanted to say a few words. It was quite unusual to interrupt the ritualistic Funeral Mass.

Millie didn't wear a lot of mascara, but most of that, which she'd applied a couple of hours earlier, was now streaking down her face. Her years of theatrical experience undoubtedly helped her to maintain control under such trying circumstances. She cleared her dry throat and began, "My son and I want to thank each and every one of you for being with us today. And special thanks to those who shared their wonderful experiences with us at the Wake Service last night. You see, I was not aware of Frank's exceptional generosity to so many people. I was married to the man for twenty-six years, but it seems there is a great deal about him I didn't know. Of course, I always knew what a good man he was; a wonderful man who was touched by the hand of God. Your celebration of his memory will always be ingrained in my heart. Now I'm going to ask that we share in this bounty of love. I would appreciate it if each of you would reach out to as many people as possible and say, *Peace be with you.*"

Millie tried to force a smile when the congregation began to do as she asked but failed miserably. She covered her face with her hands and hurried back to her seat, where Keno wrapped an arm around her heaving shoulders.

Keno tried to recall the significance of it when the priest waved a large ornamental censer to spread clouds of gray, aromatic incense. Then it surprised him to see a large share of the congregation file past to accept Holy Communion. The final refrain of the Communion Hymn penetrated through the agony and ingrained itself in Keno's mind.

After the Song of Farewell the priests and choir boys led the Recessional, following Frank's casket as it was wheeled along on the gold-plated gurney to the double doors. Once there, the pallbearers collectively hoisted it waist-high and carried it down the rain-washed concrete steps to the waiting hearse. More than one mourner observed that Luiz and Daryl Steele could have hauled the casket by themselves.

Saint Raphael Archangel's bells tolled as many of the mourners ran through the rain to get to their cars. A large number were willing to brave the weather and join the funeral procession winding its way to the gravesite. Some lingered inside the vestibule to chat, and still others decided to go down to San Rafael Joe's, as it was already a couple of minutes past 3:00 p.m., the scheduled starting time for the Celebration of Life reception.

Julie and Buzz were among those who lingered while deciding where to go next. When their searching eyes met, their heads simultaneously snapped back in surprise.

As Julie moved toward him, she asked herself: *What the heck is he doing here?*

Buzz, no doubt asking himself a similar question, closed the distance and smiled. "Hi, Julie. Nice to see you."

"You're the last person I expected to see today."

"Likewise," he replied with a slightly sheepish look.

Julie said, "I remember you asking me some questions about the accident last Sunday. Were you a friend of Mr. Flores?"

Buzz assumed a nonchalant look. "No, I'm afraid it's a little more pragmatic than that." He glanced toward Simon Bernstein, who apparently had chosen to linger with an old Jewish acquaintance, as evidenced by their wearing yarmulkes. Simon's, of course, was colorfully decorated with elaborate needlepoint. "Do you remember me telling you about my less-ambulatory client who lives in Tiburon?"

Julie's frowned, trying to remember. "Sort of."

"The man standing on an artificial leg is Mr. Simon Bernstein, whose daughter is romantically involved with Joaquin Flores, the deceased's son. But I'm sure you knew all that."

Of course, Julie had heard of Simon Bernstein. He owned the most expensive house in the county, and she had known that Joaquin was Frank Flores' son. "And how would that persuade you to attend a funeral for a man you didn't know?"

"Mr. Bernstein wanted me to stay close today. For the money he pays me, I'll sit in his lap if he asks me to." He made a guilty face before adding, "And I'll also admit to being a little curious."

The explanation sounded convincing enough. "I'm impressed. You must really have some expertise if you're giving financial advice to a billionaire."

"What about you? Why did you feel obligated to come?"

"Well, I was..." She caught herself from saying that she was at the scene when Frank was killed. "You know, it happened on our property. I mean the property I'm selling, of course. And I'd seen him around, and he seemed so nice..." She had to fight back a grimace while thinking: *What a way to start a relationship, dancing around the truth while standing in church.*

Looking a little puzzled, Buzz asked, "Would you like to join me for a cocktail this evening?"

Julie glanced at Simon. "Will Mr. Bernstein be joining us?"

"No, I'll be getting permission to leave pretty soon."

Julie smiled and said, "It's tempting, but I'd better not. We're having the grand opening tomorrow, and I've still got a lot of preparation to do."

"Call me if you change your mind?"

Wow, Julie thought, *he left his schedule open for me.* "Maybe Sunday, early evening?"

"Yeah, let's catch an early dinner this Sunday."

Buzz's cell phone rang as he was merging onto Highway 101. "What's up?"

The soprano voice exuded excitement. "Hey, Buzz, it's Timothy. I'm across the street from the Charles Chung residence, and you know what?"

"What, Timothy?"

"A really pretty Asian female, who's probably in her late twenties, just drove up in a blue Honda and went inside."

"She was really pretty?"

"She's gorgeous. Want her license plate number?"

This information lent mass confusion to Buzz's theory that Charles Chung and Lulu Simmons were having an affair. "Yes, and I want to know who this gorgeous female is."

After relating the license number, Timothy asked, "What do you want me to do now, Chief?"

"That's enough for today, Timothy. But it might be a good idea to check out the old pier tomorrow morning to see if Chung and Lulu Simmons are going fishing again."

Timothy's voice sounded tired. "How early?"

"If they go, I'm sure they'll be fishing at the Sea Lion Cove, so you don't have to be out there before eight."

Relief lowered the shrill voice a couple of octaves. "Thanks, Buzz; I'll be there surveilling them by eight tomorrow morning."

Buzz paused a few moments to consider his next move, then called his TS&T service to place an order for Ghilardi Development Corporation's telephone line at Lucas Valley Road.

Millie and Netanya each had a hand on one of Keno's big shoulders as he hobbled up the gentle slope toward the gravesite, joining the procession to the Place of Committal. Keno was surprised to see the casket resting on a platform, supported by a not-quite-hidden hydraulic lift. The area surrounding the grave had been covered with synthetic carpet, so much neater than anything he had envisioned. He wondered how Millie could have afforded the stone cross at the end of the grave. FRANK FLORES — Loved By All —was chiseled into the stone. Surprisingly, there were no dates. He realized Millie didn't know when Frank was born.

The rain fell harder as Father Sartori blessed the gravesite and performed the Prayer of Commendation. And there was no ceremonial dirt showering the casket. Instead, a long line of mourners passed by the grave, each offering the flower of his or her choice. The growing pile painted the scene with a beautiful array of colors. A fitting memorial for a man who had added so much beauty to the lives of others.

Millie could barely stand on her own, so Keno asked Netanya and Hector to help her down to the waiting limo. They understood when Keno said he wanted to spend a final moment alone with his father.

Keno stood there watching as the other mourners scrambled back to the shelter of their cars. With matted hair and drenched clothes, he waited to say goodbye to Frank for the last time. But when he turned toward the grave, he found himself looking at an amazing sight. The flowers on the synthetic carpet were wilting under the assault of the steady rain, but the flowers resting on the casket remained unblemished, almost as if bathed in sunlight, and looking so fresh they sort of glowed. As he watched, he felt something stir deep inside. That *something*, as if awakened by an emotional switch, came alive. Somehow, he knew this was a product of the special connection between a father and his son.

Flowing tears and rain soon blinded Keno. He whispered, "Bye, Dad. I'll do my best to live up to my promises."

When Keno returned to the waiting limousine, Hector gave him a powerful hug. The stocky man didn't try to hide his grief as he looked up and let the rain bathe his leathered face. "Every angel in Heaven is crying today."

Chapter Fourteen

Buzz had just taken his second sip of coffee when a TS&T com-op called to report that they had finished servicing Ghilardi Development Corporation's telephone line. The com-op also informed him that the attractive woman Timothy had observed entering Charles Chung's residence in Corte Madera yesterday was Chung's wife, Xian Li. The woman had emigrated from Taiwan to the U.S. a little more than a year ago, and she and Charles were married only four months after her arrival.

If Buzz had been attached to a curiosity gauge, the needle would have maxed out in the danger zone. His mind needed answers: *What's wrong with this picture? Charles Chung is a newlywed with a gorgeous young wife, yet he's hanging out with a plain, somewhat older married woman. If Chung and Lulu Simmons were related, my com-ops would have picked up on that. Is the threat of exposure still in the equation?*

A few minutes later, Timothy reported that the boat with the outboard motor was still tied to the old pier, and there was no sign of the Chinese fisherpersons.

Buzz had good reason to believe that Chung and Lulu Simmons had gone fishing early last Sunday. He would wait to see if they would be going again this Sunday before confronting them. He didn't want to jeopardize either's marriage without having all the facts. He told Timothy to take the rest of the weekend off—he would handle tomorrow morning's stakeout.

Buzz knew that, sooner or later, it would become necessary for Julie to divulge everything she knew about the incident. But before he confronted her, this delicate matter was going to need considerably more planning. This morning, he would go to the Marin County Sheriff's Department in San Rafael and examine Deputy Drable's report of the barn fire. Then he would go to Tiburon to meet with his employer.

Millie wasn't feeling well, to put it mildly. She'd had too much to drink at the reception, and then she'd sneaked three double shots of super-chilled vodka after Keno had gone to bed. Even so, she still managed to fix her son a breakfast that a famished lumberjack would have been proud to polish off.

When he'd finished, she sat down with Keno to have a cup of coffee. Trying her best to put on a brave face, she said, "It was a very nice funeral."

Keno could see that a vacant look had taken up permanent residence in his mother's eyes. Grief was visibly aging her, and the alcohol wasn't helping. Just as Keno agreed, "Yeah, it was incredibly nice," his new cell phone rang.

Keno greeted, "Hey girl, what's goin' on?"

Netanya's voice was devoid of its usual enthusiasm. "Daddy asked me to tell you he's going out of town tomorrow. He has a board meeting in Chicago on Monday but wants to discuss something with you before he goes." She paused before asking, "So what's up? Why does Daddy need to talk to you by himself? I tried to pump him, but he was almost secretive in a way he's never been with me before." She paused again before continuing with a chill in her voice. "I'm getting a little concerned, Joaquin. First, the two of you start spending a ridiculous amount of time together in the Data Dungeon, and now Daddy's acting all mysterious. I'm feeling totally left out."

Keno tried to imagine what Simon might want. But if his short association with his future father-in-law had taught him anything, it was that he should always have sound data before reaching a conclusion. "I have no idea, Tanya. My head is spinning with all the business practices he's been teaching me, but I have no idea why he wants to see me."

"We need to talk about how involved you're going to get with the *business practices.*"

"I think so, too. But the most important thing is to keep things good between us."

Netanya's voice perked up a little. "Thanks for saying that, Joaquin. I needed it. See you in a few."

As Keno replaced the receiver, it occurred to him that it might not be a good idea to leave his mother alone. He watched her stare into her coffee cup, slowly stirring the brown liquid with no sense of purpose. "You have any plans for today, Mom?"

She shook her head absently. "No, though I suppose I should spend some time cleaning this old house. It's been completely neglected since..."

Knowing that soon money wouldn't be a deterrent for just about any luxury, Keno interrupted. "Why don't you call a cleaning service? We can afford it."

"Are you kidding? Did you forget that I've lost my breadwinner?"

Keno considered telling Millie that he was going to marry the richest girl in Marin County but didn't want to break his promise. Besides, Netanya would want to be with him when he broke the news. "Trust me, Mom, we can afford it. We brought in more than five grand in receivables and are still in the landscaping business. Which reminds me, we need to meet with Hector and make some decisions."

Millie's face took on a curious look. "What about all the work Frank did at the Sea Lion Cove Estates? Can we collect on any of that?"

Keno made a mental note to ask Simon about acquiring the services of a good lawyer who specialized in civil matters. "You bet.

We're going to get every cent of that money, even if we have to sue." Anger flashed across his mind while considering the possibility of suing Nicky Ghilardi—he would rather settle things personally.

Millie's spirits noticeably brightened. "You know what, Sunshine? I think it's time I learned a thing or two about the landscaping business. I'm sure Milagrozo Landscaping has plenty of clients."

"That would be an excellent idea. It would keep the business going and keep your mind occupied. Hector and Luiz can do the fieldwork, and you can take care of the business end. We can set you up an office here at home, and I'll help out as much as I can. Plus, Hector knows how to make the Milagrozo mulch and a lot of other things."

Millie's eyes showed signs of coming alive for the first time since suffering her heart-wrenching loss. "Maybe we should go down to Frank's office this morning. We could get some ideas on how to get the ball rolling."

Keno felt bad about motivating his mother and leaving her hanging. "I'm sorry, but I already agreed to go over to Tanya's this morning. I guess I shouldn't have..."

She patted his hand while interrupting with: "Don't be silly. I'm perfectly capable of learning the basics by myself. I can begin by studying some of the information we found in those files. Lord knows there's plenty of it."

Keno said, "No, I don't want you to be by yourself right now. I'll call Tanya and tell her I'll be over later."

"That really isn't necessary, Sunshine. If you're that concerned, I'll call Gladys and ask her to go down to the Yard with me. She's always as worried about me as you are."

Keno studied his surprisingly upbeat mother for a few seconds before relenting. "Okay, but you have to call her right now and make sure she can go with you. Otherwise, I'm not leaving."

Millie carried the cordless phone to the kitchen counter, then made a show of dialing the number. A machine answered as Millie knew it would. Gladys had told her yesterday that she and Faye would be going to see her daughter in Santa Rosa. Millie held a pleasant discussion with a dial tone, even mixing in a little lighthearted banter.

After finishing her fake call, she smiled at Keno and fibbed, "It's all set. Gladys will be here in half an hour, so go ahead with your plans."

"Okay, if you're positive she's coming." Keno took the time to scribble his and Netanya's cell numbers on a Post-it note and stuck it to the fridge door. "If you need me for anything, just call either one of these numbers. I'll only be fifteen minutes away."

She pecked him on the cheek, and said, "Stop with all the worrying."

Millie had every intention of driving down to the Yard, but, of course, Gladys wouldn't be going with her. The cool, foggy aftermath of rain was lingering, so she put on her wool coat, picked up her purse, and started for the door. She opened the door just as a nervous young man pressed the doorbell—the timing couldn't have been better had it been rehearsed a hundred times. They both appeared petrified, each staring with startled eyes.

Awkward seconds passed before the man asked, "Millicent Elizabeth Flores?"

Millie was stunned. She couldn't recall anyone calling her Millicent Elizabeth since they'd announced her full name at her high school graduation many eventful years ago. "Yes, I'm Millicent Flores. What can I do for you?"

The anxious man handed her a subpoena, spun on his heels, and hurried down the front steps.

Retreating to the kitchen table, Millie put down her purse and opened the legal document. It boldly stated that Millicent Elizabeth Flores and Milagrozo Landscaping Company, et al., were identified as Defendants in a lawsuit. Ghilardi Development Corporation et al., herein named Plaintiff, was suing for the sum of $250,000. Millie's astonished mind lingered on the words, *Breach of Contract*.

She fought back an urge to rip the document to shreds while screaming, "You inconsiderate bastards!" The paper made a rustling sound as she placed it on the table with a trembling hand. She began to pound the table with the sides of her fists while shouting, "You killed my husband, injured and jailed my son, and now you greedy sons of bitches want everything that's left of my life!"

Her chest heaved as she fought for control. She entertained the idea of calling Keno, but what could he do? What could anybody do?

An urge to calm herself with a drink crept into her mind, then grew until it became a desperate plea. The plea intensified until it became an unyielding command. Millie found the bottle of Stolichnaya hidden beneath the lingerie in her dresser drawer. She hurried back to the kitchen where she splashed a double shot into a water glass and tossed it down. The harsh liquid burned her throat and set off a coughing fit. Wiping away tears with an index finger, she hurried to the refrigerator to get an ice tray. She slammed several ice cubes into the empty glass and poured a crystal-clear stream of vodka over them. While waiting for this liquor to chill, she placed the quart bottle in the freezer. If she were going to drink, she might as well enjoy it.

Deputy Drable happened to be sitting behind a desk when Buzz walked into the sheriff's office and introduced himself as an insurance investigator with Traveler's Insurance Company. When Buzz handed over a business card as proof, the deputy became almost embarrassingly cooperative. After providing a dramatic description of the blazing inferno that engulfed the old barn, Drable discussed the report in meticulous detail. He explained how Nicky's, Yvette's, and Javier's statements had convincingly placed the blame on Tomás Martinez, the recently fired employee. The deputy grew solemn while discussing the blood found at the scene. The rain had unfortunately washed it away before he could collect a decent sample for DNA testing. Drable then made a copy of the report for the convincing impostor.

Buzz found the most surprising part of the report to be the statement made by Javier, one of Nicky's hired hands. Buzz asked himself: *I wonder how Nicky coerced this long-time employee to tell such a blatant lie?*

As Buzz was about to leave, Deputy Drable informed him, "We've got an APB out on Martinez. Hopefully, the Border Patrol or the CHP will nab that rascal before he makes it back to Mexico."

Thinking there wouldn't be a lot of motivation to prevent an illegal from sneaking out of the U.S., Buzz held little hope that any law enforcement agency would be successful. However, he would unleash every resource at his disposal to help find the young man. If Martinez had a rock-solid alibi that could place him close to the border at the time of the fire, it would conclusively discredit Nicky's lie. "Thanks for everything, Deputy Drable. It appears as if you've done a good job handling this matter."

The deputy clearly enjoyed the compliment—he didn't get many. "Thank you, Sir. Just let me know if I can be of any more assistance."

Netanya greeted Keno with a couple of *I'm sorry for being bitchy kisses* before leading him to Simon's private office next to the library. The room, with a Danish modern motif, was simplistically striking. At the same time, it did reflect the billionaire's idiosyncrasies with an eclectic assortment of souvenirs collected from all around the world. As Keno might have expected, the collection included dozens of hats and caps, many of which might be considered outlandish.

Wearing a lime green Tam-o'-Shanter, Simon gestured toward two empty chairs in front of his desk. He rubbed his good hand over the prosthetic one—a nervous habit that exposed his excitement. He flashed a rare full smile and said, "I've decided on your wedding present."

Netanya's eyes stretched to their expansive limits. She'd been expecting some sort of tedious business discussion, so she was caught completely off guard. Delighted at this unexpected turn of events, she almost childishly bounced in her chair. "What is it, Abba?"

Though Keno was equally surprised, a more serious concern took some of the luster off Simon's disclosure. On the drive over, he was considering how to renegotiate his deal with Simon. He was worried that the business responsibilities were going to create a chasm in his relationship with Netanya.

Simon reached down beside his desk and retrieved a 24-by-36-inch picture, which was a computer-enhanced depiction. With his left hand holding one side of the narrow frame and his prosthetic hand supporting the bottom, he elevated it high enough for the young couple to get a good look. "What do you think?"

Netanya smiled and said, "Sweeeeet! It's totally awesome!"

Keno sat staring at the slightly angled state-of-the-art helicopter, which seemed ready to land at an ultra-modern heliport. This was almost too much to accept. "You're buying us a helicopter?"

"Not a helicopter, Joaquin. Two helicopters. His and Hers." Simon chuckled as he tilted the picture a little more so that he could see it himself. "Robinson Helicopter Manufacturing makes them, and they've been kind enough to make a few modifications for us. This amazing model will have four comfortable leather seats and some extra horsepower." Simon grinned gleefully, adding, "I'm also putting in a heliport, which will only be about a hundred yards behind the house."

Netanya bounded out of her chair and kissed her father on the cheek. "This is sooo cool, Daddy."

Keno shook his head, still clinging to disbelief. A month ago, he was worrying about buying gas for his Harley, and now he was going to have his own helicopter. "This is incredible, Simon."

Simon continued to exude a rare level of excitement. "You'll each have a pilot to escort you until you've gotten your own licenses and become comfortable flying these fantastic little whirly birds" He smiled and repeated, "*Whirly birds*. I like the ring of that."

"I do too, Abba." Netanya's eyes seemed to glow as she squeezed Keno's hand and whispered, "We're actually getting our own whirly birds."

"After you've gotten your licenses," Simon went on, "you will be able to fly wherever you wish, whenever you wish." He paused as if a thought had just occurred to him. "I presently have my Gulfstream parked at the Novato Airport. It will be very convenient for either of you to hop up there on one of these helicopters and take the jet to virtually any city in the world."

As Netanya took the picture to have a closer look, Simon muttered, "I may have to purchase a second Gulfstream."

Keno didn't immediately react to Simon's remark about buying a second jet—the word *convenient* was lingering in his mind. He asked himself: *Does Daddy Bernstein want to make it convenient for Netanya to attend classes at UCLA while I stay in the Tiburon mansion and learn the business? Can Simon be that controlling?*

Netanya's thoughts appeared to be moving along a similar wavelength. "It would be a cool way for me to commute to classes without spending too much time away from home." She turned to meet Keno's gaze, then shook her head consolingly. "Besides, our plans have been radically changed, Joaquin. There's no way you'll be able to leave Millie alone, at least not for a while."

Keno agreed. "Looks like you're the only one who gets to become an actor."

Simon's smile barely creased his lips. "You'll have enough to keep your mind occupied while she's away at school, Joaquin."

Keno couldn't help frowning as he studied Simon. "If I didn't know better, I'd think you planned all of this down to the smallest detail."

Netanya seemed to be studying her father, too. "You're always one step ahead of everybody, aren't you?"

"You said it yourself, my dear. Joaquin shouldn't be leaving his mother alone right now." Simon massaged his chin thoughtfully as if broaching the subject with utmost caution. "Yes, your mother is going to be very lonely, Joaquin. Perhaps we can convince her to stay here with us until the worst of her grieving is behind her."

You really are a clever old dude, Keno realized. *If she stays here in this house, then I will be under your thumb.* He shook his head in the negative. "No way, Simon. There's no chance she's going to give up our house in Mill Valley. She'd never be comfortable anywhere but there."

Netanya's frown revealed her concern. "How is Millie holding up?"

"I think she's doing a little better. She and a friend are going down to Frank's office in the Yard today. She wants to check out some possibilities for the landscaping business. I'm really hoping she'll get involved because that would keep her mind occupied."

The muscular British butler appeared at the door, pretentiously coughing to announce his presence. When Simon glanced at the unassuming man with an elevated eyebrow, the butler spoke without expression. "Mr. Aldridge has arrived."

Simon nodded. "Show him in, James."

Keno was amused to learn the butler's name was James. *How British.*

A minute later, James ushered Buzz into the office. Keno was surprised to see the man he believed was a self-employed private investigator. Buzz had given him that impression the day they'd gone to visit the accident scene at the Sea Lion Cove Estates.

Simon motioned Buzz in with his good hand. "Please join us."

Buzz offered a little wave and greeted, "Good morning, everybody."

Netanya smiled, and said, "Hi, Handsome."

Keno felt a flash of jealousy as he returned the wave. "Hey, Buzz, what's up?"

After Buzz had found a seat, Simon explained, "I've asked Buzz to meet with us this morning to discuss a couple of things. First, he and his team have been spending a great deal of time and energy collecting evidence against Nicholas Ghilardi, Jr., which will prove the depraved young man is guilty of vehicular manslaughter, and I expect we will get an update on that situation. Secondly, Buzz will be discussing security matters."

Keno couldn't contain himself. "You have a team, Buzz? What's up with that?"

Buzz glanced at Simon, silently asking for permission to respond. When Simon nodded, Buzz said matter-of-factly, "I work for Mr. Bernstein assembling information and providing security, and I've put together an effective team to perform these missions. My team members are mostly ex-FBI and ex-Secret Service. At the moment, we're concentrating our resources on collecting evidence that will reveal the truth about your father's death, Joaquin. Actually, we already know what happened that morning, but we will need to prove these facts in a court of law. Unfortunately, that portion of the mission hasn't been progressing as well as we'd hoped. Other than you, Joaquin, we only have one confirmed eyeball witness, whose cooperation we haven't yet enlisted, and two potential witnesses who aren't yet willing to cooperate."

Buzz paused a moment before adding, "Some important evidence was destroyed in a fire set by Nicky Ghilardi, which he is blaming on an illegal Mexican who has gone missing. We are doing everything we can to locate this young man and prove that Nicky destroyed the evidence, which will serve to compound his other felonies." Buzz's steely blue eyes narrowed. "When Nicky Ghilardi goes down, he's going down hard."

Keno was impressed. Simon was expending a tremendous amount of resources for his sake. "I can't tell you how much I appreciate all this, Simon."

"It wouldn't do to have a criminal in the family."

Netanya shook her head to reveal her disapproval. "It's okay to do something nice without having an underlying reason, Abba."

Simon thoughtfully massaged his chin, then turned to Buzz. "I have every confidence that you and your team will soon acquire the necessary evidence to convict young Mr. Ghilardi, so let's move on to security matters."

Buzz directed his words to Keno and Netanya. "We all know the world isn't safe anywhere these days, but security problems are exponentially compounded when wealth is involved. Big money attracts all kinds of criminals and wackos. And when we're dealing with the kind of wealth Mr. Bernstein possesses, there are many additional risks." Buzz cleared his throat and went on. "I can't express emphatically enough that your lives may depend on procedures and equipment that my team puts in place to protect you."

Buzz paused to glance at the door where the muscular butler had exited. "I'm satisfied this house is secure, but when you're out in the real world it's not so easy to guarantee anyone's safety. Other than the obvious robbery, our foremost concern is kidnapping. We've taken steps to reduce that risk by having at least two members of my team accompany Mr. Bernstein wherever he goes." He turned to face Netanya before adding, "But it has proven to be more challenging to protect you, Netanya. Since you've chosen to be in the public eye, it's difficult to shield you from every dangerous situation."

"Come on, Buzz, you're scaring me," Netanya said with her concern showing.

"I apologize for that, but I want to impress you with the potential risks. We live in a world full of crazies."

Netanya held up her wrist, exposing her stylish wristwatch. "Hellooo, I'm wearing the secret microchip."

Surprised, Keno asked, "What's that?"

"There's a computer I.D. chip in the wristwatch, as well as a magnetic coil that can activate a tiny transmitter that sends out a unique signal," Buzz explained. "This personal I.D. signal is picked up by a geosynchronous satellite and relayed to one of my team's computers. We can track Netanya's exact location at any given moment." He gave Netanya a sideways glance. "Of course, it's up to her to make sure she's wearing it and to make sure it's activated when she's someplace where she's exposed."

Keno thought a moment, then asked, "What's a geosynchronous satellite?"

"It's a global positioning satellite that orbits the earth at the same speed the earth revolves, keeping it in a relatively fixed position where it can stay locked onto the desired target." Buzz reached into his pocket and produced an attractive man's watch, studied it for a moment, then handed it to Keno. "This has your personal I.D. chip in it, Joaquin." He reached into another pocket, retrieved an ordinary-looking cell phone and handed it to Keno, too. "This contains a transmitter that activates the same emergency signal. Just hit the star key and then five, five, five."

While several thoughts were racing across Keno's mind, the easy winner was reluctance. "I don't know. This all seems like Big Brother stuff to me. I'm not sure I want anybody to know where I am every second." He frowned while adding, "This also reminds me of something I read about. It's called *function creep*."

Netanya wrinkled her nose as if she'd just smelled something offensive. "Function creep?"

"Yeah," Keno said while trying to recall what he'd read. "It's when people begin using a new scientific device for one thing, and then it winds up being used for a completely different purpose. And that different purpose is usually something that makes it easier for Big Brother to invade our privacy or the military to kill and maim people."

Simon's cough sounded a bit forced. "You're about to enter a world to which you've never been exposed, Joaquin. You will have to concern yourself with a much bigger picture from now on. Imagine the grief you would cause us if you were to be kidnapped. I, of course, would willingly pay any amount for your safe return, but simply paying money doesn't always do the trick."

"You won't have to wear the chip, or have it activated all the time," Buzz instructed. "We only want you to have it activated when there's an elevated potential for risk."

Keno shrugged and then tried on the watch, which, of course, fit perfectly. "After all the nice things everybody's done for me and my mother, and are still doing, I guess it's not too much to ask." He winked at Netanya and said, "But I'm not wearing it when I go to strip clubs."

Netanya swatted him on the shoulder and glared. "If you get kidnapped while you are at a strip club, forget about it. I won't let Daddy pay the ransom."

"That's cold," Keno replied. "Maybe I can get Buzz to go with me for protection."

Buzz's expression let it be known that he wasn't about to get drawn into that exchange. "I guess I'm done here." He shook Simon's extended left hand and gave a little wave. "See you guys. Drive carefully and be nice to people."

Simon's eye lingered on the door, obviously waiting for Buzz to be out of earshot. "There goes a very good man. I was fortunate to steal him away from the Secret Service."

Keno was impressed. "You stole him?"

"I was fortunate enough to persuade him to take charge of my security team. He formerly oversaw the former President's security detail. Thanks to his quick thinking, a couple of potentially catastrophic events were nipped in the bud without the public knowing a thing about it." Simon paused to emphasize a point. "The best security is prevention, not reaction. And let me remind you, his heroic acts of prevention came about by his having the proper intelligence ahead of time."

Keno's admiration of Simon had reached a new level. "I think it's incredible that you actually stole Buzz away from the President."

"I wouldn't say *stole*, exactly. Though I did provide a much greener pasture." Simon chuckled before adding, "A greener pasture in his favorite city. Buzz was born in San Francisco to hard-working parents who never enjoyed having a lot of money. He liked the idea of coming home and taking care of them. He bought them a nice house on the coast near Mendocino, and they're now enjoying life beyond their fondest expectations."

Buzz's story made Keno think of how he could take care of Millie in the not-too-distant future. "I could see how a cool guy like him could be persuaded to care for his parents. And I intend to take care of my mother that way, too."

"I would expect nothing less." Simon's eye moved back and forth between the young couple, indicating that they were about to be dismissed. "It's been an interesting morning, but I must go down to the Data Dungeon and take care of a few things that require my personal attention. I'll be leaving for Chicago tomorrow morning."

Keno entertained the idea of going down to the Data Dungeon with Simon but decided it would be wiser to spend some time with Netanya. "See you when you get back."

"I plan to return on Wednesday morning. Perhaps we can get together that afternoon to discuss important matters."

Keno felt as if he were already an employee. However, he would soon be one of the better paid employees on the planet. "Okay, see you then."

Netanya stood and beckoned Keno with a tilt of her head. "Come on, hunky dude. Let's trip up to my crib and rap about our plans and stuff."

Simon shook his head as he watched the young couple exit the room. His daughter's English had surrendered to the idiomatic, which was probably unavoidable considering how contemporary writers and musicians butchered the language these days. However, he realized that language had progressed in this manner since man's first meaningful grunts. He smiled while thinking: *Perhaps we're about to come full circle.*

J.P. Maloney was waiting at a remote table when Jason Bridger strolled into The Wharf a few minutes past noon. The old lawyer raised his hand in a half-hearted wave to attract the district attorney's attention. With his stomach acting up, Maloney forced a thin smile when Jason got close.

The DA gave the age-dappled hand a quick shake. "How are you, J.P.?"

Maloney ignored the gratuitous greeting. "Are you going to eat, Jason? I'm not. That miserable psychopath has ruined my appetite. And if it weren't for the devastating financial liability, I'd help you put his ugly butt away." J.P. uncharacteristically let his imagination roam for a few seconds, happily visualizing Nicky behind bars. "If there were some way you could lock the idiot up for the rest of my life for what he' done..."

Jason frowned. "Are you referring to evidence I'm not aware of? According to the deputy sheriff's report, Nicky was cleared of all charges related to the barn fire."

Maloney snorted, and said, "The bastard can be fiendishly clever, even if he is dumber than a doorstop when it comes to common sense decisions."

Jason threw up his hands, palms out, and leaned back in his chair. "Hold it, J.P. If you know he's guilty of any criminal behavior, I don't want to hear about it."

"While I have my suspicions about the fire, I was referring to the way Nicky goes about things," J.P. grunted his disgust before revealing Nicky's latest malicious ploy. "Now he's suing Frank Flores' poor widow for every penny she's got, and he's only doing it to get her son riled."

Jason seemed reluctant to accept that J.P. Maloney was exhibiting compassion. "I don't get it. Why would Nicky want to rile Joaquin Flores?"

J.P.'s face reddened from the heat of disgust. "That's exactly what I'm talking about, Jason. He doesn't have any common sense. He wants to get that young Flores pissed off enough to attack him or some such thing. Nicky thinks that if he can accomplish that, it will prove that Flores is a menace to society. Or at the very least, it will undermine his reliability as a witness to last Sunday's... accident."

Jason's humorless chuckle sounded like a series of grunts. "Yeah, I have an idea that Flores would be angry enough to go after Nicky if he were to sue his mother. That would be a natural reaction. But Nicky had better hope he doesn't get what he's wishing for. Joaquin Flores is a stud."

J.P. almost smiled. "It would do my soul good if he were to pound the bloody bejesus out of Nicky."

Jason frowned. "How am I involved in all of this?"

Maloney slipped a fat envelope across the table, which Jason Bridger quickly jammed into a pocket of his windbreaker. It was understood that it was another large contribution to the DA's campaign fund. "I just wanted to make sure we're still on the same page, Jason." The old lawyer hesitated a moment before adding, "I don't have a clue as to how any of this will play out, but I wanted to give you a heads-up about the possibility that Joaquin Flores might soon be doing something crazy. Prepare you for the worst if you know what I mean."

Jason stood and extended his hand. "Thanks, J.P., but I'd seriously consider jumping ship if I were in your shoes."

Maloney shook the offered hand. "I consider that about a dozen times a day, but I'm too damned old to jump."

The Stolichnaya had finally chilled enough, and it was going down like ice water. Millie sat holding the subpoena in one hand and the cold glass in the other, mumbling curses and swearing at the paper. Every so often, she would take a sip of vodka and then give the subpoena a violent shake as if trying to whip the words right off the page. She began to talk to the subpoena with slurred words. "If my son were here, he'd take care of you." Her head moved in small circles as she shook the paper. "If my husband were still alive, he would really fix you. His friend Gino Matteri said my husband was a real good shot with a shotgun. Frank could blow you to bits. Tiny, jagged, ragged, little bits."

Her aggressive words instigated the germ of a thought—an idea that managed to take root in the fuzz encompassing her brain. She knew where the shotgun was kept. She whispered, "Maybe I'll go get it and blow this subpoena to bits myself."

Millie placed the drink and the subpoena on the table, balanced herself on the back of the chair to gain her bearings, then went staggering toward the den. She knew that Frank had always kept the shotgun in the gun rack. The beautiful cedar gun rack that she believed was going to be a hutch for her china dishware when he first began to build it. But Frank had changed his mind. He didn't think it was a fine enough piece of furniture to put in his wife's dining room. Millie smiled wistfully as she approached the gun rack. She gently caressed the marbled wood with her fingertips and stroked it like a priceless piece of art. But Frank was wrong. It had turned out to be a marvelous cabinet—an exquisite piece of furniture.

Millie opened one of the glass-encased doors and took out the 12-gauge Remington. Surprised by its weight, she bounced the gun up and down in her hands to get the feel of it. She lifted the weapon to shoulder height and attempted to aim it, but the little round sight at the end of the barrel kept dancing all over the room.

Millie vaguely remembered that Frank had never left the shotgun loaded, so she leaned it against the corner formed by the wall and the gun rack, then fumbled around in the top drawer until she found a red box of shells. It took a while to figure out how to load the weapon, but she eventually managed to stand the gun on its end and slide five shells into the magazine. She clamped the stock under her armpit and let the barrel's grip rest on the palm of her hand. She picked up the box containing the remaining shotgun shells, then staggered back to the living room.

At first, she'd merely intended to blast the subpoena to pieces, but a much grander plan began to bloom in the fuzz. She stood staring off into the distance, first imagining the concept, then vividly visualizing her opportunity for revenge.

She found a ballpoint pen and a blank piece of paper, found Ghilardi Development Corporation's Lucas Valley address on the subpoena, and wrote it down in a big, shaky scrawl. Since she was bound and determined to blast something, it might as well be the Devil himself.

Keno and Netanya lay sprawled on her expansive bed, discussing their plans, hopes, and dreams. This important conversation had brought some light to the concerns they'd been harboring.

Netanya turned on her side to face him, then toyed with the buttons of his shirt. "I guess you didn't realize how much baggage was attached to a rich man's daughter."

"I don't mind, especially if it's big bags full of money."

She punched him and said, "Get serious."

"Okay," Keno said, "I'll admit that I had no concept of how involved it would be. All the basics of business your dad expects me to learn, and then all that security stuff..."

"Are you sorry you got involved?"

Keno wrapped an arm around her, pulled her close, and kissed her. "No way, Tanya. And I'm not complaining, it's just that it's a lot to deal with. Especially for a guy who has never had any money and never been exposed to all the things that go with it."

She wrapped her arm around his waist and squeezed with all her might. "There will be a lot of adjusting, but that's probably true for most couples."

When Keno's eyes moved down to Netanya's smooth stomach, he noticed that her jeans had slid down a little. Barely visible on her lower abdomen was a small, slightly curved scar. He touched it with a fingertip and asked, "Is that an appendix scar?"

"Yeah," she said matter-of-factly. "When I was sixteen, my appendix almost burst. They said I was lucky to the hospital just in time.

Keno felt as if a shock wave had rushed over him. Recalling the weird dream he'd had while parked at the beach with Millie, he was almost afraid to ask, "Where did it happen?"

She seemed surprised that he would ask. "I was at the beach."

"Stinson Beach?"

Netanya's forehead wrinkled with curiosity. "Yeah, I was in the surf at Stinson when the pain first hit.

Keno felt his body grow weak. *This is too weird. But I can't let myself think about it right now.*

"You okay, Joaquin?"

Keno shook his head to clear it. "Yeah, I was just tripping on going to the beach. You know, surfing and stuff."

"I'm hurt." Netanya's lower lip protruded. "You're not interested in what I have to say."

Keno playfully pushed in her lip and pulled her to him. "That's what you think. You're never completely out of my thoughts."

Their lips instinctively parted and met in a slow, lingering kiss. Netanya's smoldering eyes suggested that he'd ignited her passion, and the suggestive touch of her wandering fingers told him that she wanted to keep going, but he reluctantly pushed her hand away.

Surprised by the rejection, she asked, "What's the matter?"

He blew out an exasperated breath, releasing some of his own mounting desire. "It just occurred to me that Millie is depending on her friend to care for her today. I should check on her before we get all carried away.'

Even while wearing a look of disappointment, Netanya's expression revealed that she understood. "Good idea. You'd better check to make sure she's doing okay."

Millie didn't answer the phone at the old Victorian, and Keno got the message machine when he punched in the number for Milagrozo Landscaping. The sound of Frank's cheerful message hit him like a linebacker sandwich.

Netanya sensed something was wrong. "What's the matter, Joaquin?"

Keno took a deep breath, then blasted it out so hard that it sounded like a reed instrument. "My father's voice is still on the answering machine."

"Whoa! That must have been a shocker."

"Yeah, it totally caught me off guard."

Netanya sighed, then began to massage his chest with comforting fingers. She waited a minute before asking, "So, do you know what's up with Millie?"

"She didn't answer at either place." After a moment's deliberation, he added, "Maybe she's on the road."

"Why don't you go home and check on her? I'm sure she's okay, but you're not going to stop worrying about her if you don't know for sure."

"Good idea. Why don't you go with me?"

"Okay, cool, we'll ride in my hot wheels."

He stared at her a moment, then asked, "Remember what Buzz said?"

"Yeah, I will drive carefully, but I won't commit to being nice to people."

The recent encounters with marinas, boats, and the inviting smells of fresh salt air had begun to grow on Buzz, perhaps infusing a subliminal nautical suggestion. When he left the Bernstein mansion, he knew Julie's open house would prevent them from having lunch together. And he didn't have any hot leads to pursue at the moment, so on a whim, he decided to drive to the San Rafael Marina and check out boats for sale. His sailing experience amounted to being a helpless passenger during a few miserably wet and cold boat rides on the bay, so he was leaning more toward enjoying the seas in the comfort of a powerboat. He purposely avoided the word *yacht* in his fantasy.

Buzz had strolled about the marina, pier shopping, no more than five minutes before he was spotted by a young man who referred to himself as *an aquatic pleasures facilitator*. Buzz was about to learn more than he ever wanted to know about powerboats.

Deputy Wertz had persuaded Deputy Drable to take a ride over to Belvedere where they could check out Hans Van Exel's extravagant house. Wertz was now on a mission. Arresting this major drug dealer could eliminate some of the heat for his shady handling of Nicky Ghilardi's accident. Also, the sheriff would enjoy a lot of favorable ink in the *Independent Journal* if they busted Van Exel—that would really pile up the points. Today's drive-by with Deputy Drable probably wouldn't pay immediate dividends, but it might help somewhere down the road.

Amazingly, Millie herded the Volvo through Mill Valley's narrow streets without incident, then swerved it out onto Highway 101. She crowded the extreme edge of the slow lane while one angry driver after another leaned on their horns as they went whizzing by. Perhaps it was the time of day, the luck of the draw, or having at least one guardian angel working overtime. But Millie made it all the way to the Lucas Valley Road exit without being stopped by the California Highway Patrol or being rear-ended by any number of speeding drivers.

Millie still had enough reasoning power to realize that she'd missed the turn for the underpass and was going east on Jones Road, which was taking her in the opposite direction. She turned around at a wide spot near the golf course, then aimed the Volvo west.

She slowed to pedestrian speed to keep an eye out for the right address, but her vigilance proved unnecessary. The huge G on the massive wrought-iron gate was nearly impossible to miss, even for a lady who was close to being blind drunk. She stopped in the middle of the road, backed up, pulled the Volvo over to the shoulder, and then parked close to the ditch.

She shook her blonde mane and blinked her eyes several times, trying to assemble her fuzzy thoughts. She had not, however, considered the possibility of confronting such a formidable gate. She knew she couldn't climb over the big metal gate, and the substantial cyclone fence, with its *High Voltage* sign, eliminated virtually all possibilities of going around it. It occurred to her that there might be some opening mechanism near the gate, so she dragged herself out of the car and went staggering across the asphalt road. After a couple of minutes of searching, she came to believe that there wasn't one. Frustrated, she grabbed a couple of the gate's wrought-iron rods and shook them with all her might, but, of course, it was a wasted effort. Her aggravation mounted, along with her need for a drink.

Millie stomped back across the road to the Volvo and jerked open the door to the back seat. She unrolled the beach towel she'd used to conceal the shotgun when carrying it out of the house. Using both hands, she tugged the bulky weapon out of the car. She took a moment to glance up at the big house on the hill, wishing that the evil bastard who lived there was within range.

Hostility, frustration, grief, and a couple of other dismal emotions teamed up to bolster her determination. Millie stormed back across the road, aimed the shotgun at the locking mechanism in the center of the gate, and blasted away.

Nicky sat at his office desk, eating one of the delicious croissants Yvette had brought in. He wasn't quite lucid yet because he'd enjoyed—more correctly, wasted—another long night. He'd snorted a large amount of cocaine, and this had impaired his performance with the hooker who took him for most of his coke and five hundred dollars.

Booming blasts from the shotgun caused Nicky to recoil and drop the croissant. A stunned second later, he found himself kneeling behind the desk. Glistening beads of perspiration formed on his forehead as he guessed who might be shooting that close to his office. A frightening image of Biker Boy soon materialized in his debauched mind.

Millie put down the gun, rubbed her sore shoulder, then picked at a steel pellet which had ricocheted off the gate and buried itself in her forearm. Trying to focus, she shook her head hard enough to send her blonde hair waving and then went over to inspect the gate's lock. She grabbed two of the wrought-iron rods and jerked as hard as she could, but the pitted and cratered lock held fast. More determined than ever, she picked up the gun and went back to the Volvo to reload.

Yvette came running into the office. "Who is doing all that shooting, Nicky?"

Pretending that he'd dropped something on the floor, Nicky placed an imaginary item in his shirt pocket before struggling to his feet. He didn't want his mother to know what a coward he was.

"I don't know who it is," Nicky replied, but I'm calling Wertz to come check it out."

Deputy Wertz, who'd just turned off the freeway and was heading east on Tiburon Boulevard toward Belvedere, took the call on his cell phone. He listened to Nicky rant for half a minute, then shut off the cell. He turned to Deputy Drable and said, "Somebody's doing a lot of shooting at the Ghilardi Ranch. We'd better go over there and see what's going on."

Deputy Drable asked, "Should I call it in?"

Wertz didn't know what to expect but wanted control of any situation involving Nicky. "Let's check it out first."

A minute later, a com-op called Buzz and played Nicky's recorded call to Deputy Wertz's cell phone. Buzz thanked the aquatic pleasures facilitator for his time and information, then jogged out to his Beamer and sped toward the Ghilardi Ranch.

As Millie was blasting away the second time, Keno and Netanya were entering the old Victorian in Mill Valley.

When Keno saw a crumpled piece of paper lying on the table, he spread it open and read it. As the appalling words of the subpoena sunk in, a strange feeling came over him. The feeling was accentuated with a sense of disaster.

When he noticed an empty glass on the table, still slightly frosty, instinct led him to the refrigerator. He opened the freezer door and saw that more than half of the vodka was missing from the bottle of Stolichnaya. While peering into the freezer compartment, a frosty cloud suddenly captured his attention. He stared in disbelief as an alarming, ghost-like vision formed in the mist. When the images came into focus, he could make out Millie's face—perspiring and red with rage. Almost crazily, she was holding a shotgun and shooting at a gate with a big G on it. Not waiting for this apparition to fold in on itself and disappear as the others had, Keno slammed the freezer door shut.

With a confused Netanya trotting along behind, Keno hopped into the den as fast as his crutches could carry him. His breathing stopped when he saw one of the gun cabinet doors standing open, and his heart sank when he discovered that Frank's shotgun was missing. He grimaced and shouted, "Damn it!"

Netanya knew something was terribly wrong. "What's going on, Joaquin?"

"Millie is drunk and has Frank's shotgun." Keno's command came out harsher than intended. "Let's see how fast your Ferrari can get us to Lucas Valley Road." He realized Netanya had questions, but they would have to wait.

When everything grew quiet after Millie's second volley, Nicky found the courage to peek out to see who was doing the shooting. Even more important, to his way of thinking, was learning if he were the intended target.

He felt his mother's warm breath on his neck as she leaned close behind him. "Do you know who it is, Nicky?"

Nicky could see that it was a tall, blonde woman, but it was hard to distinguish her facial features from that distance. His hazy mind raced, but he failed to find the connection between Millie and Keno. "I don't know who the hell it is. It looks like some crazy broad. But wait a minute... It looks like she's gonna leave... She's gettin' in that old car across the road." A few seconds later, he shouted, "What the...? That broad ain't leavin'" She's headin' the car right for the gate. Look at that! She rammed right into it!"

Nicky and Yvette stared dumbfounded as Millie backed the Volvo about twenty feet, then took another run at the crippled gate. The third attempt banged it open, and the separated gate halves bounced off of the Volvo's fenders as though giant springs were attached. The Volvo's engine whined loud enough to be heard all the way up to the office as it roared through the hard-earned opening.

But the car abruptly stalled when water flooded from its cracked radiator, apparently drowning the engine. Millie ground on the starter until it finally fired again. The Volvo leaped forward, stalled a little, and then chugged up the hill toward the big house.

Javier and the other three laborers had just finished their lunch. Attracted by the gunshots, they watched from the old house. They could see that an angry lady was coming after someone—most likely Nicky. At least three of the four were rooting for her to succeed.

Nicky rushed to get the Glock 9mm out of his desk, an act that caused Yvette to go limp and feint into a pile of chiffon and white lace. Showing little concern, Nicky glanced at his unconscious mother lying on the floor while pushing the button to roll down the metal blinds. He hoped they would protect him from an assault through the picture windows. More sweat popped out on his forehead as his beady eyes darted about the room, frantically searching for the best place to make his stand.

Almost all of the water in the Volvo's radiator had spilled out on the asphalt driveway by now, and the battered car looked like a runaway steam engine. The windshield had become so blanketed with steam that Millie was forced to lean her head out of the window to see where she was going. The valiant Volvo coughed its last jerking gasp, and then died some fifty yards from her goal. Her strength waning, Millie grabbed the shotgun by the barrel and struggled to climb out of the car.

Nicky cracked the office door just far enough to slither through. Literally shaking in his boots, he pressed his body tight against the door jamb and held the pistol in front of his face with both hands.

Buzz was the first outsider to arrive on the scene. It didn't take long for his trained eyes to survey the situation and conclude that Millie Flores had gone berserk. He pressed the accelerator to the floor and sped the Beamer through the twisted halves of the wrought-iron gate.

Millie's naturally wavy hair hung limp and straight from exposure to steam; her perspiration-dampened clothes clung to her body; and her legs wobbled as if made of rubber. But none of this diminished the rigid look of determination on her grim, flushed face. A deep-seated rage drove her on as she doggedly marched up the hill, holding the shotgun in front of her breasts.

Nicky peeked around the corner just far enough to see the crazy woman who had closed to about forty yards. His breath coming in short gasps, he pressed the back of his head against the wall. Warm sweat trickled down his forehead, stinging his eyes.

About thirty yards away now, Millie stopped long enough to shout, "Come out and take your medicine like a man, Nicky Ghilardi. Come on out, you rotten little weasel!"

The speeding Ferrari's tires sent squealing sounds piercing through the tranquil valley, joining the siren's whine that grew louder as the deputy sheriff's car approached.

Buzz slid the Beamer to a stop behind the steaming Volvo and bailed out. He shouted at the top of his lungs, "Stop, Mrs. Flores! Stop and I'll help you!" Then he went racing up the hill.

Nicky reached his gun around the corner with one hand and blindly sprayed several wild shots.

Buzz instinctively hit the deck.

Undeterred, Millie kneeled on one knee and returned fire. The shotgun blasts splintered wood and shattered glass, but none of the pellets found their target. Likewise, Nicky's wild shots were only killing volunteer oat hay in the field.

Both deputies heard the gun battle raging as they drove up behind Buzz's Beamer. After exchanging raised eyebrows, they each scurried out of the squad car and crouched behind the heavy doors—wisely taking stock of the situation.

The Ferrari came screeching to a stop behind the squad car. Netanya shouted, "Look, Joaquin! Millie's up there on the road."

Keno had already spotted her. "Drive around those cars."

Netanya shrugged and obediently steered the low-slung sports car off the asphalt. Within seconds, the left front tire began to sink into the rain-softened bank. She gunned the engine and rode the clutch just enough to keep the rear tires from spinning too much. Gradually, she guided the magnificent vehicle past the other three cars blocking the road.

Millie took more shells out of her jacket pocket and began to slide them into the shotgun.

Sensing that the crazy woman had run out of ammo, Nicky grew brave enough to peek around the corner in time to see her reloading. He leaned out a bit farther and did his best to aim the pistol. Nicky opened fire just as Buzz reached out and grabbed Millie from behind.

Buzz tried to spin Millie around and shield her body with his own, but one round plunged into the back of Millie's thigh before he could get her completely turned. Another round whizzed under his elbow and penetrated her ribcage. Still, another, zinging directly toward the back of Millie's head, hit Buzz's shoulder—he'd moved her just far enough to save her life.

Buzz shouted over his burning shoulder, "Hold your fire, you idiot!" Then he turned to see how seriously Millie had been hit.

As Netanya pulled the sports car up alongside the Beamer, Keno shouted, "That punk just shot my mom!" With an incredulous look entrenched on his face, he forgot all about his crutches and hopped over to his collapsed mother.

Showing no concern for himself, Buzz looked up at Keno. "She's been hit, but I don't know how bad."

Keno noticed an expanding crimson stain on Buzz's shirt. "Looks like you've been hit, too. We need to get you both to a hospital. Think we can fit you in the Ferrari?"

Still cradling Millie's head, Buzz grimaced when a sudden sharp pain attacked his shoulder. He raised his eyebrows and said, "I doubt it. But whatever you decide to do, make it quick."

Deputy Drable had moved close enough to hear most of the conversation. He turned to Deputy Wertz, who was just now ambling up, and said, "I can get these wounded to Marin General Emergency a lot faster than if we wait for an ambulance. Let's get them in the squad car."

Wertz agreed but was reluctant to leave the scene. "Okay, you take them to the hospital. I'll stay here and sort things out."

The two deputies carried Millie to the squad car and carefully placed her on the backseat while Netanya helped Buzz onto the front passenger seat.

Deputy Drable turned on the flashing lights and the siren, then sped down the hill in reverse until he reached the county road. The squad car whipped around and burned rubber while speeding away.

Nicky didn't make a move until Wertz had joined Keno and Netanya, standing by the Ferrari. He tucked the Glock in his waistband, then put on a brave face as he sauntered out with his thumbs hooked in his cowhide belt.

Anger flashed across Keno's mind, blinding him to every other purpose except how to inflict enormous amounts of pain on Nicky. He hopped toward the malicious man as fast as he could, then swung his crutch with hopes of crushing Nicky's skull.

Nicky jumped back and pulled out his pistol, which he obviously didn't realize was empty. He shouted, "You're next, Biker Boy," and squeezed the trigger, which only resulted in a hollow clicking sound. Nicky's wide-eyed expression revealed his terror as he began to back away from the infuriated mass of muscle advancing toward him.

Deputy Wertz hurried between them, placed both hands against Keno's chest, and pushed with all his might. "That's enough!"

Keno's face felt as if someone had blasted it with a blowtorch. He pointed an index finger threateningly. "I'm going to get you, you miserable little punk. I don't know how, when, or where, but I'm going to make you pay for shooting my mother."

Nicky had apparently found a little courage while standing in Wertz's shadow. "You're just lucky I ran outta ammo, Biker Boy. An' if you mess with me again, I'll reload an' blow your big ass away."

Keno pushed Wertz out of the way and swung his crutch again. Nicky stumbled and almost fell while retreating. Wertz grabbed Keno's arm and held on with all his might.

Not convinced he could restrain Keno, Wertz threatened, "You're going to force me to arrest you again."

Netanya grabbed hold of Keno's other arm and pleaded, "Come on, Joaquin, you can't solve anything like this. Besides, we have to go see how Millie is doing."

Keno had to exhaust a couple of heated breaths before finding enough control to speak. "What are you going to do about this, Deputy? You had to see this punk shoot my mother when she was helpless." Keno paused, trying to burn a hole in Wertz with the fire in his eyes. "Are you going to arrest that ugly bastard?"

"Your mother attacked Nicky with a shotgun while trespassing on his property," Wertz said matter-of-factly. "It looks like an obvious case of self-defense."

Keno realized that Wertz wasn't going to do anything, so he directed his venom toward Nicky. "You might think you got away with shooting my mother, punk, but one way or another, I'm going to get you." He glared at Nicky for a few intense seconds to emphasize his threat, then turned and hopped back to the Ferrari.

Nicky snapped a quick glance at the deputy as they stood watching the expensive sports car speed down the hill. "What took you so long to get here, Wertz? That crazy bitch coulda killed me."

"Who would figure Mrs. Flores would go nuts?" Wertz said with a shrug—he wasn't about to accept any blame. "If it had been Joaquin, I could have taken him out. But there was no way I could shoot her, especially with Drable on the scene."

As the Ferrari zoomed away, Nicky stared after it. "That's a hot ride. I gotta get me one o' them."

Wertz was glad to change the subject. "I bet it cost more than two hundred grand, especially with that paint job."

"Ya know what? If it wasn't for Miss Rich-Bitch, I wouldn't be havin' all this freakin' trouble."

"No doubt about it," Wertz agreed. "And on top of that, Simon Bernstein gave Joaquin Flores a new Cadillac."

"Are you kiddin' me?"

"No, that rich old man must really like Flores. And it's really a beautiful car he gave him, too. It's the same color as that Ferrari. I saw it at his house in Mill Valley when I arrested him."

"Biker boy don't know how lucky he is. Without Bernstein's money, he'd still be in the slammer." Nicky paused to mull things over, then said, "Make sure you put in your report how Biker Boy threatened to kill me today.

"No problem."

"An' I'm pressin' charges against that crazy broad. You can get her for attempted murder, destruction of property, an' anything else you can think of."

Wertz suddenly felt dirty. Just standing next to the egomaniac was making his skin crawl. He was truly beginning to understand what the expression *dirty money* meant. "Yeah, I'll throw the book at her."

Nicky started back to his office, then stopped, turned, and raised his voice, "An' make sure all the news reporters get our slant on this. We don't want that old broad lookin' like a martyr."

"You got it, Nicky G. I'll call a reporter I know and have him put the right spin on the story."

As Deputy Wertz watched Nicky stomp into his office, he decided that he'd sold his soul.

Buzz had suffered a severe flesh wound that required stitches. Though extremely painful, the bullet hadn't struck any vital arteries or organs. Millie, on the other hand, was in critical condition. She was going to need surgery on both wounds.

Keno anxiously hopped back and forth in the waiting room.

Netanya could do little but sit and watch him unleash enormous quantities of nervous energy. She had called her daddy to fill him in soon after the doctor had delivered the disturbing report on Millie's condition.

Simon Bernstein immediately called Nathaniel Clay to inform him that his services would soon be required. The billionaire informed the defense lawyer that it was going to tax his vast legal expertise to extricate Millie Flores from this mess, even with extenuating circumstances.

Nearly two sluggish hours crawled by before Keno and Netanya were allowed to see Buzz. A heavily taped bandage covered one shoulder, and his arm rested in an elevated sling. He managed the semblance of a smile when the young couple approached his bed. "Thanks for coming by."

"No, thank you, Buzz. You took a bullet to save my mom, and I owe you big time." Keno shook his head for emphasis. "And I'll never forget it."

Buzz tried to divert attention from his heroics with a timeworn cliché. "That's why I get paid the big bucks."

Netanya patted his good arm and said, "Something tells me you're going to be getting paid even bigger bucks."

"How's your mom doing?" Buzz asked

Keno did his limited crutch shrug. "She's being operated on as we speak. And the doctor tried his best to convince me that she's going to make it."

"I'm sure she will. She's a tough lady."

Netanya asked, "Do you need anything?"

Buzz glanced at a plastic bag lying on the small dresser next to the bed. "No, I think I'm okay. They brought me a toothbrush and whatnot. Besides, I'll be leaving early tomorrow morning."

Netanya frowned. "The doctors are releasing you so soon?"

"Nicky Ghilardi has accelerated my plans. I need to talk to a couple potential witnesses ASAP." He glanced at Keno and said, "Don't worry, Joaquin, we'll get him."

Keno's eyes narrowed as he worked his lower jaw to release some tension. "I know we will, Buzz. One way or another, we'll get that punk."

Chapter Fifteen

Timothy didn't appreciate his telephone's annoying ring. He'd gone to a friend's house yesterday, and they'd stayed up late watching *Lord of the Rings*—with the idea of sleeping in this morning. It was the fourth time he'd watched the trilogy.

One eye remained buried deep in his pillow while the exposed eye reluctantly blinked, gradually bringing the red numbers of his clock radio into focus. It read 6:32 a.m.

He reached for the ringing phone with a big paw, awkwardly balanced it on the side of his head, and grumbled, "Yeah?"

"Good morning, Timothy."

Timothy recognized the voice but asked anyway, "Buzz?"

"Your powers of deduction continue to amaze me. Why didn't you answer your cell last night?"

Timothy sat up and scratched his rumpled head. "I forgot to charge it yesterday, so I left it on the charger." He yawned, then remembered to ask, "Didn't I have the day off?"

"Things have changed, and not for the better. I need you to come to Marin General Hospital right away. Just drive up to the front entrance. I'll be there waiting."

Timothy yawned again, long and loud. "What the heck are you doing at the hospital?"

"I'll explain when you get here. Now put wings on that big crate of yours. And bring me a sweatshirt or something."

"A sweatshirt?" An empty pause warned him not to push it. "Okay, Buzz, I'll bring you a sweatshirt, and I'll really hurry."

Buzz didn't bother to offer his usual safety tip.

Twenty minutes later, Timothy frowned with surprise when Buzz came out from behind a bush near the hospital's entrance.

Careful not to move his shoulder more than necessary, Buzz climbed in the Suburban and ordered, "Let's go."

Timothy obediently pressed his foot on the accelerator, but he had questions that needed answers. "What happened to your shoulder, Buzz?"

"An idiot shot me yesterday. Now drive out to the freeway and head north."

"What?" Timothy's jaw dropped, but he maneuvered the Suburban toward the freeway. "Which idiot shot you?"

"Nicky Ghilardi. Where's that sweatshirt?"

"It's on the seat right behind you. It's the smallest one I could find in such a hurry." Timothy frowned and asked, "Why'd that idiot shoot you?"

"I got in the way." Buzz grabbed the sweatshirt, at least three sizes too big, and smirked while considering how silly it was going to look. He slipped it over his head, then poked his unbandaged arm through a cavernous sleeve.

"Where are we going, Buzz?"

"We're going to interrogate the Chinese couple, and I'd like to do it someplace that won't cause them embarrassment. The shack at the old pier would be ideal."

"What do you mean by *cause them embarrassment?*"

"I'll explain later." Buzz glanced at his watch, angry at himself for not getting Timothy out of bed half an hour sooner. "You'd better step on it."

Timothy didn't step on it hard enough. The potential witnesses were already fifty yards away from the rickety pier when the Suburban came to a sliding stop in front of the weathered shack. Buzz went limp. Arriving just a few minutes sooner would have prevented spending hours with the inquisitive teddy bear.

Keno had slept fitfully, probably three hours at most. He couldn't escape a persistent parade of jumbled thoughts—each marching to a conflicting drumbeat. And no wonder. The past seven days had provided an extraordinary range of psychological confusion. He'd been elevated to the highest highs and plummeted to the lowest lows. He had reached the pinnacle of love; experienced excruciating grief; witnessed paranormal visions; suffered painful and life-altering physical injuries; endured incarceration; been introduced to the legal system; experienced the extremes of hate; and offered enormous wealth and power. His senses had been hammered again when he'd seen a vision of his mother in harm's way, then watched helplessly as Nicky Ghilardi shot her. And now he had to accept the possibility that Millie was mentally disturbed. *Yeah, it's been one helluva week.*

Even with the emotional storm raging within, Keno enjoyed the feeling of Netanya's warm body cuddling next to his. She'd stayed with him at the old Victorian last night, and he'd really appreciated it. Not only had she attended to his every whim, but she'd been thoughtful enough to call the hospital at least once each hour to check on Millie. It seemed his mother had come through the operation as well as could be expected, though she remained in critical condition.

Netanya had one arm draped over his stomach while purring contented sleep sounds, so he couldn't bring himself to disturb her. Besides, it was Sunday and there wasn't a lot he could do this early. He fluffed his pillow and buried his head in it—granting sleep another opportunity to rescue him.

Julie decided to go jogging instead of working out in her personal gym. Feeling the damp, foggy air on her face was invigorating, and she had a bounce in her step that had been missing for a while. She owed a lot of her renewed vigor to yesterday's grand opening, which she considered an overwhelming success. She had closed two solid deals and had another strong *maybe* pending. Having her finances under control made her feel as if an enormous weight had been lifted.

Thoughts of finances soon caused a mental image of her friendly financial advisor to pop into her mind. A warm, fuzzy feeling swept over her. She felt her smile indenting her dimples while realizing that she and Buzz were going to be together tonight. It had been a lot easier to fight off the excitement of infatuation when pressing problems had been in the way, but now....

Julie scooped up the Sunday paper on her way into the house, tossed it on the kitchen table, enjoyed a quick swallow of orange juice, and then hit the shower. If today was even half as good as yesterday, it was going to be fantastic.

Julie fixed herself a bowl of Cheerios with banana, poured a cup of her wonderful coffee, and sat down to enjoy her breakfast with the *Independent Journal.* She glanced at the front page, which featured the recurring story about a suicide bomber in the Middle East, a report on the President's latest faux pas, and another horror story about a serial rapist, this time in the state of Idaho—the usual stuff. However, when she flipped the page, a local story jumped out at her. She sat up straight to collect herself, and then read:

MARIN SHOOTOUT

A bazaar shooting occurred yesterday at the Ghilardi Ranch on Lucas Valley Road, just a few miles north of San Rafael. The shooter was identified as Mrs. Millicent Flores, a Mill Valley resident. Mrs. Flores allegedly drove her car through the security gate guarding the primary entrance to the ranch, which also serves as a construction equipment yard for the Ghilardi Development

Corporation. Mrs. Flores then allegedly attempted to shoot Mr. Nicholas Ghilardi, Jr., who was said to be working in his office at the Ghilardi residence.

Deputy Sheriff Wertz, the officer in charge at the scene, was quoted as saying: "Mrs. Flores rammed her car through the property's main gate and attacked Mr. Ghilardi with a shotgun for reasons we don't know. There was an exchange of gunfire, and Ms. Flores was critically injured during the shootout. The wounded assailant was then taken to Marin General Hospital by my partner, Deputy Grable."

Deputy Wertz refused to comment on whether this assault was in any way related to a vehicular accident in which a Mr. Frank Flores was killed this past Sunday. At last report, Ms. Flores remains in critical condition while Mr. Ghilardi apparently escaped unscathed.

In a related incident, a Mr. C.J. Aldridge was seriously wounded during the heated shootout. Mr. Aldridge was also treated at Marin General...

One hand flew to Julie's mouth as she dropped the newspaper on the cereal bowl. She reacted with an elevated level of anger toward Nicky, but then her face flushed from a sudden attack of guilt. It occurred to her that if she hadn't lied to protect Nicky, this terrible turn of events might not have happened. Her mind raced, searching for answers. *Was Mrs. Flores trying to get even with Nicky for killing her husband? No doubt about it. The poor woman probably went off the deep end. That's understandable, but what the hell was Buzz doing there?*
Julie found her phone and punched in Buzz's cell number.

Buzz and Timothy were parked next to Ghilardi Drive, where they'd gone to observe Charles Chung and Lulu Simmons who were fishing at their favorite spot in the Sea Lion Cove. Timothy had earlier leaned his head back on the driver's seat and was now sound asleep. Buzz was glad to see the big man snoozing. It was nice not to be bothered by a steady barrage of questions while pouring over a lengthy list of problems and possibilities.

When his cell phone rang, he recognized the number. "Hi, Julie."

"Are you alright?"

Buzz lied, "I'm fine. Why do you ask?"

"I just read in the paper that a Mr. C.J. Aldridge was seriously wounded at Nicky Ghilardi's ranch yesterday. You may find this strange, but I don't know any other man by that name. And I doubt that any other C.J. Aldridge would know Mrs. Flores and also be interested in Nicky G."

"Newspapers tend to exaggerate things."

Julie didn't appreciate his evasiveness. "Stop playing games. How bad were you hurt?"

"Just a scratch."

"What were you doing there, anyway?"

Buzz knew he would have to come clean, sooner or later, but preferred later. "It's a long story that I don't want to go into right now." He manipulated the truth a little by adding, "I'm with someone very important, so now is not a good time to discuss it."

"Okay, be that way. So, do you know how bad Mrs. Flores was hurt?"

Buzz couldn't minimize this response. "She took a couple of serious hits. The bastard shot her twice when her back was turned."

"I'm so sorry for that poor woman. Is she going to make it?"

It occurred to Buzz that Julie's perjured testimony had helped Nicky perpetuate his evil. He wondered whether this, at some point, might diminish his feelings for her. "She must be doing a little better. They've upgraded her condition from critical to serious."

"That's a good thing."

"Serious is still serious." He decided he wasn't ready to judge Julie for lying, at least not yet. "Are we still on for tonight?"

The thought improved Julie's mood. "Yes, I'm really looking forward to it."

"Your place about seven?"

"Seven is good. Take care, Buzz."

"Yeah, drive carefully and be nice to people."

Julie stared at the phone after she'd replaced the receiver. She asked herself: *Is it just me, or did I detect some disapproval in his voice?*

The wind on the bay picked up early, and the Chinese couple chose not to risk their lives any more than they already had in the dilapidated old boat. They'd each caught one large striped bass, so Charles Chung wasn't all that disappointed when he fired up the outboard motor and headed south toward the rickety pier.

About half an hour later, Charles Chung suspected who was doing all the banging but couldn't think of a way to avoid the confrontation. He finished chopping the heads and fins off the two fish, then went to answer the plank door. He even remembered the Special Investigator's name. "What can I do for you, Mr. Aldridge?"

Buzz walked in, and without saying a word, went over to have a look at the two large striped bass. Lulu Simmons, busily washing away guts, gave him a sideways glance but didn't say anything either.

Clearly impressed, Buzz finally said, "You two are outstanding fishermen. Or should I say, fisherpersons?"

Charles Chung scowled at this peculiar man, wearing a ridiculously oversized sweatshirt and sporting a bandage on one exposed shoulder. "Gender is not important to people who enjoy fishing, Mr. Aldridge. What can I do for you?"

Buzz met Chung's steady gaze with a menacing glare, then pointed to his bandaged shoulder. "See this? The same guy who killed Frank Flores while speeding like a maniac shot me and Mrs. Flores yesterday. Mrs. Flores, the woman widowed by that maniac named Nicky Ghilardi, is now lying in the hospital in critical condition. The only reason she isn't dead is because that idiot is such a lousy shot." Buzz paused to let that sink in, then continued with undisguised malice in his voice. "I know you and Mrs. Simmons saw Nicky Ghilardi's

Mercedes speeding down Ghilardi Drive last Sunday, and I'm sure you both saw it collide with Frank Flores' green pickup truck." Buzz's eyes hardened to blue flint. "I need you to help me put that maniac behind bars before he kills or injures somebody else."

Chung's resolve waver a little, but still insisted, "We told you that we saw nothing."

Buzz grimaced and grabbed the wounded shoulder when it was struck with a stabbing pain. This torment exorcised his last ounce of patience. "I don't have time to fool around, Mr. Chung. If you don't cooperate, I intend to expose these little fishing expeditions to your wife, Xian Li."

Lulu's head snapped around, her expression revealing fear.

Chung's reserved demeanor suddenly changed. "Do you have no principles, Mr. Aldridge?"

Buzz shook his head. "Not really. I would much rather have the two of you cooperate willingly, but I will do whatever it takes to nail Nicky Ghilardi."

Lulu cast a nervous glance at Chung.

Buzz paused a couple of beats before presenting an alternative. "I only need one of you to testify to the criminal incident that occurred last Sunday. No one needs to know that both of you were in the boat."

Uncertain, Chung responded, "I don't understand."

"I'm working to clear Joaquin Flores of bogus charges made by Nicky Ghilardi, and that's my one and only objective. I think I can persuade Joaquin to testify that he just saw one of you in the boat. His statement can be worded in such a way that it will only be misleading by omission." He paused before asking, "What do you say to that?"

Charles Chung and Lulu Simmons exchanged long, anxious looks before nodding their mutual assent.

Chung raised his chin a bit and said, "I will testify that I was in the boat that morning, Mr. Aldridge. However, I cannot lie on a witness stand if someone asks me a direct question regarding Lulu's presence."

"I understand, Mr. Chung, but if we're careful with how your testimony is worded, that's not going to happen." Buzz paused a moment, apparently letting Chung think things over. "But you did see the Mercedes speeding down Ghilardi Drive and then collide with Frank Flores' green Ford pickup truck last Sunday?"

"Yes, I must confess I did. What you just described is exactly what I saw." Chung felt a rush of embarrassment. "Now that I've learned that that terrible man has hurt more people, I feel very ashamed for not speaking up sooner."

"I'm sure you were only doing what you thought was necessary, but better late than never. And I want to thank you in advance for the good you'll be doing for the Flores family."

Lulu moved closer, evidently wanting to put matters into proper perspective. "Do not think bad of Charlie, Mr. Aldridge. He was protecting my marriage, not his. I am married to a good man, but he would never understand my friendship with Charlie. I may be going to hell for this, but my husband thinks I am at church when I am fishing on Sundays."

Buzz smiled and said, "I seriously doubt anybody is going to hell because they fib about going fishing."

Lulu nervously folded and unfolded her hands, clearly trying to find the best way to explain their improbable situation. "Our fathers were best friends all their lives, and they bought this property as partners more than fifty years ago. They always took Charlie and me fishing with them, starting when we were only about five years old. And other than a few vacations and a couple of illnesses, we have fished together at least once a week since that time. When our fathers died, they left this property to both of us. And just like they were, we are friends and partners and hope to remain so for the rest of our lives. As I said, my husband would not approve of my spending so much time with Charlie, but I don't want to give it up. Our fishing together is one of the most pleasurable things in my life."

Buzz sort of mumbled, "That's what I get for jumping to conclusions without having all the facts." He grimaced and added, "Don't worry, Mrs. Simmons, your secret is safe with me. I don't want to cause either of you any marital problems, or any other embarrassment as far as that goes."

Lulu bowed her head to show her appreciation, and said, "Thank you, Mr. Aldridge."

Chung asked, "When will you be taking my statement?"

"I'll call you tomorrow morning and arrange for you to meet with a defense attorney named Nathaniel Clay."

"Would you like my cell number?"

Buzz couldn't resist a smirk while admitting, "I already have it, Mr. Chung." As he reached the plank door, he turned and said, "Drive carefully and be nice to people."

Lulu stared after him with a befuddled look.

It surprised Keno to see that it was past 10 a.m. He couldn't remember the last time he'd slept this late. He looked around for Netanya, but she'd slipped out of bed without waking him. Now she was curled up in a chair, reading *Variety*—one of the two magazines Millie splurged on. When noticing he was awake, she brought him a cup of coffee.

He smiled and said, "Not many guys get waited on by a billionaire."

"I'm not a billionaire, silly, Daddy is. And besides—she leaned over and kissed his cheek, making a big smacking sound—"any billionaire babe would be glad to wait on a hottie like you."

"You really know how to get a guy's day started."

She tousled his hair and asked innocently, "How's my thespian potential?"

He frowned at being set up, then made a pitiful face, looking as if he were about to cry. "You didn't mean it?"

"Maybe, maybe not."

Keno remembered speaking those exact words to her. "It's payback time?"

"I've been waiting for days."

Keno enjoyed the fooling around, but Millie's plight, nagging at the back of his mind, wouldn't let the fun last. He sighed and said, "I guess I'd better get up and get dressed so we can go check on Millie."

"Yeah, we should. I called about half an hour ago, and a nurse said she's still in serious condition."

"Has she regained consciousness?"

"The nurse wouldn't tell me. She knows that you're the only immediate family member Millie has, so you're the only one she'll reveal that info to. And that's weird because the nurse on duty last night was willing to tell me anything."

"That's the difference between night and day, huh?"

Netanya rolled her eyes. "Corneeee."

Just as Keno had found his crutches, his cell phone rang. When he motioned toward it with his head and gave his best begging look, Netanya found it and then handed it to him.

When he'd finished a short conversation, Keno explained, "That was Butch, our great middle linebacker. His parents named him right because he is one tough dude. Anyway, the team has a bye this week, which means no heavy practice. Butch and some frat boys are throwing a birthday blast for Daryl Slate tomorrow night. Everybody knows that me and Daryl are tight, so they remembered to invite me to the party. Pretty cool, huh?"

"It's very cool, Joaquin. And I think it would be good for you to hang with your boys a little. Maybe escape some of the heavy crap you've been wading in lately."

"Yeah," Keno agreed, "but I haven't been wading in it, I've been swimming in it."

Keno hopped as quietly as he could with the casts, and Netanya tiptoed as they entered Millie's room in the ICU. An alarming array of hoses and electrical leads sprouted from her immobile body.

"She looks relaxed enough," Netanya whispered.

"I don't know why we're tiptoeing and whispering. It would probably take an earthquake to wake her up." Keno moved close enough to reach out and gently stroked one of his mother's hands, which were lying crossed just beneath her breasts. A disturbing thought crossed his mind. *This looks a lot like the way Frank's hands were placed in the coffin.*

However, Keno was wrong about waking her. The energy in his affectionate touch had somehow penetrated the dense fog enshrouding Millie's brain. Her mind strained to find consciousness until blurred, yellow light sneaked through the narrowest of slits. The eyelids quivered, struggling to obey the brain's intuitive command, then finally parted. A burst of bright light suddenly dilated her surprised pupils. Two blurred figures gradually came into focus, and the assimilated faces became familiar. A sensation of joy began to flood through Millie's mind, and for some unexplained reason, it was followed by a great sense of sorrow. She raised one weak hand and reached out to her son. Her muffled words tumbled out as if she had a mouth full of cotton. "Is that you, Sunshine?"

Keno leaned on the crutches and held her delicate hand in both of his big ones. "Yeah, it's me, Mom. And Netanya's here, too."

Netanya moved closer and patted the shoulder opposite the wound. "Hi, Millie."

A series of confused recollections swept across Millie's mind. Large pieces of the puzzles were missing, but she could connect enough of them together to grasp the gravity of what she'd done. "I've behaved very stupidly, haven't I?"

"No, Mom," Keno said with conviction, "you did what you thought was right. I wish you would have snuffed that ugly punk."

Millie flinched at a brief but vivid memory of the shootout. "You know I've never condoned violence."

"I know, Mom, but you've never had to deal with a s.o.b. like Nicky Ghilardi."

"Don't even worry about what happened, Millie," Netanya consoled. "All you need to think about right now is getting better."

Millie enjoyed hearing Netanya's soothing words, but her thoughts had begun to swirl and become more confused. She barely managed, "Thanks, I really do appreciate..." before her eyelids grew heavy, and the distorted yellow light returned through the weight of narrowing slits. Then everything faded to black.

Keno did his limited crutch shrug. "Looks like she's out."

"Sleep is definitely the best thing for her right now."

"No doubt." As he helplessly stared at his mother, a loud growl emanating from his stomach reminded Keno that his breakfast had consisted of a glass of orange juice. "There's nothing we can do for her at the moment, so let's go get something to eat."

"Hope you never have to choose between me and food."

He winked and said, "I hope you never make me."

As they were about to leave the hospital parking lot in the Ferrari, Netanya's cell phone jingled. She smiled when she saw her daddy's number in the window. "Hi, Daddy, what's going on? I thought you'd be halfway to Chicago by now."

"I've changed my plans." Elevated with excitement, Simon's voice was loud enough for Keno to hear. "Can you and Joaquin come to the house this morning?"

Netanya turned to Keno. "Daddy wants us to go to our house. I'm sure you can eat there if you're up for it. Is that okay?" When he nodded enthusiastically, she said, "Sure, Daddy, we can be there in about fifteen minutes."

As Netanya steered the Ferrari up the curving drive to the Bernstein mansion, Keno noticed that the gardener and the chauffeur seemed to be going through the motions of working on Sunday. He didn't think too much about it until he saw the maintenance man carrying a small step ladder and a paint bucket. This aroused his curiosity. A closer look told him that all three of these men were built like the English butler; all moved like athletes; all were about thirty years old; and all seemed extremely alert. The discovery initiated a light-hearted chuckle.

Netanya asked, "What's up with the happy sound?"

"How many times have I been here? Maybe eight or nine?"

She shrugged. "Yeah, I'd guess at least that many. But how is that funny?"

"This is the first time I've noticed a small army of security guys."

Netanya took a few seconds to examine her father's employees. "Don't feel bad, Joaquin. I've been here for years, but it has never occurred to me. I mean, I might have known it in the back of my mind, but I didn't really think about it." She shrugged and added, "Maybe I didn't want to know."

"I can see why. Sometimes, it's better not to think about living in constant danger. I don't know if it's a good analogy, but I never wanted to think about getting hurt when I played football."

"I guess it is kind of the same thing. It's all about living your life without letting fear control what you do."

Keno noticed a red BMW and a gold Porsche parked in front of the house. "Looks like your father has company. I'm pretty sure the red Beamer belongs to Buzz Aldridge."

Netanya parked near the front door and offered, "I'm sure the gold Porche belongs to Mr. Clay." A look of concern crossed her face. "Something important is going down."

Simon Bernstein was holding court in his office next to the library. This time he sported a San Francisco Giant's black and orange baseball cap along with his recent penchant for wearing patriotic yachting attire. His eyebrow elevated and a smile creased his slender face when the young couple entered the room. "Good morning, youngsters."

Keno returned the greeting, then gave a little wave to Buzz and Clay, each comfortably seated with a cup of coffee. Clay maintained his usual dignified appearance in a designer workout suit. On the other hand, Buzz needed a shave and had on a wrinkled shirt with one sleeve loosely draped over the bandaged shoulder.

Netanya smiled, said, "Hi, guys," and then gave her father a peck on the check. "You sound happy this morning, Abba."

Simon rubbed the fingers of his good hand over the prosthetic resting on the desk, a telltale sign of exciting news. "We've had a turn of good fortune. Buzz has located an eyewitness who saw everything. The man actually observed Nicky Ghilardi's Mercedes collide with the truck in which Joaquin's father was killed." Simon glanced up at Keno and apologized, "I'm sorry if my excitement has caused me to appear insensitive."

Keno shook his head in the negative while suppressing his gut-wrenching reaction to the despised name. "No, I appreciate your enthusiasm, Simon. Finding an eyewitness is the best news I've heard in a while."

Simon motioned to Buzz. "Please fill us in."

Buzz put down his coffee cup and leaned on his free elbow. "One of the fishermen you saw fishing in the Sea Lion Cove that morning, Keno, is willing to testify that Nicky Ghilardi was speeding at the time of the incident. The fisherman is an upstanding Chinese man named Charles Chung. He's a lifelong resident of Marin County and should make a convincing witness. He had a perfect angle to see everything from his boat, which was only about fifty yards out at the time of the incident. He can't put an exact number to how fast Ghilardi was going, of course, but I think his words, *a very high rate of speed*, should be convincing enough for any judge or jury." He turned to Clay. "Don't you agree, Nate?"

Clay nodded. "Yes, the most important thing is to corroborate Joaquin's testimony, which was a very limited view from ground level. And from what you've described, Buzz, Mr. Chung was in an ideal position to see the entire incident unfold."

Picking up on the word *incident*, Keno frowned. "Aren't you forgetting that I saw *two* fishermen in the boat?"

Buzz looked pensive for a moment, apparently deciding how much to explain. "The other person in the boat was a married lady who has been fishing with Charles Chung since they were little kids. It's all very innocent, but it could cause her serious marital problems if her husband finds out that she was in the boat with Chung that morning. It will be in her best interest to avoid using her testimony." Buzz grimaced and confessed, "In fact, I could only convince Chung to testify by promising to keep her out of it."

It was Clay's turn to look pensive. "Two eyeball witnesses carry a great deal more weight than merely double, Buzz. There's an exponential effect when you put two witnesses on the stand back-to-back. I know you're thinking of the woman's best interest, which I find admirable, but it may be too big a gamble for us not to use her." His face took on a business-like demeanor. "Our first priority is to clear Joaquin, of course, but the added leverage may also benefit Mrs. Flores' cause somewhere down the road."

Buzz surprised them all with his next disclosure. "I know how important it is, but I'm pretty sure I can produce the second eyewitness that you'll need to cinch the deal."

With all seven eyes aimed his way, Buzz played his trump card. "Julie Lemmon was in the car with Nicky Ghilardi the morning of the incident, and she gave Deputy Wertz a false statement for the sole purpose of landing the sales contract for the Sea Lion Cove Estates. She detests Nicky almost as much as the rest of us, but she was in a financial jam at the time and felt that she needed to do something drastic." Buzz paused before adding in a softer voice, "She's basically a good person, and I don't think she realized the consequences of allowing her ambitions to get in the way of coming forward I'm meeting with her tonight, and I'll do everything I can to persuade her to do the right thing and testify."

Simon massaged his chin with a finger and thumb. "Perhaps we can provide some financial incentive."

Netanya's jaw dropped. "You're really going to bribe a witness, Daddy?"

"Nothing quite so obscene, my dear. We'll just be encouraging her to provide the essential testimony."

Netanya wasn't buying it. "Sure sounds like a bribe to me."

Buzz glanced around the room, making a lot of eye contact. "I think I can convince Miss Lemmon to do the right thing without offering a financial incentive, but if I have to, I will. And then we'll have her, Mr. Chung, and Joaquin all telling the same story."

"That should do it," Clay said matter-of-factly. "With that kind of ammunition, I'll be able to do some serious horse-trading with Jason Bridger."

Keno frowned. "What kind of *horse-trading* can you do with a district attorney?"

"I'm sure we can get the charges against you tossed, Joaquin, but I'm very concerned about your mother's situation. It is not good, to put it mildly. However, if we have enough concrete evidence to convict Nicky Ghilardi of vehicular manslaughter, not to mention obstruction of justice, I may be able to cut a deal with Mr. Bridger."

Still frowning, Keno asked, "Why would the DA want to cut a deal?"

Buzz cleared his throat and explained, "Jason Bridger has some lofty political ambitions. He's going to run for Congress next year, and that takes serious money. His war chest has already been fattened with generous contributions from the Ghilardi Development Corporation—some legit, some under the table. But no matter how he came by it, it will influence the way he deals with the CEO of that generous corporation."

Netanya looked puzzled. "How do you know so much about the district attorney's campaign contributions? I doubt that Mr. Bridger has made that information public."

Buzz shrugged his good shoulder. "Let's just say I know which rocks to look under."

Netanya and Keno exchanged inquisitive looks, both even more curious about the workings of Buzz's team.

"Back to the matter at hand," Clay interjected. "I think we can safely assume that Jason Bridger will jump at the chance to go easy on Ghilardi when I explain that he simply has to provide equal justice for Mrs. Flores."

Keno felt his anger flare. "I hate the thought of giving that punk a break."

"None of us like that thought, Joaquin," Clay empathized, "but we have to do everything we can for your mother. I'm hoping that when this all plays out, we can get her placed in a comfortable mental health facility for a very minimal amount of time."

Until now, the seriousness of Millie's crime had eluded Keno, but the realization that his mother could be facing years in prison came screaming into his brain. Even though Marin County had long been a bastion for those with a liberal bent, the courts had been clamping down on crimes of violence. And Millie's aberrant behavior was about as violent as one could get without actually killing a person. Like it or not, Clay's suggestion of a comfortable mental health facility was probably the best he could hope for. "I'm sure you'll do what's best, Mr. Clay."

Then Keno remembered the subpoena he'd brought with him. He took it out of his pocket, unfolded it, and handed it to the defense attorney. "I don't know if you can use this to help explain why my mom blew it, but it shows the kind of evil bastard we're dealing with. Ghilardi Development Corporation owes my father's landscaping company thousands of dollars, and not only is Nicky trying to get out of paying, he's suing my mom for more than everything she's got."

Clay quickly scanned the document. "This will certainly establish aggravation, as well as enhance sympathy. Few people condone a large corporation suing a grieving widow." He passed the subpoena to a curious Simon, then suggested, "I'll have Bob Nelson take a look at this." He glanced at Keno before explaining, "He's one of my associates who deals with civil matters. He'll eat their lunch on this one."

Simon studied the subpoena, nodded his approval, and handed it back to Clay. "Speaking of lunch, is anyone hungry besides me?"

This, of course, was one of Keno's favorite questions. "Count me in."

Buzz and Clay had eaten at the Bernstein mansion on several prior occasions, and they weren't about to pass on the opportunity for gourmet dining. There were nods all around, and then all moved from the office to a glass-enclosed balcony that offered a spectacular view—a view that could sell lots and lots of postcards.

Deputy Wertz was doing everything in his power to get on Sheriff Roland's good side. Even though it was his day off, he stopped by the sheriff's office to see if there had been any new developments in the Hans Van Exel drug-trafficking investigation—an operation he had personally set in motion.

The duty dispatcher, an attractive woman of thirty-something, informed him that she wasn't aware of any recent activity. But she was purposely misleading him. She possessed important information she wasn't at liberty to discuss. Sheriff Roland had alerted the FBI to Van Exel's drug operation. The two law enforcement agencies had agreed to a joint operation and would share the publicity if a major bust ensued. Van Exel's Belvedere residence had been thoroughly bugged and an around-the-clock stakeout was in progress.

However, the dispatcher did have one interesting piece of information that she could share. "Hey, Wertz, you might be interested in a fax that just came in." She found the printout and handed it to him. "They found the Mexican guy who set that barn on fire out at the Ghilardi Ranch."

Wertz snatched the paper out of her hand and quickly read it. The fax was a response to an APB for one Tomás L. Martinez. He was presently in custody in El Cajon, California, a suburb of San Diego, about twenty miles north of the border. A positive I.D. had been established with the thumbprint on his Green Card and a Mexican driver's license issued in Tijuana, Baja Mexico.

Martinez had been in jail since Thursday night when he'd been arrested for shoplifting twenty-two dollars and fifteen cents worth of food from an Albertson's supermarket. The El Cajon Police

Department had requested follow-up pertaining to extradition. With an overflowing jail, they'd be more than happy to rid themselves of one illegal Mexican.

The El Cajon Police Department had unwittingly provided the perfect alibi for Tomás Martinez, and this would soon cause big trouble for Nicky Ghilardi. There would be nothing that either Wertz or Jason Bridger could do to cover up Nicky's willful destruction of evidence in the barn fire. Nobody was going to believe Yvette, clearly covering for her son. Then Javier, not too fond of Nicky anyway, would crack under the slightest pressure.

Nicky Ghilardi soon received a disturbing call. "You have a major problem, Nicky G." Still in bed, Nicky was just now clearing his head from another night of sex, booze, and drugs. The last thing he wanted to hear was that he had another important matter to deal with. "What the hell's the problem this time, Wertz?"

"The Mexican that you said started the barn fire is presently incarcerated in El Cajon, down by the border, and he has been since last Thursday night."

Nicky slammed the nightstand with the palm of his hand. "What the hell ya tellin' me? That freakin' Martinez has got an alibi?"

"Ironclad," Wetz responded. "It doesn't get any better than being locked in jail when the fire started."

Nicky tried to think his way out of this mess, but solutions were slow to come by. The aftermath of cocaine was affecting his brain like gritty sand in greasy bearings. "You got any ideas?"

"Sorry, Nicky G., I can't see any way out of this one. But you'd better come up with something good and do it quick. If I know straight-arrow Drable, he'll be reopening the investigation the minute he finds out about this."

"Maybe I can say it was some other Mexican who did it, an' I just got 'em mixed up." He forced a hollow chuckle. "Those beaners all look alike to me."

His voice devoid of amusement, Wertz replied, "That's not going to fly."

Nicky slammed the nightstand with his hand again, this time knocking over the lamp. "Then you think o' somethin' that will fly, Deputy Ding-a-ling. You should be doin' everything ya can to help me. Remember, you're makin' out like a bandit because o' me."

Sorry he'd called, Wertz said, "I'm trying to do you a favor. Giving you a heads-up."

"Yeah, yeah, I know. But I'll really make it worth your while if you can think o' somethin' to bail me outta this freakin' mess. I'll set you up with another house deal. I'll even give ya one twice as good."

"I'll try to think of something, Nicky G. Talk to you soon."

Nicky didn't really hear Wertz's final response. He was battling the urge to clear his mind with another line of coke.

Buzz's cell phone rang while his mouth was extracting remarkable flavors from a bite of ethereal veal—he'd never imagined that any meat could be so tasty and so tender. He found his cell but waited a few seconds to answer it. He wanted to allow his ecstatic taste buds to savor the last molecule of the delicate meat, which seemed to be vaporizing in his mouth. But his disappointment with the interruption didn't last long. A com-op had called to report on the incriminating conversation between Nicky and Deputy Wertz, and then played it for Buzz.

Buzz ended the call and smiled at the seven curious eyes aimed his way. "Terrific news. The good guys have just belted one out of the park. The Mexican that Nicky accused of burning down his barn is in the slammer in El Cajon, down by San Diego. And here's the best part, he's been in there since last Thursday, which provides him with an ironclad alibi."

Simon leaned forward and said, "Enlighten us, Buzz."

Buzz had earlier reported the facts surrounding the barn fire to his never-miss-a-thing employer, but he knew Simon liked reviewing every detail. "The Mercedes Nicky Ghilardi was driving the day of the incident was in a barn at the Ghilardi Ranch. It contained positive proof that Nicky was drinking and using cocaine, so he burned down the barn and everything in it to dispose of that incriminating evidence. Then he blamed the arson on a young Mexican he'd recently fired for taking a siesta. Now we know that the young Mexican was in jail at the exact time of the fire. This emphatically points the finger back to Nicky and completely undermines his fabricated yarn."

Pensive a moment, Simon then asked, "Why is the young Mexican in jail?"

Buzz rewound the tape in his head. "He shoplifted twenty-two dollars' worth of food from a supermarket."

Simon massaged his chin for a few seconds, then turned to Clay. "Can you arrange to get the young man released from jail?"

Clay nodded. "Yes, I'll request a copy of the arrest report for our purposes and then make a couple of calls to get it done."

"I would appreciate it, Nathaniel." Simon thought a moment, then added, "And see that the young man gets a couple thousand dollars while you're at it. After all, he is helping our cause, and he shouldn't be going hungry."

Netanya flashed her pretty smile. "That is so cool, Daddy."

Keno remembered Simon's argument against expending resources to feed the poor. It would only make them stronger long enough to procreate, thereby increasing their number and creating an ever-enlarging circle of poverty. It sounded good in theory, but hungry people weren't simply statistics, and Simon couldn't remain so calculating and aloof when it got personal. "Yeah, that is totally cool, Simon."

Keno and Netanya returned to the hospital about an hour after the exceptional lunch. Other than an occasional fright-induced grimace, or a muffled cry of desperation emanating from somewhere deep within her dreams, Millie maintained a blank expression. She lay with her hands folded across her chest, which slightly rose and fell with each soft, lingering breath. Though it was under the most difficult circumstances either could have imagined, the young couple used the quiet time to talk about their plans, their hopes and dreams. It was something they'd been needing to do.

Julie Lemmon had bagged two more sales, and her new salesman had landed one sale and got another strong *maybe*, all before 4:00 p.m. Satisfied with all this success, she closed her sales office early—something she hadn't done in years. Her new salesman didn't mind: made more than a grand his first day on the job.

However, Julie hadn't closed early to pursue personal pleasures. She needed to address the guilt that relentlessly nagged at her. It was one thing to profit from false testimony, but it was another thing entirely when the lie had made it possible for a maniac to nearly kill a grieving widow and, adding insult to injury, shoot the man she was extremely fond of. No, she admitted to herself, in love with.

But could she relinquish this golden opportunity just to satisfy her guilt? It was an opportunity to make hundreds of thousands of dollars. Opportunities like this come to struggling real estate brokers rarely more than once in a lifetime, and usually not even that often. The bottom line is that it came down to money versus morals. She battled with the dilemma for the better part of three vacillating hours.

Julie spent about an hour debating with herself in front of the mirror, ending up with a favorable result—she looked quite gorgeous. Her auburn hair flowed with silky smoothness, contrasting nicely with her emerald eyes. An ultra-light layer of make-up in strategic places, a couple of touches of mascara, and just the right soft shade of lipstick were all the camouflage required. She wore a sinuous beige jumpsuit with a long, narrow V that extended down to the bottoms of her proud breasts; the smooth material delicately clung to every well-exercised curve.

Buzz arrived at 6:55 p.m. He believed in being punctual, but tonight he had to fight against being too early. He'd tried to watch a preseason football game that afternoon but barely remembered the names of the teams, never mind the final score.

He took one look and said, "Wow! You look fantastic."

He had shaved and done his best with a loose-fitting shirt but was far from looking his best. Even so, he still looked good to Julie, whose vision was undoubtedly distorted by infatuation. She invited him in and kissed him as passionately as she dared. She suddenly felt the need for liquid courage. "I'm having a Margarita. Want to join me?"

Buzz rarely drank anything but Johnnie Walker scotch, Black Label, but smiled and said, "I guess it can't hurt to apply a little extra wax to the skids. Bring it on."

Julie put out bowls of salsa and guacamole, plus a big bag of corn chips, which unintentionally became dinner. Three-quarters of a Margaritas pitcher later, they were feeling very little pain. It was, however, only a brain-dimming disguise. Important issues were still struggling to surface.

Julie was beginning to feel frustrated. Buzz had deftly parried her probes, which searched for the reason he was at the Ghilardi Ranch when he got shot. Unaware that he had attended Hastings Law School in San Francisco, she said, "You should have been a lawyer. You are really good at evading a direct question."

He cocked his head and studied her face. "You know, you really are beautiful."

Julie rolled her slightly bloodshot eyes. "Thank you. I'm glad you think so, but you just confirmed my opinion. You would have made a great shyster."

He laughed and said, "Yeah, I guess I am pretty good at keeping things in gray zones. There seems to be very little black and white in my profession." He let his gaze linger on hers a moment before asking, "What about you? I'll bet a real estate broker can become good at deception when it becomes necessary."

Julie nodded without realizing he was leading her down the Path of Absolution. "For sure. My business requires a lot of rose coloring, not so much black and white. But we have to be careful to paint those rosy pictures without being completely dishonest."

Buzz's face took on a wistful look. "Wouldn't it be great if we could be completely honest all the time?"

"Yes, it would." She glanced at him thoughtfully and made a decision. "I'm glad you raised the subject. There's something I really need to get off my chest. I've been battling with it for hours, but I'm afraid if I come clean, you'll think I'm a terrible person."

Buzz smiled and encouraged, "Come on, out with it. I doubt you can say anything to make me think you're terrible."

"I'm not so sure about that." She took another swallow of Margarita, and when their eyes met, she felt hers leaking tears. "I've done a terrible thing, Buzz. I lied to protect Nicky Ghilardi, one of the most awful, rotten people on the face of the earth. And I did it because I'm a greedy person."

Buzz's expression exposed his sense of relief. He put his healthy arm around her shoulders and consoled, "It's okay, Julie. It's nothing that can't be set straight."

"Nicky was going extremely fast that morning when he hit the truck Frank Flores was driving. And I signed a false statement that said Nicky wasn't speeding." She sniffed and went on. "Nicky gave me a huge sales contract for covering his ugly little butt. And now the rotten bastard shot you and Mrs. Flores." She sniffed and said, "I'm so terrible."

"We all do things we're not proud of Julie. At least you're trying to make things right."

"Do you hate me, Buzz?" Julie's sobs had subsided, but her eyes were still flooded with tears. "I know I don't deserve somebody like you."

"Somebody like me?" His chuckle was short on humor. "Let's wait until you hear my confession before we decide which one of us is worse."

"Your confession? What have you got to confess that could even begin to compare with my lying?"

Buzz removed his arm from her shoulders and his eyes met her questioning gaze. "Do you remember that old TV show, *I've Got a Secret?*"

She searched for a moment. "I think so. But what's that got to do with anything?"

"Well, I really do have a secret. I'm not a financial advisor."

"I sort of knew that. I mean, you're always at places you shouldn't be… and you're always asking all sorts of questions…" Julie's face took on a quizzical look. "So, what do you really do?"

"I supervise a team that provides information and security for Mr. Bernstein. But if you tell anybody, I'll have to waste you."

"Oh, my God!" Julie wiped her teary eyes, then chuckled. "I can't tell you how glad I am to learn that you're a liar, too, Buzz." Her lips found his with a wet, lingering kiss. "Such accomplished liars like us were meant for each other. You know that don't you?"

He returned the kiss and said, "Yeah, and just think of the children we can have. Definitely successful politicians."

"Or big-time CEOs" she said gleefully.

Buzz nodded his agreement. "We could have kids with enough prevarication potential to make it to the White House."

She took another sip of Margarita, then shook her head. "Nah, that would have to include heartless, and we wouldn't want that."

Chapter Sixteen

Keno arrived at the hospital at 7:30 a.m., just two minutes before Millie began to scream.

Two nurses had gone into ICU, unplugged her, moved her onto a gurney, and then transported her to one of the better private rooms, as per the chief of staff's instructions—Simon Bernstein had made a phone call for the upgrade No sooner had the nurses placed Millie in the new adjustable bed than she began to shriek at the top of her lungs. She kept repeating, "Fraaaaaank, get me out of heeeeere!" and then followed each desperate plea with a high-pitched and long-winded, "Aaaaaaahhhhh!"

Just as Keno had found the new room, a grim-faced nurse rushed out and trotted toward the nurses' station. A combination of emotions—mostly related to dread and curiosity—swept over Keno as he hurried in as fast as he could hop, skip, and jump. He moved close to the bed and reached out to comfort his mother. Millie was having none of it. She jerked her arm away and let out another piercing scream that penetrated to the core of his being.

Keno resisted an urge to cover his ears while making eye contact with a second nurse, who was frozen in place on the opposite side of the bed. The befuddled nurse stared out through thick glasses with wide, frightened eyes.

After another excruciating scream had subsided, Keno asked, "Do you know what's wrong with her?"

The myopic nurse shook her head. "Not a clue. She started screaming right after we moved her into this room."

Keno waited until the next scream had faded. "Can't you do something?"

"Diane went to get a doctor. I think he'll sedate her."

The grim-faced nurse, Diane, came rushing in with a frail doctor whose hair brought porcupine quills to mind. The doctor rushed to the side of the bed, waited for Millie's next scream to subside, then rattled off the name and quantity of a sedative.

Diane was prepared. She almost magically produced a vial of medicine and a syringe, which she loaded and emptied into the plastic tube leading to the I.V. taped on Millie's arm.

As seconds gradually became minutes, the screams diminished in volume but not in frequency. The doctor's face took on a perplexed look while instructing Diane, "Better hit her with another ten milligrams."

The second dose proved to be successful. It provided Keno with a certain amount of relief when he saw his mother resting comfortably. But the experience had taken a heavy toll joining the disturbing mix of emotions fighting for recognition. Chief among them was the smoldering hatred aimed at the punk who'd caused this.

On his way out, the doctor was kind enough to stop and lend a comforting word. "Your mother has suffered a severe panic attack, which can be upsetting for all concerned. I'm not a psychiatrist, but I've come to learn that these attacks can happen to almost any patient, anywhere, anytime. We may never know the exact cause of your mother's episode, though emotional trauma is most likely responsible." He rested his chin on his closed fist and pursed his lips, indicating he'd just recalled something. "I did have a similar incident a couple of years ago when I had a patient removed from the ICU. I've had it explained that a patient can be subconsciously aware that they're getting the best possible care, and then when they're abruptly moved, they feel like they've been disconnected from a comfort zone. I suppose it could be as fundamentally traumatic as a baby leaving the womb."

He shrugged, indicating that this was the best he could offer. "I think your mother will be fine after she regains consciousness and becomes familiar with her surroundings. However, we do have a psychiatrist on our staff who I've heard is really sharp. It might be a good idea to have him look at her."

"Thanks, Doctor," Keno replied while struggling with the possibility that Millie was going to need a shrink. "How long do you think she'll be out?"

He shrugged. "I can't say for sure, but she'll probably be missing lunch."

Keno hopped and skipped out to the Cadillac, which he'd parked in the lot next to the hospital. He was glad it was cool and foggy outside. The cool air felt especially refreshing after suffering through that agonizing experience.

When Buzz called Nathaniel Clay to reveal that Julie was willing to offer testimony beneficial to Joaquin Flores, the defense lawyer informed him that he had already arranged to meet with Charles Chung at 9:00 a.m. the following morning. They would be meeting at the Holiday Inn near the Marin County Civic Center, and since time was of the essence, it would be a bonus if Julie and Buzz could join them. Clay then suggested they might as well go all the way and add Joaquin to the mix.

Buzz immediately called Keno to invite him to the meeting. While he was at it, he related the need for Keno to testify to seeing only one fisherman in the boat that Sunday morning. When he explained that this was only a slight omission of fact, Keno made it clear that he didn't care for the deception. However, he agreed to go along when he was reminded that a marriage might depend on it.

Julie was beside herself. She'd made an irrevocable decision, and, like it or not, she was stuck with it. Easing a guilty conscience would probably cost everything she'd worked for her entire adult life. She thought: *Hoisted on my own petard. What the heck is a petard anyway? Didn't I read somewhere that it was an old French bomb? Didn't Shakespeare use that as a metaphor to imply that a big fart lifted up somebody's butt?* She found the reflection amusing, even in her troubled state of mind. She forced herself to complete a grueling workout, and practiced some fictitious testimony during a long, hot shower.

Julie looked composed by the time she sat down at the breakfast table with Buzz. Almost casually, she said, "You don't look so good."

"Thanks a lot." He stared at her sitting there with no make-up and her wet hair hanging straight down. She still looked great. "I wish I could say the same for you, but I swore off lying."

"I didn't mean that you're unattractive. I meant that you don't look as healthy as you should. Is your shoulder hurting you?"

In truth, the shoulder was hurting like hell. Since it had woken him two hours earlier, nerve-searing pain zapped him almost every time he moved. "Don't worry your pretty wet head about my shoulder. It'll be just fine."

"I'm surprised they didn't keep you in the hospital longer." Julie glared at him suspiciously. "You did get the okay to check out of the hospital?"

Buzz's feigned innocence, but he might as well have signed a confession.

Julie stared with an open mouth. "Buzz?"

"Going straight is not all it's cracked up to be."

"They didn't officially release you?"

Buzz shrugged his good shoulder. "I had an emergency to deal with."

"There's going to be another emergency if that wound gets infected. That's nothing to play around with, Mr. Tough Guy. You're just begging for gangrene."

A stabbing pain suddenly supported her side of the argument. "I'll go see my doctor right after the meeting."

"Promise?"

"Yeah, for what it's worth, you have my word on it."

Nathaniel Clay did almost everything with a touch of class, and this morning's meeting with prospective witnesses would do nothing to tarnish that image. The meeting was held in an impressive conference room at the Holiday Inn, just north of San Rafael. At one end of a long, glossy table were six stylish place settings, each with a china plate, a matching cup and saucer, a juice glass, and brightly polished silverware resting on carefully folded cloth napkins. Placed within easy reach were three baskets of enticing pastries, one glass pitcher containing orange juice and one containing tomato juice. There were also three large thermoses of coffee—one decaf and two regulars.

Clay remained standing while greeting each arrival as he would welcome an important guest to his home. After Buzz, Julie, Keno, and Charles Chung had entered the conference room, Clay introduced them to his associate, Amelia Winford.

Taking a page out of her mentor's book, Amelia went around shaking hands with each person as if she were truly delighted to meet them. Amelia had slate-black skin, as if tempered with gunpowder, and she flashed a luminescent smile that brightened the already well-lit room. Her cheery disposition seemed to infect everyone with a happy virus.

After everyone had found a seat, Clay led the attack on the foodstuffs. After swallowing a bite of Danish and washing it down with a healthy swallow of orange juice, the gracious defense attorney remarked, "Amelia is my most competent associate, and I'm ashamed to admit how much I've come to depend on her. I will warn you, however, she can be a bit aggressive. Don't be surprised if she interrupts you with a sharply pointed question." In an almost casual way, Clay added, "She'll be recording our conversations, but don't let that alarm you. Everything we say here will be held in the strictest confidence. And I expect you will respect that confidence as well." Clay purposely made individual eye contact to emphasize his point. "I can't stress that enough."

When each rapt listener had nodded to confirm they'd grasped the importance of his warning, he proceeded with an all-business voice. He established the time of day, who was present and where they were meeting—obligatory facts recorded by Amelia. He explained that pressing time concerns required him to collect this testimony as a group, which he lightheartedly referred to as *Team Flores*.

Clay realized it was a tactical gamble to have each of the witnesses share his or her testimony in front of the others. It could cause any among them to withhold embarrassing information. However, he liked the Team concept. He hoped it would inspire them to unite in the admirable concept of pursuing truth and justice. This was, after all, a classic case of good versus evil.

With the preliminaries satisfied, Clay looked around the table, and said, "I suppose we should begin with Joaquin."

Keno hunched his shoulders questioningly. "Want me to just tell what I saw the day my father was…?"

"Yes, but for formalities sake, begin with your name, address, occupation, and relationship to the deceased. Then tell us everything you witnessed after arriving at the Sea Lion Cove Estates that Sunday morning." Then Clay thought to add, "Which, for the record, was one week ago yesterday."

It occurred to Keno that he was an unemployed ex-student who lived at home with his mother, and his primary source of income was now dependent on marrying the richest girl in the county. However, he only admitted to the unemployed ex-student part. He had to pause a moment before reliving that tragic Sunday morning, which seemed like weeks ago, not merely eight days. His eyes glistened with moisture when he'd finished recounting the painful experience that had resulted in the needless death of his father.

He noticed that all but Amelia had lowered their heads, each seeming to find something interesting on their plates, in their coffee cups, or on their fingernails. Keno concluded his testimony by describing his conversation with Julie that morning and his encounter with Nicky Ghilardi. But not sure about something, he caught Clay's attention with a glance. "Do I need to tell you about my hassle with Deputy Wertz and going to jail?

"No, that's a separate matter that I'm dealing with."

Amelia glanced at her notes. "I would like you to clarify something, Joaquin. Are the casts you're wearing the result of injuries incurred the morning of the incident?"

"Yes, I really hurt my knee when I trashed my bike."

With her pen poised over a yellow legal pad, she frowned and said, "You said you *ran* over to where your father was lying on a bed of flowers."

Keno replied, "I didn't exactly run over, but I hurried over as fast as I could. I guess my adrenaline was really pumping because I don't remember feeling much pain."

Amelia made a note before asking, "And when you had the altercation with Nicky Ghilardi, you weren't able to stand and fight him?"

"No, I wasn't. I went down after I punched him once in his pot gut. But that was several minutes after the accident, so the adrenaline had probably worn off by then."

"And Nicky kicked you when you were lying on the ground?"

"Yeah, that's what the ugly punk did.'

Amelia made a face to reveal her disgust, and then she glanced at her notes. "You described Julie Lemmon's hair as... the word you used was *frizzled*."

"Yeah, that's the best way I know how to describe it."

When Amelia leaned back with a prim smile and slightly raised eyebrows, Clay knew she was satisfied, at least for the moment. He scanned the table, then said, "I suppose we should hear from Miss Lemmon next."

Julie's mind had been racing during Keno's testimony. She'd been caught up in Clay's team concept, but there was no way she would admit to all that had taken place inside the Mercedes that morning. She asked herself: *How can I explain that Nicky was speeding to a place where I was going to satisfy him sexually? How can I admit that I was fondling his crotch just seconds before we hit the truck? How am I going to explain how Nicky's vomit splashed on my hair? What if Nicky finds out about my testimony and decides to get back at me by revealing everything?*

With a curious expression, Clay leaned toward Julie. "Miss Lemmon?"

After rattling off the relevant personal information, Julie decided to confess to a couple of sordid details, hoping these would detract attention from the worst of things. She cleared her throat and began. "I'm not proud of the fact that I partied with Nicky Ghilardi the night before the accident. I was trying to land a huge sales contract the only way I knew how. My real estate company was hurting financially, and I was desperate to do almost anything to bail it out. I arranged for a friend to introduce me to Nicky soon after I'd learned that he had control over the primary sales contract for the Sea Lion Cove Estates. Getting that contract would guarantee that I could rescue my failing business. Stupid me, I agreed to go out with Nicky the first time we met, even though he was the most unappealing man I've ever been that close to. But, as I said, I was desperate. We started drinking early that Saturday night and then continued until the following Sunday morning. But Nicky wasn't only drinking, he was also doing a lot of cocaine."

Amelia's intelligent eyes narrowed—she'd picked up on something. "Excuse me, Miss Lemmon, but I find it curious that you used the word *doing* to describe Mr. Ghilardi's drug use. Can you be more specific about the quantities of cocaine that he was *doing* during the hours leading up to the incident?"

At first, Julie didn't know what to think about Amelia questioning her for using a specific verb. But when it occurred to her that *doing* implied familiarity, she responded with an off-handed denial. "I don't know the first thing about cocaine or how to measure it, but Nicky had a plastic baggy that looked to have about half a cup in it. When we were alone, he would put a line on a small mirror, chop it up with a single-edge razor blade, and then snort it. But when we were around other people, in a club or whatever, he had a little gadget that looked like a silver bullet with a hole in one end. He would twist a little knob on the side of the gadget and snort from it every once in a while. Looking back, I think he was using cocaine most of the night."

Amelia's eyes flashed to her notes, suggesting she'd picked up on the switch from *doing* to *using*. "Please tell us about Mr. Ghilardi's alcohol consumption while you were with him."

"He started off with a few straight shots of Jack Daniel's, but then switched to beer. I would guess he drank at least a dozen beers, maybe more. He was still at it the next morning. Anyway, at around midnight he insisted that we go bar-hopping to a couple of topless joints. And that was really a nightmare. He embarrassed me to tears by..."

"Excuse me, Miss Lemmon," Amelia interrupted. "If you don't mind, let's cut to that Sunday morning at the Sea Lion Cove Estates when Mr. Ghilardi first drove his Mercedes onto Ghilardi Drive. Tell us why the two of you were there and what you were doing prior to the accident."

Julie nodded while thinking fast. She realized she'd have to be careful with every word now. "I apologize for getting sidetracked. Anyway, we were driving out to the Sea Lion Cove Estates to finalize the details associated with the sales contract, look at the model homes, and get an overall view of the property. I wanted to get a handle on the sales plan and everything it was going to entail." Julie paused to review the edited testimony in her mind. "As soon as Nicky turned onto Ghilardi Drive, he pressed the accelerator all the way to the floorboard and sent the car racing down the street. I yelled at him to slow down, but he just laughed like a madman and swerved the car from side to side. I think he was doing it to scare the hell out of me, which he succeeded in doing. He thought it was funny. I thought it was insane."

"Do you know how fast he was going?" Amelia asked.

"I didn't look at the speedometer, but I heard Joaquin say he was going at least eighty at the time of the accident. I think that's probably about right."

Amelia jotted down a note and encouraged, "Go on."

Julie sighed, and said, "Stupid me, I didn't even have my seat belt buckled. Then everything happened really fast. I got a glimpse of Joaquin and his motorcycle just before Nicky swerved the car hard to one side. I think the momentum threw my head toward Nicky's lap just before we hit the truck, which I never saw until I got out of the car."

Amelia leaned forward. "You didn't see the pickup truck prior to the collision?"

"No, I didn't. For one thing, we were heading right into the sun, which was blinding."

"I see," Amelia replied while scribbling, *Sun?* on the legal pad. "Then your head was close to Mr. Ghilardi's lap at the moment of impact?"

"Probably very close to it when an airbag slammed into the back of my head."

"And then Mr. Ghilardi vomited on you?"

"Yes, my face hit something hard when we crashed, which I'm guessing was Nicky's huge belt buckle. That's when he threw up on me. And then I crawled to the back seat and wiped myself off with his jacket. I'm sure that's why my hair looked so... frizzled."

Amelia nodded as if it all sounded perfectly logical. "And that's when you went to assist Joaquin Flores?"

Julie was glad to hear something positive. "Yes, I went to see if there was anything I could do, which basically amounted to using my cell phone."

"And you called the Marin County Sheriff's Department?"

"Yes, I called them and told them to send an ambulance immediately. Nicky didn't like me doing that, and that might be what started the fight between him and Joaquin." She shrugged and said, "That's about it."

Wearing a pensive expression, Clay said, "Thank you, Miss Lemmon. That was very informative."

Clay next directed his attention toward the stoic Chinese man, and said, "We'd like to hear your version of that morning's events, Mr. Chung."

Charles Chung had issues of his own. He worked as an electrician for Thompson Electric, which subcontracted all the electrical work for the Sea Lion Cove Estates. Chung didn't personally know Frank Flores but had seen him around and knew that most of the other construction workers liked him. He had also seen Nicky Ghilardi a few times at the job site but had never heard anyone say anything good about him. But he hadn't related this information to Buzz because he had good reason to believe that testifying to this would jeopardize his job, even though he'd been employed by Thompson Electric for the past nineteen years.

Charles Chung nervously rubbed his damp palms together, then began. "The morning of the accident, a week ago yesterday, I was fishing at Sea Lion Cove, a place where I have fished since I was a small boy. I believe my boat was about fifty yards from Ghilardi Drive. It was a bright, sunny morning, and I was in a good spot to see everything that took place. It was also very calm and quiet out there, which made it easy to hear things. Out on the bay, a noise fifty yards away can sound as clear as if it were coming from only fifty feet away. This is why the first thing I noticed that morning was the distinctive sound of a motorcycle. It was a pleasant rumbling sound. I recall looking over and watching the motorcycle slowly come down the street. A minute or so later, I heard a car approaching very fast. I could tell it was speeding because it was making a very high-pitched noise. Then I looked over and saw a big black Mercedes come racing down the street. I was immediately concerned that it was going to hit the motorcycle. But Joaquin Flores reacted very quickly. He leaned over and put the motorcycle on its side, sliding out of the way. The big Mercedes swerved to miss him and crashed into Frank Flores' green pickup truck, which had been stopped in the middle of the street. The impact sent the pickup almost flying until it crashed into the picture window of a model home." Chung leveled his gaze at Clay. "And that is what I saw."

Amelia had clearly picked up on something. She did some lip gymnastics and then asked, "When did you learn that Frank Flores was the man driving the pickup truck?"

Chung blew out a deep breath. "I think it was the morning after the accident."

Amelia frowned. "How did you know the car was a Mercedes?"

Chung looked confused. "I may have learned that the next day as well."

"Why am I feeling that you're not telling us everything you know, Mr. Chung? Am I wrong to think that you seemed familiar with Frank Flores and the make of the car? Perhaps a little too familiar?"

Chung stared at her for a few seconds, then his body visibly sagged. "Because if I tell you everything I know, I will probably lose my job." He shrugged and offered a look of resignation. "My boss will probably fire me as it is."

Clay was not surprised at Amelia's amazing perception. She seemed to have a sixth sense when it came to detecting when a witness was holding something back. He'd seen it in action several times before. However, he felt it was his place to address this cooperative man's concerns. "There's no reason to fear telling us everything you know, Mr. Chung. What you say here this morning will be held in the strictest confidence. And we can protect you in any legal manner imaginable. If your employer attempts to terminate you for providing honest testimony, we will make it very expensive for him, and quite profitable for you. You have my word."

"That's right, Mr. Chung," Amelia put in. "Tell us what you're holding back, and we will make sure it doesn't cause you any trouble. None whatsoever."

Chung looked deflated. "I told you that I'm an electrician, but I didn't tell you that I have been working at the Sea Lion Cove Estates for the past several months. The owner of the company, Mr. Thompson, contracted to do all the electrical work there. That Monday morning everyone at the job site was saying how Frank Flores had driven his truck out in front of Nicky Ghilardi's Mercedes, but I knew better. At lunchtime that day, I went to see my boss and told him what I had seen. He told me I had better not breathe a word of it to anyone because it could mean big trouble. All the workers could lose their jobs if Ghilardi Development got sued and lost everything. The whole project could get shut down. There isn't a lot of construction in Marin County these days because of the building moratorium and all the environmental impact studies. I didn't want people to lose their jobs, especially hard-working union people, so I remained quiet. But when I learned that Nicky Ghilardi had shot Mrs. Flores and Mr. Aldrich, I realized I had made a terrible mistake." His eyes darted around the table. "I am very sorry, and I apologize for not coming forward sooner."

Everyone sat silent. It was as if, each in their own way, were contemplating how this one tragic event could affect so many lives in so many ways.

Amelia cleared her throat and said with convincing empathy, "Thank you very much, Mr. Chung. Your testimony is greatly appreciated."

Clay glanced at Buzz. "Do you have anything to add?"

Buzz had been contemplating whether to bring up the phony real estate transaction, which amounted to a payoff to Deputy Wertz. But he knew it would almost certainly cause Julie legal problems, to say nothing of the humiliation. He decided that if this information became necessary to convict Nicky, he would introduce it at that time. He shook his head while figuring out how to answer without resorting to a lie. "Nothing at the moment."

Clay leaned toward Buzz and stared at him as if it were the first time he'd seen him all morning. "Are you feeling alright? You don't look so good, my friend."

"Thanks, I really needed that." Feeling shaky, Buzz got to his feet and grabbed the back of his chair when a sharp pain stabbed his shoulder. "I think I'll be going now. See you all later. Drive carefully and be nice to people."

Julie jumped to her feet, put an arm around his waist, and escorted him outside. When they reached her Jaguar, she scowled and ordered, "Get in the car, Buzz Aldrich. I'm taking you to the hospital."

"I thought you had people waiting."

"My future at the Sea Lion Cove Estates is dubious, and that's being optimistic. So just get in the car. I'll sweat the small stuff later."

His shoulder felt even worse, and, on top of that, the three-day-old dog bite wound had begun to hurt. A trip to the hospital suddenly seemed like a grand idea. "Lead on, fair maid. Sir Lie-a-lot is at your mercy."

After starting the Jaguar, she said, "Thanks for not saying anything about the Wertz deal."

"What Wertz deal?"

Charles Chung returned to work at the Sea Lion Cove Estates and did his best to remain his stoic self. He hadn't been late once in nineteen years, and some of his fellow electricians had come to believe that *Dependable* was actually his first name. When he hadn't seen him for a couple of hours, Thompson Electric's foreman assumed that *Dependable Charlie* had to be somewhere correcting an unexpected problem.

Keno went straight to Marin General Hospital to check on Millie, who remained comatose. With little else to do, he spent most of the next thirty minutes on his cell phone talking to Netanya. Much of the conversation centered on whether he should go to Daryl Slate's birthday party in Berkeley later that night.

Two floors down, Buzz was getting an earful from an annoyed assistant administrator while a seemingly sadistic nurse was cheerfully injecting a large dose of penicillin into one of his muscular buttocks.

Clay and Amelia remained in the conference room after everyone else had departed. Hoping she was right, Amelia said, "I think that went rather well."

"Yes," Clay agreed, "we've garnered some compelling evidence. And, by the way, I'd like to commend you on the way you handled the witnesses, especially after having the case thrown at you on such short notice."

Amelia unleashed her dazzling smile. "Thank you, Mr. Clay. What do you suggest we do now?"

"First, I suggest that you start by calling me Nate. And then I suggest we arrange a meeting with Jason Bridger, ASAP." Clay mulled it over for a moment. "In fact, I'm calling his office right now."

"Okay…" It took a moment for Amelia to force out, "Nate." Her smile revealed that she enjoyed saying his name. "I'll condense all the testimony into a couple of pages so that Mr. Bridger can see just how compelling the evidence is."

Forty-five minutes later, Clay and Amelia entered the district attorney's office in the Marin County Civic Center.

Though naturally apprehensive, Jason Bridger was more than a little energized. Going up against one of the better defense attorneys in the state, if not the country, instilled a certain amount of awe-inspired anxiety. However, it also presented a challenge of major proportions, and Jason was curious to see how he would measure up.

As he invited his professional combatants into his office, Jason wondered what kinds of cards Clay was holding. Their brief phone conversation led him to believe the imposing lawyer probably had an ace or two up his sleeve. Following the introduction with Amelia, and after both had politely refused his offer of coffee or something to drink, Jason asked offhandedly, "To what do I owe the pleasure?"

Amelia presented Jason with three pages of condensed testimony, which only revealed numbers in lieu of the witnesses' names. She spoke with an air of confidence. "These pages contain overwhelming evidence that will prove beyond a shadow of a doubt that Nicholas Ghilardi's Mercedes was traveling at an extremely high rate of speed when it collided with Frank Flores' pickup truck that Sunday morning. The testimony will prove that Mr. Flores' truck was stopped at the moment of impact. In addition, one reliable eyewitness has testified that Mr. Ghilardi was inhaling large quantities of cocaine and drinking excessive amounts of alcohol for several hours immediately prior to the time of the incident." Amelia pointed out Julie's *topless joints* comment without her name attached. "And it will be rather easy to locate more eyewitnesses who will corroborate his excessive alcohol consumption."

Jason had been gifted with the ability to speedread. He whizzed through the three pages, then looked up at Clay. "Where are you going with this?"

"I'd say some horse-trading is in order."

It surprised Jason to hear such an archaic term emanating from such a suave and erudite man. He forced a chuckle. "From what I've read here, your horses are pulling hard against Nicky Ghilardi, but they aren't doing much to lighten the burden from your other clients."

Clay shook his head as if he were about to scold a naughty boy. "I appreciate the burden of guilt pun, Jason, but let's not beat around the bush. We both know your war chest is polluted with Ghilardi money."

Jason hadn't expected Clay to trump him with the dubious money card, at least not so soon. "I'll admit that I've accepted money from Ghilardi Development, legal campaign funds by the way, but that will not influence the performance of my duties."

"No one is accusing you of any wrongdoing, Jason."

Jason liked the sound of that. "Then what are you asking for?"

"We want all the charges against Joaquin Flores dismissed, and for Mrs. Flores, we want probation and limited confinement in a mental health institution of our choosing."

Jason grimaced. "If I throw out the cocaine possession charge against Joaquin Flores, I'd be admitting that we have a dirty deputy sheriff who planted evidence."

"I suppose so," Clay agreed. "But as they say, the truth hurts, and the truth is bound to come out if we go to court."

Jason was no fool. He'd had some serious reservations about Deputy Wertz's veracity from the beginning. "I can probably make the charges against Joaquin go away, but there is absolutely nothing I can do about Mrs. Flores' situation. She went on a shooting rampage witnessed by two deputy sheriffs, Mrs. Yvette Ghilardi, and a very reliable employee. The shootout even got a write-up in the *Independent Journal*, which reported every flagrant detail. There's no way I can sweep that much dirt under the rug."

Clay turned to Amelia. "Would you mind getting me a drink of water? My throat suddenly became a bit dry."

Amelia took the hint and hurried out.

Clay narrowed his eyes and leveled his gaze. "I would have a field day trying Mrs. Flores' case, Jason. An out-of-control drunk and cocaine freak not only killed her husband, who just happened to be one of the nicest men on the face of the earth, the bastard is also suing the grieving widow to boot." Clay shook his head in disgust. "I can produce a dozen witnesses who will relate heart-wrenching stories about what a wonderful man Frank Flores was. Get real, Jason, you won't be able to run for dog catcher after I get through making you look like a Nazi executioner."

He paused to let Jason chew on that for a moment, then went on. "Now here's how the cow ate the cabbage. You give me what I want, I'll ask Simon Bernstein to bankroll your run for Congress. If you don't cooperate, I'll convince him to back your opponent, whoever the hell it is. Do it my way; it's a win-win. Any other way, it's lose-lose."

Jason felt as if he'd just been knocked stupid with a sucker punch. "Are you saying I'd have Simon Bernstein's backing to help my run for Congress?"

"I'm not prepared to make a definite commitment, of course, but I'm quite confident he would be willing to support you. Mr. Bernstein has informed me, in no uncertain terms, that he's willing to go to virtually any extremes to exonerate his future son-in-law. He also instructed me to do everything I can to help Joaquin's poor widowed mother."

Jason sat silent for a few seconds, feeling as if Clay were playing ping-pong with his thoughts. "Can I have a day to sort this out?"

"Sure, Jason, we can agree on specifics at this time tomorrow." Clay glanced at his watch, then walked out without offering a handshake, much less a parting word.

Jason sat at his desk, confused and feeling more than a little inept. The heavyweight champ had just knocked the crap out of him, winning by TKO after only one round.

Jason wasn't a heavy drinker, but the encounter with Nathaniel Clay encouraged him to have an early lunch at The Wharf, beginning at the bar with a dry Beefeater's martini. Unfortunately, he only had time to enjoy one good sip of comforting gin before he felt a tap on his shoulder.

The reflection in the mirror behind the bar belonged to J.P. Maloney, one of the last people on the planet he wanted to see today.

Jason took another sip of his drink, then spun on the stool to greet the sly old fox.

"Good morning, J.P. How's it going?"

J.P. forced the corners of his mouth to curl a little, almost managing a smile. "You're at it a little earlier than usual."

Jason shrugged. "I'm having one of those days."

J.P. motioned with a quick jerk of his head. "Let's grab a table."

Grudgingly, Jason relented. "Sure, lead the way."

When they'd each found a chair, J.P. asked, "What's going on with that Mrs. Flores situation? From everything I've learned, she's gone completely off her rocker."

Jason recognized a loophole he just might wriggle through. "Yes, Mrs. Flores apparently went wacko when she got a subpoena informing her that Ghilardi Development was suing her for two hundred and fifty grand. Add that to her husband's tragic death, and her maniacal behavior almost seems justifiable."

"Trying to kill someone with a shotgun is never justifiable, Jason." J.P. looked even more hateful than usual. "You're starting to sound like some lily-livered liberal."

It occurred to Jason that the old rascal had probably done the legal work and filed the appalling lawsuit himself. "Do you know anything about that lawsuit, J.P.?"

J.P. didn't like having his motives questioned, especially since Nicky had created the mess. "Sometimes we're forced to do things we don't like to protect our investments. And sometimes the best defense is a good offense." J.P. glared at the DA, then went on. "But my reasons for doing anything shouldn't concern you, Jason. What should concern you is how you're going to convict that crazy bitch."

Jason was tired of being defensive. He tossed down the rest of the martini, then met J.P.'s surly glare with a determined look of his own. "Nathaniel Clay came into my office this morning with solid evidence that proves Nicky was drinking, using cocaine, and speeding like a maniac when he killed Frank Flores. He wants to use this convincing evidence to leverage a horse-trade Those are his exact words. *Horse-trade."*

Jason leaned back and ordered another round.

J.P. rarely exposed weakness, but this information caused his jaw to drop a little. "Solid evidence?"

"Rock solid. For starters, three eyeball witnesses."

J.P. had not foreseen this scenario. He gulped down the rest of his wine. "How's it going to play out if you do some of that... hors-trading?"

"Joaquin Flores walks. Mrs. Flores gets a big probation just for show, and then does some time in a mental health institution." Jason decided not to reveal, *of their choosing.*

"What can you do for Nicky?"

For the first time in recent memory, Jason felt he was dealing from a position of strength. And it felt good. "I haven't made up my mind yet, but he certainly has to be held accountable. After all, he sense-lessly killed a man while under the influence of alcohol and cocaine." Jason paused, then added a little salt to the open wound. "And from everything I've heard, Frank Flores was a damned good man."

J.P.'s face was growing grayer by the second; his atrophied old heart couldn't quite keep up with these shocking revelations. He pounded the table with the bottom of one fist, making glasses and silverware jump. "Dammit, Jason, we've been very generous with you. You'd better damned well figure a way out of this mess!"

Jason had begun to enjoy himself. Knowing he was going to have Bernstein's money behind him for his political campaign gave him an almost intoxicating feeling of power. And the chilled gin wasn't hurting. He took a long sip of his second martini, then shook his head helplessly. "I know you've been very generous, J.P., but maybe you didn't realize you weren't buying my office. I'm still the district attorney of this county, and I still have an obligation to the people. You know I'll be fair with Nicky, but I just can't turn my back on such extreme criminal behavior."

J.P. suddenly envisioned a multi-million-dollar wrongful-death suit sucking the life out of the Ghilardi Development Corporation. He used the table to get to his feet. "If we go down, you're going down with us."

Jason turned up both palms and shrugged. "I wish there were something I could do, old pal, but I'm backed into a corner on this one."

J.P.'s expression indicated he was about to complain, but he suddenly turned on his heels and stormed out, mumbling something about corrupt politicians.

As he watched the sly old fox slink away, Jason smiled contentedly for the first time in days. He took another sip of his martini and began to consider how he could make political hay out of prosecuting the CEO of the Ghilardi Development Corporation. The public always loves to see the big boys go down. *Yes,* Jason thought almost smugly, *Nicky Ghilardi's butt will make a nice stepping-stone to a Congressional office in Washington.*

Then Jason realized that J.P. could cause him problems if he revealed the under-the-table cash donations. *No,* he reminded himself, *nothing is ever easy when it comes to politics,*

Chapter Seventeen

J.P. called Nicky the minute he climbed into his Lincoln. He didn't share any details but told him they needed to meet as soon as possible, and he strongly suggested that Nicky invite Wertz.

Decked out in black cowboy clothes, as he'd taken to wearing lately, Nicky sat at his desk with his boots resting on one of Julie Lemmon's recent sales contracts. He tipped his black Stetson back with a thumb and asked, "Okay, J.P., what's so damn important that I had to interrupt my busy schedule?"

Busy schedule? J.P. wished he were forty years younger. Hell, even thirty. He would beat the arrogant brat to within an inch of his life. He cast a sideways glance at Deputy Wertz, then directed his reply to Nicky with some extra venom. "Your freedom and the corporation's solvency are what's so damn important, Nicky." The old lawyer glared, pleased that he'd gotten the idiot's attention. "Nathaniel Clay has presented the DA with solid evidence that you were drinking, using cocaine, and speeding like a madman when you killed Frank Flores."

Nicky seemed surprised. "I thought you were supposed to have my ass covered with the DA?"

"That ungrateful traitor has changed his tune. I suspect that Clay has either bought him off with Bernstein's money or scared the piss out of him. Perhaps both."

Nicky scowled. "What's up with that solid evidence crap?"

"Clay has three rock-solid eyewitnesses, and he plans to use them for some horse-trading Joaquin Flores is going to get off scot-free, and Mrs. Flores will be getting some show probation and a little quiet time in a funny farm."

Nicky's mind raced. *Three eyewitnesses? Joaquin Flores is one for sure. Who are the other two? The only other people at the accident scene were Wertz and Julie Lemmon. She is probably number two, but could Wertz be number three?* He glared at the visibly concerned deputy. "Did you rat on me, Wertz?"

The deputy's head jerked back as if Nicky had punched him. "Hell no! You think I'd jeopardize my chance to make some big money on our house deal?" The accusation had released some suppressed resentment. "Don't be talking to me in that tone of voice, Nicky G, and don't ever accuse me of that kind of bullshit again."

Nicky believed Deputy Wertz; his reaction was too real and too angry to be phony. "Okay, I believe you. So let it go." Nicky paused, then said, "But I know damn well Julie Lemmon has stabbed me in the back. She's the only one who knows for sure I was drinkin' an' doin' coke that night." He slammed the desk with a palm. "That broad is toast!" He turned to J.P. and snapped, "Figure out some way to get her for breach o' contract or whatever it takes. I want that bitch outta the Sea Lion Cove Estates before sundown."

J.P. smirked in response to the cowboy lingo. "I doubt if we can do it legally, Honcho. But even if we could, we don't know for sure that she's one of the witnesses."

Nicky didn't know what to think about the *Honcho* remark, so he ignored it. "I know for sure she's one of 'em, an' that's all that counts. If you can't do it legally, I'll do it my own damn way."

Wertz raised his hands in protest. "Hold it right there, Nicky. I've gone along with you on everything so far, even ignoring the fact that you use coke and know a big-time drug dealer, but I can't stand by and let you physically harm anyone. Especially a woman."

Nicky glared at the deputy, then got up and paced behind his massive desk. He rejected one idea after another until he found what he considered a viable solution. He put his hands on his ample hips, squared his narrow shoulders, and nodded his head. "Awright, you ding-a-lings, I got it." He directed his attention to J.P. "You said Clay was gonna do some horse-tradin'.' Well, we can do some o' that tradin' our own damn selves." Nicky chuckled. "An, we're gonna get us a big stud to trade with."

Wertz made a face, as if too afraid to ask. "What do you have in mind, Nicky?"

Nicky smirked and performed his bobblehead doll routine. "We're gonna frame Joaquin Flores with a totally real lookin' kidnappin'.' Then we can work out a deal with that dimwitted DA an' that hotshot lawyer."

Wertz and J.P. exchanged *Are you kidding me?* looks.

J.P. cleared his throat and said with disdain, "Haven't we gone down this road before? The frame-up with the cocaine is bound to backfire on you and Wertz as it is."

Wertz frowned. "How could that come back on me?"

J.P. glared at Wertz as if he were a brainless idiot. "Gee, let me count the ways, Deputy Dog." He shook his head and said, "A first-year law student could prove that the accident report you filed was inaccurate, to put it mildly. If they've turned Julie Lemmon, she's had to admit that she and Nicky were lying about everything. And, old pal, that will place the shadow of suspicion directly on you. Don't you think they're going to be just a little skeptical of you finding cocaine in the motorcycle's saddlebags only one day after you filed a false accident report?"

Wertz grimaced. "Yeah, it is going to look bad if Joaquin Flores walks."

"Real bad," J.P. agreed. "You might start thinking about a career change."

"There ya go," Nicky said. "We gotta keep Biker Boy from walkin'." He glared at his captive audience of two, and said, "An' I ain't goin' to prison for nobody."

Wertz shot J.P. a nervous look. "I wouldn't make it in prison. It's not a good place for former officers of the law."

The thought of prison sent shudders through Nicky. "Nobody's goin' down. Not if we can do somethin' about it."

J.P. recalled reading an article about the high incidence of birth defects incurred by in vitro babies and wondered if these problems included brain damage. That might explain some of Nicky's behavior. "Okay, Honcho, let's hear your cockamamie scheme."

Nicky didn't have the slightest idea of what *cockamamie* meant but proceeded as if it meant something grand. He smiled devilishly while working his hands together. "Okay, here's the deal. We know Biker Boy has been drivin' aroun' in a brand-new Cadillac that belongs to ol' man Bernstein. An' almost everybody in the county knows he's super-pissed at me for shootin' his mama. An' we're gonna use that against him. We'll get him to come to a certain place at a certain time, an' then we'll set him up an' make it look like he kidnapped me."

Nicky chuckled as the malicious scheme unfolded in his imagination. "I got this idea from a movie Robert Redford was in. You guys tie me up an' put me in the trunk o' the Cadillac after we bust out a taillight. Wertz, who has another deputy with him to make it look totally legit, stops the car to give Biker Boy a fix-it ticket. While Wertz is checkin' out the taillight, the other deputy hears me kickin' an' screamin' in the trunk. They make Biker Boy open it up, an' bingo, there I am. A helpless victim of a heartless kidnappin'." Nicky chuckled again. "Everybody will believe that Biker Boy was out to kill me. Gettin' revenge for killin' his daddy an' shootin' his momma. Besides, doin' crazy crap runs in their family. Look at how his nutso mamma tried to shoot me."

J.P. massaged his forehead, hoping it would diminish the sharp pain stabbing at the back of his eyes. For a moment, he thought he was having a stroke for the same reason Big Nick had probably suffered one—putting up with Nicky. Suddenly feeling very tired, J.P. struggled to his feet, glared at Nicky as if he were retarded, then headed for the door. He glanced back over his shoulder and grumbled, "Deal me out, boys. I'm too old for this foolishness. You two idiots are on your own as far as I'm concerned."

Nicky slammed the desk with an open palm and said, "Go ahead, walk out on me you ol' goat. I was plannin' on gettin' rid o' your decrepit ol' ass anyway."

Deputy Wertz sat contemplating the situation. Doing nothing almost certainly meant that Nicky would be arrested and charged with several felonies. And Wertz imagined his own arrest wouldn't be far behind. Nicky would stab him in the back to get his sentence reduced for as little as one day—hell, even an hour. If Nicky's plan had even a remote chance of success, it would be better than waiting around for the inevitable. Besides, he had too much to lose to make a run for the border. And living the life of a wanted man is not that much better than serving time. He'd once returned a prisoner to San Quentin after he'd been on the lam for two years. The guy wouldn't have looked any loonier if he had spent those years in solitary confinement. No, if he were going down, it might as well be for taking a shot at avoiding a prison sentence, which would probably be fatal anyway.

"Okay, let's talk about your cockamamie plan. It sounds to me like it might have some serious holes in it. How are you going to know where the Cadillac is at exactly the right time? And another thing, how are going to get into the trunk? I used to be able to get into cars with a slim jim, but not anymore. These new luxury cars have anti-theft security systems that I can't begin to touch."

Nicky smirked, and said, "Don't sweat it. I got all that stuff figured out. First off, Biker Boy's mamma is in the hospital. I'll figure out a way to get the devoted son there exactly when we want him there. So, there's your time an' place." He paused for a moment, as if searching for more answers under the brim of his cowboy hat. "An' as far as gettin' into the Cadillac's trunk, I know just the cokehead who can handle that for us. Travis Cobb, who happens to own North County Towing, owes me big time. That slob ratted me out to my best coke dealer, and now either he cooperates, or I'll blow his fat ass away."

Wertz shook his head, and said, "I told you I won't tolerate any physical violence."

"Okay then, we'll plant some coke at his place an' you can figure how to get him arrested for dealin.' An' he won't have no hot shot lawyer to save his big lard ass."

Wertz was amazed at the logical solutions that sprouted from Nicky's devious mind. "So, what I basically have to do is have another deputy with me when I stop Joaquin Flores for a broken taillight. Then we discover you in the trunk?"

"That's about it, other than helpin' me persuade Cobb the blob to go along with the plan. An' remember, I'm takin' all the risks. I'm the one whose hide will be on the line."

Wertz exhausted a long, slow breath. "I can't see any other way out of this mess. Either I help you pull off your cockamamie plan, far-fetched as it is, or I go to prison and lose everything I've worked for, including the house deal. I guess I don't have any choice. Let's give it a shot. When do you want to pull it off?"

Nicky grinned to hide his mounting paranoia. "We can't afford to wait. They could be comin' after me at any time. I say we go ahead an' do it tonight."

Wertz's folded his arms to hide his trembling hands. "Can we get everything in place that fast?"

Nicky bounded out of his chair, snatched his pistol out of a desk drawer, and jammed it into his belt. He grabbed a full-length leather coat off the coat rack, jerked his head toward the door, and said, "Follow me up to Cobb's place in Novato."

Wertz felt queasy. "I'll be right behind you."

When Millie finally regained a semblance of consciousness, Keno, who'd been dozing off and on, saw her turn her head a little. He slipped on his crutches and moved to the side of the bed, cautiously studying her face to see whether she was going to suffer another panic attack.

She fought for recognition, and then smiled weakly. "Hi, Sunshine." She reached out with a shaky hand until her fingers found his.

"How ya feeling, Mom?"

She stared for a moment, as if considering the question. "I've been better."

With hopes of implanting a positive thought, he told a white lie. "I can tell you're improving. You're sure looking a lot better."

She forced a little smile. "If this is considered improvement, I must have been in terrible shape."

With an armload of fast food, Netanya arrived just in time to rescue Keno from another fib. Her big eyes telegraphed her delight when she saw that Millie was awake. "Hey! You're awake. I'm so glad to see you, Millie."

Millie moved her shoulders and arms, testing to see how much feeling they had in them. But pain quickly established limits. She grimaced and said, "You mean you're glad to see me alive."

Netanya smiled and replied, "Especially that." She waited until Keno had found a chair, then said, "You'd better eat this stuff before it gets cold Joaquin," and handed him two Whoppers, a large bag of fries, and a chocolate milkshake.

He eagerly agreed. His breakfast had consisted of orange juice and a few pastries.

While Keno munched, Netanya went to the side of the bed. She gently stroked Millie's shoulder and commiserated, "Things have been really rotten for you lately, Millie, but you're one tough lady. You're going to get through this."

Millie patted the back of Netanya's hand and said, "Thanks for being here, Tanya. I appreciate everything you've done." She glanced at Keno, who sat munching. "If the two of you ever get married, always remember that the big lug can be controlled with his stomach. If he gets out of line, threaten to hide the food." A cough interrupted her weak chuckle.

Netanya smiled, waiting for the coughing spell to subside. "That's really cool, Millie. No matter how bad it gets, you never lose your sense of humor."

When a nurse came in to take Millie's blood pressure, Netanya went over and sat down next to Keno. "I know you haven't been getting any sleep, Joaquin. If you want to go home and take a nap, I'll be glad to stay here with Millie."

"I was going to ask you to keep her company if I decide to go to Daryl Slate's birthday party." He shrugged while mulling it over. "But I probably shouldn't go."

"I think you should go, Joaquin," Netanya told him. "You need a break from all the heavy stuff that you've been dealing with. I'll be glad to stay with Millie tonight, but you still need to rest this afternoon."

"I don't want to be taking advantage of you."

She leaned over and kissed him on the cheek, then whispered, "Hey, she's going to be my mother-in-law. I need to get on her good side."

"You're already on her good side." Netanya's suggestion of a nap, combined with the heavy food, suddenly made Keno feel as if weights were attached to his eyelids. "Yeah, maybe I could crash for an hour or so."

"Cool. Go home and grab a nap. You'll feel like a new man." She grinned devilishly and whispered in his ear, "It might be a blast to have a new man."

He playfully cuffed her shoulder. "Don't even think about it." Then he climbed on his crutches and hopped over to the bed. "I'm going to go grab a nap, Millie. I'll be back in a little while."

"Get some rest, Sunshine. I'm not going anywhere."

A few minutes later, a nurse brought Millie a tray that held a skinless chicken breast, wheat toast, cottage cheese, lime Jell-O, tea, and apple juice. Millie nibbled but didn't have much in the way of an appetite. When Netanya saw that Millie wasn't going to eat any more she moved the table arm out of the way and helped adjust the bed to a more comfortable position. Then Millie closed her eyes and drifted off to sleep.

Netanya had brought along a Grisham novel and soon allowed her imagination to take her on a thrilling adventure down in Mississippi.

When Nicky moseyed into Travis's shop he looked as if he might be heading for a shootout at the O.K. Corral. His black Stetson was pulled down close to his dark eyebrows, his black leather coat hung open enough to reveal the pistol in his belt, and his cowboy boots made a clomping sound as he stomped his way inside. Nicky was feeling brave, and it showed. In addition to the loaded Glock, he had a two-way radio hidden inside his coat collar. The radio was switched on, and the volume turned up to the max. Wertz was listening to every word, and Nicky could instantly summon the deputy parked across the street at the 7-Eleven.

Travis Cobb sat on the stool in front of his workbench, concentrating hard on attaching a clamp to the end of a cable. The rhythmic clomping of Nicky's boots eventually pounded their way into his coke-dimmed brain.

Travis spun around and scowled. He'd heard about the shootout at the Ghilardi Ranch and quickly considered the possibility that Nicky might start blasting away at any time. "What the hell you want, Ghilardi?"

Nicky stopped just short of arm's reach, put one thumb in his belt, fondled the Glock's grip with his other hand, and narrowed his beady eyes. "I come to get even for you rattin' on me."

Travis immediately noticed the pistol. He quickly weighed his chances of getting to Nicky before he could pull the gun. But when the fat man considered his athletic limitations, he didn't like the odds. "What the hell are you talking about?"

Nicky inched the gun out a little. "Don't lie to me, butthead. Van Exel ratted you out when he cut me off." Nicky's mouth twisted into a humorless grin. "A rat rattin' out another rat. That's about as low as rattin' gets, ain't it?"

"There was nothing I could do about it, Nicky. I didn't have a choice. Van Exel was worried about you talking too much, and he threatened to kill me on the spot if I wasn't straight with him."

Nicky's hand fidgeted on the gun, obviously enjoying it when the fat man flinched. "You owe me big time for that rattin,' an' I'm here to collect."

"What could you possibly want from me? I ain't got no coke left, and I ain't got much cash neither."

Nicky stared for several seconds, clearly enjoying making the fat man sweat. "I need you to unlock a new Cadillac."

Travis frowned and stared, not believing that he could get off the hook so easily. "That's all you want from me? Unlocking a Cadillac?"

"Can you open the trunk of a brand-new Cadillac?"

Travis still couldn't believe that was all Nicky wanted. "That's it?"

"Can you positively guarantee you can open one o' them new trunks?"

"Well, yeaaaah." Travis shook his big head from side to side. "What the hell do you think I do all day? I can get into any car ever made." Then the possible downside occurred to him. "Are you stealing a new Cadillac? If I got caught doing something like that, not only could I go to jail, I could lose the family business."

"I ain't stealin' nothin,' ya lousy rat, but never mind that. You just have your fat butt out at the sales office of the Sea Lion Cove Estates at eight o'clock tonight."

Travis was totally confused. "Is there going to be a Cadillac parked out there?"

"No, dimwit, that's where I'm going to leave my Mercedes 'cause there won't be any witnesses out there at that time o' night. I'm goin' in the sales office and break up some stuff. Then I'm gonna leave my car door open an' my keys layin' on the ground to make it look like

I was kidnapped. You're gonna pick me up out there, then tape me up an' put me in the trunk of a Cadillac. It's goin' to be parked at Marin General Hospital."

Travis shrugged, still not fully comprehending the plan. But it did seem like an easy way to get Nicky off his back. The alternative could be getting blasted by the ugly idiot, who was acting even crazier than usual. "Okay, I'll meet you at the Sea Lion Cove Estates at eight o'clock."

Nicky glared for emphasis. "That's exactly eight o'clock tonight, butthead. If you're one minute late, I'm gonna come gunnin' for your flabby hide. An' I'm serious as a heart attack. I'll come back an' blow you away if you don't show. Ya got me?"

Feeling somewhat relieved, Travis nodded. "Don't sweat it, Nicky. I'll be there."

Across the street, Deputy Wertz felt a sense of relief and an even stronger sense of admiration. This was the first he'd heard of the abduction scene. While he regretted getting in bed with the Devil, it was good to know that the Devil could be very clever.

Julie decided to go about her business as if nothing out of the ordinary had happened. It pleased her to find that Robbie, the new salesman, had taken the initiative. He'd opened the office and helped the new secretary, Pam, make coffee and begin to get acclimated.

There were no obscene messages from Nicky, so Julie assumed he still didn't know she'd betrayed him. She put on an enthusiastic face and encouraged, "Alright, you guys, let's sell some houses today."

Julie couldn't have been happier with her new hires. Even though they were short on experience, they worked together with uncommon enthusiasm. While Robbie openly displayed effeminate tendencies, he was a natural charmer. He had a way of making potential buyers believe he was their best friend doing them a favor. And Pam, the ambitious secretary, caught on to things faster than Julie could teach them.

The team had obtained two signed contracts and two strong maybes by the time Nicky barged into the office that afternoon. All eyes snapped toward the door when he kicked it open with a cowboy boot. Julie was at her desk, reviewing a contract with Pam, while Robbie and a middle-aged couple were discussing house plans in the living room.

Nicky stomped in, put his thumbs in his belt, and elevated his voice. "I want everybody outta this office." When all five remained stunned, and no one made an effort to move, he shouted, "Didn't anybody hear me? I said everybody get the hell outta here, an' I mean now!"

The married couple didn't bother to wait for an explanation. They exchanged quick glances and were out the door.

Robbie, clearly upset about his potential sale escaping, walked across the room to stand beside Julie. "What's the deal with Cowboy Bob?"

Nicky quickly sized Robbie up. "Who asked you to butt in, you freakin' fag?"

Julie's jaw muscles locked her clenched teeth. Her nostrils flared as she jumped up to confront Nicky. "You can't just come into my office acting like John freaking Wayne. For one thing, you don't measure up." Her nostrils flared again. "If you're not out of here in five seconds, I'm calling a lawyer and suing you for breach of contract."

"Up yours, bitch. I know you stabbed me in the back. An' ya did it after I gave you a helluva good deal. Now *you* havta go."

Robbie, who'd boxed for a couple of years in Golden Gloves, stepped in front of Julie. "I think you're the one who has to go, you phony drugstore cowboy. I'll beat the snot out of you and throw your ugly behind out of here if I have to."

Nicky stepped back and pulled the leather coat apart to expose his pistol. "I don't know who the hell you are, but I'm Nicky G. I own this property, includin' the floor you're standin' on. Now get your swishy butt on outta here."

Pam suddenly spoke up. "I've got 911 on the phone, Julie. What do you want me to tell them?"

Nicky leaned over to look past Robbie. When he saw the plucky secretary holding the phone shoulder high, he warned, "I'm gettin' your traitor butt outta here, Lemmon, one way or another." Then he turned and kicked the door on his way out.

Julie turned to her secretary, and said, "Thanks for the quick thinking, Pam." She shrugged and added, "If you didn't know, that was Nicky Ghilardi, who calls himself Nicky G. He's the CEO of Ghilardi Development Corporation. He has issues." She shrugged and told them, "Actually, he's an egomaniac fruitcake who likes to play cowboy. I do have a binding sales contract to justify my staying, but I'll understand if either of you want to leave..."

Robbie shook his head with a look of determination engraved on his effeminate features. "That goofball could decide to come back and hassle you, Julie. I'm not leaving this office until you do."

Pam nodded her agreement. "I'm not leaving either. I need this job, and you need our support."

Julie wished Buzz were well and would take care of Nicky G. "I can't let you guys risk your lives. Let's finish what we were doing and call it a day. I'll do everything I can to get a restraining order by tomorrow morning. I know a very good lawyer who I'm sure will handle this. I'll let you know as soon as I get it done."

Panic suddenly overwhelmed Millie's dreams. She began to thrash about in the bed, and a few seconds later her scream assaulted Netanya's distracted mind. She was deeply engrossed in the Grisham novel, which caused the scream to become a shocking jolt back to reality. She sat petrified for a moment—unsure of what to do. Then she noticed the call button and hurried over to press it.

The duty nurse had been forewarned. A little more than a minute after the warning light flashed, she rushed in with a loaded hypodermic. Millie was soon snoozing peacefully.

When Keno arrived half an hour later, Netanya had to deal with a dilemma. She didn't want to withhold the truth, but if she told him about the panic attack, brief as it was, she was sure he wouldn't go to the birthday party. She realized that Millie was going to be out for hours, and even if she were to have another attack, the nursing staff had everything under control. She decided she would tell him about it tomorrow. "Hey, Joaquin."

"Hey, yourself. How's Millie doing?"

Netanya shrugged. "Sleeping like a baby. She's so weak, I'm sure she'll be out of it a lot during the next few days."

"Sounds like a good diagnosis, Doctor Bernstein."

Netanya had formulated a plan to make it easy for Keno to attend the party. "I'm going home for a couple of hours, and then I'll come back and take over so that you can go tonight."

"You sure? I don't feel right about partying while you're stuck here."

She moved close and put one arm around his waist. "Listen, bub, you're going to go enjoy yourself, or I'll torment you so much that you'll want to be someplace else anyway."

Keno smiled. "You always get your way, don't you?"

"Better get used to it." She kissed him and then gathered her things. "I'll be back in two hours. In the meantime, kick back and relax." She tipped her head toward the bed. "Millie is."

Deputy Wertz caught up with Deputy Drable just as he was leaving for the day. "Say, old buddy, I got a solid lead on that Van Exel case. Can I count on you for backup if I need it later?"

Drable stared at Wertz with a look of frustration. "How much later? I was planning to spend some time with my kids."

"It won't be that late. I got a solid tip that a male nurse at Marin General is making a big buy around eight-thirty tonight."

"Where'd you get a tip like that?"

Wertz shrugged and showed Drable both palms. "Sorry, buddy, I can't reveal my source." He winked and added, "It would be politically incorrect, if you know what I mean."

Drable stared without the slightest idea of what he meant. "If you know for sure that something is going down, call me on my cell. Otherwise, I'm hanging out with my kids."

"Thanks, buddy. I will be calling you."

Wertz had to locate the Cadillac, which was the best way he knew to keep tabs on Keno. And that proved easy enough. The distinctive car was already parked at the hospital.

At 7:35 p.m., Keno and Netanya went out for pizza. He wanted them to spend a little time together, away from the depressing hospital room.

When Netanya reached for her third slice, he asked, "You're not pregnant, are you? I've never seen you eat more than two slices.

"Now that I'm getting married, I don't have to worry about how my bod looks. I can totally chub out if I want to."

He stared for a few seconds. "You know what? You are one ornery babe."

"Oh, Joaquin, my darling," she said dramatically. "I'm so glad you're beginning to understand me."

He shook his head, wolfed down his fourth slice, and then stared at the last slice on the tray. "You want that one, Tubby?"

She whacked him on the shoulder. "I'm not tubby yet, but just wait 'til we're married."

"In that case, I'm taking preventative measures," he said as he grabbed the last slice.

A little while later, they walked out hand in hand, happier after spending some upbeat time together.

She drove him back to the hospital parking lot, where they spent a few tender minutes enjoying each other's touch, smell, and feel. She suddenly pushed him away, and said, "Hold it right there, Bub. I'm not letting you get all horny just before you go partying."

"Don't sweat it, there aren't going to be any babes at the party. Besides, there's not going to be any babe but you for the rest of my life."

"Thanks. Joaquin. I believe you. Now go have some fun with your boys. Visiting hours will only last another hour or so, but I'll stay with Millie until they kick me out."

Keno had managed to shower and get dressed with the cumbersome casts in the way, and he'd just started to brush his hair when the house phone interrupted. He debated whether to answer it but finally surrendered to the persistent ring. "Hello?"

A muffled voice asked, "Mr. Joaquin Flores?"

"That's me."

"You need to get to the hospital right away. There's been an emergency."

Keno's heart pounded, and a sudden surge of blood flooded his brain. A little dizzy and short of breath, he asked, "Has something happened to my mother?"

"Cardiac arrest. You'd better hurry."

Keno slammed down the phone and hurried as fast as he could hop, skip, and jump. It usually took him fifteen minutes to get to the hospital, but this time he made it in ten.

With his mind and pulse racing, Keno burst into the hospital. He hopped over to an elderly woman sitting behind the Information Desk and shouted, "Where would they take a patient if they just had a heart attack?"

The graying woman stared at the wild-eyed young man. "Are you telling me that one of our patients has had a heart attack?"

Keno's jaw clenched, and then an impatient breath blasted out. "That's exactly what I'm telling you. It's my mother, Millie Flores. She was in 417 D."

His intensity apparently impressed the woman. She picked up the phone and hurriedly dialed the nurses' station. Several anxious seconds ticked by before she was connected with the nurse who would know the answer. When the information lady asked about the patient in 417 D, Keno overheard the curious voice convey that Millicent Flores was resting comfortably.

The information lady frowned at Keno, then spoke consolingly, "I don't know where you got your information, young man, but thank God, it was wrong. Your mother did not have a heart attack."

Keno felt a tremendous sense of relief. But for his own peace of mind, he needed to verify that his mother was okay. He went to the elevator and pushed the "4" button. During the trip to the fourth floor, he wondered: *Who would put me through this? Who would make such a cruel phone call?* By the time he'd hopped and skipped into Millie's room, he'd settled on the answer.

Netanya looked startled when she looked up from her Grisham novel. "What's up, Joaquin? I thought you'd be in Berkeley by now."

When Keno saw that Millie was sleeping soundly, he glanced at Netanya with fire in his eyes. With both fists doubled, he spat, "Nicky!"

Ready to make their move, Travis Cobb and Nicky acted in only a matter of seconds after Keno had skipped and hopped his way into the hospital.

His hands, feet, arms, and legs already bound with duct tape, Nicky ordered Travis to pull his tow truck up behind the Cadillac and open the trunk.

Working with tight-fitting latex gloves, Travis managed to pop the lock on the Cadillac's driver-side door in a matter of seconds. But he had activated the security alarm, which announced the illegal entry with a pulsating screech that could be heard half a mile away. Nicky's loud cursing didn't seem to affect Travis as he proceeded in a confident, professional manner. The fat man was in his element. He hit the hood release, calmly took out his wire cutters, and put an abrupt end to the annoying alarm. He then reached inside the door and pressed the button that popped the trunk lid. He snipped a wire leading to the taillight, and then cut the emergency escape tab hanging near the trunk's locking mechanism. Satisfied, he turned and gave a thumbs-up to Nicky, signifying that everything was all set.

Travis's face took on a look of genuine pleasure as he lifted Nicky off the tow truck's passenger's seat and placed him in the Cadillac's spacious trunk. The corpulent man stared at Nicky lying there, and said, "I think it would look a helluva lot more convincing if I put a little duct tape over your mouth."

"Just shut the trunk, an' get the hell outta here."

Travis ignored Nicky's protests. He found the roll of duct tape and peeled off a long piece. Nicky squirmed, twisted, and cursed, but Travis managed to wrap the sticky tape around his face. For good measure, Travis repeated the process. He nodded his big head and said, "Now that looks a helluva lot more convincing." He took one final satisfied look, winked with a smug expression, and then pushed down the Cadillac's trunk lid, which closed with a hydraulic swishing sound.

Deputy Wertz had picked up Deputy Drable at 8:22 p.m., allowing for a comfortable margin of time to reach Marin General Hospital. Wertz slowly cruised the squad car around the parking lot with one eye on the purple and yellow tow truck. When the loud car alarm went off, Wertz hit the squad car's accelerator. It was all he could do to prevent Drable from spotting the Cadillac.

Drable craned his neck, trying to locate the source of the alarm. "Can you tell where that alarm is coming from?"

When it suddenly went quiet, Wertz breathed a sigh of relief. "I'm sure somebody set it off accidentally. And if you ask me, those damn things are worthless. They go off so easy, nobody pays any attention to them anymore."

Just as Drable responded, "Yeah, that's the truth, they..." the dispatcher's shrill voice suddenly interrupted.

Her almost hysterical words exploded over the squad car's radio. "Shots fired! Code eleven ninety-nine! Officer down! All units respond!

Shooting in progress! Proceed to fourteen thirty-four Mallard Street in Belvedere! Eleven ninety-nine! Officer down! I repeat, all units proceed to fourteen thirty-four Mallard Street in Belvedere!"

Dumfounded, Wertz stared at the radio. The dispatcher had just shouted out Hans Van Exel's address.

Drable swatted him on the shoulder. "Hey, what are you waiting for? Let's go!"

Wertz didn't have a choice. He flipped switches to activate the squad car's flashing lights and screaming siren, then aimed the powerful vehicle toward Belvedere. He considered calling the Highway Patrol to alert them to the Cadillac's missing taillight but realized that such a warning might sound suspicious—if not downright absurd.

Keno was still steaming over Nicky's rotten trick when he climbed into the Cadillac and headed for Berkeley. He finally decided to let the anger go, wanting to get in a party mood—no, needing to get in a party mood. He put on his favorite radio station and cranked up the volume. His head began to bounce in time with a catchy beat, and soon his shoulders began bouncing, too. He cranked up the volume a little more and said, "Yeah, I'm gonna party tonight. It's been a while."

Nicky had expected a ten-minute wait before Keno returned to the Cadillac, but he didn't expect to wait for more than a couple of minutes before Wertz pulled the car over. He began to grow concerned when he felt the Cadillac accelerate to highway speed. He asked himself: *Where the hell is Wertz?* As minutes turned into miles, his concern progressed to fear. The tires hummed faster by the second. Something had gone terribly wrong. It was getting a lot warmer in the trunk, and it was hard to breathe. Nicky felt a lump rise in his throat when he thought the Biker Boy might find him in this vulnerable position. He mumbled to himself: *That freakin' Travis, tapin' my mouth so I can't breathe right, let alone yell for help. I'm gonna get that puss-gutted rat for this.*

Nicky tried to twist his hands free, but the resilient tape dug deeper into his skin with each angry tug. He rolled onto his stomach and kicked at the trunk lid but couldn't quite reach it. He felt helplessly trapped. Even the loud rock music began to irritate him. His cheeks ballooned, and his nostrils flared as he fought for breath. Panic consumed his racing mind. He imagined that he smelled exhaust fumes creeping into the trunk. He could feel it getting hotter by the minute. He was sure he was going to die of carbon monoxide poisoning. Tears scalded his cheeks. Terror took control. He wet himself. He tried to shout, "Momma," but his jaw couldn't move.

As the deputies approached Belvedere, an ambulance raced in the opposite direction with its siren wailing. Deputy Drable turned and watched it speed past. "I bet they're taking the wounded officer to the hospital. Hope he wasn't hurt too bad."

Wertz grimaced. "Yeah, he was probably a local who didn't know what he was getting into." He stopped the squad car about thirty yards down the street from Hans Van Exel's house, quickly observing that he and Drable were the first Marin County Sheriff's Department deputies to arrive at the scene.

Neighbors of all ages, sizes, and shapes scurried away from the shootout as fast as their legs could carry them. Officers of the California Highway Patrol blocked off the west end of the street with cones and flares. FBI agents, wearing blue jackets with bold yellow lettering, used a van and an unmarked car for protection. Several uniformed officers from the Belvedere/Tiburon police department crouched behind three squad cars, the braver locals snapping off a couple of quick rounds before ducking down again. The FBI agents unleashed a steady hail of gunfire—a couple of them blasting away with shotguns—but Hans Van Exel's bodyguards were better armed with bullet-spewing weapons.

Wertz had cruised around Van Exel's property several times during the past couple of days, so he knew the layout almost as well as anyone who lived in the area. After studying the situation, he drove his squad car around the block and turned into a long, narrow alley. At first, Deputy Drable thought his partner was chickening out, trying to avoid the raging gun battle. But it was easy to grasp Wertz's plan when a silver Corvette came roaring out of an ink-black space, some twenty yards down the alley.

Wertz shouted, "Hang on!" and aimed the squad car at the speeding sports car. Van Exel attempted to swerve past the heavier car, but there just wasn't room—Newton's law about objects not occupying the same space at the same time prevailed. Metal and concrete crunched expensive fiberglass. The squad car's left front fender dug into the Corvette's driver's door while an inflexible concrete wall pinned the passenger door.

With both his car doors blocked, Van Exel's only chance to escape was to shoot his way out. He aimed his Uzi at the Corvette's windshield and blasted away. But it was wasted ammunition.

The deputies scrambled out of the squad car's passenger door and waited until Hans began to climb through the jagged veil of safety glass. Doing what they were trained to do, Wertz and Drable moved in, and when Van Exel found himself in a defenseless position the deputies collared him.

Granting interviews to the media and handling the booking consumed Wertz's next couple of hours—heady stuff for a deputy sheriff who desperately needed to bolster his shaky career. Celebratory beers at Lucky's Tavern with Deputy Drable and several others from the sheriff's department naturally followed.

It was well past midnight, while parking his car in his garage, when it dawned on Wertz that he'd abandoned Nicky. At first, he thought he would just forget about it; there wasn't anything he could do at this late hour. However, a little curiosity and a lot of concern for self-preservation wouldn't let it rest. He couldn't ignore the probability that he and Travis Cobb were the only people on the planet who knew that Nicky was locked in the Cadillac's trunk. He blew out some beer-contaminated breath and reluctantly punched in Travis's home number on his cell. He had to hit *redial* four times before the fat man finally answered.

Travis had just snorted his last line of coke, and, as far as he was concerned, there was nothing worse than having his high interrupted. "Call somebody else," he barked into the receiver without caring who it was. "I can't help you right now. My truck's broke down."

"Hold on, Travis. This is Deputy Wertz."

"Wertz? What the hell do you want?"

"You know where Nicky Ghilardi is?"

Worried that he might be in serious trouble, the fat man lied, "No, I got no idea where that ugly retard is. Why you asking me?"

"Nicky's missing, and I'm calling everybody I can think of."

Travis's drugged mind conjured up an image of Nicky lying dead in the trunk of the Cadillac, and an amused chuckle escaped. "I got no idea where he is, but I hope somebody snuffed him."

Wertz suddenly assumed that Travis probably didn't know that he was involved in Nicky's kidnapping plan— which now appeared to be a failed plan—and he wasn't about to reveal any details. It also occurred to the deputy that Joaquin Flores might have found Nicky by this time. Wertz decided that Travis's *snuffed* hope might not be such a bad conclusion. In fact, it would be an excellent solution. If Joaquin Flores had snuffed Nicky, his problems would have been eliminated along with him. Nobody could prove anything.

Grudgingly, the deputy drove to Mill Valley to see if Joaquin Flores had parked the Cadillac at the old Victorian, but, of course, he hadn't. When a drive-by at the hospital proved fruitless, Wertz recalled that J.P. had called it a *cockamamie plan*. The grouchy old lawyer had nailed it.

With the thought that Flores might be spending the night with Bernstein's daughter, Wertz decided to check out the Bernstein mansion. At 1:20 a.m., he reached the front gate, but that was as close as he was going to get. Like an extraterrestrial beam piercing the foggy night, a bright spotlight encircled the squad car. An authoritative voice resonated from a hidden speaker: "Stop the car and place both hands on the steering wheel."

Wertz powered down the window before placing his hands on the steering wheel. He leaned his head out and shouted, "This is Deputy Wertz of the Marin County Sheriff's Department. Extinguish that damned light!"

"You are on private property, Deputy Wertz. You cannot proceed without a warrant."

"I'm here on police business. I don't intend to search anything, so I don't need a warrant."

The authoritative voice asked with a hint of sarcasm, "What is the nature of your *police business* at this late hour?"

It took Wertz a moment to come up with a credible answer. "I'm looking for the Cadillac that Joaquin Flores was driving. It might have been involved in a hit-and-run accident. Is the vehicle on the premises?"

There was a pause, leading Wertz to believe that the person with the assertive voice was conferring with someone else. "Neither the car nor Joaquin Flores is currently on the premises. Does that conclude your police business?"

Wertz didn't bother to reply before whipping the squad car around and speeding away. He took another slow drive by the Flores' residence and another tour of the hospital parking lot. He even drove out to the Sea Lion Cove Estates to make sure Nicky's Mercedes was still at the staged abduction scene, which it was. With no sign of the Cadillac and no other realistic place to look, Wertz decided it was time to go home and collapse into bed. It had been a long and eventful day. Even so, the question still nagged at him: *Where the hell is Nicky?*

Chapter Eighteen

Most of Keno's body ached when he awoke on the used and abused frat house couch, but he decided the punishment had been worth it. Daryl Slate's birthday party had been a major blast. Since the football players had a couple of days off due to the teams' bye week, several players joined the fraternity brothers to celebrate. Keno had consumed more beer than he intended to, but it had felt good to cut loose with his friends and escape the depressing circumstances recently overwhelming his life.

He stretched, yawned, massaged the top of his throbbing head, and looked around. He didn't see a single friend or frat brother. It was amazing how so many guys could be there raising hell most of the night, and then just disappear. It was as if the first rays of sunlight had caused them to run away and hide like beer-sucking vampires.

Keno found his crutches and headed for the bathroom. While standing over the commode, he glanced down and noticed a jagged crack in his ankle cast. He frowned, trying to remember how it had happened. The replay quickly came to mind. Butch Duggins, Cal's bruising middle linebacker, had accidentally kicked one of his crutches out from under him, causing him to take a header down a flight of stairs. This dastardly deed had led to an emergency convening of the kangaroo court. The frat judges found Butch guilty of *cruel and unusual battery* on a handicapped brother. Harsh justice was promptly meted out. Butch had to fetch Keno's beer for the rest of his life, or 6:00 a.m., whichever came first.

Keno went into the kitchen and opened the fridge. It still contained a few cans of beer but little in the way of food—at least food that didn't have something green growing from it. However, he did find a quart of tomato juice, which was exactly what the doctor ordered. He downed half the bottle without stopping.

He went back to the couch to look for his blue and gold letter jacket where he'd left his cell phone in a side pocket. When he found the jacket lying in a nearby corner, he noticed several assorted stains splattered on it. Not bad, considering the high probability of total disaster. He found the cell phone and tapped in Netanya's number.

She apparently had her cell close; she interrupted the second ring. "How's the party animal?"

"Oooowwwooo," he howled. "You shouldn't have let me out of my cage."

She rewarded his theatrics with a melodious laugh. "Was it worth it?"

"It was a total blast. But I won't be partying like that again for a while."

"I'm glad you had fun, you definitely needed it. So what's on for today?"

"I guess I need to see the bone doctor. I broke my ankle cast last night."

"You what?" She paused a few seconds, then said, "Never mind, I don't even want to know. Can you drive?"

"Yeah, that won't be a problem."

"Okay, just come to my house, and in the meantime, I'll call Doctor Sanford's office. If he's too busy to see you, I'm sure he'll hook you up with somebody."

A prior commitment wormed its way into Keno's hazy thoughts. "Uh oh, I'm supposed to meet Hector this morning. I promised to meet him at the Yard to go over some jobs."

"Then we'll go to Plan B. I'll meet you at the Yard, and we'll go from there."

"Plan B sounds good. We'll hook up there, go see how Millie's doing, and then you can take me to the doctor."

"You got it, Joaquin. And later we'll go to Plan C. I'll do whatever you want today, then you can be my pleasure slave tonight."

"Plan C was always one of my favorites."

After giving he directions to the Yard, Keno hopped out to the Cadillac. He'd parked the car about twenty-five yards down the hill on the opposite side of the curving street, which was a slender strip of asphalt. An isolated piece of ground beneath a eucalyptus tree had been his private parking spot for the past two years. He'd wrapped a heavy chain around that perpetually peeling tree to secure his old motorcycle and recently his Knucklehead. Amazingly enough, the slightly rusted chain was still there.

Nicky woke when he heard the Cadillac's engine come to life. He blinked his blurry eyes, and then bit his swollen tongue when he tried to swallow. Lying curled in the fetal position, his body began to twitch and tremble, palsy-like. He didn't have the vaguest idea of where he was, what time it was, or, even more disconcerting, what was going to happen next. However, he did know that he'd just suffered through the worst night of his life.

Nicky had lain awake for hours, hearing frequent outbursts from a wild party and listening to sticky tire sounds when an occasional car passed by on the fog-dampened asphalt street. Tortuous hours later, there had been a brief flurry of vehicles and people leaving the party. Then it had grown deathly quiet. Not a sound for hours. Or were they just slow-moving minutes? In total darkness, with his hands bound behind his back, there was no way to tell. His expensive Rolex was worthless.

Nicky had tried kicking anything within reach to attract passersby's attention, but everything he managed to hit with his cowboy boots had seemed padded. He'd even resorted to banging his head against the trunk's lid to make noise, but that ill-conceived strategy had been rewarded with a throbbing headache. Then, with hopes of dislodging the duct tape covering his mouth, he'd steadily worked his lower jaw up and down a millimeter at a time. With a surprising display of determination, Nicky didn't quit until his jaw had become too tired to move. He next tried scraping his face on the trunk's carpet, but that soon resulted in a stinging rug burn. No matter what he tried, he couldn't loosen the sticky tape enough to yell for help or scream the way he desperately wanted.

Nicky figured there had to be some connection between silence and cold. The quieter it got outside, the colder it got inside the trunk. He'd tried rolling back and forth to keep warm, but he could only sustain that effort for a couple of minutes at a time. When he grew tired of rolling, he would curl his body into the tightest ball he could manage. And this led to a systematic exercise of rolling back and forth, then curling himself into a ball—roll and curl, roll and curl.

After physically exhausting himself, Nicky's imagination began to chase after bizarre rationale. He conjured up all sorts of scenarios for Wertz not stopping the Cadillac. The deputy could have been seriously injured or even killed in a car wreck. Maybe he had an attack of appendicitis, or all the excitement had caused him to have a heart attack. Perhaps somebody had shot him during a robbery. Or worse, maybe Wertz had simply thrown him to the wolves—the main wolf being Biker Boy.

When he felt the Cadillac accelerate to highway speed, Nicky allowed himself a glimmer of hope. He assumed that Biker Boy was driving back to his house in Mill Valley. And this might give Wertz the opportunity to see the Cadillac and find him before he died of thirst, or his runny nose plugged and shut off his air supply.

Keno and Hector met at the Yard about an hour after Keno had left the Bear Cave in Berkeley. After exchanging their familiar banter, they went inside the house trailer/office to formulate a plan. Both felt a responsibility to service Milagrozo Landscaping's loyal customers. However, the planning and scheduling turned out to be a lot more involved than either had anticipated, and they soon realized how much they missed Frank's guidance.

As they were conversing, Keno got the impression that Hector was purposely holding something back. "Is there something that you're not comfortable with?"

Hector let go a reluctant sigh. "I don't know how to tell you something about something I don't know anything about."

Keno didn't quite grasp that one. "What?"

"Frank was doing something… *como se dice, secreto?*"

Surprise intensified Keno's confusion. "Frank was doing something secret?"

"Si, Frank was working on something in the hothouse that he didn't want nobody to know about. He said he would show us when he was ready." Hector raised his eyebrows for emphasis. "And he worked in there a lot lately."

Keno felt his own eyebrows elevate. "When we're finished in here, we'll go see what he had going on. "

Even though the gate was wide open when she arrived, Netanya didn't know if she should drive on into the Yard. Taking no chances, she stopped and honked the annoying Italian horn. And then she drove on in when Keno leaned out of the small aluminum door and waved her on over to the house trailer/office. She parked beside the Bernstein Burgundy Cadillac and cheerfully sauntered inside.

Keno greeted her with a smile from behind the desk.

Hector politely tipped his straw hat.

Netanya smiled and said, "Hi, Hector, I'm Netanya. I saw you at Frank's wake. Your eulogy was very touching."

Hector gently shook her offered hand, then looked down, visibly embarrassed by the compliment. "Thank you, young lady. It is very nice to meet you."

She kissed Keno on the cheek. "You doing okay?"

"Yeah, we're just about done here. I won't be long."

"No problem, I'll wait outside until you're finished."

When Netanya went back outside, thinking she'd take a stroll around the Yard, the powerful aroma of decay attacked her long-sheltered sense of smell. She climbed in the Ferrari, started it, and turned on the fan, but it didn't help very much. With no way of knowing that Nicky was in the Cadillac's trunk, some ten feet away, she turned up the volume on her headphones, then leaned back and closed her eyes.

As promised, Keno came hopping out a few minutes later. Hector followed him out, then waited until Keno had dropped his big body onto the Ferrari's passenger seat.

Hector suggested, "Maybe we can go into the hothouse, mañana."

Keno grimaced and said, "Yeah, I totally blanked on that. But we will definitely check it out mañana."

Wertz blinked open his eyes, glanced at the clock on the night-stand, and then took a minute to relive his exciting night. When he recalled making the arrest, which many regarded as a heroic feat, he felt a rush of exhilaration laced with a heavy dose of pride. He'd done good, real good. Sheriff Riddle—an extremely excited and very pleased Sheriff Riddle—would probably see that he got a medal. At the very least, he'd get a commendation and a healthy cash bonus.

While breathing in the sweet air of triumph, an uninvited thought of Nicky's disappearance crashed his private celebration. An image of the miserable brat slowly dying in the Cadillac's trunk let the air out of his happy balloon. Wertz wished he'd never met Nicky G—the hateful psychopath was ruining his life. Even so, Wertz couldn't let the mystery remain unsolved. The more he thought about it, the more he felt compelled to learn about what had happened to Nicky.

With the wind out of his hero sails, the deputy got dressed and grabbed a quick cup of coffee. He couldn't help himself. He had to go looking.

Keno and Netanya had walked into Marin General Hospital only seconds before Wertz cruised by in his Crown Victoria, searching for the elusive Cadillac. The deputy soon spotted the Ferrari, which he recognized from the shootout at the ranch. The sports car told him that the Bernstein girl was at the hospital, no doubt visiting Mrs. Flores. *But where in the hell was Joaquin Flores and the Cadillac?*

In a morning of near misses, Keno and Netanya entered one elevator just as Julie Lemmon stepped out of an adjoining one. Julie had been to see Buzz, who had developed a serious infection as she'd feared he would. Even so, Buzz had insisted on helping Julie get a restraining order that would force Nicky to honor the sales contract and prevent him from interfering with her business.

Buzz, of course, had called Nathaniel Clay, confident that his friend and colleague would come to Julie's rescue.

Aware that Julie's testimony had caused her considerable embarrassment, Clay felt indebted to Julie for coming forward. In addition—since Nicky Ghilardi must have learned about her statement through Jason Bridger, or at least through his contact with J.P. Maloney—he felt more than a little responsible for her current predicament. Eager to rectify matters, he promised to meet with Julie immediately after today's meeting with the DA.

Keno and Netanya were pleased to see Millie wide awake and propped up in bed. Her smile appeared genuine as she greeted, "Hi, you two. Good to see you."

Keno hopped over and kissed Millie on the cheek. "You're looking way better."

Millie seemed to believe him. "Thanks, Sunshine. I do feel much stronger today."

Netanya smiled, and said, "You really are looking better, Millie. You'll be back on your feet in no time."

Millie's face suddenly clouded. "I wonder what fate awaits me then."

Keno held her hand, and said, "Don't sweat it, Mom. Mr. Clay is taking care of everything."

Millie sighed and looked off into the distance. "I remember some of what I did, which seems terrible in the harsh light of sober reflection. I broke the law, and I expect I'll have to pay for it."

Netanya seemed sorry that she'd initiated this depressing subject. "Everybody knows about the mitigating circumstances, Millie. No judge or jury is going to hold you responsible, especially when they learn about all the cruel things Nicky Ghilardi has done."

Hearing that name caused Keno to seethe inside, but he worked hard at hiding it. His mother had been exposed to more than enough emotional turbulence. "Netanya's right, Mom, but you shouldn't be thinking about that. You just concentrate on getting well."

Millie patted her son's big hand. "How are you doing, Sunshine?"

"I'm good. Hector and I planned a few landscaping jobs this morning, which he and Luiz are going to take care of. Then last night I went over to Berkeley and partied with a bunch of my friends." He glanced down at his cast. "I got a little carried away and broke my ankle cast, and now I have to go get it replaced."

"I'd like to reprimand you for drinking too much, but I suppose my bouts with vodka have rescinded the privilege." She sighed and asked, "Were you hurt?"

"No, I didn't even feel it." He did his limited crutch shrug. "This cast is supposed to come off in a few days anyway. If my ankle is healed enough, the doctor can put on a walking cast."

Millie leaned over as much as she dared and glanced down at the broken cast. "You should get a new one put on right away. This one is probably doing more harm than good.

Keno bent down and kissed her forehead. "Okay, Mom. You take it easy and don't worry about anything. We'll be back as soon as we can."

Nathaniel Clay entered Jason Bridger's office exactly twenty-four hours after he'd left it. The DA didn't seem surprised by the impressive lawyer's punctuality.

When his offer of coffee was refused, Jason folded his hands and asked, "Where would you like to begin?"

Clay compressed his lips, figuratively biting his tongue. He wanted to chastise the DA for revealing yesterday's conversation to J.P. Maloney but decided it wouldn't serve any purpose. "Let's resume where we left off yesterday. If you recall, I offered Simon Bernstein's support for your political ambitions. In return, I want all charges against Joaquin Flores dismissed, and for Mrs. Flores, I want minimum probation and no more than three years of controlled treatment in a facility of our choosing."

"I don't recall you mentioning a specific time of incarceration for Mrs. Flores."

"You're right, I didn't. But three years in a mental health facility is more than reasonable under the circumstances. And I would prefer that we use the word *treatment* rather than incarceration."

Jason accepted the request with a nod, then replied, "As I told you yesterday, I don't see a problem with letting Joaquin Flores walk. But it's not going to look good for a man running a tough law and order campaign to go easy on a woman charged with several felonies. Especially when one of them happens to be attempted murder."

Clay had anticipated Jason's position and had his usual ace in the hole. The cash the DA had received from Ghilardi Development wasn't entirely clean, which left Jason caught in the middle. He and J.P. Maloney could use it against him, and Jason knew it. "If you publicly discredit Nicky Ghilardi and throw the book at him, your constituents will think you're tough on crime. And the liberal element will think you're a fair man if you handle Mrs. Flores' situation as I've suggested. If the P.R. is manipulated properly, you can look good on both sides of the street. And there's an additional bonus in it if you cooperate. Simon Bernstein is willing to provide you unlimited access to a high-powered public relations firm in San Francisco. Those people can make you look like the proverbial white knight in shining armor."

Jason nervously ran his hands through his thinning blond hair. Can I share something in confidence?"

Convinced that he already knew Jason's dirty little secret, Clay nodded. "What we say in this room stays between us."

Jason spent a few seconds agonizing over the decision, then exhausted a deep sigh. "I know it's not a legitimate excuse, but I've recently had some serious financial setbacks." He shrugged. "A sick pregnant wife, a stupid investment in a dot.com loser, and a couple of other minor catastrophes I won't bore you with. The point is, I've already gone through the cash I received from the Ghilardi Corporation. Actually, I got some under-the-table money from a lawyer named J.P. Maloney, and if I play ball with you, I'm sure he will want to expose me. And even a cursory investigation will reveal that I've tapped out my campaign fund."

Hearing exactly what he'd expected, Clay nodded. "I suspect that Mr. Maloney's primary concern is that Mrs. Flores is going to file a wrongful death suit. I'm sure she would stand to collect a very healthy sum if Nicky Ghilardi is found guilty of vehicular manslaughter, along with committing arson to suppress evidence and obstruct justice. I have no doubt that this kind of suit could cripple the Ghilardi Development Corporation."

"Yes," Jason agreed, I'm sure J.P. is only concerned with the corporation's exposure. I don't believe he has any emotional attachment to Nicky." Jason let go a little chuckle. "Or anyone else, as far as I can tell."

Clay tapped the tips of his fingers together as if searching for the best solution. "Okay, here's the deal. If you accept my offer, I guarantee no lawsuit will be filed against the Ghilardi Development Corporation. Joaquin Flores will someday be one of the richest men in

Marin County, so money won't be an issue for his mother. However, Joaquin will want his pound of flesh. I have no doubt he'll want Nicky put away for a long, long time."

Jason expelled a sigh of relief. "Sounds good, but I just can't let it appear as if I'm letting Mrs. Flores off with a slap on the wrist. How about five years of treatment in the mental health facility and five years of probation?"

Bartering for years of people's lives was the part of Clay's profession he least enjoyed. "I'll go for the five-year probation. I seriously doubt that Mrs. Flores will be shooting at anyone else with a shotgun. However, I will only accept two to five in the mental health care facility. Just say you're leaving the final determination to the shrinks, which is hard to argue against."

"Okay," Jason agreed, "I suppose that's acceptable. My only concern now is how I'm going to convince J.P. that a lawsuit is not going to happen."

Clay stood and said, "I'll personally see to it."

Jason blinked in surprise. "I really appreciate that. Your personal guarantee will carry a lot more weight than anything coming from me."

The imposing defense attorney extended his hand and said, "Nice doing business with you, Jason. And good luck with your run for office next year. I believe you are an honest man at heart."

Jason shook the offered hand with genuine enthusiasm. "Thank you. I appreciate having the opportunity to prove I'm worthy of the people's trust." He smiled while adding, "And thanks for teaching me a thing or two about horse-trading."

Clay met Julie in the Holiday Inn's main dining room, not far from the conference room where Team Flores met the day before. When he saw the attractive woman sitting in a booth, smiling in his direction, he recalled a disturbing part of her testimony. He had to suppress a shudder when he thought about her having to date Nicky Ghilardi to land a sales contract. He couldn't help thinking: *The poor woman must have been desperate.* He returned the smile and extended his hand. "Good morning, Julie."

"Thanks for seeing me, Mr. Clay. I know how busy you are." He'd barely taken a seat before she pushed her sales contract in front of him. Catching herself, she apologized. "I'm sorry, I should've let you order something before I pounced." She glanced at a plastic pitcher sitting on the table. "Care for some coffee?"

"Yes, but that's about all I'll have time for."

Julie frowned, obviously deciding how she was going to explain something that was bothering her. "I don't know how he found out. But when Nicky came storming into my office yesterday, he already knew I'd testified against him."

Clay knew the leak had originated with Jason Bridger and felt personally responsible for allowing it to happen. Nevertheless, he didn't have time to delve into that convoluted set of circumstances. "I'm sorry you had to endure Nicky Ghilardi's abuse, but I'll put an end to it. Believe me, it won't happen again." He offered his most convincing look before adding, "I want to tell you again how much I appreciate your testimony, Julie. It gave me the clout I needed to wrap things up the way I'd hoped. Now the least I can do is provide you with protection from that scum bag."

"I'm just glad I could help."

Clay picked up the sales contract and began to read. A minute later, he shrugged and said, "I don't see a problem with this."

She stared hopefully. "Can I get a restraining order?"

"Absolutely. Nicky Ghilardi has no right to interfere with your place of business." He picked up the sales contract and gave it a little wave. "Can I take this with me?"

"Sure, that's a copy."

Clay took a healthy sip of coffee, then sighed. "Nicky Ghilardi is a name I'd soon like to forget."

Julie grimaced and said, "You're not the only one."

The moment Deputy Wertz entered the Marin County Sheriff's Office, an almost delirious Sheriff Riddle summoned him back to his office. The sheriff was clearly exuding excitement from the great publicity he'd garnered from last night's major drug bust. Wertz had barely closed the door behind him when the sheriff held up the front page of the *Independent Journal*. He made a show of turning it so that Wertz could see the bold headlines:

COKE KING BUSTED

Wearing a fixed grin beneath his graying mustache, the sheriff grabbed Wertz's hand and pumped it. "How's my hero doing this morning?"

Wertz could only remember shaking hands with the sheriff once before, and that was nearly ten years ago, the first time he'd met him. "I'm fine, Sheriff."

"Good! Great! A TV crew from Channel Five is coming over from the City in a little while. They want to do a story about you and your involvement in the drug bust." The sheriff's face beamed. "Now, don't be bashful, Wertz. Tell them how you were the first to get a lead on the Van Exel case; how you came to me with it; how I contacted the FBI; how I assigned you to surveillance; and how we all worked together and coordinated everything to set the trap. Describe what a great team effort this office put together. And don't be afraid to tell them how you used your quick thinking and professional intuition to capture Van Exel—the kingpin of the largest cocaine ring in the history of Marin County."

Wertz nodded, realizing that the sheriff had already scripted his impending interview. "Right, Sheriff. I'll be sure to tell them everything you just said."

The sheriff couldn't shed his grin. "Later on, I can make a statement about your heroism under fire and how I'm putting you in for the Medal of Valor."

Wertz shook his sleep-deprived head to make sure he wasn't dreaming. "Thanks, Sheriff, I appreciate it."

Channel Five's T.V. crew, headed by an attractive Japanese reporter, arrived fifteen minutes later. The initial interview took the better part of an hour, and then the persistent reporter explained that she would need some *viewer-enlightenment* footage at the crime scene. She asked Wertz to accompany her, telling him he could provide the viewers with professional insight. She encouraged, "Be sure to elaborate on how last night's shootout in Belvedere shattered the tranquility and terrified the residents of that wealthy bedroom community."

Wertz consciously added this suggestion to the sheriff's input, then replayed the entire script in his mind.

The sheriff had insisted that Wertz spend as much time with the reporter as she required. He also rewarded the heroic deputy with the rest of the week off and an as-yet-to-be-determined bonus.

Wertz felt as if he'd grown wings. Though unfortunate for Nicky, this gratifying experience had eclipsed all thoughts regarding the deputy's missing partner-in-crime.

Yvette Ghilardi's alarm was accelerating by the minute. Nicky had occasionally stayed out all night, but he'd never failed to check in at some point. Her baby had never stayed away this long without letting her know the reason why. She dry-washed her hands as she paced. She was trying her best to fend off a parade of tragic scenarios that persisted in assaulting her imagination. Though difficult to accept—especially through the zealous shield of adoration—Yvette had come to realize that some of Nicky's recent behavior had not been entirely rational. She worried that this had led to some evil people exacting revenge. Also, she had personally witnessed some of Nicky's recent violent behavior, which now seemed unnecessary in the bright glare of hindsight. In addition, she'd overheard some things regarding Biker Boy that she obviously wasn't supposed to hear. And nagging questions about the barn fire weren't going away.

Yvette surrendered to her fears. She called the local hospitals, the California Highway Patrol, the Marin County Sheriff's Department, and even a few police stations in neighboring towns. She learned absolutely nothing from all these calls—not a thing. At first, she considered this a good thing, but then more questions loomed, and the protracted minutes of not knowing became progressively more challenging to deal with. And with no place else to turn, she begrudgingly called J.P. Maloney.

"Hello, J.P., how are you today?"

J.P. held the telephone away from his ear and glared at it. Yvette had not called him in all the years he'd known her—not once. And now she was addressing him as J.P., not the affected "Mr. Maloney." "What do you want, Yvette? Is Big Nick alright?"

"Big Nick is getting stronger and more alert every day. But this call isn't about him."

J.P. knew who the call was about, and, more than likely, it had something to do with the hateful brat's cockamamie plan. "What's going on with Nicky this time?"

Yvette's voice cracked as she said, "I'm afraid something terrible has happened to him."

J.P. considered the possibility that Joaquin Flores had caught onto Nicky's plan and had violently disposed of the pathological fool. The sly old lawyer fought back a chuckle while asking, "What makes you think so?"

"He hasn't been home all night, and he hasn't called. That's not like him. And I've already called the hospitals, the Highway patrol, the police..." Her sniffles delayed the conversation for several seconds. "I know he isn't a saint, but Nicky has always been very considerate of my feelings. I know he wouldn't worry me this way." She sniffed louder. "Not if he could prevent it."

"I'll make some calls and get back to you, Yvette. If he doesn't show in the next couple of hours, we'll file a Missing Person's report."

"Thank you, J.P., I really appreciate your help."

"Yeah, okay, goodbye." J.P. cradled the phone without the slightest intention of inquiring about Nicky's welfare. His mind began to explore what life would be like without the hateful brat. Grand and cheerful possibilities loomed…

A minute later, J.P. received a phone call that he would have never anticipated—not in this lifetime. "Yeah?"

"Mr. Maloney?"

"Yeah, who are you, and what do you want?"

"This is Nathaniel Clay, and I have some important matters I'd like to discuss. Is this a good time?"

J.P. massaged his unhinged jaw to collect himself. His shrewd mind searched, but he couldn't pin down one reason why the renowned criminal defense attorney would be calling him. "I guess it's as good a time as any. What's on your mind?"

"As you probably know, I represent Joaquin Flores and his mother, Millicent Flores."

"What's that got to do with me?"

"We have mutual interests, Mr. Maloney. We face common problems that could become complicated, embarrassing, expensive, and detrimental for all parties concerned if they aren't dealt with." Clay paused, allowing that input to sink in before adding, "I believe these matters can be resolved with a little common sense. Are you interested?"

J.P. wasn't used to such forthrightness. "I'm listening."

"I've reached a tentative agreement with Jason Bridger concerning pending criminal charges, but he's afraid you won't be comfortable with the agreement unless I can provide you with certain assurances."

J.P. was leery of a trap. "Go on."

"You and I both know Jason has suffered severe financial difficulties, and he's had to use the money your corporation donated to his campaign fund. So I'll get right to it. Neither of my clients will sue Ghilardi Development Corporation or its shareholders if you agree not to expose Jason's misuse of campaign funds."

J.P.'s ever-dubious mind couldn't fend off an enormous sense of relief, but he still couldn't quite grasp where Clay was coming from. "I'm intrigued, Mr. Clay, but in my experience, these deals usually come with a catch. What haven't you told me?"

"Nicky Ghilardi has to be sacrificed."

J.P. wanted to chuckle—so hard his shoulders and stomach were shaking—but he managed to hold it in. "You're asking me to sacrifice Nicky?"

"That's exactly what I'm asking. And I'll spell it out for you. Charges will be dismissed against Joaquin Flores, and Mrs. Flores will plead guilty and receive five years' probation and serve two to five years in a mental health facility. Nicky Ghilardi will be charged with vehicular manslaughter, obstruction of justice, and arson. The bottom line is that Jason Bridger has to look good to satisfy his political aspirations."

Not used to smiling for more than a few seconds at a time, the corners of J.P.'s mouth were beginning to ache. "And Ghilardi Development won't have any financial liability if Nicky is convicted?"

"That's correct. No liability whatsoever."

J.P. realized that if Nicky were convicted of the three felonies, Yvette would be legally bound to relinquish control of Ghilardi Development Corporation. And if Big Nick remained incapacitated, she would be compelled to relinquish control to him—J.P. Maloney. He would have complete control of his corporation, his baby. "Okay, Mr. Clay, I accept. If you agree not to sue, I will cancel the lawsuit against Mrs. Flores, which I argued against filing in the first place."

"I understand, Mr. Maloney. Then we have a deal?"

"I trust you implicitly, Mr. Clay, but I feel obligated to get something in writing for the corporation's sake. I could croak at any time, and you could get run over by a truck. Know what I mean?"

"Of course. I'll draft a letter forfeiting all claims relating to the Frank Flores incident, effective the day the criminal charges against Nicky Ghilardi are filed by Jason Bridger."

It occurred to J.P. that the criminal defense lawyer hadn't requested a guarantee from his side. But then he asked himself: *Who had the balls to cross that brilliant s.o.b.?* "Thanks, Mr. Clay, you've gained an admirer today. I wish more lawyers would use their common sense to resolve these kinds of affairs."

J.P. replaced the telephone receiver and smiled again. Two extraordinary opportunities for being shed of Nicky loomed. The brat would be killed by young Flores or sent to prison for a long, long time—excellent prospects both.

He fantasized about running Ghilardi Development Corporation without having Nicky around to screw things up. J.P. began to whistle a happy little tune, something he couldn't remember doing for years—possibly decades.

Chapter Nineteen

Nicky had gnawed a hole, slightly more than an inch in diameter, through the duct tape covering his tender mouth. He sucked in several deep breaths and then, just because he could, he poked his tongue through the hole. Though psychologically suspect, it provided a tiny sense of escape.

It took the planning of his real escape, however, to suppress the intense thirst and escalating hunger. The first step of his new plan required him to kick off his cowboy boots. Then he could bend his knees enough to slip his feet through the duct tape binding his wrists together, and this would allow him to maneuver his hands and arms in front of his face. And then he could chew through the tape binding his wrists. Nicky had gotten quite proficient at chewing duct tape, but the thought of swallowing more glue made him sick to his empty stomach. He wiggled his toes and performed limited foot gymnastics as he scraped the ostrich leather boots together, edging his feet out with an up-and-down motion. This rubbing action caused a lot of pain to the insides of his ankles, each growing more tender with every stroke. But he kept himself going with the belief that he was gaining about an inch every four or five minutes.

It was late afternoon before Doctor Sanford's physician assistant had finished constructing a new lightweight walking cast for Keno's ankle, which was healing faster than expected. The P.A. warned against putting too much stress on the slower-healing knee but okayed limited amounts of walking with the cane.

Keno was starving by this time, so he suggested that Netanya drive them to Alioto's Grotto at Fisherman's Wharf in San Francisco for a late lunch. She seemed more amused than embarrassed while watching him consume two complete crab cioppino dinners, which included a basket of French bread, a garden salad, a side dish of sliced salami, a large bowl of minestrone soup, and a heaping dish of ravioli.

When the check came, Keno offered a sheepish look. "I feel like a pimp."

"Not many hookers could afford to feed a pimp who eats as much as you do."

"Yeah," he agreed, "but I need lots of protein to take care of you."

She smiled seductively and teased, "Maybe you should have a dozen oysters for dessert."

He grinned as he rubbed his belly. "I wouldn't mind having some for a snack later."

"That can be arranged. You know what a great chef we have, and Daddy is in Chicago, so I'm home alone."

Keno mentally flashed on the muscular security guards roaming the Bernstein mansion and knew she was never home alone. "I'll tell you what, we'll stop by the hospital to check on Millie, and then we can go do some of that *pleasure slave stuff.*"

"You're just full of good ideas today. Let's get outta here and go see Millie."

J.P. Maloney put a damper on Deputy Wertz's fantastic day. When the deputy answered his cell phone, J.P. didn't concern himself with niceties. "I read in the paper that you're a freaking superhero."

"I collared Van Exel, and everybody's making a big deal out of it."

"Good for you, but somebody we know has disappeared while you were out there saving the planet. Do you know where that repulsive brat is?

"No, I sure don't."

"Did you guys try to pull off that cockamamie plan?"

"I guess you could say we tried to pull it off, but things didn't go exactly as planned. I was riding with Drable when the shooting started at Van Exel's last night, so I didn't have any control over what happened next. I felt bad about deserting Nicky, but it couldn't be helped. I had to go with Drable when we got an officer-down call. As far I know, Nicky could still be in the trunk of Bernstein's Cadillac."

"I figured something like that. You planning to do anything about it?"

"I don't know what else to do, J.P. I've looked everywhere I can think of, and there's no sign of Joaquin Flores or the Cadillac."

"I almost wish I hadn't called." J.P.'s sigh didn't convey any disappointment. "Well, keep me posted."

Wertz also wished J.P. hadn't made the call. Now he felt obligated to go looking again.

Millie was sound asleep when Keno and Netanya stopped at the hospital to check on her. The young couple peeked in on Millie and listened to her light snore—mindful of a cat's purr. They exchanged suggestive looks and then hurried to the Bernstein mansion.

Nicky finally managed to wriggle his feet out of the cowboy boots. He felt good about completing the first step of his plan, even though that demanding accomplishment had produced several raw spots on the insides of his ankles. He cursed his pot gut as he twisted, turned, and strained to get one foot through the triangle formed by his arms and tightly bound wrists. Huffing and puffing, he half-succeeded with his second goal. With his taped wrists positioned between his legs, he paused for some much-needed rest. But the biting duct tape, cutting into his wrists and pressing up against his urine-soaked crotch, urged him on. Several minutes later, he managed to strain enough to get the second foot through the triangle. But this, too, came at a price, albeit more disgusting than painful.

Netanya lay back on her luxurious bed, smiled dreamily, and said, "I think I'll take up smoking."

Keno frowned. "Why take up that stupid habit?"

"You always see people in old movies smoking after they had sex. It's sooo cool."

"You know what? I think I'm going to have you checked out by a shrink before I take the final plunge."

She turned and put an arm around his waist. "You really are a good straight man."

"Now what?"

"I really could have pounced on *final plunge*."

He let out an exasperated breath. "Really, Tanya, would you consider seeing a shrink before we get married?"

She strategically placed her hand. "I got your shrink right here, Bubba."

"I surrender." He laughed and kissed her forehead. "I hate to ruin things by getting all serious, but I'm starting to feel guilty. My mom is lying there in the hospital, seriously wounded mentally and physically, and I go partying all night and then spend the afternoon having fun and great sex." He made a guilty face before adding, "It doesn't seem right."

Netanya reached up and kissed his chin. "You're really a good guy, Joaquin, and I'm glad you're worried about your mother. But guilt doesn't look good on you."

"Maybe not, but it's still there."

"Okay, if it will make you feel better, we'll go to the hospital and spend some time with Millie."

"That would be cool. And know what else?"

"What else?"

"I really blew it on this one. We should have stopped in to see Buzz Aldrich when we were there. He really did a lot to help us, and now he's back in the hospital because he took a bullet for my mom." He playfully swatted her behind. "And it's all your fault for distracting me."

"So now I'm just a distraction."

"But a totally fun distraction."

"Okay, I'm going to take a quick shower, and then we'll go deal with some of that guilt you're obsessing with."

Nicky had become very proficient at chewing duct tape. He gnawed, pulled with his front teeth, gnawed, and pulled some more. At last, the tough, sticky tape binding his wrists came apart. He jerked his hands free, and then rolled on his back and spread his arms as wide as he could, reveling in the feeling of liberated limbs. He stretched his arms and legs in the big trunk and waved and kicked as if making a snow angel. Then he sat up with the back of his head pressed against the trunk lid, ripped the rest of the tape from his wrists, and searched for the edge of the tape that encircled his neck and mouth.

But try as he might, he couldn't find an edge to unwind the tape. He knew he couldn't break the resilient material by simply pulling on it, and it would have required more chewing—a lot more chewing—so he resorted to scraping it from his face with his fingernails. After much painful and methodical scraping, and tugging on little separated strands, he managed to get it loose. The twisted and gnarled strands of duct tape hung around his neck like a ludicrous gray necklace. His scratched and scraped face felt as if it had been scorched with a blowtorch, but at least he could open his mouth wide and exercise his jaw. A big yawn had become a pleasurable thing.

This time, Keno and Netanya thoughtfully stopped in to see Buzz Aldridge in the hospital. He appreciated the thought, but he wasn't prepared for visitors. He explained that the infection was causing a lot of pain, for which the doctor had prescribed morphine. But never having used anything stronger than aspirin, the narcotic had turned his muscles to Jell-O. Looking spaced out, he added, "That stuff really messed with my mind."

Keno knew a little about consuming opiates when a body wasn't used to them. He smiled, and said, "We'll catch you later, Buzz. When you return from orbit."

It took Buzz a moment to get it. "Oh, right. Thanks for stopping by. You guys drive carefully and be nice to people."

Millie was eating dinner when they reached her room.

"Way to go, Millie," Netanya said. "It's good to see you eating again."

Millie swallowed and smiled. "Yeah, I was a little hungry for a change."

Keno, now more ambulatory with the assistance of a cane and the walking cast, moved close to the bed and scrutinized his mother's tray. He leaned over and snatched a little tomato out of the salad. "Is that yellow stuff custard? Are you going to eat it?"

Millie playfully swatted the back of his hand. "You should be ashamed of yourself, you big lug. I can't believe you would steal food from your bedridden mother."

"He's an animal," Netanya said. "He inhaled two complete crab cioppino dinners for lunch, and now he's stealing stuff off your tray."

Millie's eyebrows arched knowingly. "Remember what I said about controlling him with food?"

Keno put on a pained face. "Hey, it was way past lunch when I ate today. And it's not fair for you to be ganging up on me."

"I think it is," Millie said. "You're as big as both of us."

Netanya smiled. "I know his appetite is bigger than both of ours."

Millie agreed, "That's for sure."

"Hey, I missed breakfast. I had to catch up."

Netanya made eye contact with Millie. "Is he serious?"

Millie nodded. "Yes, if he misses a meal, he finds a way to catch up."

Keno found a wheat cracker and popped it into his mouth. "All this talk about food really is making me hungry."

The visit continued in a lighthearted vein, all three sidestepping Millie's impending legal problems. A nurse came in and gave Millie her medicines, and she soon dozed off.

Netanya glanced at her watch and remarked, "It's later than I thought. I bet you really are hungry by now."

"Hey, I wasn't kidding about that when we got here two hours ago."

"It hasn't even been an hour, silly man."

He grinned and said, "It seems like three."

"What do you want to do about getting the Caddy?"

"How about you take me to pick it up at the Yard, and then we can go to Marin Joe's for dinner?"

"Sounds like another Plan A."

When they arrived at the Yard, Keno remembered that he'd left his keys in the house trailer/office meant that he didn't have a key to open the gate.

He started to get out of the car, but Netanya objected. "You shouldn't be walking on gravel if you don't have to. I'll open it." The fog had moved in, and it had grown fairly dark, but the Ferrari's headlights made it easy to find the key under the third rock. She opened the gate, put the key back where she'd found it, then got back in the car and cautiously drove across the gravel road to the house trailer/office.

Keno leaned over and gave her a quick kiss. "I'm going to go inside and check on a job that Hector and I might have forgotten about when we made our plans this morning. She's one of Frank's oldest customers, and I don't think she got included."

"Want me to wait?"

"No, that's okay, go ahead and get us a table. I'll be there in a few minutes. "

"Okay, but I don't want to be there waiting by myself."

"No problem, see ya in a few."

Netanya waited with the Ferrari's headlights lighting the way until Keno found the key under the third rock, unlocked the small metal door, and flipped the light on inside the house trailer/office. She gave the annoying horn a couple of quick beeps, waved, then backed the sports car out and slowly left the Yard.

Keno leaned out the door and watched the powerful car negotiate the slight bumps in the road. As Netanya drove away in the Ferrari, the car's headlights became two slender spotlights diminishing in size as they cast golden-hued cones in the fog.

Nicky had drifted off to a hazy place, somewhere between nightmarish dreams and tortured consciousness. But the beeping Italian horn had caused his eyes to snap open. He listened to the big engine's rumble as it idled for a while, then soon powered the sports car away. Questions sprouted: *Have they driven off and left me again, or did somebody come to get this Cadillac? And is that somebody Biker Boy?*

The combination of thirst, hunger, and misery overwhelmed Nicky's fear of physical harm. As far as he was concerned, nobody, not even Biker Boy, could inflict more pain and suffering than he'd already endured. One way or another, it was time to do something about this appalling situation.

Nicky began to scream at the top of his lungs, but his parched throat only allowed a squawking noise, something like a distressed crow. Convinced that this pitiful effort wasn't helping his cause, he angrily ripped a cowboy boot free of tangled duct tape, slipped it on, and began kicking at the trunk lid.

Keno knew something wasn't right. He could have sworn he heard erratic noises coming from outside. He went to the door and listened. There they were again—muffled thumping noises. It took a while to determine the direction. With curiosity mounting, he grabbed his cane, stepped down from the small metal door, and limped over to the Cadillac. The closer he got to the trunk, the louder the thumping noises became. Surprised, curious, and concerned, he put one hand on top of the trunk lid. Sure enough, he could feel and hear the pounding. He instinctively took a step back to think about this aberrant discovery. He had no idea whether it was man or beast.

With very mixed feelings, Keno shouted, "Hey! Is somebody in there?"

Nicky immediately recognized the questioning voice—he'd heard it shout at the scene of the accident. Unfortunately, it belonged to Biker Boy. He thought fast and armed himself with a cowboy boot, his wide leather belt, and the big silver buckle. "Get me outta here," he squawked. "I'm dyin' o' thirst."

Keno didn't recognize the dry, croaking voice. His head spinning with a confusing combination of bewilderment and anxiety, he hopped inside to find the Cadillac's key fob. It only took a moment to locate it on the desk. While picking it up, he thought: *This is crazy. How could somebody be trapped in the Caddy's trunk?*

Heavy fog had moved in and made it darker outside. It occurred to Keno that all he had to do to solve the mystery was press a button to open the trunk. He held his thumb over the button for a moment, not knowing what to expect. He pressed it, the lid popped open, a dim light came on, and a terrible stench escaped. The awful smell gagged him and made his eyes water. For reasons unknown, it caused a brief flashback to a sun-ripened Porta Potty he'd once entered at a construction site. While holding his breath, he quickly came to realize that the stench belonged to none other than Nicky Ghilardi.

Nicky pounced like a cornered wolverine attacking a befuddled grizzly. He swung his cowboy boot as hard as he could. The heel struck the bridge of Keno's nose and momentarily blinded him. Then Nicky swung his belt—the big buckle laying open a gash above Keno's left eye. Keno raised his arms in self-defense and tried to move away, but he stumbled and fell.

Like a man possessed, Nicky unleashed a three-pronged attack. He kicked with the boot on his foot, flailed away with the boot in his right hand, and, with his left hand, swung the belt with the flesh-tearing buckle. Then, as if he didn't have enough weapons, he spied Keno's cane lying on the ground. Believing the heavy cane would make it easier to render Biker Boy unconscious, he snatched it up and began to beat the bigger man about his head and shoulders. Keno instinctively put his hands in front of his face to ward off the devastating blows, but it didn't help much. Nicky knew he was fighting for survival and relentlessly sustained the barrage.

Rage eventually overcame Keno's shock and pain. His anger ignited a deep, turbulent aggression, which spread through his bloodstream like flame shooting across napalm. His anger diminished the effect of the blows coming from every direction, but his resolve reduced them to the level of insect bites. Keno grasped hold of Nicky's ankles, clamping them with vise-like arms. Nicky continued to flail away with the belt buckle and the wooden cane, but Keno had him in his powerful grasp now. He tackled the much smaller man and overwhelmed him with brute strength. He twisted Nicky's body under his and began to pound away with sledgehammer fists.

Still fighting for his life, Nicky buried his teeth into the trapezius muscle between Keno's neck and shoulder. Like a desperate bulldog, he clamped down and twisted with all his might, doing his best to tear away a mouthful of flesh.

The piercing pain only fueled Keno's rage. He hit Nicky so hard that it cracked a rib, and another mighty blow knocked the last ounce of air from his lungs. Still, another separated the smaller man's jaws in a silent howl of pain—Nicky didn't have enough air left in his lungs to generate an audible scream. A final blow separated Nicky from consciousness.

Keno had become a crazed animal. His swollen eyes narrowed to murderous slits. Blood streamed from his mouth and both nostrils; more blood oozed from a multitude of belt cuts; and a multitude of cane welts swelled on his face, arms, and shoulders. Like a battered gladiator, he stood over his defeated foe considering how to deliver the mortal blow. He lifted Nicky high above his head, and, while shaking the limp body like a rag doll, he let go a primal scream. "Aaaahhhhhhhh!"

He threw Nicky over his shoulder and shuffled down to the tool shed. He dropped the limp body on the ground like a sack of potatoes and searched for the key, which, as expected, he found under the third rock. He opened the tool shed, found the chain saw, and fired it up to make sure it was working.

The saw's terrifying growl filtered through to Nicky's consciousness. When he slowly opened his eyes, he was convinced he was having a horrible nightmare. He couldn't believe that the bloodied and battered big demon holding a screaming, revving chain saw could be real. But biting his bottom lip convinced him that the horror was genuine, and a terrified whimper escaped.

Keno stared with crazed eyes—blood red replacing the last remnants of white—and laughed maniacally. "Now you're going to get yours, Nicky Ghilardi. I'm going to cut you up into little pieces, and then I'm going to feed you to Gonzo."

Nicky didn't know who or what Gonzo was but suspected it wasn't a good thing. "Don't hurt me anymore," he begged. "I'll do anything ya want."

Days of pent-up loathing exploded in Keno's brain. He sneered and spoke with a guttural growl. "You killed my father, one the best men who ever lived, and now my mom and I will be missing him every second of every day for the rest of our lives." Keno's snarl revealed perfectly white teeth that contrasted with the blood and grime on his face. "You not only shot my mother, you ugly little punk, you totally ruined her life." He used the back of one hand to wipe away saliva bubbling at the corners of his bloodied mouth. "And you've caused me nothing but pain and misery." His chest heaved, and heated blasts of breath escaped. "You don't deserve to live for another minute."

Nicky whimpered, then tried to scoot away on his belly like a snake looking for a hole to hide in. Keno grabbed him by the scruff of the neck and dragged him, kicking and screaming, into the tool shed. His rage overwhelming his thoughts, Keno found a roll of duct tape and bound Nicky's hands behind his back.

"Don't! I can't stand anymore o' that freakin' duct tape," Nicky sniveled. "I'd rather be dead than all taped up again. Just go ahead an' kill me. Just get it over with."

"You're going to get your wish, you rotten punk" Keno threatened. "Only I'm going to do it slow, real slow. First, I'm going to cut off your feet, one at a time, and then I'm going to make you watch me feed them to Gonzo. Then I'm going to cut off your hands and make you watch Gonzo eat them. And then your arms and legs, one at a time. The last thing Gonzo eats will be your ugly head." He fired up the chain saw again and revved it to maximum R.P.M., only inches from Nicky's face.

"Please don't cut me up like that," Nicky begged. "I'll give you a million bucks. No, two million."

Keno revved the chain saw again for effect, and said, "The hell with your money." Then he carried the menacing weapon to the Gonzo shed and set it down beside the door. He looked under the third rock, but the key wasn't there. Just to make sure, he looked under the second and fourth rocks, too. Still, no key for the Gonzo shed. Hector must have forgotten to put it back. He cursed under his breath when he realized that he'd have to get the one in the house trailer/office.

As Keno went limping up the hill, Nicky shouted after him, his cowboy accent forgotten. "I'll sign over everything I own to you and then leave the state. Please, Biker Boy, I'll give you everything I have. I'll even leave the country."

Keno ignored the pitiful pleas. He'd already begun to dwell on how he was going to dispose of Nicky's remains. But getting rid of finely chopped body parts wouldn't be a problem. He would mix the little pieces with different piles of Milagrozo mulch. Then cleaning the stainless-steel Gonzo machine wouldn't be that difficult, either—he knew where Hector kept the hose he used to clean equipment. He would run enough brush through to absorb the worst of the mess and then hose down the machine. And just to be on the safe side, he would run through two or three barrels of leaves for a final polishing.

Absorbed with finding the key to the shed, Keno stormed into the house trailer/office as fast as he could hop. He soon found the right key hanging on the board on the wall where Frank had meticulously placed all the tagged keys. But when he tugged at the key, it seemed to be glued to the brass hook. He tugged again, but it stubbornly refused to come free. Contracting his powerful muscles, he gripped the key with all his might and yanked. The key didn't come free, but the hook came right out of the board. It took every ounce of his strength to keep twisting the key until it finally came free from the hook.

As Keno turned to hop back toward the small aluminum door, his walking cast caught on a loose piece of carpet, and he tripped. As he lunged forward, he reached out with one hand to break his fall, and this act of self-preservation caused him to knock some things off Frank's desk. But still fixated on the thought of disposing of Nicky, he struggled to his feet and reached for the door's handle. Keno twisted, but the small aluminum alloy handle wouldn't budge. He twisted harder, but he still couldn't free the door latch. His patience exhausted, he gave the handle a desperate yank. He couldn't believe it when it broke off in his hand without freeing the lock.

Keno stared at the handle in his hand, then at the door. It occurred to him that this could present a problem. He tried to fit the handle back into place, hoping to turn the broken handle shaft, but a couple of minutes of poking and jiggling proved futile. Frustrated beyond any semblance of control, Keno leaned over and charged the door, slamming it with his mightiest shoulder block. Amazingly, the small metal door held fast. A few more of these desperate attempts yielded the same result, only with added injury to his body.

He studied the windows but soon realized that none were big enough to squeeze his big body through, even if he could break out the glass. Short on options, he limped over to get Frank's old metal chair. Using it as an unwieldy hammer, he slammed the chair against the door. The door still didn't budge. He futilely pounded away, smashing the little door again and again, only giving up when exhaustion overwhelmed him. Feeling defeated, Keno collapsed on the floor.

Glancing around, Keno discovered that he was sitting close to some of the items he'd knocked off of Frank's desk. He noticed a penholder, a notebook, and Frank's tattered Bible. The Bible had fallen open to where a purple cloth bookmarker separated the pages. As he looked down at the open Bible, an eerie feeling came over him. A powerful presence—like a ghostly visitor—seemed to be sitting beside him. It seemed so real that he was afraid to turn and look. As he stared down at the open Bible, he felt as if someone, or possibly an eerie spirit, was telling him to pick it up and read. The compelling urge intensified until he became convinced that he had no choice. He swallowed hard, then picked up the Bible.

It was opened to the Book of Romans. He scanned the page and then stopped as if directed to a specific passage. He read: *Recompense to no man evil for evil.* He skipped down to the word he was looking for. *Avenge not yourselves, but rather give place unto wrath: for it is written, Vengeance is mine; I will repay, saith the Lord.* He skipped some more. *Therefore, if thine enemy hunger, feed him; if he thirsts, give him drink; for so doing thou shall heap coals of fire upon his head.*

Keno's body sagged, and he rested his shoulder against the desk, feeling as if every last ounce of his strength had been drained. For reasons he couldn't explain, he'd been intimidated by what he'd just read. He shuddered, thinking that finding the Bible open to those exact passages was too convenient to be an accident. While trying to absorb these inexplicable feelings, his mind connected this mystical event with his father's dying words and his own paranormal visions. *Could Frank be talking to me? Is he telling me to cool it?* Then he questioned his sanity out loud: "Am I totally wacko, or what?"

Netanya decided that waiting thirty minutes at Marin Joe's was at least fifteen minutes too many. Several reasons for Keno not being there as he'd promised crossed her mind. Though feeling a little miffed, part of her was concerned for his welfare as she sped the Ferrari back toward the Yard. She became convinced it was a total lack of consideration when she saw the Cadillac still parked where it had been all day; the light still on in the house trailer/office; and another light glowing in a small shed. He'd probably got caught up in doing something that he thought was important and had forgotten all about her.

Netanya opened the little metal door to the house trailer/office and barged inside, ready to give her inconsiderate fiancé a piece of her mind. But she wasn't prepared for the site that greeted her. "Oh, my God!"

Keno didn't know where to begin. "I'm sorry, babe..."

"What in the world...?"

"I guess things got out of control."

"Are you alright?" She went to him and stroked his wounds with cautious fingertips. "What happened, Joaquin? You're all bloody, and beat up, and dirty..." Then she made a face, as if confronted with something repulsive. "What's that awful smell?"

"That's rotten, Nicky. You're not going to believe this, but right after you left, I found Nicky Ghilardi in the Cadillac's trunk."

Her mouth fell open. "Alive?"

"Yes, unfortunately, alive and kicking." He raised his shirt and revealed several welts and abrasions. "Really kicking."

"Oh, my God! That's awful." Clearly perplexed, she shook her head and asked, "So how did he get in the trunk?"

"Not a clue, but I think he might have been trying to set me up again."

"Where is he now?"

"Down at the tool shed where I left him taped up."

"Did you beat him up, too?"

"Yeah, but I think I got the worst of it."

"I still can't believe he was locked in the Caddy's trunk."

"I have no idea how the idiot could have gotten in there. But from the way he smelled, he must have been in there for quite a while." When pain reminded him of the physical punishment he'd suffered, Keno exhausted a heavy breath. "I almost wish we hadn't come back to get the Cadillac tonight. He probably would have been dead by tomorrow morning."

"You're not serious?"

Keno shrugged. "I don't know what to think anymore."

"Come on, Joaquin. I know Nick's a total jerk, but he has probably suffered enough. I can't even imagine being locked in the trunk like that."

Keno decided it was time to come clean. Maybe sharing everything would help—it was all too heavy to keep to himself.

"Honestly, Tanya, I was going to cut Nicky up and feed him to the Gonzo machine, and then I was going to hide his stinking little pieces in different piles of Milagrozo mulch." He paused, not sure how to explain the chilling, paranormal event. "I know you'll find this hard to believe, but I think I had a heavy religious experience that stopped me from going through with it."

Netanya looked frightened as she asked with uncertainty in her voice, "The Gonzo machine chops things into little pieces?"

"That's what it does."

"And you were going to chop Nicky up?"

"Yeah, I was."

"Are you kidding me?"

"No, I'm not. I was going to make him suffer, and then make him disappear."

"And then you had a spiritual experience that prevented you from killing him?"

"Yeah, a bunch of weird stuff happened when I came into the office to get a key for the Gonzo shed. First, the key felt like it was super-glued to the hook, and then I tripped and fell on the way out. Then the door latch wouldn't budge when I tried to open it, and then the latch broke off in my hand when I twisted it." He glanced at the bent and broken metal chair. "I even beat the hell out of the door with that chair, but it still wouldn't open.

Netanya frowned while digesting his frightening narrative. "You're telling me that a paranormal force trapped you in here?"

"Yeah, I definitely think so. When I collapsed on the floor, I noticed that the Bible had fallen off the desk, and it was conveniently opened to the Book of Romans. That's where it says *vengeance is mine.* I know this sounds totally crazy, but it seemed like a ghost was sitting right here beside me. And then it felt like it was calming me down and talking some sense into me."

He offered his most convincing look. "I swear, Tanya, there was some kind of spirit in here with me." He stared at her for a few seconds, allowing her time to consider his astonishing words. "I think it might have been Frank."

Netanya visibly shuddered. "This is scary, Joaquin."

"Tell me about it. But when you think about the big picture, it did keep me from killing that rotten punk."

Keno paused to consider how much to share about Frank's dying words. "There's something else I haven't told you, or anybody else as far as that goes. When my father died, he told me I was meant to do good things for the world. He said I was supposed to teach the world to feed itself with something called Tierra Milagro. He also warned me that evil would try to stop me, and then he made me promise I wouldn't sacrifice my destiny to be an avenger of blood."

"You definitely would have been killing Nicky for vengeance."

"My dad also admitted to being clairvoyant," Keno told her. "I don't know; maybe he was a prophet or something."

Visibly stunned by all she'd just heard, Netanya stared at Keno while collecting herself. Finally allowing herself to blink, she took the Bible and read the passages he had described. "This does seem apropos. If you think about it, a lot of the Bible is made up of prophesies that Jews, Christians, and even Muslims buy into. And who says there can't be prophets anymore? Who says your dad couldn't have been one? Everybody knows he was a really good man. I even heard people saying he was a saint."

Keno blew out a big breath. "I'm not sure about anything except that I definitely felt a presence here. And whatever it was, or whoever it was, it did prevent me from becoming a killer." He shook his head while considering the magnitude of it all. "What do you think we should do now?"

"Well, the passage does say to give your enemy food and drink. If Nicky was in the trunk for who knows how long, he definitely needs them."

Keno shrugged. "It also says doing so shall heap coals of fire on his head. You find him some food and drink, and I'll see what I can do about digging up some hot coals."

Netanya stared with an incredulous look. "I can't believe you're joking at a time like this." She shook her head and said, "I'll see if there is anything to eat around here."

Keno made a pained face. "I don't know. Being nice to that punk is asking a lot."

Netanya shot a glance at the Bible. "It depends on who's doing the asking."

Keno still retained a sense of unease. The powerful grip of the supernatural presence had dissipated, but something had caused a significant change to come over him. "The more I think about everything, the weirder it gets."

Netanya discovered unopened packets of soda crackers in a cabinet and then found a plastic bottle of orange juice and several slices of cheese in the half-size refrigerator. "Let's just go with it, Joaquin, and do what the Bible says."

"Alright, Keno agreed, "but my knee is totally swollen inside this cast. I'm going to need my cane, which I'm hoping is out by the Caddy."

Netanya found his cane and helped Keno limp down the hill to the tool shed. But Nicky wasn't there.

Netanya shouted, "Nicky! We're bringing you some O.J. and some things to eat. Come on out. Nobody is going to hurt you."

When they went inside the tool shed, Netanya saw several small pools of blood, the shed in total disarray, and a pile of twisted duct tape. "It looks like a combat zone."

"I was really pissed, and I guess he was desperate."

Keno found a powerful Maglite, and then shone it over the ground in a grid-like pattern. It didn't take a lot of searching to find footprints leading down to the hothouse. In fact, for the briefest of moments, Keno felt a little suspicious. An almost unbroken small groove in the ground, as if something was being dragged, seemed too easy to follow.

While noticing that several rocks in front of the main entry were overturned, Keno flashed the light on the hothouse door, which stood slightly ajar. "It looks like Nicky found the key and went inside. He must have seen me find the key to the tool shed and then figured out that a key would be under one of the rocks." Keno's shrug contained a hint of respect. "I guess he's not a total idiot."

Her face appearing radiant in the yellow-tinted light, Netanya called out, "Nicky. We have some food for you." She shrugged and added, "We come in peace. Promise."

Keno pushed the door open with his cane, took a moment to make sure it was safe, and limped inside. He clicked the light switch, but nothing happened. "I wonder why the light's not working."

He looked to his right and noticed a door leading to an office. Feeling Netanya's nervous breath on his neck, he stepped inside and swept the bright light over the room and its new furnishings. "Look at this, Tanya. Frank must have just put in all new office furniture, a new computer, and even a new printer. It's all so new, most of it is not even hooked up yet."

"Looks like he was catching up with the future."

"No doubt." Following the circular beam around the room, Keno noticed a glass-encased cabinet with an older-looking cedar box inside. On closer inspection, he could see that the box, with a plain wooden cross on its top, had been placed on a stand covered with fancy red and gold velvet. It appeared as if the box were a prized trophy provided with a special place of honor. As he shone the light on it, the marbled cedar box seemed to reflect more light than it should have.

Feeling a slight chill, Keno said, "Maybe this is what Frank was waiting to tell me about."

"Waiting to tell you?"

"Never mind, I fill you in later. Let's go check out the rest of the place."

"Good idea. Nicky's not hiding in here."

Next, Keno swept the Maglite's beam over the interior of the main building, then danced it over some exceptionally large plants. Their brilliant colors jumped out, even in the restricted light. "Wow! Look at the size of these plants!"

Netanya, a couple of steps behind, exclaimed, "And their colors! It's like an exotic jungle in here."

"Yeah," Keno replied. "It looks like my dad was into growing some incredible vegetation." He stepped closer and observed, "And the plants are growing out of things that look like bathtubs."

"They really are bathtubs," Netanya said as she lifted the bottom of a bright red tomato with her fingers. "Look, Joaquin, this tomato is almost as big as a cantaloupe."

Keno replied, "Yeah, and this cantaloupe is the size of a watermelon."

Netanya moved close to another plant and questioned, "Is this really a string bean? It's almost as big as my arm."

When he thought he heard some heavy breathing, Keno was reminded of the reason they were in the hothouse. He lowered his voice and asked, "You hear that?"

Netanya cocked her head to listen. "Yeah, I do."

Wearing a look of resignation, Keno called out, "Believe it or not, we're here to make peace, Nicky. Tanya even brought you some food and O.J."

The metal end of a shovel suddenly sliced through the beam of light, viciously striking the cast supporting Keno's swollen knee. Mind-numbing pain pierced Keno's surprised brain, provoking a tormented bellow.

By now an expert at escaping duct tape bindings, Nicky held the shovel in a threatening parade-rest position when he appeared in the Maglite's beam.

Netanya let go a shrill shriek and hurried to Keno's side. Her expression of surprise appeared frozen on her face as she knelt to help him.

Nicky swung the shovel and struck the back of Netanya's head with a brutal blow. When she fell, seemingly unconscious, Nicky smiled and let go a contented grunt. He then turned and cast a sneer at Keno before going to retrieve the chain saw, which he had left behind a nearby plant. He had considered using the terrifying tool for his initial attack but realized its loud noise would have eliminated the element of surprise.

Nicky had never operated a chainsaw, so it took a few moments to figure out how to start it. By the time he had it revving, Keno was sitting and glaring. Though he was suffering a lot of residual pain, that didn't suppress Nicky's evil grin. "Now it's my turn, Biker Boy. Before I vamoose outta here, I'm gonna do some o' that cuttn' you was talkin' about doin' to me."

As Nicky began to close the distance, Keno grabbed his cane and began to roll away as fast as he could. He wanted to take advantage of the dark.

Nicky shouted, "You can roll, but you can't hide, Biker Boy."
Amused by his own wit, Nicky chuckled. He found the Maglite and
went stumbling after Keno.

Keno rolled into a partition between two bathtubs and then
struggled to lift himself up and support his weight on one leg. Forced
to lean against one for stability, he held the cane at his side with the
idea of using it as a weapon.

Nicky flashed the light around until he located Keno. Confident
that his prey was immobile, he wedged the Maglite at the base of
a nearby plant, then tilted it up at just the right angle. With Keno
centered in the makeshift spotlight, Nicky raised the chain saw, revved
it, and closed the distance.

Keno lashed out with the cane, but Nicky angled the chain saw
and abruptly sawed Keno's hope in half. Nicky's villainous laugh
echoed through the hothouse "I'm startin' with your arms first, Biker
Boy, 'cause I know you can't run."

Aware of his limitations, a look of desperation grew on Keno's
battered face.

Nicky couldn't have been more surprised when Netanya pounced
on him from behind. Working her long nails like an angry eagle's talons,
she ripped at Nicky's eyes and face with astonishing fury. Momentarily
blinded, Nicky cried out and staggered back. He stumbled and flopped
backwards, clumsily landing on top of Netanya.

The chain saw, running at maximum R.P.M. with Nicky's finger
still squeezing the trigger, fell backwards, too. The speeding chain made
contact for less than a second, but it instantly chewed into Netanya's face
and ripped away a strip of beautiful flesh. The unforgiving chain had
dug a nasty gouge. Gory-looking tissue was laid open on her cheekbone.

Obviously aware that something terrible had happened, Netanya's
hand flew to her face. She moved her hand away and saw it covered
in blood a horrified moment before losing consciousness.

Keno screamed, "Noooooo!"

When Nicky's vision cleared, he saw Netanya's gruesome-looking face lying just inches from his own. Shocked senseless by this close-up, Nicky could think of nothing but a rapid escape. He scrambled to his feet, scurried out the door, and trudged up the hill. He couldn't believe his good fortune when he saw the Ferrari's key fob lying on the car's console. Not bothering with the seat belt, he started the magnificent vehicle and sped away.

For a moment, Keno was too stunned to breathe. He crawled to Netanya's side and examined the horrific gash, not quite hidden under her limp and bloody hand. A feeling of déjà vu zapped his mind—he suddenly remembered envisioning the grisly wound the day he'd proposed. Consciously putting that disturbing thought aside, he slipped off his shirt and tore it into strips to fashion a makeshift bandage. While moving her hand, he spotted the watch containing the global positioning device. He knew it would be difficult, if not impossible, to get her to the hospital in time to save her life. To ensure getting a better signal, he ignored the assault of pain and carried Netanya outside. He quickly activated the device, hoping beyond hope that Buzz's security team would respond quickly enough.

Hearing the Ferrari's powerful engine in the distance reminded Keno that Nicky was getting away. The heavy rumble pummeled his mind with regret. When he glanced up and saw the full moon's pale blue face breaking through the foggy night, *something* awakened at the root of that regret. That *something* sent energy coursing through him again, but this was different—it was an energy of heart-rending anguish.

As if taking a page from his brief acting experience, Keno looked up to the sky and shouted, "Why, God? Why? Why didn't you let me kill that evil bastard? If vengeance is yours, you'd better damn well take care of him, or I swear, I will!"

Keno's anguish—energized by that *something* springing from the core of his soul—caused him to unleash a long, woeful cry. Bringing to mind a mournful wolf's howl, the distressing sound pierced the tranquil night.

As Nicky sped the Ferrari along the curving, two-lane asphalt road leading away from the Yard, he felt a sense of power—a growing sense of invincibility. He'd overcome enormous odds, and he'd won. He couldn't resist an urge to brag, and shouted into the night, "I really got Biker Boy and his rich bitch Jap, that Jewish American Princess. That'll teach 'em to mess with Nicky G." He let go a fiendish giggle, then asked rhetorically, "Who has the last laugh now?"

The sleep-deprived young woman, a sophomore at the College of Marin, had a habit of increasing her headset's volume a little more after each delivery. Her head bounced and swayed to the Hip-Hop beat while the thumping base blasted hard enough to keep her eyelids open. The volume maxed out, and her mind elsewhere, she almost subconsciously steered the commercial van through the fog. She was about to make her last delivery of the day for FLOWERS EXPRESS.

Nicky's eyes expanded to their limits when he realized he was on the wrong side of the road. Suddenly, like a giant creature leaping out of the dark, a pair of gleaming headlights sped directly toward him. He yanked the steering wheel hard to the right and stomped his foot on the gas pedal. The Ferrari responded quicker, much quicker, than any car he'd ever driven. The spectacular sports car, obeying his commands faster than he could blink, accelerated straight into a weathered power pole. The violent impact sent Nicky's head flying over the airbag and above the convertible's windshield.

The collision severed a live electric wire connected to an insulator situated near the top of the power pole. Like an enormous sparkler dancing on a string, the wildly skipping wire sent sparks shooting and spraying from everything it touched in the fog-enshrouded night. The frolicking wire soon found the top of Nicky's exposed head. The fleeting connection caused his thick black hair to sizzle, then smolder, like a bed of hot coals.

Epilogue

Five Years Later

Keno swooped the Bernstein Burgundy helicopter in low, leveled it over the Jeep convertible, and then rocked it from side to side, waving an aerobatic hello. He smiled and saluted, then banked the sleek craft on a steep angle and zoomed across the backyard to the heliport.

With Netanya behind the wheel and Simon and little Francisco sitting in the back, the electric powered jeep raced to meet Keno at the landing pad. The excited little family watched with happy anticipation as their favorite pilot expertly set the chopper down on the white landing marker, only inches off dead center.

Keno climbed out of the chopper and limped toward the jeep, but Francisco had already closed the distance, meeting him halfway. "Poppo," the boy shouted, and then he leaped wildly, confident that his big, strong father would snatch him out of the air. "Take me for a ride in the hello-chopter."

Keno smiled and hugged his three-year-old son. "Maybe tomorrow." He straightened Francisco's Greek sailor cap, then held his pride-and-joy high over his head.

"Wow, Cisco, you have really grown. You're getting to be quite a load."

"Yeah," the boy replied gleefully, "I'm getting growed now."

His son's joyful face overwhelmed Keno for a moment—he'd seen an emaciated boy of about the same age die of malnutrition just a couple of days earlier. It wasn't easy to let go of that other boy's heartbreaking image, even as hardened as Keno had become by the years of observing unmitigated misery and seeing acres of graves occupied by thousands of those who'd died in a similar fashion.

He hugged Francisco so hard that it squeezed out a protest. "Owww! You're strong, Poppo."

Keno fought back the emotion swelling behind his eyes while letting go of his son.

Netanya reached a slender hand around Keno's tanned neck, then planted a warm kiss on his smiling lips. The kiss unleashed a flood of feelings. "So good to see you, Joaquin. The past six weeks have seemed like six months." Her almond eyes stared into his while massaging his bearded chin. "No, more like six years."

He pulled her close and kissed her again, slowly and tenderly, the way he'd been dreaming of doing since the day he'd landed at the Lilongwe Airport in the impoverished sub-Saharan African country of Malawi. "Definitely more like six years."

She caressed his cheek with her fingertips while scrunching her freckled nose and grimacing. "I feel guilty for even saying it, but I don't want you going away anymore."

Keno nodded. "I know the feeling. It's getting harder all the time."

Francisco tugged at his father's pants leg and said, "C'mon Poppo. We gotta go see Nanno."

Netanya didn't want to let go. She gave Keno one final squeeze, stepped back, and subconsciously flipped her hair, which was purposely shaped to hide Nicky Ghilardi's egregious mutilation. The discolored scar was still visible, though decidedly less so after several plastic surgeries. She said, "Take it easy, Cisco. We're not going to see Nanno until after lunch."

The boy took his father's hand, glanced up, and asked, "Can we eat lunch early?"

Netanya grinned, and said, "Definitely his father's son." Her face turned serious as she added, "Buzz, Nate, and Doctor Singh are waiting, Joaquin. We're having a short meeting before we go see Millie's exhibition."

Keno recalled that his mother was having an art exhibition in Mill Valley. During one of their recent phone calls, Netanya told him about helping with the arrangements. Though the excursion to Malawi for The Frank Flores Foundation had been exhausting, and the long flight home had sapped him, nothing would prevent him from missing this momentous event. After years of living in darkness, it was Millie's day to shine. "Okay, let's get going."

Simon stoically waited in the back seat, watching the happy reunion. As Keno got close, the wise older man couldn't help noticing the look in his son-in-law's eyes. He'd seen that look many times before. It was the distant, vacant look people had when they'd seen too much human suffering—suffering beyond the mind's ability to process it. Simon had seen that look in the eyes of Holocaust survivors and in the eyes of Sasha's mother after witnessing Stalin's wrath. And on a personal level, he'd seen it in the eyes of those virtually enslaved miners who'd helped make him rich—a source of guilt from which he could never escape.

At first, Simon was not thrilled with supporting The Frank Flores Foundation. He thought it would distract Joaquin from his business matters. But a remarkable development had dramatically altered that notion. Simon couldn't have been more surprised to learn that Joaquin was using the charitable foundation's public image to gain entry into arid and impoverished countries. The foundation was effectively a front for the implementation of the Tierra Milagro project.

He raised his glossy oak cane in greeting. "Welcome home, weary traveler."

Keno noticed that Simon was wearing a Greek sailor's cap identical to Francisco's, except, of course, for size. "Good to see you, Simon."

"How goes your battle for the downtrodden?"

"The battles are going okay, but I'm not convinced we're winning the war." Keno considered relating the disappointing results of his latest adventure. As he'd been doing in many third-world countries, he'd gone to Malawi to set up a trade school. But the local males seemed more interested in obtaining cash than learning a skill that wouldn't immediately pay off. Since their little democracy was heavily supported by foreign aid, they'd come to believe that foreign organizations—notably UNICEF, the World Food Programme, and Save the Children—were there to hand out money. Who could blame them? The average Malawian earned less than two dollars a day, and their life expectancy was just thirty-nine years. Feeling Simon's questioning eye, he chose to change the subject. "I've been warned that I might be excommunicated."

Netanya, now a Catholic herself, asked, "What's up with that?"

His son's presence compelled Keno to choose his words carefully. "I've been accused of aiding and abetting the Presbyterian Church in the sinful act of dispensing birth control pills." He reflected on three dirty-faced kids with swollen stomachs. These impoverished and uneducated children were shooing flies from their faces while their parents were blissfully enjoying sex just beyond a makeshift wall—perhaps unwittingly bringing another child into a world of deprivation and misery. "And I'm forced to plead guilty."

"Misguided church doctrine will eventually be rectified under the uncompromising weight of knowledge and necessity," Simon said without a lot of conviction.

"I hope you're right," Netanya put in. "But Jesus might be a good example of that. He definitely changed the rules when he came along."

Netanya's brutal injury had shattered her dream of becoming an accomplished actor, but the disappointment was considerably minimized after joining Keno's cause. Soon convinced of the plan's merit, she'd become captivated by the realistic opportunity to help change the world. Moreover, she discovered that the demanding and secretive challenges aroused her competitive spirit. Not only had she inherited Simon's head for business, but she had an uncanny gift for making the right decisions at the right time. Under her dynamic stewardship, Bernstein's wealth had increased far faster than Simon's most optimistic projections. At first, she'd become immersed in business to escape the public's eye, but now she privately held to a more selfish reason. She wanted to provide the foundation and the Tierra Milagro project with enough resources so that her husband could stay home and let others fight the battles on the front lines.

Since Netanya had liberated Keno from business concerns, he was free to devote his abundant energies to fulfilling the promises he'd made to his father. The Frank Flores Foundation had rapidly gained international recognition, and hundreds of thousands of acres across the world had secretly fallen under the control of the Tierra Milagro project.

While Netanya had effectively become the primary benefactor for Keno's ambitious goals, Simon had contributed mightily. He had enlisted the aid of several wealthy businesspeople—many of them competitors who were leery of rousing his wrath. Simon had also planted the seed for the charitable foundation's slogan: *Teach the world to fish.* Not only was the foundation teaching people to fish, it was also teaching them many skills and crafts. While effectively wearing two hats, one quite public and one quite secret, Keno had come to realize that guilds, union apprenticeships, and wise fathers imparting knowledge to their children were largely things of the past. Viable training grounds to carry on existing know-how had been vanishing for years. Expertise developed over centuries was in danger of being forever lost and forgotten. The Frank Flores Foundation has established job-training centers in twenty-seven countries thus far, with no intention of stopping there. The foundation provided training grounds for dedicated people to become instructors of important crafts and skills, and then these qualified people cultivated numerous other devoted mentors, teachers, and instructors, and so on. The Tierra Milagro project, however, was considerably more complex in its approach to helping.

"Let's go, Poppo," Francisco said in an impatient, almost demanding voice.

Netanya shot him a look. "Cool it, Cisco. Sit down and buckle your seat belt."

After a jovial round of greetings, Nathanial and Amelia Clay, Buzz and Julie Aldridge, Doctor Garish Singh, and Keno followed Simon into his magnificent library. Before joining the others, Netanya arranged for James, the muscular butler, to see that Francisco was provided a healthy snack and then turned loose on a new batch of Legos.

When everyone was seated in the library's comfortable leather chairs, Simon cleared his throat and, in his own way, brought the meeting to order. "I've called us together today for a review of the Tierra Milagro project. Duty has kept us apart for too long, and I would personally like to offer my heartfelt thanks for the valuable time and the wonderful work each of you has contributed." Simon looked up toward the ceiling, adding, "I only wish my lovely Sasha could have lived to see this remarkable project come to fruition." He turned and said, "Please lead off, Joaquin."

Simon had called the meeting, but a quick glance at all the respectful attention directed his way reminded Keno that he was in charge. He made a dramatic show of glancing at his watch, then said, "I can't believe it's been more than four years since we met in this room to lay out the master plan for the Tierra Milagro project. And I would also like to thank everyone for the demanding work you've done. But believe it or not, everything is finally falling into place. And today we'll all have a chance to learn where we've been, where we're going, and how soon we're going to get there." He thought a moment, then continued "As most of you know, Tanya and Julie have been working together on acquisitions. With Julie's real estate expertise and Tanya's business acumen, they've become a real dynamic duo. Would you ladies like to give us an update?"

Netanya subconsciously flipped her hair before pushing buttons on a remote to illuminate a plasma screen, and then another button to expand it. "I'll begin by showing you a 3-D globe that shows our areas of interest. You'll notice that the lands we've purchased are outlined in gold, and the lands we've leased are outlined in red. The major waste dumps we've contracted to remove are outlined in icky brown." As the globe on the screen slowly turned, she commented, "These are the first lands Tierra Milagro is going to change, or, as we like to call it, *transform*. These lighted areas may look small, but they represent thousands of acres."

Netanya handed the remote to Julie and said, "But Julie is the real estate whiz, so I'll let her take over."

Julie pushed buttons that shut off that screen, brought another plasma screen forward, and expanded it. "This will give you a better idea of what the properties look like. You'll notice that the properties are all close to large bodies of salt water, and none are in cold climates."

Pictures of barren and arid lands—most of which would be classified as desert—appeared on the screen as if she were flipping through pictures taken from several thousand feet. "I'm taking the liberty of rounding off numbers. There you see Iraq, where we've acquired ten thousand square miles... here's Ethiopia, twelve thousand... Egypt, eighteen thousand... Tunisia, fifteen thousand. And so it goes in South America, Mexico, and a couple states in the southwestern U.S."

Julie clicked more buttons, and pictures of giant garbage disposal sites appeared. "The biggest waste dumps are outside of Cairo and Rio de Janeiro." She punched a button and zoomed in on a site with small mountains of trash and waste. "If you look closely, you can see poor people digging through that filthy stuff, mostly trying to find something to eat. And we're getting paid big bucks to haul this waste to our project sites."

Netanya's disgust lingered as she interjected, "Fortunately, a lot of rich and famous people have recently gotten involved in huge environmental programs. Maybe it's as simple as some fat cats satisfying their egos and buying themselves a legacy. Or maybe there are just some nice rich people, but whatever, buying up huge tracts of land has suddenly become a popular thing to do. One rich apparel magnate recently bought thousands of acres of the Patagonia, which he said is to keep the land wild forever. Most of the big purchases are meant to conserve forests, wildlife preserves, and even cattle ranges. Giant timber and energy corporations are fighting them tooth and nail. But, so far, we're flying under the radar because we don't fit any demographic profile."

Julie picked up on Netanya's subtle signal, indicating it was time for more real estate input. "To date, we've purchased more than two million square miles and obtained long-term leases on another nine hundred thousand of what most sensible people would consider worthless land. And we have millions of tons of garbage and waste at our disposal, no pun intended. Our land purchases have averaged about three dollars per acre, and the average yearly cost of leased properties is currently two dollars per acre per year. A significant percentage of the land costs can be absorbed with monies collected from our waste removal contracts. If the Tierra Milagro reclamation succeeds as well as projected, the value of the land holdings will be... astronomical. I can't begin to count that high."

Netanya added, "Of course, that part's going to create a problem when the big boys figure out what we're up to."

Keno sensed that the women were finished. "Thank you, great presentation Mrs. Aldridge and Mrs. Flores." He paused, and said, "And they know what they're talking about. When our land reclamations become visible on a large scale, there's going to be hell to pay. I'm sure we'll see greed on a scale compared to those controlling oil, gold, etcetera. Governments and mega-corps are going to be after us." Keno turned to the Clays and asked, "Can you calm some of our fears?"

Nathaniel Clay grimaced as he studied the picture of the gigantic waste disposal site still showing on the plasma screen. "It is abysmal." He tapped the tips of his fingers together and explained, "I'll preface my remarks with my usual disclaimer: Amelia and I would not be involved with this shady legal maneuvering but for the incredible humanitarian potential. But that said, we haven't done anything unique. The protections we have put in place have become standard practice for numerous mega-corporations, though we might have gone the extra mile. In truth, the old *layers of an onion* metaphor quite accurately describe our skullduggery. We have created layer upon layer of corporate ownership regarding individual properties." Nate smiled wryly before continuing. "I hate to admit it, but Amelia has enormous talent when it comes to manipulating the system. We've set up a separate law firm that deals strictly with International Law, and Amelia has excelled at managing it."

Clearly quite pregnant, Amelia adjusted her weight in the seat and flashed her contagious smile before explaining, "The corporate ownerships we've layered evolve until designated persons of a particular country assume control of a local company, or as is more commonly known these days, *acquire managerial responsibilities*. Ironically, we've learned that it's easier to gain control of properties if the powers that be think we intend to drill for oil or mine for minerals. Or, for that matter, almost any financial purpose other than being there to protect and improve their environment."

Amelia shrugged and went on. "However, should an investigation or a challenge of ownership by an unfriendly government or local power broker become imminent, the targeted company is promptly and conveniently sold to a different layered corporation. The former owners file for bankruptcy, lose records, pay bribes, or simply disappear. This concept used to be known as setting up dummy corporations, but I think the process has graduated to *smarter incorporated*."

Keno smiled and said, "Thanks, you two. That makes me feel a little better about our legal protections. So, what about it, Buzz?

Can you provide us with a confidence boost regarding matters of security?"

Buzz pursed his lips and shook his head from side to side. "I would never imply that Frank Flores' death and Netanya's terrible wound were anything but tragic. But someday we may look back at the evil that Nicky Ghilardi, the Devil's little helper, created and consider it to be insignificant. Maybe something like getting a mosquito bite compared to being fired on by a division of elite assault troops. I hate to sound so negative, but I'm convinced that the Tierra Milagro project is too big for any conventional security measures. I will need an army of Timothy Morgans if it comes down to using force."

Buzz exhorted a sigh of resignation. "As I've cautioned many times, we must avoid confrontation at all costs, and the best way to do that is to keep potential adversaries in the dark. Nate and Amelia have done an exceptional job of doing just that so far, legal-wise. However, I can't predict what is going to happen when deserts start blooming all over the world. The powerful and greedy will see the potential for enormous profits and use every weapon at their disposal to gain control of these new Shangri-Las—be it with political, commercial, or military means."

Buzz glanced around at his visibly discomfited audience. "I believe our best hope rests in the power of the people. We'll need to nurture strong local leaders. Principled people who will make the populous realize how much their lives will improve, and, idealistically speaking, not let any entity rob them of their new hopes and dreams."

"I think you nailed it, Buzz," Keno said. "We'll need to develop partnerships with local leaders, especially ones that aren't associated with fanatical religions, corrupt governments, or greedy corporations."

Keno then turned to Garish Singh, Doctor of Microbiology and Senior Administrator of Simon's privately owned Emeryville R&D Laboratory. "We've heard about acquisitions, legalities, and security, Doctor Singh. So now let's hear how our project is actually going to work at ground level. Tell us what's happening down in the dirt."

Doctor Singh's eyes revealed even more white than usual and his brilliant smile, contrasting with his dark complexion, revealed sparkling teeth, almost too white to be real. Looking at least a decade younger than his fifty years, the doctor's clipped manner of speech exuded the same excitement as the expression on his intense face. "I can't thank you enough for permitting me to be a part of this wonderful project. I have been blessed with the opportunity to do what I've enjoyed doing most of my adult life. Working with Tierra Milagro has rewarded me in ways beyond my wildest dreams." He paused and asked rhetorically, "Where to begin...?"

The doctor appeared to have just discovered something when he raised a finger and exclaimed, "Ahah! I believe this project all began with an amazing box. It's actually a small cedar chest, which Frank Flores had kept with him since he was a child. And I just happened to have brought it with me."

The doctor retrieved the special box from a leather case, removed protective bubble wrap, and held it up for all to see. He raised the lid with the plain cross attached, removed a wooden tray, and said, "As you can see, the tray resting on top concealed a larger space at the bottom of the box. I suspect that someone in the past filled the tray with cremated ashes to discourage inquisitive minds. However, we now know that the box contained something far more interesting than cremains. The bottom portion of the box held a unique clay container that was lined with a thin layer of goat skin. And the box contained rich, black soil that was inundated with unknown varieties of bacteria. I found classes of unicellular microorganisms integrated with one another in ways unknown to science." Doctor Singh looked off into space and mumbled, "Unusual idolatersgen ion exchanges... cations of a base... combining with other protons to form new substances...."

The doctor blinked back to the moment and continued. "But I found it fascinating that the cedar box is approximately five hundred years old, the tray and the cremains are only about two hundred years old, the goat skin liner roughly nine hundred years old, while the clay container is relatively ancient. Utilizing testing methodology that includes carbon dating, I concluded that the clay container is more than two thousand years old."

Clearly, at a loss, Doctor Singh threw up his hands and said, "Unfortunately, I can't explain this perplexing assortment of conflicting dates. But back to my findings. So far, I've isolated hundreds of classes of bacterium, most of which are Schizomycetes. Apparently, the bacteria sealed in the clay container were in a state of suspended animation. We've known about amazing bacteria from the Great Salt Lake that have been aroused after being dormant for millions of years, and living bacteria were recently found three kilometers deep in a South African gold mine, and still others are capable of eradicating oil spills. However, our little guys put them all to shame. When exposed to air and a very small amount of salt water, they become free-living organisms that go on feeding frenzies and multiply exponentially; they procreate and metastasize similar to the way cancer cells do. They devour rock, sand, vegetation, and even plastic, and, fortunately, their by-product happens to be the rich, black soil in which they were found. Thank God, they are not pathogenic. In fact, they seem to have an aversion to animal tissue, human or otherwise." The doctor's mind seemed to drift off again. "Justifies goat skin lining..." Apparently searching for reasons, he mumbled, "Proteolytic enzymes... ion exchange... zeolites... molecular filters..." before returning to the moment.

"While I'm learning more about this complex process every day, it seems that Frank Flores somehow gained a working knowledge of all this years ago. He discovered that he could remove a minuscule amount of the black soil teeming with these marvelous bacteria and microorganisms, and by merely adding a small amount of salt water, he could create an organic matter that greatly accelerates plant growth. I find it even more astounding that he knew to reseal the clay container to preserve the dormant state of the main body. Frank Flores also kept remarkably detailed records which have proved invaluable to my research." Doctor Singh shook his head in admiration. "He mentioned finding unique pods of glass-like crystal, like little potatoes, in the root systems of certain leguminous plants grown in sandy soil." Doctor Singh shrugged and said, "It's beyond my expertise to explain."

Simon Bernstein coughed, perhaps to gain attention, and said, "Not everything can be explained by our limited human understanding of things, Doctor Singh. I've come to believe that some unexplained cellular behaviors you've just presented here can and should be labeled *miraculous*. Shakespeare described a miracle as something *wondrous strange*. One might assume that *wondrous* suggests divine intervention and that *strange* implies a substantial challenge to science. And from what I've gathered, Tierra Milagro most certainly qualifies as something *wondrous strange*."

"I like the way Shakespeare put it," Keno interjected. "And I do appreciate all your research, Doctor Singh, even if we don't know exactly how or why they can do what they do. But it really doesn't matter. We just need to put these little rascals to work."

Doctor Singh smiled and remarked, "I believe these *little rascals* enjoy waking up to eat and multiply. And from what I've gathered, you have enormous quantities of waste for them to consume and vast open spaces in which they can propagate."

Wearing a serious expression, Netanya said, "Just think, gross human waste can be transformed into much-needed food and create beautiful landscapes."

Keno paused a moment to reflect on the way Frank had saved that special box all those years after surviving a powerful hurricane. And how his parents had defied astronomical odds to meet in Puerto Rico; then how fate had guided him to meet Netanya and how their falling in love had led to his relationship with Simon; then how Frank's senseless death had brought together the amazing talents of Buzz, Julie, Nate, Amelia, and Doctor Singh. It was all too convenient for coincidence. It occurred to him that none of this would have happened if Frank had not been killed. The ultimate sacrifice. With all thirteen eyes locked onto him, he commented, "I'm sure there is a *wondrous* hand behind all this."

J.P. Maloney had to read the article again, this time paying much closer attention.

Palo Alto Doctor Fathers Over 200

Serious criminal charges were filed yesterday against W.G. Krysknace, M.D., a long-time Palo Alto pediatrician. The doctor stands accused of replacing donor sperm with his own. Allegedly, the prolific pediatrician has fathered more than two hundred children with the in vitro fertilization procedure. His offspring purportedly range from six-month-old babies to adults now in their late twenties. Extensive DNA testing has positively confirmed...

J.P. glanced over the article with amusement the first time he read it, thinking: *The planet is spinning out of its orbit.* Then something about the story rang a bell. And the doctor's name was doing the ringing. "Krysknace," he mumbled to himself. "What the hell kind of name is that?"

J.P. thought about it a little more, and, at least in his own mind, his suspicions were confirmed. Yes, he remembered now: *This was the doctor who had performed the in vitro fertilization procedure for Yvette.* He shook his head and mumbled, "I'll be a monkey's uncle." As if trying to inform everyone in the county, he shouted, "Doctor Krysknace is Nicky's father!"

J.P. ripped the page in half, carefully folded it, and put it in his pocket. He simply couldn't help himself—he had to share this spectacular bit of news with Big Nick.

As he often did these days, Big Nick was sitting out on his balcony. He took great pleasure in watching the Doberman pinschers run and cavort. And these Dobies were living in style. With the help of his old construction ramrod, Jack Murphy, Javier had done a remarkable job building the kennels and putting in a unique maze of dog runs.

He enjoyed thinking: *Yes, old Javier pampers these Dobies just about every way a dog can be babied, especially Caesar and Cleopatra. I only wish I'd have been healthy when Nicky shot them to cover his butt. Thank God they recovered. I don't know what I'd have done to that idiot if they hadn't.*

When a blue Lincoln came roaring through the gate, it caught Big Nick's attention. He hadn't entertained many visitors recently—especially visitors who could open the gate. When the car got closer, Big Nick recognized J.P.'s emaciated body slumped behind the wheel. He was surprised to see the grouchy old lawyer so soon after he'd undergone triple bypass surgery.

Though he wanted to, J.P. didn't smile when he extended his hand toward his old friend and partner. In fact, he wanted to let go of a big belly laugh, which happened about once every decade. He fought back an urge to pull out the folded newspaper page instead of sitting and indulging in some dreaded small talk. "The dogs are looking good, Big."

With one side of his face still showing the paralyzing effects of the stroke, Big Nick smiled like a proud father. "I'll say. Javier has become one of the best trainers in the business. He won Best of Breed at Eukanuba, and I think he's going to do real good at the Nationals."

J.P. felt a twinge of loss as he looked down to where all the massive construction equipment used to be parked. He missed those big cash cows for reasons even he didn't fully understand. "How many dogs do you have now?"

"Sixteen, give or take a couple. I leave all the sales decisions to Javier. He hates to part with any of them, and he's damned fussy about who he'll sell them to."

J.P. thought he saw some fuzzy colors moving out in the field. He scowled as his aging eyes struggled to bring a small herd of animals into focus. "I thought you got rid of your cows."

Big Nick chuckled and leaned toward the rail. He gazed out at the field and offered, "I did. You're looking at a herd of goats."

"Goats? What possessed you to buy stinking goats?"

"I didn't buy them. They belong to my new neighbor, Bob something-or-other. He pays me rent to let them graze, which is good for me in a couple of ways. I make a few bucks, plus they eat down the grass and volunteer hay, which helps reduce the threat of fire." Big Nick leaned back in his chair, then gave J.P. a knowing look. "But I wouldn't be making fun of them goats if I were you. They're walking cash cows. This Bob something-or-other uses goat milk to raise Holstein calves, and they grow a helluva faster on it than they do on cow's milk. Plus, the calves grow up healthier."

J.P. had exchanged all the small talk he could stomach for one morning. Without bothering to comment on goats' earnings potential, he retrieved the newspaper article from his coat pocket and spread it out on the patio table. "Take a look at this, Big."

Big Nick shot J.P. a curious glance, then fumbled for his reading glasses. He bent close to the creased page, then read slowly. He sat up in his chair, looked off into the distance, leaned over, and, even slower this time, read the article again. Big Nick frowned, shook his head from side to side, and then whispered, "I'll be go to hell."

J.P. could finally let go of the belly laugh he'd been holding back. "Doesn't that top just about anything you ever heard of?"

Big Nick shook his head again while letting the information sink in. "To tell you the truth, I'm glad to know the little bastard didn't come from an Italian bloodline."

Just then, Yvette, wearing all black since her son's accident, pushed Nicky out onto the balcony in an ultramodern wheelchair. A quadriplegic, Nicky's physical abilities were restricted to limited hand and head movements. As he and his mother closed the distance, Nicky managed to turn his contorted right hand enough to wave his middle finger at the old men. Then a strange noise, sounding remarkably like an angry parrot's screech, erupted from deep within his throat.

Yvette smiled politely, straightened Nicky's cowboy hat, and then offered her translation. "Nicky says, 'Good morning, gentlemen.'"

J.P. flashed back to that foggy night when Nicky drove the Ferrari into a power pole. It was a miracle that Deputy Wertz— just happened to be looking high and low for the jerk—found him just in time. J.P. had privately kept his fingers crossed, hoping that Nicky wouldn't come out of the four-month coma. He thought at the time: *The idiot might as well not have. What good is being a quadriplegic that can't even talk, let alone being completely helpless?* Yes, in an abstract sense, justice had been served, and this was just about the worst punishment J.P. could have imagined.

Also, these cruel injuries had made it convenient for Jason Bridger—who had gone from Marin County DA to serving in the U.S. Congress—to secure Nicky a life sentence of house arrest. The old lawyer nodded and grunted, "Tell him I said good morning yourself."

After listening to his mother deliver the greeting, Nicky screeched with greater agitation and volume. Eager to help, Yvette translated again. "Nicky says, 'It is especially nice to see you looking so well, J.P.'"

J.P. doubted that Nicky had ever entertained a courteous thought about him in his life, let alone conceiving one in his present condition. He gave Big Nick a wry look, then nodded at Yvette. "Tell Nicky I'm glad he's still got some spunk left in him."

Quite content in her role as mother, nurse, and companion—which virtually gave her total control over her son's life—Yvette was convinced that she alone could communicate with Nicky. She slowly reiterated J.P.'s message with perfect diction. After paying close attention to his reply, which amounted to even louder frenetic screeching, she turned and said, "Nicky said, 'Thank you for offering those considerate and encouraging words.'"

Still smiling, Yvette noticed the newspaper page lying open on the patio table. Her curiosity got the better of her, and she moved closer before asking, "Is there something interesting in the paper?"

J.P. grimaced and muttered, "It's nothing important," then turned to fold the page before she could read it.

Big Nick had other ideas. He placed a big hand on the page, making sure it stayed right where it was. Perhaps for a little payback for her mindless doting on Nicky, he wanted his wife to read the article. "Take a look at this story, Yvette. It has some very interesting information."

Yvette expanded her little heart-shaped smile, then leaned over to read. Her naturally pale face turned ghostly white, her eyes rolled back in her head, and she fainted into a fluffy pile of chiffon and black lace.

Millie's art exhibition occupied a considerable share of Mill Valley's town square, which sat among an inordinate amount of greenery and a surprising number of redwood trees. The square was bordered by several small businesses—most of which sold things that smelled good. Tantalizing aromas of fresh coffee and bakery goods enticed people as they drifted through the air.

Mill Valley was usually a quiet town, a true bedroom community, but today's exhibition had attracted a good-sized crowd. Many people knew Millie through her volunteer work at the hospital; some through her history with the local theatre; some through Frank and Milagrozo Landscaping; some through the Bernstein connection; and others through Keno and The Frank Flore Foundation. Then, of course, there were the nosy types who still remembered the notorious shootout at the Ghilardi Ranch.

Keno harbored guilt for seeing his mother so infrequently during the past few years, but, thankfully, each of those visits had provided new encouragement. Millie would never get over losing Frank but immersing herself in painting with oils had brought a ray of light into her life. Not only that, Keno was pleasantly surprised by her mastery of that difficult medium.

Millie's paintings, sixteen pieces of various sizes, were mounted on tripod easels and, thanks to Netanya's attention to detail, they were strategically scattered about the square. Though still emotionally scarred, Millie seemed happy and lighthearted as she strolled about the exhibition, politely chatting with diverse groups gathered at the paintings. When asked about the price of a particular piece, she suddenly had somewhere else to go. Several would-be buyers even called after her—a few offering substantial sums—but she never seemed to hear.

With little Francisco bouncing along behind, beside, and in front, Keno and Netanya made the rounds. They were glad to see Hector and Luiz, who had brought along their wives.

Hector had a thousand things he wanted to discuss about Milagrozo Landscaping. "I need your help, Jefe. We have too much business now. It's more than me and Luiz can handle."

Keno playfully cuffed the stout landscaper on the shoulder, and said, "That's a good thing, amigo. I'll meet you at the Yard in the morning to talk about some new people we're hiring. You and Luiz are going to teach some very special people how to become good landscapers, and that's going to help us in a lot of ways."

Curious about the *very special people* remark, Hector said, "Getting more help is a good idea, Jefe. I'm getting too old to be digging in the dirt."

They next crossed paths with Nathaniel and Amelia Clay. Nate said, "Millie couldn't have chosen a nicer day," then tousled Francisco's hair. "How's it goin', big guy?"

Francisco ran a hand over his hair to straighten it while scowling up at Nate. "Don't do that, mister. My mom combed it. She wants me to look good for Nanno."

Nate made an apologetic face. "Sorry, Cisco." He winked at Netanya and said, "There's a boy nobody is going to mess with."

Netanya agreed, "Yes, he's got linebacker written all over him."

Nate added, "I want to commend you on your recent accomplishments in Africa, Joaquin. I don't believe many other charitable organizations understand how important it is to elevate those peoples' esteem. You've taken aid to a higher level by offering much more than the immediate needs of food and medicine."

"Thanks, Nate. I can't tell you how much we appreciate all you and Amelia have done. And are still doing as far as that goes.'

"You are providing phenomenal rays of hope, Joaquin," Amelia said with genuine admiration. "It must be very rewarding to know you're improving so many lives."

Keno felt the little rush of the joy he used to experience when his odyssey first began. "Yes, Amelia, my work can be very rewarding at times."

"I know it takes enormous sacrifice," Nate said. "I could never summon that much resolve."

"If there is one thing Joaquin has plenty of," Netanya interjected, "it's resolve."

"By the way," Nate said, "our friend Jason Bridger, I should say Congressman Bridger, has taken a page out of your book. He recently introduced legislation for funding job-training centers in low-income regions across the country."

Keno was aware of Jason Bridger's pending legislation, and he also knew that Nathaniel and Amelia Clay were the inspiration behind it. "I'm glad to learn that he's a good guy after all."

Amelia smiled and asked with a curious expression, "Isn't Millie selling any of her work? Nate and I saw a piece we absolutely loved and made a generous offer, but she didn't seem the slightest bit interested in discussing it with us."

Netanya nodded knowingly. "Millie paints from the heart, and it seems that she's emotionally attached to each and every painting."

Nate's face took on a determined look. "We're not going to surrender that easily. Our negotiating skills have been challenged. We'll see you later."

Buzz and Julie emerged from the crowd, smiling their hellos. Julie lugged a large bag containing baby paraphernalia while Buzz pushed his nine-month-old twin daughters, sitting side by side in a double-seated baby stroller. The friends exchanged pleasantries and watched as Francisco tiptoed close and studied the girls, who smiled, jabbered, and waved their hands gleefully. This, of course, ignited a cheerful exchange among the amused adults.

Across the way, Simon had managed to corner Millie one-on-one. He had assigned two of his top procurement agents to buy as many pieces as they could for the highest prices possible. But, so far, they had failed to acquire a single painting.

While holding a painting up to inspect, Simon said, "Millie, my dear, I'm going to insist that you let me purchase this marvelous landscape." He shook his head with admiration as he studied the colorful pastoral setting from different angles. "You have a rare talent. I liken it to a brilliant merge of Gauguin and Monet. And I'm convinced there is going to be a huge demand for your work in the not-too-distant future. Not only do I want to purchase this piece because it will fit so well with my collection, it will be a prudent investment."

Millie made a congenial face that didn't reveal anything. "Let me think about it, Simon, and I'll get back to you." Then she shifted gears. "When I was at that place, I had a lot of free time on my hands. I spent a lot of time studying the Bible and other religious writings, which I found to be a wonderful source of comfort. During my reading, I came upon something that I found remarkably interesting. I read that a devout Jew named Simon cradled the infant Jesus and recognized him as the Messiah shortly after he was born. I suppose it would have been a very courageous revelation at the time."

Simon was caught off guard. He knew *that place* was the mental health facility where Millie had spent the better part of three years. He also knew of the Biblical passage but considered it irrelevant on a personal level. "Yes, I am aware of the passage. I only wish I were as sure about the Messiah as that particular Simon was. However, that's a matter we can discuss at a different time and place. Let's get back to your selling me this painting…"

Though Netanya's injury had eradicated her aspirations for an acting career and plunged her into the world of business, it had also allowed her to enjoy being a wife and mother. Then, too, she had recently scratched the thespian itch with nominal participation in the Marin County Repertory Theatre. But the thrill of the lights had beckoned with more intensity than she'd counted on. She would soon be making her directorial debut with *Auntie Mame,* and she was trying to convince Julie to play an important character, possibly even the lead.

While their wives discussed theatrical possibilities, Buzz casually directed Keno to a quiet place out of earshot. He had security issues that needed to be addressed. "You're really making life difficult for me, Joaquin. You just can't keep exposing yourself to all those crazies in all those uncivilized places. And sometimes the local police are more dangerous than the crooks and terrorists"

"I don't know why you're so worried, Buzz. I've got the *Timinator* protecting me."

Buzz couldn't fight back a smile. Timothy Morgan, now looking like a young Arnold Schwarzenegger, oversaw Keno's security detail, and he'd proved to be more than an adequate man for the job. Buzz knew of at least five incidents when the Timinator had saved Keno's life. And there were at least two other occasions where the former teddy bear—now turned lean and mean animal—had intercepted elaborate plans meant to attack the foundation's facilities. "I'm aware of how good Timothy and his team are at what they do, but that doesn't relieve you of your obligation to stay out of harm's way.

"I gotta go where the jobs take me."

"I'm also concerned that Timothy hasn't told me everything that's happened during your travels and travails. Have you instructed him to suppress certain events? Keep things from the home security team?"

Keno had done exactly that, but he wasn't about to admit it. Also, he couldn't reveal that he'd experienced visions that had helped him warn Timothy of impending attacks.

Keno grinned and said, "If I had directed Timothy not to report certain things, I would have sworn him to secrecy. And I would never confess to any suppression of events, no matter how hard you tortured me."

"It's not funny," Buzz warned. "I have ways of learning things."

"I'll tell you what, Buzz. One of these days when I have the time, we'll sit down and go over the highlights of the past few years. It might make a helluva story." Then, with a tone that told Buzz he was through discussing security, Keno said, "Let's go take a look at Millie's paintings."

The first few paintings Keno and Buzz looked at included brilliant arrays of flowers, scenic pastoral settings, and oceanic scenes. Then they stopped near one painting that seemed out of place.

Millie had masterfully portrayed a beautiful view of the Sierra Madres. Buzz leaned closer to the painting titled *Forever a Mountain and* studied it carefully. His trained eyes had apparently caught something. He stepped back, rested his chin on his fist for a few seconds, then asked, "Do you see that?"

Keno shrugged. "It is different, but I'm not sure that I'm seeing what you're seeing."

Buzz smiled and said, "Take a closer look."

Keno frowned as he studied the painting. Then his eyes suddenly widened with discovery. "Yeah, I see it now. It's a face… It's embedded there on that steep slope."

Buzz frowned and asked, "Whose face is it?"

"It's Frank!" Keno exclaimed.

They hurried to another painting and found the face again; then found it in another; and ultimately, in every painting they looked at. They found Frank's face hidden in flower beds, grassy fields, and in billowing clouds.

When Keno's knee began to throb from all the scurrying, he stopped to remark, "That's incredible. My mom has managed to get Frank's face in every painting."

"Yes," Buzz agreed, "that takes some serious talent. I believe it required a touch of genius."

His eyes growing moist, Keno confided, "I still miss Frank, too, but Millie is never going to let him go."

"No wonder she won't sell any of her paintings."

"I don't know why this is affecting me like this. But for some reason, I'm suddenly curious about Frank's background." Keno's face took on a wistful look. "You know what I mean? Where he came from, who his parents were, all that genealogy stuff?"

Buzz mulled it over, then gave Keno a knowing look. "I'll bet I could find out."

"You really think so?"

"It will take some time and money, but with all the new genetic technology, I'm pretty sure I can get it done."

Keno frowned and said, When you stop to think about it, none of this would have happened if Frank hadn't miraculously survived a hurricane. He wouldn't have met my mom, and they wouldn't have had me, and then I met and married Netanya through my mom, and then you, Simon, and Nate wouldn't have been involved. And then events made it so that Tanya and I didn't get to try our hand at acting…."

Buzz said, "Lots of coincidences."

Keno replied, "Feels more like a plan. Maybe God's?"

Buzz shrugged. "That's too deep for me."

Keno glanced over and saw Millie standing alone by a painting set apart from the others. She was looking a bit tired, so he decided to go offer his support. "Nice talking with you, Buzz. See ya later."

Buzz nodded and said, "We'll probably be leaving soon. The girls are a lot like their mother, which means they get bored easily. Drive carefully and be nice to people."

Millie did her best to smile when her son limped up. "Hey, Sunshine, glad you finally got around to visiting with your crazy old mom."

Keno kissed her on the forehead, wrapped her in his arms, and held her close for a comforting moment. "You should say my genius mom. Your paintings are incredible."

"I'm glad you like them."

"It's not just me. Everybody thinks they're beyond great."

He moved closer to look at a painting that she'd kept separate from the others, suspecting it might be something out of the ordinary. When he studied it, he could see that his mother had convincingly captured a magnificent sailboat in the midst of a violent storm. Near the top of the painting, a golden light divided the dark, angry clouds.

"This is fantastic, Mom. I think it's the best one yet. Is that golden light supposed to be the sun symbolizing the hope-through-the-storm kind of thing?"

Millie elevated her eyebrows thoughtfully. "I suppose you could say that."

Keno smiled and said, "We're on to you, you know."

The picture of innocence, she replied, "On to me? What are you talking about?"

"All the faces." Keno winked and confided, "Buzz figured it out."

He studied the painting some more, deliberately dissecting it inch by inch. However, this face was much harder to find because he was looking for the wrong one.

Keno shook his head in admiration. Ingenious strokes shaped subtle hues—spectacular and flawless blends of color converging with light. Suddenly, his eyes popped open. There it was. The angelic face had materialized just beneath the imposing curl of a majestic wave. "Whoa! That's Frank when he was a boy named Francisco."

Millie smiled wistfully. "Yes, or Chico Milagro, whichever you prefer."

Seeing the innocent face caused *something* to stir at the core of Keno's soul. But it wasn't a mysterious feeling anymore. He'd learned what that *something* was years ago and had learned to live with it. As Frank lay dying that tragic day, he'd passed on to his son the capacity to embrace almost unlimited passion—the ability to feel things at a level shared by a special few. Keno had learned, however, that this extraordinary passion could peak at both ends of the scale. He had the capacity for violent anger if he surrendered to it. Fortunately, his internal contests were mostly won by his good side. However, his enormous empathy often caused him to suffer heart-wrenching pain, but that seemed a small price to pay for spending his life doing the work he so enjoyed. Endowed with a profound sense of spiritual resolve, he'd been granted the pleasure of spreading hope and joy throughout the world—fulfilling his destiny with uninhibited love.

THE END

Acknowledgements

I have been blessed that so many people have cared about me, helped me, and inspired me. I wish that I could name them all.

Here are a remarkable few:

- Robin Quinn, the bright editor/proofreader who clarified scenes, fact-checked, and polished this story.
- Ghislain Viau, the gifted artist who created the stimulating cover and expertly completed the formatting.
- Tom and Mellisa Massey, my dear friends who are always there when I need them.
- Alice Grossi, a special friend who provided the incentive for me to finish this novel.
- And the enduring love for my three sons—Darren, Nathan, and Tracy—has continually encouraged me.

About the Author

Theodore Lane Miller ("Ted") has worn many hats during an adventurous life. He is a retired General Contractor who lives in Las Vegas, Nevada, where he enjoys writing and playing golf. He served in the U.S. Marine Corps, shortly after which he married a homecoming queen, and together they had three remarkable sons. He attended Santa Rosa J.C. (California) at night while employed as a lab tech applying thin film coatings in vacuum. He next worked as a painter on the SF/Oakland Bay Bridge while attending Heald Engineering College at night. Using his engineering education and his bridge painting skills, he became a steel painting contractor. Some of his work included the Alaska pipeline, the Carl Vinson aircraft carrier, the Palos Verde nuclear plants in Arizona, and several large bridges in the Northwest. He then became a General Contractor with jobs in several western states. After retiring, he became an assistant editor for the *American Contractor Magazine*, wrote poetry, and patented two inventions. Then being shut in with Covid 19 and winning a long battle with cancer provided him the time and opportunity to accomplish one of his life-long goals—writing and publishing a novel.

9 798218 455194